Granite Justice

A Belle Evans Mystery

Susan Lanning

To Leslie & Chris, fellow writers — and great friends. Susan —

Granite Justice
A Belle Evans Mystery

Copyright © 2013 by Susan Lanning

ISBN - 13: 978-1491 222 805
ISBN - 10: 1491 222 808

ACKNOWLEDGMENTS

Reading mysteries is one of my first loves, but up till now I've shied away from writing a straight detective mystery. So here is my first detective - Belle Evans - a combination of my paternal grandmother's first name and my maternal grandmother's last name.

Having moved, like my heroine, to the new and wondrous state of Arizona, I have done my best to capture some of its beauty and mystery. The people, however, are no different from all people everywhere, striving to cope with life as it's been handed to them. Which makes them even more wondrous than the scenery.

Writing in general takes a lot of work, and a lot of help from others. I'd like to thank the Yavapai Sheriff's Department for taking time to explain regulations and equipment to me. I would like to thank my husband Bruce and my sister Laurel, also mystery fans, for their help in editing. And I would especially like to thank our daughter-in-law Lisa for helping me with the cover design. We're so lucky to have such talent in our family. In fact I would like to thank all my family. They have never complained about my pursuit of writing over the years.

Last of all, I would like to commend you, dear reader, for your interest in strong characters and their stories. May they live forever in our hearts.

1

A brittle dawn wind rushed down the mountainside a hundred miles southwest of the San Francisco Peaks to whip up the parched earth of the Arizona high desert. It swept through stands of ponderosa and piñon pine on the slopes, whisked past prickly pear and juniper clinging to the arid valley floors, gouged the empty arroyos that scored vast stretches of land and formed a flurry of dust as it fought to escape the granite walls of Lame Horse Canyon. Beside the canyon road, wind lashed the shirttails of the boy who lay still and cold in the growing light.

Arms sprawled, his sightless eyes were aimed at the mauve streaks of cirrus against the deepening blue. Large pools of blood had soaked into the hard soil beneath him from the bullet hole in his head and another in his chest. A raven circled above on the uplift of wind. From a bear grass thicket a striped lizard scurried past the lifeless hand to warm itself on a rock as the sun emerged.

The clatter of a motor pierced the stillness of the canyon. A Ford pickup, forty-some years old, its color unrecognizable now, its innards in dire need of repair, rattled along the canyon track, throwing up dust caught and scattered by the wind. As the truck drew near, the sound echoed around the walls of the canyon, the vibrations scaring the lizard who ran for cover.

The vehicle rounded the bend and clanked to a sudden stop, its chassis jiggling with the rumble of the motor. A moment went by before a man stepped out, leaving the door ajar. He stumbled around the front to stare down at the still form at the side of the road.

Unwashed jeans and a flannel shirt flapped in the wind against the man's emaciated body. His battered felt cowboy hat covered a nearly bald head while whiskers stained with tobacco camouflaged the wrinkles of age and hard living. His pale eyes squinted down at the body.

Virgil Hibbits was the town scavenger whose only home was his '67 Ford pickup. They also called him 'Crack' since it was said he'd fried his brain on the stuff some years ago up in Flagstaff. Hibbits made his morning rounds looking for lost items to sell. This canyon was a favorite rendezvous for teens looking to get laid. In the throes of passion they often dropped more than their pants. So Hibbits made the trek out here a couple of times a week.

Now he searched the ground around the body, checking for any leavings. Next he knelt down to search the pockets, swearing as his muscles and bones complained. The boy, almost a man, was dark – black hair, olive skin, a 'Mex' to Hibbits. The bullet to the head had split the skull part way with the impact, spilling more than blood. Flecks from the wound dotted the boy's hair and the ground beneath. Ants had already discovered the morsels.

Hibbits thought he might have seen him out here before, maybe with the Poole girl. But his own brain didn't hold onto details. They seemed to elude him the way dreams often did on waking.

He found a wallet with a driver's license but no money, a handful of change and some car keys. He took the change, left the wallet and, since he didn't see a vehicle around, stuck the keys back where he'd found them. Getting to his feet, he stared at the body a long time before it occurred to him to report this. The sheriff would want to know. They might give him a reward for the information. This was big news. Maybe they'd stick him on TV. Him, Virgil Hibbits.

He climbed back into his pickup, slammed the door, made a U-turn, running over one leg of the body by the side of the road, and headed back down the track to town. Wind scattered the dust trail he left behind.

Late August and the stark morning sun, already high, warmed the interior of the maroon Honda as Belle Evans drove along Miner's Creek Road toward Granite High School on a mission. She had to save Ned Stambaugh's ass. Again.

Belle ran a hand through her cap of curly brown hair, the gray washed out with Nice 'n Easy. Cool when she first got up, the temperature had reached the eighties already at nine o'clock. She knew she'd have to invest in a white vehicle now that she'd moved to a land where the sun actually *did* shine. And one that wouldn't break apart on the dirt roads, more prevalent around here than paved ones. Maybe one of those huge white pickups that seemed to spring upon the landscape like growth during the monsoons.

Ned Stambaugh, the high school counselor, had called her office at the school board building this Monday morning and said he needed her. He didn't say why. With Ned it could be anything. Why couldn't he manage any of his own problems? How in hell had he managed before she came? She found herself spending more time at the high school than at any other building.

Barely two weeks into the school year in her relatively new position as Security Counselor and there was trouble already. Maybe another proposed fight between a Chicano gang and their white counterpart; she was fast realizing the extent of hatred and prejudice in this state. Or a bomb threat. Those happened all the time back East. No, he didn't sound that frantic. And Ned, she was learning, sounded frantic when anything big was afoot. Still, Belle's position required that she check out every call.

She turned up Spring Street, taking in her breath yet again at the sight of the crystal sun washing boulders and piñon pines along the roadside as she climbed the hill toward Granite High. Stark, rugged, hostile even, and yet infinitely compelling was this Southwestern landscape.

This winter she'd made the biggest move of her life. She'd left behind not only Cleveland, Ohio, but her two grown children who insisted they could lead their own lives without her immediate presence, and husband Larry, whom she'd finally gotten up the gumption to ditch after the last and most humiliating fiasco. A trial separation only, he'd reminded her, but one she was looking to make permanent.

Now she was out here, a world apart from what she'd always known, in the place she'd dreamed of living. Don't ever get used to this land, she told herself. Never take this place for granted.

Belle pulled into the parking area of the school and stopped in the teachers' lot. Time to see what species of ant Ned had up his ass today.

Granite High School, housing fifteen hundred plus students, was built like a campus, not like the single building schools back East. Five two-story buildings, letters A through E, ranged around a courtyard of grass and small pines and dotted with concrete benches and tables. It was known for the pile of granite boulders at one side looking a little like a haystack made of rock. Belle always had the feeling of entering a college. Until she checked out the kids.

Typical high school. Boys' pants – shorts this time of year – hanging around their crotch, girls' be-ringed bellybuttons crying 'check me out.' Tattoos ruled. Then she thought about some of the friends of her daughter Ellie at college in Cleveland and decided that maybe the two levels weren't so different after all. Stambaugh's office was in Building A. She waved at a group of students she knew and headed for it.

"The girl won't talk to me," Ned told Belle, jumping up from the desk the minute she appeared in his office. It was a Spartan place, painted an indiscriminate tan, files and records housed neatly in cubbyholes and drawers, a picture of the Grand Canyon on one wall, a group of awards on another. "She says something's wrong but she won't tell me what."

Ned, in long-sleeved shirt and tie, in spite of summer, was tall and muscular, clean-shaven and good-looking. Belle guessed somewhere in his late thirties – maybe ten years her junior. He had the appearance of a football coach. But she'd learned early on that his appearance didn't even reach his second layer of skin. The real Ned Stambaugh was a fussy man, forever afraid of criticism and rejection. He was married but his wife was busy with her career as the manager of the local Dillard's. No children.

When Belle had first met Ned the third Monday of January – her beginning day on the job – he'd cowered at the very mention of the administration, all but genuflected as Superintendent Cummerford suggested he show Belle the ropes.

She'd discovered that Ned's specialty was scheduling and helping kids get into college. He seemed genuinely concerned for his charges, never stinting in his efforts to alter schedules, provide a haven from stress, allow students to discuss their differences. But his understanding of the human psyche was sadly limited. He apparently couldn't comprehend the inner workings of kids, why they behaved as they did. Why they weren't all like him.

Belle, on the other hand, knew teenagers were a mass of raw emotions. No longer children but not yet adults, they saw issues as black and white with no in betweens. And they latched onto first impressions with savage permanence.

"Maybe this girl just needs a woman's touch," Belle suggested. "Where is she now?"

"In my conference room." He nodded toward a closed door in the office, looking nervous and out of his realm. "I tried sending her back to class but she wouldn't go. I'm just not sure what to do with her."

He handed Belle a student folder which she looked over briefly. Lily Poole, age seventeen, a junior, grades good, no prior office referrals. Then she followed him to the door, not sure how she could help the situation if Ned couldn't handle it. Wait – what was she thinking? Ned handle it? She opened the door and walked in.

The girl was tall and lithe with long auburn hair and hazel eyes that swam with sorrow. In worn blue jeans and a flowered blouse that looked like it had been pulled from the bottom of a laundry basket, she appeared wretched. And she had a fresh bruise purpling her jaw that she'd tried to cover with make-up. At sight of the bruise, Belle swung a hard glance at Ned and he shrugged, looking as lost as the girl. Just like him not to mention this little tidbit of information.

"Mrs. Evans, this is Lily Poole," Ned said. "Lily, Mrs. Evans is a counselor in our school system. She works in all the schools to coordinate –" He halted, obviously uneasy with the phrase 'school security.'

Belle helped him out. "I coordinate counseling problems that are district wide." No one in the system was comfortable with the necessity for security in their school. They'd hired her last January because she'd convinced them of their need for her services. Previously the school had tried having an officer from the police department visit on a regular basis, but he'd apparently come on as the heavy and the students had shied away from him. Besides, uniforms made kids skittish. Still, hers was a tenuous position, her first twelve months here a trial run. No pressure there.

Belle took a seat next to the girl. Ned's conference room was bare, unwelcoming. A round table and four hard chairs furnished it. Vinyl flooring, fluorescent lights and no pictures made it seem more like a police interrogation room than a school facility. She wondered how he ever dealt with students in such an atmosphere. She nodded at Ned to leave, took a breath as he closed the door and turned to Lily Poole.

"Mr. Stambaugh says you're upset about something, Lily." The girl glanced at her folded hands, her complexion pale in spite of the Arizona tan. Belle waited for her to speak. When nothing was forthcoming, she said. "Can you tell me about it?" Still nothing. "Does it have anything to do with the bruise on your jaw?"

This time the girl turned away, shoving auburn hair behind her right ear.

Belle sat back, crossed her legs, moved into a position of ease. "I understand you're a junior this year, Lily. Do you like school?"

Lily, face still averted, nodded. A response.

"Do you get good grades?"

Another nod.

"Any classes you like in particular?"

"English." The voice was tentative.

"Teachers?"

Eyes back on the folded hands, she said, "Miz Perez, my English teacher."

Belle didn't know anything about Ms. Perez but she could have her sit in if necessary. She said, "My favorite teacher was Mr. Becker in sophomore chemistry. I was pretty lousy in science but he made me feel good about it anyway." She scratched the back of her neck, wondering where that memory had come from.

"Miz Perez, she's from Mexico. She's awesome. Tells us all about her life there."

"What about?" Belle eased the question in gently as though coaxing a rabbit out of the brush. She'd worked enough years with kids to know when to pounce and when to tread lightly.

For a moment Lily was mute again. Then she said, "About when she was a girl, how she cried over the poverty down there. She watched little kids die of hunger." Lily turned to Belle, her eyes brooding. "It was so awful."

"And you feel it as though it were happening to you?"

The girl didn't seem conscious of wringing her hands. "Miz Perez, she makes you see things, makes you understand about the world. Like Julio does."

Suddenly tears came and Lily turned away.

Belle let the silence stretch out. How many times had Ellie needed this kind of prodding to release her daily tragedies? How many times had the two of them sat at the supper table like this after the 'men' had finally left them alone? And then it came gushing out.

"Please Miz – "

"Evans."

"I don't know what to do. I don't know who I can talk to." Lily whipped around in her chair, her eyes awash with tears, grasping her hands before her. "I'm so scared."

Belle handed her a tissue box from the table. "Tell me, Lily. I'm here to help."

"Julio," she cried, hands to her face. "Oh my God! Julio. It's all my fault. He's – he's dead. My dad killed him!"

Cold washed through Belle's chest. Lily cried in earnest now so Belle got up and pulled the girl into her arms, letting her sob against her in pain and panic. When Ned peeked in the door, she shook her head to make him go away.

As the girl's crying subsided, Belle held her at arm's length and said, "Can you tell me about it?"

Lily hung her head, desperation oozing from her. "My dad hated him cause he's Mexican. My dad hates Mexicans," she spit out, her voice rising. "He's a damned racist! I wish I could run away and leave him to rot."

Belle let her go on for a few moments more, spewing out the anger and bile. Handing her the tissue box again, she sat her back down. "What about your mother, Lily?"

"She's dead, too. *He* killed her."

"He killed your mother? How do you know?"

"He pushed her when he was drunk. Pushed her against the counter. She – she –" The girl's whole demeanor deflated.

Belle was at a loss. "What about brothers? Sisters?"

"I don't have any."

"So you live with your father?"

A nod.

Belle took in air, let it out. "Okay. Lily, how do you know your father killed your friend?"

"Julio? He was my lover. We were going to be married, Miz Evans."

A new bout of sobbing began. Belle waited it out. When the sobs quieted, Belle said, "Can you tell me about it?"

Lily's chest continued to heave but she managed to get her story out. "Julio asked me to meet him over by Lame Horse Canyon last night. That's our meeting place – when I can't see him at school. He said he had something to tell me. He was – he was –" She broke down again, devouring tissues.

Belle prodded her.

"He said he was going to get enough money so we could run off together. He's been working like crazy to make money for us."

"Your dad, is he abusive? Does he hit you?" Belle glanced at the bruise on the girl's jaw.

Lily hesitated. "He didn't used to be mean like that. Just since Julio and me've been dating. He never liked any of my boyfriends, but mostly Julio because he's –"

"Mexican."

Lily's eyes burned with anger, then softened. "Julio said he'd have money soon and we could leave – leave my racist shit of a father, leave this place that doesn't understand people like Julio. Miz Perez knows how it is. She's helped us, talked to us sometimes." She swept hair behind her ears with hands that shook.

Belle made a mental note to check out Ms. Perez who apparently left a strong impression on Lily. Maybe even influenced her choice of boyfriend. "All right, you met at the canyon. What happened?"

"Do you know Lame Horse Canyon? There's only one way in and it's hidden from the road. So we didn't see my dad's pickup until it was too late. He jumped out and started swearing at us. He called me a whore and he called Julio a dirty Spic rapist! He –he –"

Belle ran a hand over her mouth. "Is that where you got the bruise on your jaw?"

Lily nodded. "He began to beat Julio. I screamed at my dad but he didn't quit. When my dad hit me, Julio hit him back and knocked him down, then told me to get out of there, to go." The girl grabbed Belle's arms. "I didn't want to leave him there – leave him to deal with my dad. I saw the gun in my dad's belt. I was so afraid, but Julio insisted. He yelled to get out of there fast. I didn't know what to think so I – I just ran to my Jeep and drove away."

Belle let it sink in. She got to her feet, walked the small space across the room, came back. "How do you know Julio's dead, Lily? Maybe they just fought and that's all."

"He's dead," Lily told her with a cold finality that chilled the conference room air. "He didn't call me afterwards and I couldn't get hold of him. Then this morning I heard it on the radio. 'Julio Morales, found beaten and shot to death in Lame Horse Canyon.'"

2

"Can't we call the police?" Belle asked Harold Ramey, the principal of the high school. His office was also in building A, just down the hall from the counselor's. He and Ned had sent Lily to the nurse's office to lie down and were now in a three-way conference with Belle over the matter.

"The authorities already know about Julio Morales's – death. A sheriff's deputy called here to see if Lily was at school," the principal said. "We don't need to get further involved."

"Have they arrested Mr. Poole?" she asked.

"Not to my knowledge. Why would they? On a girl's hysterical ravings? She didn't actually witness the killing." Ramey was a large, morose man in his fifties with small eyes and jowls that quivered. Belle found him forever guarding the high school from 'sticky situations.' He shifted in the conference chair, adjusting his bulk in the navy suit he wore while morning sun from the window behind reflected off the bald circle on the back of his head. "I don't want the school involved any more than it is already. As soon as Lily has recovered, we'll send her home. The police can deal with her there. We don't want the other students upset by this."

"Send her home?" Belle was almost out of her seat when Ned gave her a warning look. Ramey lifted his head as if in question.

Ramey had been Belle's first road block when she got the job last winter. It was as if his girth were a wall across any path she tried to follow. In February she'd wanted to pull a group of boys out of class to snuff the rumblings of a fight. Ramey had vetoed it, saying it would disturb the teachers, and the fight had occurred, disturbing not just the teachers but everyone. In March he'd refused to call the police on a possible drug violation, and the kid had ODed on meth. Not the school's fault, he'd maintained. But the boy was dead.

The story of Ramey was that a group of parents had tried to sue him about eight years before over an incident in which he'd used less than his normal amount of caution. Apparently he'd accused some students of intimidating a teacher in class so badly that the fellow had quit. Ramey had stood up for the man during his one heroic stance and had been beaten down mercilessly in a lawsuit claiming slander of the students. The parents hadn't won the financial settlement, but the damage had been done. Harold Ramey had drawn in after that.

Belle tried again. "I just think that if Lily's afraid of her father – if her father did have anything to do with it –"

"It's not our concern, Isabel. I don't want us to be a part of this situation."

"We can counsel Lily, of course," Ned suggested, as though trying to bridge the gap. "We can help her deal with it."

Belle did her best to remain reasonable. "Lily's father may hurt her if we send her back. She already has an ugly bruise on her jaw. His doing."

"According to her. It may not have been her father who did that." He had the grace to look disconcerted but his decision was embedded in one of the granite boulders in the courtyard. "If there's a problem of abuse, we'll let the authorities deal with it. The school isn't responsible for what goes on at home. Report what you know to the police. Otherwise we stay out of it."

It was like swallowing rocks to take this in. What was wrong with Ramey? Had that lawsuit eight years ago stripped him of his entire backbone? Was she looking at jelly-fish Harold now?

Ramey threw out a few more statements, all of them unenlightened to Belle's way of thinking. Ned played the good little boy and nodded agreement. Visions danced in her head of the last incident husband Larry had caused her, and she sat there, anger roiling and determination seething, until she could burst out of this room and do something about it herself.

Jenny, the principal's secretary, was a gum snapper. Forty something, platinum blond from a bottle, clothes that probably came off Wal-Mart racks. In spite of a girth to match her boss, she was quick on her feet. And she was immensely interested in everyone's business. Belle had heard her referred to as the "Granite High School Courier." She was the one who'd related the details of Ramey's lawsuit story.

"Rosa Perez? I think her prep period is – " Jenny got up from her desk, cordoned off from the others by a screen covered with Disneyland posters. She went to a master schedule near the door to one of the offices and checked. "Here it is. Third period. Starts in twenty minutes. She's in Building C, second floor, room 245."

Belle nodded. "Thanks, Jenny."

"Is this – " Jenny came back to her desk inside the cubicle, glanced around to see if anyone was within earshot. "Is this about Lily Poole? She was so upset this morning."

"What do you know about Lily?"

Jenny snapped her gum, giving Belle a covert glance. "Nice kid but real unhappy. Father's pretty – well, you know – hits the bottle." She tipped her hand to her mouth. "I heard about her boyfriend getting shot. God, can you believe it? Had to be her father, don't ya think? He hated Julio cause he was – you know – Mexican."

"Did you ever meet Mr. Poole?"

"No, not really," Jenny moved in close like she had a secret. "I only know about him because of Lily. Seen her bruised couple-a times."

"You have?" Belle straightened. "How many times?"

"I don't know, two, maybe three. It seemed to start this year mostly."

Belle nodded, thanked her, and went across the courtyard to Building C to wait until third period.

Rosa Perez looked up from her desk when Belle entered the room. Small, striking features were accented by caution and intelligence in her eyes. The woman appeared to be about Belle's age, her late forties.

The classroom was filled with color and mood in the pictures and posters, in the student creations filling the walls and bookcases – busy and vibrant. It literally sang with life in all its bright and dark forms.

"Can I help you?" the woman said with only a slight accent. Then she stood and came forward.

Belle introduced herself and told Rosa Perez why she was here. "Lily Poole mentioned you. I take it you know what's happened"

Rosa Perez glanced away, fighting some emotion. "Julio Morales. He was killed. Shot to death."

Belle nodded. "I've been talking to Lily about it. You're apparently important to her, so I thought I'd come see what you might know about the matter." Belle sat on the edge of one of the student desks. "Mr. Ramey doesn't want the school to get involved, but I hate to leave Lily to the wolves, have her go back into a situation that may be harmful to her."

An ugly curl of the lip altered Rosa's features. "Ramey, that one. His entire brain has been used up in his feeding habits." She all but spit. "I'm so sorry about Julio. He was going to do something with himself, you know. A few years back he came to America to live with his aunt,

Mrs. Hernandez. She adopted him so he'd have a chance to make a life for himself. Seven other kids at home in Mexico. He had plans to help them. He said he was going to make enough money to bring them all to America. Such high hopes, high ideals."

"Lily said he wanted to run away with her, get her free from her father."

Rosa nodded grimly. "Poole is a pig when he drinks. Which is most of the time now. He doesn't deserve a daughter like Lily, but she takes care of him all the same. I don't know how she does it. He begs for her pity, then gets drunk and takes out his anger on someone. Lately it's been her. I think because of her attachment to Julio."

She perched on a desk near Belle. "Julio wouldn't have taken Lily away until he could support her. I've known them since the beginning of last year. He showed me pictures of his family back home. He and Lily asked me to help them send letters to his family. They'd come and talk, or listen to me go on about my childhood in Mexico City. A sweet couple but drowning in sorrow."

Belle looked around the room at the student work. Several miniature dioramas depicting literature selections sat on a table. She recognized the balcony scene from *Romeo and Juliet* and an abstract she was sure came from *Of Mice and Men*. "What about Lily's mother? Lily said her father had killed his wife."

"They called it an accident," Rosa told her. "Lily was only nine. There was an inquest, I understand, but no indictment. Since then it has been just her father." Rosa got to her feet, her expression one of deep concern. "Mrs. Evans, can you do anything for her? If her father really did kill Julio – "

"Do you think he could have?"

"I hate to say it of anyone, but I wouldn't be at all surprised. Not the way he is when he drinks."

"No evidence, though, according to Ramey," Belle reminded her. "He says it's only speculation on Lily's part."

Rosa nodded. "And if this town follows form, they'll let it go at that. The man will be free and Lily will have to go home to live in fear." She walked to a window and looked out at the mountains in the distance. "My life here in America has been so superior to my childhood in Mexico, I sometimes feel ashamed to complain." She turned back to Belle. "But there is injustice even in this advanced culture. There is hatred and terror and wrong done to people every day. It breaks my heart to see it happen to Lily Poole."

3

"Does Ramey know you're taking me home?" Lily Poole asked from the passenger side of the Honda. Her hands were folded tight between her legs, her back rigid.

"No, but I'm sure he'll find out." Belle kept her eyes on the road. Lily didn't have transportation. She'd come to school with a friend that morning because her father had messed with the engine of her Jeep. Ned Stambaugh had arranged for someone from the school to take the girl home so Belle stepped in. Harold Ramey wouldn't be happy.

They had to drive through part of the town. Almost noon and the streets were crowded. Belle was struck all over again at the uniqueness of this rugged, starkly Western, mountain town, so different from where she'd lived all her life. Granite, Arizona, had a population of some forty thousand according to the latest census and was built on a series of hills like a roller coaster among the Olmsted Mountains and other smaller ranges. The townspeople boasted their elevation at a mile high just like Denver.

Granite was actually a description of the rock formations in the area rather than a conceived name for a town. But the town was established soon after President Lincoln had commissioned Fort Malone to be built during the Civil War. And, as was often the case, the description ended up doubling as the town's name. Now, Belle had been told, Granite had nearly tripled in size during the last ten years alone. A lot of people looking for good weather and cheap land, and maybe a chance to start a new life, like her.

She switched on the radio to see if she could put Lily at her ease. News: some traffic crisis in Phoenix on East 101 causing one of their frequent delays, August thunderstorms on their way toward the Peaks at Flagstaff. Neither would affect the town of Granite, close to a hundred miles from either city.

The local news was mostly political these days with the state primaries less than three weeks off. A big rally was planned for one of the U. S. Senate candidates on the steps of the Crook County Courthouse in the middle of downtown Granite which seemed to be taking up everyone's attention.

"And Morgan Andrews challenges Lloyd Pruitt to a debate over the issues," the newscaster announced. "'It's time this state knew what's at stake, and what we as candidates stand for,' Andrews, running for the U.S. Senate, told reporters. He also plans a rally in Granite at the –"

"Guess that's not too uplifting, is it?" Belle said, switching the radio off.

"I hope you won't get in trouble 'cause of me, Miz Evans," Lily said, her voice quiet but with underlying strength hauled up, no doubt, from some resource within her.

"Don't you worry about me, kiddo. Let's concentrate on your situation. Will you be all right at home?"

Lily shrugged, though not with conviction. "My dad can be fine sometimes. But he was pretty mad this morning when my friend picked me up. You never can tell with him lately."

The Honda reached the edge of town and Miner's Creek Road heading west. The road went up one hill, down another, around curves, with the Juniper Mountains ahead in the distance. Patches of high desert juniper and piñon pines contrasted with yucca and agave. Scraggly bushes of cliff rose bloomed and manzanita sprawled precariously along rock ledges. Late morning sun baked them all indiscriminately. Belle gazed ahead of her, looking for the turnoff for Stagg Road and Lily's home.

In spite of the warmth, Lily shivered as she watched Belle, that quiet desperation in her face. Finally she spoke. "I don't know, Miz Evans. If my dad's been drinking he'll – he'll be mad as hell that I told anybody."

"We won't mention that. At least not until the police get there to protect you. They've been called." Belle glanced at the girl. "I'll stay till then if you want."

"Would you? Oh God, I'd feel a lot better if you would. My dad, I used to be able to handle him better, but now he gets so –" She shoved hair behind her ear and huddled.

Handle him? Belle took in a deep breath. She reached over and squeezed Lily's arm, trying to give the girl reassurance she didn't feel herself. Who the hell was this man anyway that he could strike his daughter and get away with it? Maybe even kill a boy? A spark of fear ran up her back but her anger doused it. And too many past episodes with Larry fed the fumes.

Ramey – he was a piece of useless lard – just like the police. She'd only had dealings with them a couple of other times. Late March was the first time when the school had had to call in the Granite Police on a charge of drug possession. After the other boy had died from meth use,

Ramey had finally consented to call in the authorities. The police had bullied the three boys involved and carted them off.

Then in April Tom Drake had brought a gun to class out in Knoll Valley because a gang of boys had threatened him. Knoll Valley, the small town east of Granite, was part of the school system but under county law enforcement jurisdiction. So this had been Belle's introduction to the Crook County Sheriff's Department. Sheriff's Department, Granite Police – how many times had it broken her heart thinking about what kind of world these kids had to grow up in today?

After her experience back in Ohio, getting shot in the arm by an irate father and Larry's extreme reaction to it which lost her the job, she'd enrolled in the local police academy. Then, kissing her disastrous marriage good-bye and coming out West, she'd latched onto this idea of Security Counselor from some of the Eastern models, talked the school system here into giving it a try, citing the Newtown killings in Connecticut and all other past school shootings. These were dangerous times for students, while Congress, with NRA money flowing freely, fought any new gun laws that might protect them. And Arizona allowing guns anywhere any time. Belle looked over at Lily and shuddered. Now Ramey was sending this girl back to the bosom of a possible killer. He'd make a good candidate for Congress.

They turned onto Stagg Road, twisting through boulders and a scattering of chaparral, each in their separate closet of rumination.

Ralph Poole was an angry man blaming the world for his woes. Some told him his brain had been addled by too much liquor. There'd been a time early on when he thought his life had been pretty good, when he felt the world hadn't bitten him in the ass every chance it got. He'd done okay in the construction business until the Tucker Highway project ten years ago. He'd gotten his leg crushed under a dozer. Still had a nasty limp. And they'd given him nothing. Disability, same as welfare. Chicken shit.

That's when things had gone sour. Drinking had become his only release. Trouble was he couldn't control himself at those times. When he ended up killing his wife eight years ago by shoving her in one of his tirades, the police called the circumstances suspicious, but they'd never made the case against him. It was an accident. He hadn't meant to push her so hard. He had a gimpy leg. He'd lost his balance.

After that he'd sworn off liquor. Insisted he'd never drink again. But that hadn't lasted long. Life on government handouts sucked the big one. Drink was his only friend. The police claimed his disability didn't prevent him from picking fights in every bar in Crook County and sending several men to the hospital. He'd been brought up on charges often enough but had gotten off with a few nights in the county jail and a warning. Nursing his bottle of whiskey, he'd stay holed up in his mobile home off Stagg Road. Lily always took care of him. He needed her to look after him.

Ralph Poole was at the door of the run-down trailer as Belle drove up. The place screamed of poverty – trash in the yard, paint peeling off the old fifty by ten single wide. A Jeep, once green, and a white Chevy pickup, splattered in so much mud and dust you could hardly tell the color, were parked askew off to the side near a fat juniper. Around the other side, a large Doberman barked viciously, caroming off the restraints of his pen, teeth bared. Belle wondered how this girl could have come from such an environment.

Lily pressed herself into the back of her seat, hands gripping the sides, her face taut. Belle reached over and touched her hand.

"I'm here, honey. He wouldn't dare do anything while I'm here."

Lily looked unconvinced so Belle got out of the car, shoved down her own apprehension and headed for the man at the door of the trailer.

Thin and wiry, unshaven, eyes bleary with drink, Poole sneered at Belle, taking in her dress and flats, his face belligerent. "You got some business here with my daughter?" he asked, his words slurred. The dog continued to heave its body at the fence, snarling and barking. Poole turned on the animal. "Shut the hell up!"

Belle stood her ground. "I brought Lily home, Mr. Poole. She wasn't feeling well at school."

Poole peered at his daughter in the car, then thumped down the steps, his left leg almost unbending and impeding his progress.

"Lily girl, you okay?" He hobbled forward. "I'm sorry I hit you like that last night. You know I'm sorry, Lily. It's just that damned drink. Makes me lose control. I ain't mad at you no more, honey."

Lily remained where she was and turned away from him.

"Aw, come on, girl. I'm your ole man. Don't that mean nothing? I can't get along without ya, you know that."

Belle stepped in front of him as he neared the car. "Mr. Poole, your daughter is very upset. The boy she loved has been killed."

He stopped, glaring down at Belle. "Loved, shee-it. He was a goddamned Spic. She couldn't love him." Back at Lily. "Come on, girl. I'm real sorry. Honest I am."

Lily's head snapped around, her eyes aglow with anger and pain. "You killed him, you bastard. You shot him!"

Poole staggered back, almost tripping from the bad left leg. "Lies. Them's lies!" When he saw the unrelenting ferocity in her, his face got mean. "You been whoring around with that damned Spic to spite me. Is that it? You was gonna leave with him? Leave your ole man? How'm I supposed to I get along without you?"

Lily leaned out the window. "Think I'd stay with you now? You killed him, damn you!"

His eyes grew small and flat and his snarl increased as he moved forward. "What's she been saying? What lies you been telling people, girl?"

Lily shrank back in the seat of the Honda.

"She was sick at school. That's all I can tell you," Belle said, not liking this turn of events at all.

"About me?" His voice reached a higher pitch. "She been telling lies about me? You telling lies, Lily?"

Anger came to Belle's defense. She stood her ground, ignoring the Doberman and faced the man. "Mr. Poole, I've informed the authorities under what conditions I was bringing your daughter home. They're going to be keeping an eye out for her, so I suggest you quell your temper. I'd hate to report anything unfavorable." She'd left a message at the Granite Police Station but wasn't sure anyone would follow up. She didn't know if Poole would call her bluff.

"Ya know, lady, you got some gall coming out here to *my* house with *my* daughter and talk this-a way to me. How'd you like it if I was to sic my dog on you?"

The Doberman leaped against the fence as though in response, yapping, baring foam-coated teeth.

An ugly situation, this. A man – maybe a killer – who was out of control, with a vicious dog and possibly a gun, if he hadn't disposed of it. She had her police training and a lot of her dad's stories on the job as a Cleveland cop to back her up. But a few Karate moves and a basic knowledge of self-defense wasn't much.

"Mr. Poole, if I have to, I'll take Lily to a shelter and you can deal with those people as well as the police," she told him, glancing back at the girl in the car with, she hoped, a reassuring look.

"You threatening me, lady?"

For a man with one bad leg, he was fast. He grabbed Belle's arm, fingers biting into her flesh in a painful grip, and yanked her so close his face nearly touched hers. Odors of stale sweat and alcohol engulfed her, making her head reel.

"Lady, don't never fuck with me," he hissed. "This here's my daughter. Not you nor the police nor anybody else got anything to say."

At that moment Lily jumped out of the car. "Stop it!" she cried and shoved at her father. "Leave her alone, you bastard!"

The dog, sensing an attack, jumped high into the air, bombarding the fence. Adrenalin came to Belle's rescue. With a quick twist of her body, she snapped free of Poole's grip. But the next moment he had hold of Lily. The Doberman barked furiously.

Belle faced the man, her gaze nailed to his. "Let go of her, Mr. Poole. Right now. Let go of Lily."

She was never sure if he'd have backed off because another sound intruded on the background, drawing nearer. Tires crunched the gravel as a car came up the track. Was this good or bad? Belle didn't dare turn away from Poole. But he paused at sight of the vehicle. Then let go of his daughter as it came to a stop, his eyes slits now and cautious. As Belle turned, her legs went limp with relief.

Behind her was a sheriff's department Chevy Blazer, white with the gold county seal painted on the side and a bar of lights on top. As she watched, Sheriff McFarland himself turned off the motor, opened the door and stepped out.

McFarland, in khakis, a pale blue shirt and his tan Stetson, never seemed to be in a hurry, as though there were plenty of time for necessities and no need to rush into life. He took in the situation – a livid Poole, Belle dressed for school, Lily panting at her side. And the dog trying to break from its prison.

"Poole, what's the problem?" He had a slow, easy voice and a gait to match as he swung the door shut and moved toward the three of them. "Mrs. Evans? You got a reason to be here?"

Belle eased her muscles out of the tight stance. But as he watched her, she grew uneasy again. She knew these police were jealous of their jurisdiction and anyone getting in their way – the Granite PD patrolled their town; Janos, north of Granite, kept a tight rein on their own people; and the Crook County Sheriff's Department had most of the outlying areas; and nobody touched the reservations, no one dared step on the jurisdiction of the BIA. Ramey had contacted the GPD; she'd even called them herself. But out here on Stagg Road was county territory.

"I brought Lily home from school. She was sick," Belle told him.

McFarland nodded slightly, sucking on a tooth. He glanced around, looked pointedly at the Doberman attacking the cage, then at Poole.

"Shut up!" Poole yelled. The dog barked once more then quit.

The sheriff stood, hands slung on his hips just under his utility belt that held the Smith and Wesson double-action revolver. The tan Stetson shaded his rough face leathered by years of Arizona sun. He was an unprepossessing man, tall, thin, relaxed, but apparently he had a reputation of tough justice after his many years in law enforcement. Ever since Belle's acquaintance with him back in the spring when Tom Drake brought the gun into Knoll Valley Junior High, she'd listened when people talked about him. They seemed to trust him, but still he wasn't an easy man to deal with. She'd found that out several times since. And her own paranoia over the domineering male figure always clicked in.

McFarland turned to Poole. "I need you to come to the sheriff's office with me. Got some questions I want answers to."

Poole's face screwed up, defensive now and edged with fear. "What for? I ain't done nothing. You got no call to take me in."

"Questions," the sheriff said, relaxed, his expression unreadable. "Best you just come along."

"What's it about?" Poole demanded, not budging. "It's about that Spic, ain't it? The one they found dead. My daughter was whoring with that sonofabitch. Hell, they ain't human. Just dirt to wipe off the bottom of your feet."

Lily's eyes flashed anger and Belle's chest heaved, but McFarland barely blinked. Belle stood watching both men.

"I've got questions, Poole. You need to come along with me." He nodded toward the Blazer.

Poole stood his ground, the Doberman taut but quiet. "Just questions?" he said finally.

McFarland nodded.

"Shee-it," the man spit out. He heaved past Belle, his face suddenly pathetic as he stuck it in Lily's. "Lily," he said, "you be here when I get back. You be here."

Belle moved toward him then. "You know, Mr. Poole, I don't think I'd go demanding anything of your daughter under the circumstances. Especially in front of the sheriff."

Poole turned on her, shoved his face into hers again, the alcohol on his breath staggering and expression venal. "Lady, you kiss off. Don't you never interfere with me again. And you leave my daughter alone. You got no business here."

"Poole," said McFarland, "in the car." He didn't raise his voice but there was steel in it.

Ralph Poole kept his face in Belle's a moment more, eyes yellow, pupils dark with menace. Then he straightened and moved toward the patrol car.

McFarland came to meet Belle. He had a quizzical expression on his face. "Looks like Poole doesn't like you, Mrs. Evans."

"Does he like anyone?"

"What's happened?"

Belle looked at Lily, near tears. "She was upset at school over Julio Morales. She thinks her dad had some hand in his death and was afraid to come home. So I brought her. He already hit her last night."

He nodded. "Granite police were called. They called me – my jurisdiction."

"I see." She looked at the patrol car. Poole was standing beside it. "If you let him go, he'll come back home and maybe hit her again. Or worse."

The sheriff glanced off at the mobile home and the dog. Then he looked over at Lily. "I can't hold Poole without evidence. But there's a half-way house at the edge of town on Forest Road. They'll take her for a few days. If there's a question about it, have them contact my office."

"I know the place," she said. "What about the dog?"

He gave a snort of laughter. "You wanna take it?"

Belle glared at him.

McFarland glanced at the dog again. "If we hold Poole overnight, I'll send a deputy out here. Anything else you're concerned about, Mrs. Evans?"

Belle winced. "I just don't like to see animals go hungry. No matter how god-awful they are."

Wiping a hand across his leathery face, he took her in, the gray eyes inscrutable under the Stetson. Then he nodded, pulled at the brim of his hat and took off for the Blazer in long, easy strides.

Belle watched him check Poole for weapons, watched him get the man settled in the back and start up, watched as he turned the patrol car and disappeared down the road, leaving a dust cloud behind. Then she went to Lily, still huddled into herself. "Get what you need from the trailer. You don't have to stay here. And make sure your dog has something to eat and drink."

"That dog can damn well take care of himself. I hope he starves." But she looked contrite as she entered the mobile home.

Belle waited outside, glancing around the place. Besides the big juniper there were a couple of sad looking piñon pines in what she took to be the yard. Rangeland dotted with scrub oak and bear grass stretched out for a good two or three miles before giving way to hills of ponderosa. A small herd of pronghorn antelope grazed in the distance. A harsh land. Belligerence seemed to ooze from it. And yet she felt the pull in the same way one feels a disobedient child crying out for understanding.

She'd been to Arizona a number of times over the years, to visit her sister Louise in Phoenix. First with her family, then later making the trek by herself. And each time she'd started home, she'd felt that pull from the land pleading with her to stay. Later, escaping a crumbling marriage, she'd headed West. Now she lived here, halfway up the mountains from her sister and practically on the other side of the world from her family.

Lily came from her house carrying a duffle and some dog food. She slopped water in the dish from the hose while the Doberman nosed her, looking for affection. But Lily wasn't ready to give it.

4

Eli McFarland turned onto Stagg Road, heading for town. The Juniper Mountains lay to the West, the Olmsteds towered to the south. The air hung clear and hot but with clouds gathering. Could be rain this afternoon. And August was the time for dove hunters to show themselves – which meant more work for him with those gun-happy fools shooting at anything that moved. If the bullets hadn't been so precisely positioned and up close, he'd wonder if Julio Morales had been a hunting victim.

They'd gotten the information on the Morales kid this morning early. Virgil Hibbits had found the boy out at Lame Horse Canyon and come in to report it. Hibbits, or "Crack" as people around town referred to him, lived in his ancient truck. He parked it on one piece of public land or another, or trespassed on private property if he could get away with it.

But Hibbits hadn't actually seen the shooting. And if any of the love birds who frequented the canyon saw it, they weren't giving themselves away. "Think any of those young punks want their girl's ole man knowing they were screwing her brains out?" His chief detective Carter had muttered. So they had no witness – except, apparently, for a hysterical girlfriend who despised her father and insisted he'd done it. Not a lot to go on.

He glanced at Poole in the rearview mirror. A real piece of work who'd been in and out of the county jail half a dozen times in the last year alone. An angry man, despising himself and a world that made him what he was. And sometimes taking it out on others.

First his wife. Her death had occurred before McFarland had been in office. She'd died from a trauma to the head, a severe blow to the back of her skull when she fell against the corner of the room divider between kitchen and living room. An accident, they said. Apparently there'd never been evidence of anything else. Then there was Poole's daughter whom it looked like he'd slapped around a few times. Now maybe this Morales kid was another Poole victim. He'd have to send Carter out with a warrant to do a search. But for now, just get Poole the hell out of there before someone else got hurt.

Mac had been doubly concerned after he and Carter visited the Hernandez family this morning to inform them about their nephew's death. Big dogs barked and bared their teeth; the smell of poverty permeated the house.

Carlos, the oldest son, had stood speechless for a minute or so, then suddenly exploded, insisting that someone had shot down his cousin because Julio was a Mexican, a *Spic*. The dogs had set up a row and Carlos had babbled something about revenge until his father had shut him and the dogs up. But the look in the boy's eyes had been telling.

"Jesus, Mac, those animals wanted a piece-a me," Carter said after they left.

"That's cause there's so much of you," he told his detective. "Look at those muscles of yours. All the animals could think of was 'steak.'"

He knew he should have sent a deputy to do this job with Poole. Probably should have left Carter and his partner to inform the Hernandez family, too. Trouble was, the situation here looked volatile with the daughter. His people referred to him as the 'hands-on' sheriff, always getting involved himself. What the hell – might as well keep up his image. Besides, murders were an oddity in Crook County.

Mac, as his friends had called him all the way back to high school in Tempe, was a closed man, though he hadn't always been. His four year stint as an Air Force pilot in some unsavory conflicts had soured him some but his experience in law school at Columbia had reinforced his ideals. However, ten years with the DA's office in D.C., and four years as chief of police back home in Glendale had turned what he now considered his Pollyanna outlook on the world bitter. "Too tight-assed for your own good," his buddies used to tell him. "Hell, Mac, life's a bitch. You gotta let up – do what it takes to survive." He'd tried looking the other way but it hadn't worked. Too many cover-ups, too many under-the-table deals made him feel like he needed a bath and a strong disinfectant.

But the real topper had been the death of his son Jamie from meningitis twelve years ago and the subsequent ruin of his marriage with Kathy two years later. Broken and in pain, he'd returned to Arizona. His four years in Glendale and some of the city corruption he'd encountered had only made the wounds fester, so he'd climbed the mountain to Granite, taken the sheriff's job and kept pretty much to himself. People up here didn't seem to mind.

Poole shifted in the back seat. "Ain't had nothing to do with that Spic got killed," he barked. Bullet-proof glass separated him from the driver, a steel mesh partitioned him from the passenger side. "He was screwing my girl. I warned him off is all. Maybe hit him a few times. Shit, I'm a father, ain't I?"

"Could-a fooled me," Mac muttered.

He glanced at Poole again. He'd searched him but hadn't cuffed him. Didn't want a scene if he could avoid it. Belligerent cops always ready for a fight that wasn't necessary didn't last long on his force. Keep it as simple and calm as possible.

Damn the school for letting that Evans lady get involved. He understood what she was trying to accomplish here – how she'd talked the school board into hiring her as Security Counselor for the system. Not a bad idea when the Granite PD was too damned cheap to provide more than a part-time probation officer at the high school. What good was that going to do? But she had no business confronting Poole. A dangerous situation. He'd have a talk with Harold Ramey when he got back to the office.

Late afternoon sun streaked across store fronts and sidewalks as Belle barreled down the street from the high school, hot and fuming. Apparently McFarland had called Ramey to let him know just how the department felt about teacher interference. Damn the man. And he'd seemed so easy-going. Hah! He could kiss off if he thought she was going to let Lily Poole down just because the macho ego in this wild west territory couldn't handle a woman's involvement. She'd had enough degrading from her husband over the years to choke an entire herd of horses.

Poor Lily. She'd looked so lost when Belle had taken her to The Pines Halfway House. It was a decent enough place, clean, spare but comfortable. She'd checked it out herself, gone on a tour with Mrs. Rivera, the chubby little matron, and questioned the woman about how she ran the establishment.

"We are very watchful here," Mrs. Rivera told them in her thick Spanish accent. "Much care is given to our girls. And we provide security here. We do not want anyone coming in who will harm them." Her body seemed too soft for the job she had, but there was steel and determination in her eyes.

Belle had had plenty of experience with halfway houses back in Cleveland. It went with the job as counselor, finding places for the battered and abused kids of the world. Some places were fairly nice and some she'd had to report to the authorities. This appeared to be one of the better ones.

Carrying the old duffle of possessions she'd gathered in a hurry – brush, make-up, clean jeans – Lily had moved in a daze, her eyes pleading with Belle not to leave her. And yet some stubborn pride held her upright, probably that strength that had kept her going when things got tough at home.

"Will I have to stay here long?" she asked.

Belle took her aside. "It's all right, Lily. You'll be fine here. I'll be in touch daily. And I'll check with the sheriff's office about your father." Then she'd given Lily a hug. It was still acceptable for female employees to give the girls a hug.

Lily clung to her as though she were drowning and Belle was the life raft. After all, she'd just lost Julio, her one hope for the future. But Mrs. Rivera took over, led her away to meet some of the other girls and allowed Belle, with one last look around, to be off.

Belle had decided afterwards to confront Ramey with what she'd done – against his orders, of course. Damn it, they'd hired her for her expertise in counseling and her police training. And she'd done what she knew was best. So, screw Ramey, and that lousy sheriff, too.

Almost six o'clock as she pulled into the driveway of the apartment she rented. Towering, ultra white cumulus clouds, heavy with moisture, obscured some of the sun. Humidity during what they called the monsoons in Arizona didn't begin to compete with the heaviness of the year-round air near Lake Erie. Still, she could feel the weight of it in her lungs and forty-seven year old joints.

Summer in the Southwest had been an exhibition of wonder for someone who'd lived her life in northern Ohio. Here, up in the arid mountains, over-heated days turned into cool evenings and mornings, the wind whipping up in sudden blasts that drove tree branches sideways, or dying to a breeze that dried the sweat and cleared the mind.

Then suddenly, out of nowhere, warm, wet air would move in off the Baja Peninsula or from the Gulf of Mexico causing storms the likes of which she'd never experienced. Gully washers, some called them. Micro bursts of wind, and lightning like a Fourth of July display were common, causing flash floods and forest fires. Then the calm would return and the air would shimmer. Crisp and clear. This summer had been dry according to Arizona standards. But Belle had witnessed a few storms last month that had been decidedly memorable.

Belle's apartment sat at the end of Quail Run. It took over the upper half of a light gray Victorian house of moderate size. She'd loved it at first sight and hadn't changed her mind in her eight months of living here. It helped that she'd talked down the price of the rent.

Her landlord, Adrian Good, had bought the place as an investment and had the upstairs made into an apartment with an entrance at the back. An art dealer with a precise eye for detail, he'd refurbished it to its original plans – turret, lacy trim, materials, color.

The house stood on a hilltop at the end of the street surrounded by trees and overlooking an arm of Miner's Creek some twenty feet below. The creek, lined with old, gnarled cottonwoods like a corps of ancient giants huddled along the banks, ran through the entire town on a bias. It actually had water flowing through it year round, even in a drought like the present.

Sycamores and big tooth maples shaded most of the backyard except for a spot where Adrian had planted a combined flower and vegetable garden. The garden looked as if it had been clipped and pasted from a Sunset Magazine. Belle decided that in a land of desert two thousand miles away from where she'd spent most of her life, 696 Quail Run was a damned good find.

Adrian Good worked in the garden now, pinching back spent blooms on the massive hemispheres of mums. He looked up when she got out of the car. Adrian was in his mid-thirties, short and a little on the hefty side but with manicured hair. He wore an Izod shirt, Ralph Lauren stone-washed jeans, and had an angelic face that masked a knife-edged tongue.

Adrian lived with Bernard Wozak, his significant other of eleven years. Belle didn't see as much of Bern, a tall, muscular man, maybe forty, who worked construction for the Freemont Development Company in town. Adrian and Bern were an unlikely pair – one sleek and unbearably handsome, the other plodding and looking a lot like a boxer after too many fights.

They'd been a godsend to her, though, when she'd first come to town – alone in an alien world. She didn't have a lot of friends yet. When you departed from your hometown of forty-seven years, you left all that behind. But she and Adrian had struck up an immediate friendship.

"Hey, girl, you're home late," he scolded, dusting off the gardening gloves he wore. "Where the hell have you been? I've been worried."

"Heavy day," she told him. She grabbed her satchel and shut the door of the Honda.

He raised an eyebrow, taking her in critically, then sauntered forward, peeling off his gloves. "Looks like you need a good, stiff drink, love. And you can tell Mama all about it."

Belle had to laugh. He was shorter than her and probably a dozen years her junior, yet he insisted on mothering her. Did she really seem so pitiful? He'd met her sister a number of times and together he and Louise had clucked their tongues over Belle.

She was about to decline the drink, wanted only to hide away and forget the day, but she changed her mind. "Maybe you can set me straight on a few things," she said and followed him into the house.

They parked themselves in the kitchen, a replica of the turn-of-the-century style with brick and wood surfaces, but with every modern convenience skillfully camouflaged. Adrian got out the gin and vermouth.

"I couldn't let her go home alone, Adrian. Jesus, you should have seen the man. Half drunk even in the morning. God, he smelled. And mean – I'm telling you, he would have hurt Lily. He almost hit *me*." If the sheriff hadn't come along, of course. She took a swallow of her drink to down the resentment.

"So, you took her to The Pines, did you?" he said. "I've met the proprietress of that place, love. Trust me, the girl will be safe there. Don't nobody mess with Mrs. Rivera lessen they want their ass kicked all around town." He shrugged. "At least, that's what I've heard."

"Well, that wasn't the end of it. Needless to say, Ramey had words with me over the whole thing. Especially when the sheriff called to give the good principal a piece of his mind."

Finally after one of Adrian's generous martinis and all the details of the day laid out for him, she felt somehow better. Even Ramey and McFarland seemed less threatening.

"Please, darling girl, don't tell me that principal of yours is such a stupid fool he'd consider firing you for – well, for what? Keeping him from getting his very large ass sued? They do have child protection laws here. For all our colorful, cowboy ways, we're not quite that primitive," Adrian said.

He held up his glass for inspection, then took another hefty swallow. "And the sheriff, now what, pray tell, is he going to do? Throw you in jail? Just for helping him do his job? Belle, sweetie, that ain't gonna happen. I doubt if he's got the balls."

"Oh, he's got 'em," she said.

A truck pulled up in the driveway and a minute later Bern Wozak came in the kitchen door, jeans caked with dirt, T-shirt barely recognizable as white now. He swung his black lunch pail on the counter and nodded at Belle.

"You two having a nice chat?"

Adrian looked him over and threw a hand to his face. "Don't even bother to put that sexy ass of yours in a chair, Tarzan. Go directly to the bathroom, do not pass go, do not collect two hundred dollars."

Bern grinned at Belle. "Bossy, ain't he?"

Belle laughed.

"Go," Adrian said, pointing the way.

Bern grabbed a Michelob from the refrigerator, blew Adrian a kiss off and went. In a few minutes they heard water running.

After further talk and more gin, even Poole became a distant memory. But for Belle the image of Lily still hung vivid and painful.

"I don't know what to do to help her," she told Adrian. "I feel so useless in a situation like this. If her father is freed – if the halfway house sends her home – what do I do?"

Adrian polished off the rest of his martini. "Instincts, dear girl. Just follow your instincts. From what I've observed, yours seem to be cutting edge."

Belle gave a laugh that lacked humor. "If my instincts were so damned good, I wouldn't have lived a life I regret."

"Well, let's just say yours were a long time sharpening."

She laughed again, this time for real. "Good point. I can live with that."

5

Belle's apartment had been made into two bedrooms and bath to the front, a living room and kitchen at the back, overlooking the yard and Miner's Creek below. Nice view. Adrian and Bern had furnished it well, finding pieces of the Victorian period that were somehow more comfortable than the usual spindly couches and chairs. The entrance opened onto the living room. Belle kicked off her shoes and tossed her jacket and satchel on the couch then went into the kitchen and checked the refrigerator for supper. She had leftovers from some noodle concoction she'd made the day before, a couple of pieces of the roasted chicken from Sunday and some asparagus spears she could steam. Easy, filling – that was all she needed.

Larry would never have accepted that as supper. Forget leftovers. He wouldn't touch them. Noodle concoctions? In another lifetime. Maybe. And he hated asparagus, one of Belle's favorites. Good God, how had she allowed herself to live with him so long? She couldn't think of anything she liked that he did. Well, except for the kids.

But you didn't split up a family over differences in tastes like food, entertainment, ideologies. Only when you were being beaten down by a psychological bully. And then only when the kids were grown and out of the house.

Larry had lost her, What? three jobs over the last twelve years. The first in Bay Village because his stopping by two or three times a week to question her principal had finally been too much and she'd been asked to resign. Even when she found a job on the east side of Cleveland away from Larry's work, he'd managed to do the same thing. Then this last one – his storming into the superintendent's office and telling him in a strident voice which carried throughout the building that Belle was quitting. She and Larry had fought horribly after that, upsetting Ellie who was still at home.

Belle took the dish of noodles and the chicken from the refrigerator, started cleaning the asparagus and turned on the answering machine for her messages. The first was from Ned Stambaugh.

"Belle, I'm not sure where you are right now so I'm leaving a message at your house. Harold Ramey has found out you took Lily Poole home and wants to talk to you. I don't think he's happy."

"Thanks, Ned, baby," she told the machine, "but you're too late." She stuck the noodles in the microwave.

The next message was from her optometrist's secretary saying her new contacts were ready for her to pick up. "We'll be here from nine till four weekdays."

"Let's see –," Belle tossed the asparagus in a steamer and added water, "seems to me I'm doing something then. Oh, that's right. I'm *working*." Why did doctors think you could get off work any time to go see them?

The third message made her stiffen. "Isabel, this is Larry. I hope by now you're regretting this rash move you've made. Living out in that desert all alone. No one to take care of you. I never thought you'd be so foolish as to go through with it."

A kind of sick dread moved through Belle from habit, sinking down into her legs and lodging there.

"Neither Ellie nor Will have heard from you in almost a month and they're worried. Naturally, they won't tell you, so I thought I needed to. Will you please do the decent thing and contact them? It's the least you could do after your abandonment."

The microwave beeped and Belle reached up automatically to open it. "Make me feel guilty, you son-of-a-bitch." Even when she knew it wasn't true – Ellie had called yesterday and they'd talked for an hour – he could still do that to her. She grabbed the bowl, burned herself from the steam and swore. Hell, he'd done it to her all during their marriage. Why would a mere separation change things?

Before she could wallow in anger, though, the next voice stopped her. "Sheriff McFarland here, Mrs. Evans. Thought you should know, we couldn't hold Poole. If you've got a minute, give me a call. I'll be here till five-thirty." He reeled off a number.

"Oh God," Belle spat. Almost six o'clock now. She picked up the phone and dialed. There was a series of rings, then a recording. Her heart sank.

The next moment the sheriff's voice came on. "McFarland."

"Belle Evans, calling you back."

"I was almost out the door," he said. "I'm glad you called, Mrs. Evans. I see you got Lily Poole settled at The Pines."

Belle told him all about it, trying to keep the emotion from her description. "But they can only keep her a short while. They're full up. Why couldn't you hold her father?"

She heard him let out a long breath. "No evidence. My boys didn't find anything at the trailer. Can't hold him without sufficient reason."

"But Lily's sure her father killed Julio. She says she was there when he began to hit the boy. Said he had a gun. And he hit her, too."

Another sigh. "Detective Carter talked to her already. The gun used on Julio was a .38 special. But if Poole owns one, it isn't registered. And my people couldn't find a gun in the mobile home. They searched everywhere. Besides, there must be five or six hundred .38s sold yearly in this county alone."

"What about tire tracks?"

"Maybe ten vehicles had been in and out of the canyon before we got there. Besides, tire tracks don't prove murder and we already know Poole was there."

"But they were fighting. He had a gun. Lily saw it."

"She didn't see the actual shooting. According to her, she left while Julio was still alive."

Now Belle let out a sigh. "She said Julio sent her away."

"And she left. Even so, how reliable is her testimony? She was planning to run away with Morales."

Belle rubbed the back of her neck, trying to think. "There's got to be something to tie that man to Julio's death."

"Until we can find the gun –"

"What about Lily? She could be in real danger when she goes home. I mean, if Poole killed the boy and Lily knows it –"

"Mrs. Evans, she's at the halfway house for now. She's got protection." McFarland cleared his throat. "I have to ask you to stay out of this. This isn't in your job description as I understand it."

Belle's anger rose to the surface. "I'm sure Ramey set you straight on that," she snapped. "Or did you set *him* straight? Whichever it was, he didn't hesitate to let me know about it. Thank you very much, Sheriff."

A pause on the other end. "He chew you out?"

"You might say."

Another pause. "Look, I'm sorry about that, but I've got my hands full here without adding you to the case load."

"I've had training, you know. I'm not helpless."

"If Poole did kill the Morales boy, he probably wouldn't stop at trying the same with you. And, training or no, you aren't authorized by the police force to do our work for us. Please, Mrs. Evans, let's both stick to what we're paid to do. Gotta go now. Check in with Lily Poole, but confine your involvement to that." And the phone went dead.

Muttering to herself, Belle turned down the heat under the

asparagus and put the leftover chicken in to warm. She supposed McFarland was right, that she should keep out of this thing. But something about Lily Poole pulled at her. It seemed to pull at Rosa Perez. And apparently at Julio Morales who had defied a man like her father in order to be with her. Face it, the girl had a fatal charm.

All at once that didn't seem funny. Julio died because he wanted to protect Lily. What about herself? Ralph Poole was free and, as far as she could tell, dangerous.

God, what would Larry say if he knew she'd put herself in this position? "Forget what Larry would say, Isabel. You've taken the step, you're standing on your own. Larry does *not* control you anymore."

Like hell, she thought. He controlled her through guilt. As he'd always done. And since he couldn't use himself any longer, he used the kids. But Ellie and Will were absorbed in their own activities – Will married and in law school in Michigan, Ellie a sophomore majoring in history at Case Western Reserve, both completely immersed in their lives and having full confidence in their mother's.

Ellie, Will and his Lora had all visited during their various spring breaks, were thrilled with her new location and, since their Aunt Louise and Uncle Matt were but an hour and a half away, not worried about her at all. "You know Daddy, though," Ellie had told her. "Mom, you did the right thing. Will and I are grown up now. We take care of ourselves. Time you lived your own life."

Time she did, Belle told herself. Larry could go crap himself. She'd finally come of age. High time she took the reins for herself and kicked off the last vestiges of control.

She strained the asparagus and threw it in a bowl, stuck the other dishes on a tray, grabbed a fork and carried it all into the living room to the coffee table. Then switched on the TV. She should use a plate but the effort of getting one and having it to clean up afterwards seemed too much at the moment. The six o'clock news from Phoenix had already started.

"— shooting death of Julio Morales," the anchorman was saying. She stiffened. "His body was found this morning in Lame Horse Canyon just north of Granite by Virgil Hibbits. The young man, 19, had been severely beaten and shot two times, once in the chest, once in the head. Police don't as yet have a suspect, but there has been some speculation that this was a racist act of violence. Last fall two Hispanic men were beaten and left for dead in a barn outside Casa Grande. Two of the members of the white supremacist group calling themselves The Black Falcons were charged with the crime. Officials say the Morales killing has the appearance of such a crime.

"The shooting has roused indignation among several of the equal rights groups in the state. Even Morgan Andrews, one of the Republican candidates running for the U.S. Senate, has taken up the fight. He was questioned today at his home in Paradise Valley."

Andrews came on camera. He looked like the perfect candidate for Arizona – a kind of ruggedness to him, yet with intelligence and compassion in his face. Belle normally didn't trust someone who looked that good, especially anyone running for office or selling cars. But she'd liked this man the first time she'd seen him, even though in her heart she hated politics.

Andrews stood outside his home, tall, erect, gray hair blown by the constant Arizona winds, wearing a Polo shirt and jeans. "We've got to put a stop to this kind of hatred," he said. "This problem has to be dealt with. Who did this boy hurt? Why did this senseless death occur? Because his skin was dark? Because English was his second language? Arizona's a big enough state to hold everyone."

He went on a little longer, the usual political jargon, then the anchorman was back. "Morgan Andrews will hold a political rally on September seventh on the steps of the Crook County Courthouse in Granite. A number of our state's political leaders plan to attend the rally to give their support to the candidate."

A few more details were given, then the news turned to a major traffic accident on I-10 outside Phoenix, and Belle relaxed the grip she had on her fork. So, the politicians were sticking their noses into the killing of a no-name young man up here in Granite. It made her skin crawl to think how they could use some tragic event as a political wedge. Anything to get them one step closer to a vote.

And there was poor Lily Poole, alone and frightened and unable to go home. Who cared about her?

6

Mac hung up the phone and rubbed his eyes with the heels of his hands. That Evans lady was going to be a damned thorn. He could tell the first time he'd had dealings with her. Crusader Rabbit. That was all he needed.

He walked over to the window in his office that overlooked the side street and stood staring out through the Venetian blind. Streaks of the lowering sun hit the rooftops of the buildings across the way. The old Church of the Sacred Heart, turned records office, faced him on Apache Street. A print shop was next to it and a Wendy's beyond. Branches of maple and ash threw long shadows over the sidewalk. A couple wandered by in one direction walking their chocolate Lab. A patrol car drove past going the other way. The dog lifted its leg to pee against the trunk of a maple, then moved on.

Irritation nettled Mac. But if he was honest with himself, he knew it wasn't because of Belle Evans. It was Poole and the fact that he'd had to release the man. Mac needed to talk to Lily Poole about the Morales kid. Carter had barely gotten her to speak and hadn't gotten anything out of the father. He hadn't done any better himself with the man.

The boy had been beaten severely and Poole had some nasty bruises on him, too. The fight had to have been a hard one, equal blows given on both sides, it looked like. Then a shot to the chest and one to the head had finished Morales. Al Yazzie, the medical examiner, found one of the bullets embedded in the chest, a .38. Poole swore he didn't own a hand gun, just his shot gun, which Mac had confiscated.

No guns were registered to Poole at all. But then half the guns in the state weren't registered. Mac wasn't against more gun laws, never had been. But they weren't a damned bit of good if you couldn't enforce them. Out here there were more gun shops than grocery stores, and not enough money in law enforcement to hire the man power to clamp down on the sellers. People insisted the police keep them safe. They just weren't willing to pay for it.

Carter, his partner Taggert and a couple of deputies had searched the trailer home.

"We didn't find jackshit," Carter'd said. "I swear, Mac, we took that place apart from foundation to gutters. Pile-a crap, too. How can anybody live like that?"

Rolly Carter was a big, burly Scotsman, two hundred eighty pounds of mostly muscle with red hair and a mustache to match. Mac always pictured him out on an Olympic field wearing a kilt and throwing a discus.

"Whatever the hell he did with that gun, it's not at his place."

Mac nodded. "Check out where he was last night. He said he was bar hopping. Check out the garbage cans, anything he might have tossed it in."

And Carter had done it. Nothing.

In the end they'd had to let Poole go, but he put one of his deputies on the man's tail. "Let me know if he so much as pisses in the wrong direction. I want to know where the hell he's stashed that gun."

Mac pulled out his keys, turned out the office lights. Sarah, his civilian aide, had left already. The night shift had come on. He nodded to some of them, checked dispatch, then went out to the parking lot.

Sitting in his Jeep Cherokee, he felt suddenly tired. But he knew he had to talk to Lily Poole. The cold beer and steak at Wilma's Diner that lured him would have to wait. Not that the Morales kid's death would be top priority in this county. But maybe because he was a no-name Mexican, Mac felt more of a need to solve the murder.

So, instead of heading east up High Street toward food and companionship, he headed west to The Pines Halfway House.

The Pines was located where the far end of North College Avenue met Forest Road on the way out of town. Several large Ponderosas graced the front yard of the seventy-some year old brown two-story. A full front porch softened the look of austerity. It had been built in the early thirties by a banker who wanted a retreat from town. Gradually the town had grown out to meet it, the banker had died, and the place had been bought up by a madam and turned into a brothel, catering to the local cowboys' need for some Saturday night release. Now it was a haven for abused girls.

Mrs. Rivera stood broad and dubious, blocking the entrance to the halfway house. Black hair pulled back in a bun, her ample bosom tugging at the dark flowered dress. Even with the gun strapped to his waist, Mac felt outnumbered. Already he had a bad feeling about this interview.

"Can I talk to Lily Poole?" he asked, pulling off his tan Stetson.

Mrs. Rivera considered him a moment, taking him in bare head to boots like a prison guard. He decided the girls would be safe with her in charge. Lily's father wouldn't get past this mini-Valkyrie any time soon.

"Lily is very upset," she said, her accent thick. "I do not know if she will talk to you. She has been hurt badly already." She didn't budge.

Mac nodded. "I need to ask her some questions."

Mrs. Rivera remained resolute. "I will ask you one. Where is that brute of a man who says he is her father? Do you have him locked up in your jail?"

Not a hopeful beginning. Mac knew nothing would be served by enlightening her, but there was no point in lying, either. "That's the problem. We haven't any evidence to hold him. I'm hoping Lily can help us out."

"You mean he is not in jail?" The woman's eyes flared and she took a fighting stance. "I work very hard to keep my girls safe and you let the people who harm them go free? What kind of protection is that? *Policía!*" she spat.

Mac set his shoulders and rubbed the brim of his hat. "Trouble is we've got rules we have to follow. I need evidence. And I need Lily to help me with that. Can I talk to her, please?"

The woman considered him a long moment. Finally she said, "I will see." She didn't invite him in but he followed her into the hall just the same. To his right was the dining room, left was a parlor, and in front were the stairs. Mrs. Rivera started up them like an avenging bulldozer, puffing steam and anger as she went. Mac ambled into the parlor. A couple of teenage girls came through the dining room. When they saw him they giggled and darted up the stairs.

He looked around. The Pines was typical of these kinds of places. Shabby with age, furniture castoffs, carpet worn, a few pictures of the usual kind, several religious, a couple of landscapes. But in spite of the worn-out look to it – the stains around windows from weather and a little sagging in the ceiling – the place was clean. The white glove test would never trip up Mrs. Rivera.

She came back into the room followed by Lily. A pretty girl, reddish brown hair and hazel eyes, and a bruise on her jaw a day-old purple. Mrs. Rivera wore a defensive posture like a suit of armor and kept herself between man and girl. Lily moved into the room, glancing at Mac with a look of sick pain.

"Lily, I'm Sheriff McFarland. We met at your place this afternoon," he said, easing into the interview. He nodded at the sofa and she took a seat. He sat opposite her but her bodyguard remained at attention. Mac let it go. He wanted to keep things as calm as possible and sat back easily.

"I know this is hard for you to talk about, Lily, but you're the only one besides your father who saw Julio Morales just before he died."

She didn't look up, didn't acknowledge him in any way.

Mac tried again. "Detective Carter talked to you earlier today. You told him you hadn't seen the shooting, is that right?"

She nodded ever so slightly.

"And there was no one around who might have been a witness?"

A shake of the head so nebulous he wasn't sure it was real.

Mac sat forward, forearms resting on his thighs, holding his hat between his legs. "See, the trouble is, we have no real witnesses, no real evidence that your father shot Julio Morales. And we can't find the gun you claim you saw."

Suddenly Lily jerked forward on the couch, eyes defiant and nostrils quivering. Mrs. Rivera moved in as though tied to the girl. "My dad killed Julio. He shot him. He did it!"

A couple of faces peeked around a doorway, then disappeared.

"He's a killer. He hated Julio. He wanted him dead!" Her eyes glowed, her face grew livid. "God, if I had a gun – "

Mrs. Rivera came down beside her, comforting her, glaring at Mac for upsetting her. "It is all right, Lily. You are safe here."

Lily gave way to tears, sobbing against the wall of woman beside her. "He killed my mom, too," she cried. "And he went free. So he could kill Julio." More sobbing. "He'll probably kill me and you'll just let him!"

Mac sank back, defeated. Didn't look like he'd get anything from the girl tonight. She was broken-hearted and scared. And if Poole really had killed his wife in a rage, she had reason for both.

He remembered the case. It had happened maybe six months before he'd taken this job. The stench of it had hung on the air of his new office, defiling the walls and furniture. Sheriff Colburn had handled it – badly, people seemed to think. They said Poole should have been tried for manslaughter. But Colburn never brought a case against him.

Now this. Damn, he needed the evidence. If he didn't get Poole this time the old hostilities around town would bubble to the surface again. He looked Lily over, now engulfed in Mrs. Rivera's arms, sobbing.

Mac rose to his feet, hat in hand. "Looks like I'd better come back another time when Lily's calmer."

Mrs. Rivera glared at him again as though he and Poole were equally tainted. The two faces peeked down from the stairway as he set his Stetson on his head and let himself out the front door.

Overhead an angry red streaked the mass of clouds like fire across the sky. A testament to his mood? Or of things to come? Somehow, supper at Wilma's Diner wasn't going to go down so good.

7

Belle reached her office early the next morning. Tuesday, what was on her schedule? She felt vague and unfocused. No wonder, she hadn't slept much last night, tossing and turning with pictures of Lily Poole and Ralph always before her. But now she had to get to work.

They'd given her a cubbyhole at the board building downtown on Ocampa Street, a small niche with no air conditioner and one three-by-four window. The window, with dust gathered in the corners outside, looked out on another building across a small concrete courtyard with a weeping willow between. She could just make out the distant mountains through the lace of branches that shimmied in the ever-present breeze. The sky, an incredible baby blue, was dotted with cloud puffs. And a family of great-tailed grackles, oblivious to the beauty, chattered away in the tree.

She'd done her best to fix up this tiny space, tacked up some posters of the places she loved best – Lake Erie at sunset, the Rockies in winter, Key West during a storm. She'd hung a banner about the importance of a child's mind and stuck a few old mementoes and family pictures on her desk. A couple of bookcases lined one wall interspersed with several uninviting, wooden chairs. It wasn't much but it was home during the main hours of the week.

Gazing out the window she took in the courtyard, the brilliance of morning sun against the neighboring building, so bright it made you ache for joy. Not like Cleveland. In Cleveland this crystal clear air was a rarity – maybe in June, never in August. A couple of stray sunflowers and some camphor weed brightened cracks in the concrete pavement. But her mood wasn't so shiny bright. All she could think of was that terrified girl and the man she called her dad.

Belle checked her calendar. She was giving a talk on safety this afternoon to the kids at Jackson Elementary. Fourth and fifth graders. Her speech was ready along with her kit of demos, what kids should be looking for and reporting to their teachers. She had a short video to show them, too, though God knows they'd seen plenty of school violence reported on TV. Still, it didn't hurt to remind them what could happen.

This morning she had to make out a report on Lily. And she wanted to get back to the high school. See if she could talk to some students who had known Julio. She picked up the office phone and called.

"Ned, can you pull a few of Julio's friends from class today so I can question them?"

Silence. She could almost see Ned Stambaugh on the other end of the phone juggling her request. Help Belle with Lily versus placate Ramey. "We're not supposed to involve ourselves in this affair, Belle. Mr. Ramey won't like it."

"Damn it, he doesn't have to know." She eased the irritation out of her voice. "Look, I couldn't send Lily home alone. I had to try to help her."

"You weren't supposed to take her yourself. Mr. Ramey was very upset when he found out. He accused me of plotting with you."

"I didn't mean to leave you to deal with him," she told him, "but you should have seen her. All alone to face this. And the sheriff let her father go, did you know that? The man is running loose, for the love of God. Who knows what he'll do to her."

"But I don't see –"

"I just want to discover what I can about this whole thing. Maybe figure out some avenue for the law to follow up on. They don't seem able to do it themselves." Again she had to stuff down her agitation. "Please, Ned, help me out here."

More silence. Finally, "Well, Mr. Ramey has a conference to attend in Flagstaff. He's leaving at lunchtime. What about this afternoon?"

"Can we make it after two o'clock? I have to be at Jackson for a few hours."

Ned agreed. "But I really don't feel right about involving ourselves in this matter."

"We wouldn't have to if the damned sheriff's office would do their job and lock that bastard up."

A shuffling at the door made her turn. McFarland. Hat in hand, his tall, gaunt frame leaning against the doorjamb, he just looked at her. Belle said a quick good-bye and hung up the phone.

"If you eavesdrop," she told the sheriff, "you're bound to hear unpleasant things."

"Is that how it is?" He pushed away from the frame, stepped into her cubbyhole office, glanced around. "Those your kids?" He nodded at the pictures on her desk, one of Ellie, another of Will and Lora.

"Can I help you?" she asked.

He considered her, trying to come to a decision, it looked like. Then he nodded. "As a matter of fact, you can."

"Stay out of this thing, right?"

He thought a moment more. "Actually, I could use your help with Lily Poole."

Belle's defensiveness, trickled away. "How?"

"Well, I tried talking to her last night. Wanted to see if she could give me something I could use to lock up her father. But I got nowhere."

"Why did you let him go?"

He rubbed the brim of his Stetson. "Mrs. Evans, maybe you aren't aware of the fact that we can't hold a man in jail without charging him with something. We had no evidence he committed the crime except for the say so of his daughter who has reason to feel prejudiced against him."

"My dad was a cop in Cleveland all his life. He'd have found some reason to hold that man."

McFarland shrugged. "This isn't Cleveland. Arizonans don't like us playing fast and loose with the law."

"Yes well, Clevelanders don't like killers running free."

He watched her with a bland expression – no irritation, no emotion at all. She was pretty good at reading people but this man eluded her.

"I'm sorry," she told him. "I was awake half the night worrying about Lily. Guess my temper got away from me."

"I still need to talk to her. I thought maybe she might be more willing if you were present. Will you come with me?"

"When?"

"Now."

Belle checked her schedule. Just some reports to write and general planning.

"You think she'll talk if I'm there?"

McFarland placed the Stetson on his head. "We'll give it our best shot."

On the ride to The Pines Halfway House McFarland related a little of his conversation with Lily the night before. Belle listened with as much sympathy as she could muster for the man who hadn't managed to keep the father in jail. Of course Lily was upset, and no wonder. She explained the situation to the sheriff who took it in wordlessly.

They reached the halfway house and Belle grew tense as they climbed the steps to the porch. How was Lily coping? How would she react to the sheriff's visit? Mrs. Rivera met them at the door in a purple pants outfit, the flowers of the over-blouse brilliant reds and greens and golds. She glared at the sheriff but had a warm hand for Belle.

"Lily, she has had such a bad night. She has cried much." Another glare at McFarland but he seemed to take it in his stride.

"Do you think she's up to talking about it?" Belle asked. "Sheriff McFarland needs to find out everything he can in order to help her."

Mrs. Rivera looked skeptical, but she let them in and went upstairs to see if Lily would come down. Belle and McFarland went to wait in the parlor, the smell of breakfast still lingering on the air. With most of the girls at school now, the house had that morning silence of old homes. Wind rustled the pines outside in the yard, now and then a car passed, and a large wall clock ticked away the seconds in the dining room across the hall.

The two of them waited in the parlor, standing uncomfortably, not looking at each other. Before long Mrs. Rivera appeared with Lily. Lily looked worn and defeated, eyes red from crying, auburn hair hanging lifeless over her shoulders. Belle gave the girl a hug, long and hard. Partly because Lily seemed to need it and partly because she needed it herself.

Belle led her to the couch, keeping an arm around her, and nodded to Mrs. Rivera who relaxed and went off to the back of the house. McFarland, hat in hand, sat across from them.

He gave Belle a glance that asked for help, so she began. "Lily, the sheriff wants you to answer some questions. Do you think you're up to it this morning? He needs to find all the evidence he can to put your father behind bars. So far nothing's been found to convict him. Sheriff McFarland thought maybe you could give him some clue where to look and what to look for." The sheriff gave her another glance, this time quizzical. Belle quit.

Lily acknowledged the question with a slight nod, her eyes focused on her lap.

McFarland rubbed his jaw. "Lily, let's start at the beginning. You told Detective Carter that Julio called you the night before last. Where was he calling from?"

Lily seemed to steel herself. Belle could see her force the tears back.

"He called me from his house – his uncle's house, where he lives – lived."

"And you were at home?"

"My *dad's* home." Her face screwed up. "He told me it was *his* place and I'd better never forget it."

"What time was that? Approximately?"

Lily hesitated, her forehead wrinkled in thought. "I'm not sure. It was almost dark so maybe around seven or eight, I guess."

He looked encouragingly at her. "What state of mind was Julio in when he called? Excited, worried, upset?"

She glanced at Belle, uncertainty in her eyes, then at the sheriff. "He – he just sounded like himself. Maybe excited. I didn't think about it at the time."

"We hardly ever do," he acknowledged. "And what did Julio call you about?"

"He had something to tell me. Wanted me to meet him at our usual place."

"Lame Horse Canyon?"

Her nod turned into a shudder.

McFarland glanced at his hat. "Now, your father, where was he when Julio called?"

Resentment colored Lily's features. "He was in the back bedroom, nursing his bottle of liquor. Like he always is. What else?"

"So, he didn't hear you talking to Julio?"

"Not at first," she told him. "The phone's in the kitchen, and I kept my voice way down. Julio doesn't call me at home too much because of my dad. *Didn't* call me." She took a moment to swallow, eyes filling again. "My dad always hated any boys I knew, but especially Julio. Always calling him names, like he's good enough to lick Julio's *feet!*"

She straightened, rubbing both her arms. "But sure as anything, he heard me when I started to leave. He gets pissed off at everything when he's like that. He asked me if I was going to meet my Spic boyfriend. I told him we needed milk for breakfast. That I was going out to get some. But he just swore at me and called me a whore. Said I was a liar, too. I guess I was –"

Lily's tears came and Belle moved closer, letting her use a shoulder. After a moment, Lily pulled old tissues from her jeans pocket and blew her nose. "Sorry," she said. The sheriff waited her out.

Grudgingly, Belle had to admire this man. He was cool, easy with the girl. Well, maybe not last night.

When Lily seemed to have a grip on herself, he asked, "So, you went to meet Julio? Your father didn't try to stop you?"

"I just left. He wasn't fast enough to stop me."

"How did you get there?"

Lily eased back a little. "In my Jeep. I still had the keys to it then.

My dad took them away from me yesterday morning and messed up the engine somehow so I couldn't drive to school. Said I could damn well walk. I got a ride from Kimmy. That's when I heard – on the radio –" The tears came once again and Belle comforted her while McFarland waited.

Finally he sat back in a relaxed mode which seemed to relax Lily a little. "Lily, I need to know how much of the fight between Julio Morales and your father you actually witnessed."

She nodded slightly.

"Now, when you drove to Lame Horse Canyon, Julio was there already?"

An affirmative from her.

"Did you know how he got there?"

"His cousin's truck, I guess. I didn't see it but he uses it sometimes to get to school and to work. Other times Carlos takes him and drops him off. I figured he had it hidden behind the bushes like he always does."

The sheriff nodded. "That's where we found the truck Monday morning. Mr. Hernandez identified it." He looked over at Belle, then back at his hat. "When you met Julio, what did he have to say? Why did he have to meet you out at the canyon?"

"He said – he said he'd soon have enough money so we could run away together and – and get married." She sniffed.

"Have money? How was Julio planning to get it?"

"He didn't say. He just told me we could get away from my dad pretty soon and not to worry anymore."

The sheriff rubbed the brim of his hat. Belle began to recognize the gesture when he was concentrating.

"Lily, how long have you known Julio Morales? How long have you two been going together?"

"About a year. I'd seen him around school sometimes. But he was a grade higher than me."

"So how did you meet him?"

"A party Monica had. He came with Monica's boyfriend. Ricardo, he's Mexican, too. Julio and me, we just, I don't know, seemed to hit it off right away. He was so quiet and gentle. Didn't try to show off or nothing – *anything*. You know how most guys are – strutting around like they're big shots, like they got bigger, well, you-know-whats than the others. Not Julio. He was just so sweet. Strong and sweet at the same time."

Belle thought they'd lose her again, but Lily pulled herself together quickly.

McFarland waited until she was ready. "I'm going to ask you something and you have to be honest with me. It's important. Do you know if Julio had ever done anything illegal?"

"No. No." She jerked forward. "He never did anything wrong. He wasn't like that."

"No drugs?"

"No."

"Not even marijuana sometimes?"

"No," Lily insisted. "I know everybody does it, but he was clean. Honest to God. That was one of the things that was so great about him."

He looked her in the eye. "Fights? Did he get into fights?"

"If guys picked on him, sure. You know, racists like my dad? I heard he used to get into fights back when he first moved here. Kids razzing him for not knowing English. Like that. But most of the guys at school respected him. They didn't mess with him about being Mexican, or being older than the other kids in his class."

"Can you think of anything at all he had trouble with? Traffic tickets? Drinking? That sort of thing?"

She shook her head vigorously. "No way. He was clean. Sweet. Honest. Just the best."

"I see." McFarland took a breath. "Where did Julio work?"

"At Mile Hi Earth Movers. He drove some of their bulldozers. He thought it was a great job, loved working there. He worked every day after school and on weekends. They paid him pretty good money."

"Did he ever complain about his boss? People he worked with?"

She shook her head. "Not to me. He liked his job and got along great with everybody."

"Now, when you met him at the canyon, what else did he say?"

"Nothing. My dad drove up in his truck almost as soon as I got there, so we didn't have a chance to talk." She breathed fast and her lips paled.

Belle moved in closer. "Are you all right, Lily?"

The sheriff sat forward. "I know this is hard for you, but I need to know exactly what you saw while it's still fresh."

Lily straightened as if in resolve, determination and a large amount of anger in her eyes.

"Okay, now, your father came. Tell me what happened."

"He stumbled out of the truck, yelling and swearing. I don't even know what he said, it was hard to understand him. He just started at us, yelling things like 'whore' and 'Spic.'"

"You said it was almost dark. How well could you see?"

Lily ran hair behind both her ears, concentrating. "My dad's headlights were on, shining right at us, like a prison spotlight, like we were caught in a plot to escape." A sob made her stop.

McFarland waited while she found her voice again.

"He came up to Julio, yelling at him. When Julio tried to say something, my dad hauled off and punched him in the stomach. I tried to stop it but he hit him again. Then he turned around and hit me, too." Her hand went to the bruise on her face. "Julio went ballistic. He told me to get out, get away. The next time my dad hit him, he let my dad have it, good and hard in the gut. It made me feel so good that Julio wasn't going to take it."

She was breathing heavily, reliving the scene.

"Did you leave then?"

"I – I didn't want to, 'cause I saw the gun sticking out of my dad's pocket."

"Gun? Had you seen this gun before?"

She nodded vigorously.

"Do you know what kind it was?"

She shook her head. "I don't know anything about guns. Except they kill."

"But you'd seen your father with it at other times?"

She looked uncertain. "Well, I've seen him with a gun *like* that. I guess it was the same one."

"When?"

"He liked to get it out and clean it – usually when he was mad about something. Like he was thinking about using it if he could get up the guts to do it."

"What other weapons does he own?"

"That shotgun he carries in the back window of his truck." Her revulsion was evident in her face. "He's got a couple of hunting knives, too. I've seen him skin a jackrabbit with one. You'd-a thought he was making love the way he did it."

Belle's stomach churned.

"Were you afraid for Julio?"

"You bet I was. I was afraid my dad would use the gun on him if he got mad enough."

"Had you ever seen your father use his gun on someone before?"

She shook her head. "When he's sober, he's okay, I guess. Tells me I'm his lifeline, keeping him going. But when he's drunk you can't tell what he's going to do."

"So, why did you leave the canyon?"

Lily checked her hands. Belle could feel a sense of guilt edging in on the girl.

"Julio kept yelling at me to get out of there. My dad hit him and he hit my dad. And he kept yelling to leave."

"So you did?"

She nodded, lips gripped in her teeth.

The sheriff rubbed his hat. "Have you ever known Julio to carry a gun?"

"No. He's not like that. He wouldn't even think of it. He never liked guns either." She stiffened. "Maybe if he had, it would've been my dad on the news the next morning. I wish to God it had been."

At this she broke down in earnest. The interview was over.

8

Belle couldn't get Lily out of her mind, that tragic tilt of her head, the pulling in of her body. She glanced over at McFarland, driving his Jeep Cherokee, and had to admit he'd been perceptive, hadn't pushed Lily too hard. But the girl was still a bundle of emotion. Bad enough that she lose the boy she loved. And he'd died in such a violent way, too. Ordinary people seldom understood the effect of violence on friends and relatives of the victims.

They were heading back to Belle's office when she got a ring on her cell phone. She pulled it out, glanced apologetically at the sheriff – What was the protocol when you rode in an official's vehicle? – and turned it on.

"A fight," she heard from the female counselor at Monroe Middle School. Mae Grubber. A nice lady and very competent. Why wasn't she at the high school instead of Ned Stambaugh?

"What do you need me for?" Belle asked.

"It's racial. A gang of boys beat up on a new Hispanic student. Thought maybe you could talk to them."

When she hung up, McFarland glanced over at her with a question in his eyes.

Belle let out a tremendous sigh full of sadness and frustration. "Seems Monroe Middle is harboring a bunch of young Ralph Pooles."

At her office, Belle checked for any other messages, then went out to her Honda and headed for the middle school. She had a way of handling issues of prejudice among kids. She'd developed it back in Cleveland as a regular high school counselor. There hadn't been a lot of racial issues in the suburban systems where she'd worked. Back East in the middle and upper-class schools it was socially unacceptable to be openly prejudiced, a big difference from when she was growing up. But in the inner cities it still ran rife, and she'd had to handle it with the kids who'd recently moved out to the burbs. As for her dad, he'd dealt with it all the years he'd been with the city police force.

Here, though, the taboos against prejudice didn't seem as pronounced. The Indians had always been part of this land, of course, but the Mexicans were a more recent problem. Wanting only to feed their families and have a piece of the American pie, they swarmed across the border in droves, taking on jobs at slave wages, the second and third generations demanding changes in education and law.

A lot of hard-nosed, independent types who had lived in Arizona all their lives without restricting laws to pen them in and few people around to force change on them were rebelling. They were clinging fiercely to that independence, that old way of life in the face of a huge surge in population. Not just from Mexico, but new people from the East like her and Californians from the West, bringing with them their different standards, their special interests, encroaching on the land. These were the issues that brought on hatred.

So Belle had to use the methods she'd developed for helping kids to understand cultural changes, try to sympathize with the newcomers, deal with a changing society. Trouble was, it didn't work on the Ralph Pooles of the world. They were forever stuck in their hatred and spitting venom at a government gone soft and impossible to comprehend.

After lunch Belle drove to Jackson Elementary for her session with the fourth and fifth graders. She dwelt more heavily on racial issues than she'd intended. Get 'em early, she decided. Clear off the debris before it could solidify and rot away their humanity. Then she went on over to the high school, her adrenaline pumping, on her hunt for the truth.

The halls at school brimmed with activity during pass period, kids hurrying to the next class. A gaggle of girls by the lockers cooed over some hot football player passing by. Three boys came bounding from the bathroom jostling each other in a hilarious game of 'let's knock each other senseless.' A macho-looking kid near the drinking fountain asked a mousy girl if he could copy her term paper. "Nobody'll know," he said.

"I'll know," Belle stopped to tell them.

The two stared at her, then at each other and finally took off in opposite directions.

When she reached Ned Stambaugh's office he greeted her like a nervous hen, still not sure he was doing the right thing. She refused to listen to his arguments and wanted to hear from Julio's friends.

"Who are they? I thought you'd have them here waiting," she said, depositing her purse on a chair.

"Apparently the Morales boy was pretty thick with Jeremy Gibbs and Tom Kelliker," Ned told her. He fidgeted with some papers on his desk. "That's what the other kids have told me."

At her insistence he sent a runner with a note to one of the classrooms for the boys to come to his office.

"I just don't know if we should get involved," Ned said, combing a hand through sandy hair. "If Mr. Ramey finds out we're doing this –"

"Helping a student?"

"He feels we shouldn't interfere. The sheriff even called him and told us to stay out of it."

Belle sat down in one of the other four chairs that lined the wall opposite Ned's desk. "I don't think that's a problem anymore."

After a short while the two boys were led into the room by the girl who'd been sent to find them. They looked at the counselors, then at each other. Guilt colored their faces, the universal reaction of kids being called to an administrator's office.

"It's okay, fellas," Belle said. "I just need your help."

They relaxed a little, but still weren't willing to let go of the possibility of punishment and the need to make a quick exit. Who knew?

Belle led them back to the conference room and got them seated. She didn't close the door but Ned, after checking them out, apparently decided not to have any part of this.

Jeremy Gibbs had stringy blond hair to his shoulders. He was short and heavy, jeans slung low on his hips, a sizable belly stretching the black T-shirt. He had nervous hands: flexing, gripping, sticking them under his thighs then pulling them out again. His eyes never quite met Belle's, as though the light in hers was too bright.

Tom Kelliker, tall and thin and dark, had an acne problem, his face dotted with old scars and new eruptions. In worn jeans – worn from use rather than from a manufacturer's acid wash – and a green T broadcasting his hatred of hard work, he appeared to be the no-nonsense one, eyes sullen, a grimness fixed on his jaw.

Neither looked like the quarterback on the football team nor like they had a problem fighting off the girls. Belle smiled sympathetically at the pains of teenagerhood.

"Man, I can't believe what happened to Julio," Jeremy told her, his hands working nervously. "He's such a nice guy. Who'd wanna do that to him. Man, that sucks the big one."

"Bet it was Lily's ole man," Tom said. "That bastard – sorry ma'am. Hated Julio. Called Lily all kinds-a terrible things. Bet it was him did it. I just bet it was."

Belle let them talk.

"Hadda be that creep," Jeremy said, pounding his fist in his hand. "Man, the way he treated Lil sometimes –"

"Was him killed her mom," Tom said.

Belle nodded. "Julio must have wanted to help Lily – with her situation."

"Julio, he was gonna get her away from that ole fart ass if he could. You know what I'm saying?" This from Jeremy.

Tom agreed. "Told us him and Lily was gonna run away and get married."

"Did he have specific plans?" she asked.

"Worked hard at Mile Hi, keeping his money just so's he could get her away."

Jeremy sat forward, his stomach protruding over his belt, hands gripping the arms of the chair. "Julio told us he wanted to get Lil outta there 'fore she got what her mom got. 'Cept he got it first. Man, that is so ghetto. They ought-a string up ole Poole!" He pantomimed pulling on a noose, seemed to think he'd gone too far and slid back in his chair, head bent.

"Did he tell you how he was going to get enough money?"

Jeremy stuck his hands under his thighs. "Just work is all I know. Right, Tom?"

Tom nodded. "Work. Saved all his money. He'd-a done it, too, give 'em time." The boy looked on the verge of tears. "Too bad it wasn't the other way – Julio killing that bastard." He turned away.

Belle cocked her head, taking them both in, assessing them in order to understand Julio Morales. A clock on the wall ticked. The noise of a group of students rushing in and out of Ned's office made the boys jump a little, then everything settled down.

"How long had you two known Julio?" she asked.

Jeremy thought about it. "Sixth grade, I guess. That's when he come to Granite. Moved in with his aunt and uncle. Sixth grade, right, Tom?"

Tom nodded. "Not best friends or nothing back then."

Jeremy grinned. "He used to get into some fights, man. Guys picking on him all the time cause he was from Mexico. Harsh! But Julio, he showed 'em. If he couldn't speak English good, he sure knew how to fight. Then, 'course, his older cousin Carlos'd come looking for them guys that started it. So after a while they stopped picking on him."

"When did you fellows become friends?"

"Freshman year," Tom told her, rubbing at a large pimple that seemed to irritate him. "Been buds since then."

"And you're seniors now?"

They both nodded. Jeremy said, "Julio, too. Course he's a little older than us. Was," he added quietly and looked away. "Got a late start cause of not knowing English. But he sure caught up. Know what I'm saying?" The hands were animated again.

"Last year and a half we didn't see him as much," Tom added. "'Cause of him working weekends and then Lily. But we always hung at school."

"Yeah, he sure was a great friend, man," Jeremy added. "Last year he got us outta trouble with the gym teacher. The time we soaked all the football team's jocks in kerosene. Sweet! Gym teacher liked Julio so Julio said he done it when it was really me'n Tom. He got suspended for three days for it. Whoa, man!"

Tom gave a small laugh. "He spent them days working at Mile Hi and earned big bucks. Thanked us for the chance to do it."

Jeremy laughed, too. Then his eyes got wet and he brushed his face irritably. "Man, he rocked."

Belle cleared her throat. "What do you know about Julio and Ralph Poole? Had Poole ever attacked Julio before?"

Jeremy's hands started dancing. "Julio stayed away from that dickhead. Lil made him."

"So, they had never met? Never had dealings?"

Tom shook his head. "Julio talked about it sometimes, how he'd like to beat that bastard to a pulp."

"But as far as you know, that never happened?"

This time both heads shook.

"Too bad, though," Jeremy stuck in, his face hard with anger and hurt. "Julio should-a beat the crap outta that man long ago. Know what I'm saying? Maybe this wouldn't-a happened."

Belle talked to them a little longer but neither boy seemed to know what occurred the night Julio was killed. Finally she thanked them and sent them out. Ned wrote them passes and they left.

Belle remained where she was for a while, wondering if she'd learned anything of importance. Julio had two staunch friends in Jeremy and Tom, a girl who loved him, and a teacher who was friend to both. Rosa Perez, she'd want to know what Lily's present situation was.

Belle waited around till the end of the school day then headed across the courtyard for Building C. Rosa was talking to a student. She looked up and waved Belle in. When the girl left, Belle came on up to the desk.

"I heard you were at the school," Rosa said.

"I was talking to Jeremy Gibbs and Tom Kelliker."

Rosa shook her head, a wry smile on her lips. "There's a pair for you. Julio's best friends. Goof-offs if there ever were any. I had them in my class last year. But no harm in them." She walked around the desk.

Belle nodded. "That's the impression I got."

"Do you know what's happening with Lily?" Rosa asked. "That tub of lard Ramey won't tell us anything."

Belle filled her in and Rosa grew white around the mouth. "When will she come back to school?"

"In a few days, I think," Belle told her. "She seemed a little better today. Mrs. Rivera's being very protective of her, according to the sheriff."

"No child should have to go through all this."

Belle nodded and glanced out the windows at the mountains in the distance. Afternoon clouds gathered over them, some virga descending – rain that evaporated before it could touch the ground. The courtyard was slowly emptying of students.

"What was Julio like?" she asked Rosa Perez. "What kind of person? You said he wanted to help his family. I know he wanted to help Lily. What else can you tell me?"

Rosa's mouth puckered for a moment. "He was very polite in class, seemed thoughtful of people, though he kept to himself a lot. He had to work hard at language, learning English. When he came here in the sixth grade he knew so little."

"Did he have a temper or anything like that?"

Rosa gave a half grin. "Enough so the kids who used to pick on him learned to leave him alone. Julio was usually quiet and respectful, but you didn't want to cross him."

"When did you have him in class?"

"I first had him his sophomore year. And then again last year when he was a junior. I teach tenth and eleventh grade literature and composition." Rosa's eyes lit up. "I remember his sophomore year early in the fall; a couple of other Hispanics were in the class, having trouble with the lessons. One day they swore in Spanish as if I couldn't understand them, right? Said they didn't know why they had to learn the language. Wasn't Spanish good enough?"

She waved her hand at the classroom walls, English posters covering them. "Julio got right in their faces and told them in Spanish that if they wanted to live in the United States, they damn well better learn its language and stop whimpering about it like babies. Otherwise, get the hell back to Mexico." She laughed outright. "I'm here to tell you, the boys did not argue about learning English again – at least not in my presence. Or in his."

Rosa's laugh died a cold death. "So now I'm worried about Lily. She's a strong girl but she has a lot to deal with."

"You could visit her at The Pines," Belle suggested. "She thinks a lot of you. She'd probably be grateful to see you."

"I'll do that. If that fat Ramey won't tell us anything, I'll find out for myself."

Back at her office Belle checked her messages. All quiet on the Western Front. She sat for a moment, staring out her small window through the willow, beyond the building next door, to the mountains. The afternoon sun on the tops of tree and building was a mellow orange – normally a peaceful hue. But peace wouldn't come to her.

Poole was still out there. McFarland had said he had someone watching him, but how effective would that prove? Mrs. Rivera was taking care of Lily, but she had other girls and other duties keeping up the halfway house.

Why had Poole picked that time to kill Julio? Why not at the beginning of his daughter's relationship? Lily had said they'd been going out now for about a year. Why hadn't Poole attacked him before this? Another question – if the father had been so abusive, why hadn't Lily and Julio just gone ahead and left?

The second question had been answered by Rosa – Julio's sense of responsibility. He wouldn't take Lily away unless he could support her. For some reason he apparently felt he'd be able to do that soon. How had finances changed for him? Did he have a benefactor? Was he planning a robbery? How would he get his hands on a lot of money? A lot for him, anyway.

McFarland seemed to be wondering, too, when he asked Lily if Julio had dabbled in something illegal. Lily had been adamant, insisted Julio wouldn't do anything like that. But then Lily was in love with the boy – so who could tell?

Maybe there was some answer at Mile Hi Earth Movers where Julio worked. Tomorrow she'd take her lunch hour and go talk to them.

"Ramey and the sheriff be damned," she told the air. Only it came out cockier than she felt.

9

Briefcase in hand, Belle headed out the door of her apartment the next morning. Her landlords were in the driveway, Bern Wozak apparently getting a late start. Around here construction workers were on the job by six-thirty and it was nearly eight o'clock now. He waved at Belle coming down the outside staircase, grabbed the lunch bucket from Adrian, who gave him a hug, then climbed into his mud-splattered, Chevy pickup.

Adrian blew a kiss as he watched Bern drive off, then turned to Belle. "Did you sleep better last night, love?" he asked.

Belle lifted an eyebrow at him.

"Darling girl, you live right above us. I can tell when you're pacing the floor, for God's sake."

Belle let out a laugh. "Got no secrets from you, huh?"

"This is an old house. What can I say? I'm sure it was in the lease – 'No secrets kept here.'"

"Oh God, Adrian. What a lousy world this is sometimes."

He came over to her, deep sympathy in his face. "How's the Poole girl doing?"

"All right, I guess. I gave Mrs. Rivera my cell phone number. Told her to call me no matter what." Belle flipped a hand. "So far I haven't heard anything. I'll check on Lily sometime today."

Adrian took hold of her arms and looked straight at her. "We do what we can in this world, Belle. No guarantees, just perseverance and dumb luck. Lily Poole wasn't lucky. Until she met you."

She shook her head at him. "That remains to be seen."

Belle made her Wednesday morning rounds to the schools on this week's list – the two middle schools and Red Rock Elementary over on Gila Lane – setting up schedules for grade level talks with their principals and counselors.

Back at the board building at ten she got a call from Harold Ramey's office. Jenny, his secretary, was on the line.

"He'd like you to be here at 10:30, Ms. Evans," she said. "Don't know what it's about. Just seemed urgent. Mr. Ramey gets – well, you know – kind of insistent about things."

"Yes, I do know," Belle said, already on the defensive.

"Could be about Lily Poole," Jenny suggested. "How is that poor girl doing?"

"As well as can be expected. I called to check on her at the halfway house this morning. Sounds like she might be back in school tomorrow. I'd better give Ned the heads up."

Jenny snapped her gum. "Hard to believe, isn't it? I mean – you know – the murder and all."

After finishing today's report – that was one of the stipulations of hiring her, to keep records of all activities so the board could evaluate the success of her position – she took off for the high school feeling like a lamb to the slaughter. She figured Ramey would chew her out again. He probably found out about her questioning Julio's friends and was undoubtedly mad as hell at her for not letting this go.

She tried to relax and allow herself to be dazzled by the August sunshine flooding the streets as she drove. It washed the adobe Wells Fargo building and the new post office with lustrous white light, shone on the plumes of pampas grass and flower stalks of Russian sage lining sidewalks, warmed the back of an old man on a bike, blinded two others with backpacks hoofing it. She wondered if this much pure sunshine could addle the brain. Was hers already pickled, taking on this case?

Entering Building A, she headed for the main office. Jenny's large body was decked out in a pink polyester skirt and vest combo. She gave Belle a conspiratorial glance, her head to one side as though talking in secret. "Mr. Stambaugh's with Mr. Ramey now," she said. "*And*, would you believe it, Morgan Andrews is in there. You know, running for the U.S. senate? Him and that manager of his."

"Morgan Andrews?" Belle's eyes grew round.

"I know," Jenny whispered as though someone might overhear. "Could-a knocked me over with a feather. Mr. Andrews' manager called first thing this morning. But Mr. Ramey never told me about it till the man walked in – right here in the office. Couldn't-a been fifteen minutes after I called you." She giggled. "What a surprise, huh? Then Mr. Ramey calls Mr. Stambaugh into his office. After that I haven't – you know – heard a thing." She leaned across her desk, whispering again. "Kind of exciting, don't you think?"

Belle couldn't feel so optimistic. Was Ramey going to chew her out in front of this big-name politician? Was Ned there to corroborate her meddling? She probably shouldn't have talked to Julio's friends. At least not in Ned's office. Damn. She resigned herself, knocked, and entered the inner sanctum.

Morgan Andrews was somehow bigger and grander in person than he was on TV. Usually it was the other way around. His political ads didn't do him justice. He was taller than she'd thought, in his fifties, the salt with a little pepper in his hair, startling against his tan. Did he have his own makeup specialist? His gray eyes captured hers, radiating sincerity and honest concern – a trick of the trade, she knew. He wore jeans and a forest green short-sleeve shirt open at the collar, looking like just one of the boys. He got up and came forward, hand extended. Was she being unfair to him?

"Belle Evans?" he said. "This is the woman who's been working on the Morales murder case? Protecting the Poole girl? Belle, I'm proud to shake your hand." And he did it vigorously in a two-handed grip.

Belle stood stunned, letting her arm be pumped. This was a congratulatory meeting? How was that possible? He led her to another man at the table who stood up to greet her.

"My manager and good friend, Paul Cochran," he told her.

Cochran held out a hand to shake. "I'm glad to meet you, Ms. Evans. We think what you're doing is so important, so self-sacrificing."

Belle took him in, assessing him in connection with his boss. Tall and thin and younger, maybe forty, with dark hair and horn-rimmed glasses against pale skin. And a quiet rigidity in his stance. He exuded intensity like radiation, and idolatry for the other man filled his eyes. Wearing a suit, he gave the appearance of attending a different kind of function from that of Andrews.

Andrews pulled out a chair for her at Ramey's table and held it while she sat down. Harold Ramey and Ned were already seated, a cowed expression on both their faces. Belle was too amazed to laugh.

Andrews sat down himself. "Now, Belle, I want to know all about the case from your point of view. Tell me what's been happening."

Belle swallowed to make sure her throat would work. "I – um – was told to let it alone, actually."

He nodded. "I've discussed it with Harold,"

"Well, not just him."

"Mac."

"Who?"

"Eli. Sheriff McFarland." He grinned. "Mac and I are old friends. We go back all the way to high school in Tempe. Played football together. Stayed in touch ever since. He was best man at my wedding, Godfather to my son."

"I see." She raised an eyebrow at Ramey and Ned.

"I understand Mac's concern," Andrews told her. "He doesn't want any more people hurt. But I have to tell you, Belle, I admire the way you've stood up for Lily against a racist father like hers."

Again she glanced at the principal.

Andrews sat back, one ankle propped on the other knee, his gray hair catching light from one of the windows in the office. "Ned's been filling me in on this case, haven't you, Ned?"

Ramey beamed artificially at Ned and the counselor looked shyly proud.

"Belle, I understand Ralph Poole threatened you."

Belle glanced at Ned. She'd dumped all the details on him, trying to make him feel guilty enough to develop a little pluck. "Actually, his threat to me was all talk, I think. It was mostly the Doberman and the possibility of a gun. And a lot of swearing. The real threat is to his daughter. I'm more afraid for her."

Ramey sat forward. "She's at The Pines Halfway House now, isn't she, Mrs. Evans? Isabel? She's being taken very good care of."

Belle looked Ramey in the eye. "They can't keep her for long. They're full up so it's a temporary fix. The real solution would be putting Poole in jail. *Which* hasn't happened yet."

Ramey hunched back in his chair.

Andrews' expression changed. His voice became quieter. "It's the hate groups. They have too much influence in this state – this brutality towards Hispanics and Native Americans. Paul knows. It's one of the key issues in our campaign."

Ah yes, Belle thought, but quelled her reaction to the realization of why she was here.

Cochran nodded. "Morgan has always struggled for that issue to be dealt with. It's been one of his biggest efforts. Once in the senate, he'll finally have a chance to get justice for these crimes."

"I have personal reasons as well as public," Andrews said quietly as though moving into some private world. "I've seen first hand what hate groups can do."

He grew silent and Cochran looked on the verge of taking over for him, but Andrews lifted his chin.

"We need to put an end to crimes of hate. We need to yank prejudice out by the roots. The Black Falcons in Gilbert were the group responsible for the two Latino men killed in Casa Grande last year. Dragged them behind a truck, then hanged them from the rafters of an abandoned barn. It was sickening. Two of them were arrested, but I'm sure the others were behind it."

"Brutal," Cochran said, his glance hardening.

Belle remembered the case, something that had happened just before she'd moved here. It had made her wonder if her choice to come to Arizona was the right one.

"Hate crimes are a cancer feeding on our society," Morgan Andrews told them. "Time to get tough on them."

"I've heard of the Black Falcons, naturally," Ramey said. "But we've never had trouble like that up here in Granite."

"Until now."

Ramey didn't look convinced. He gestured toward Belle. "That's one of the reasons we've hired Isabel, to work with our students before such gangs develop. Isn't that right?"

Belle conceded the point.

Andrews glanced around the table. "Something interesting – according to our sources, Poole's been known to attend one or two of the Falcon meetings. I've already informed the authorities." He settled himself in the chair. "That's the trouble with my opponent Lloyd Pruitt. He's actually spent time and money working *against* the Mexican and Indian communities in this state. It's like handing hate groups like the Falcons a free reign."

Belle saw his conviction and wondered if this was going to turn into a political speech. But in the end, they got the shortened version. After all, only three voters in the room.

When he finished, he turned to her. "Channel 5 news is covering the murder, Belle. Would you be willing to do a spot with me concerning this matter?"

"Oh wait." She jumped, almost upsetting her chair. "I'm sorry, Mr. Andrews. I –"

"Call me Morgan."

"I'm sorry. I just couldn't do a television spot."

He moved his chair nearer. "You'd be a wonderful promotion for antiracism. Wouldn't she Paul?"

Cochran nodded. "You'd be perfect, Ms. Evans."

Andrews hit her with his intense gaze. "I can see your conviction in your face. I can see how much this issue means to you."

"Honestly, I couldn't," she insisted. She looked to Ramey for help. "I need to keep a low profile in this job to be effective."

"You helped out Lily Poole," Andrews reminded her.

"That's right," Ramey joined in. No help there.

"But that isn't widely known." Belle stood resolute. "No, I really couldn't. But thank you for having so much confidence in me. And thank you for supporting us in this matter," she said, taking in Ramey and Ned. She could be politic, too.

Andrews tried one more time to convince her but she turned him down. No way would she go on television. Wouldn't let herself be used as a pawn for someone who was running for office.

Ned seemed floored by the whole episode. Ramey had that cold, administrative glint in his eye. She didn't care. With a quick good-bye to Andrews and Cochran, she left the meeting.

Jenny asked what had happened but Belle didn't want it telegraphed around the school in Jenny-fashion.

"I'll tell you about it later," she said and made a fast exit, thanking God for a narrow escape.

10

Mile Hi Earth Movers had its establishment outside the town limits of Granite on Piñon Road out beyond Benton's car dealership and Potter's Nursery. The road moved through boulders and small growth as it climbed and wound its way toward the summit. Mile Hi sat at the top.

Huge fingers of buttermilk clouds spread across the sky like an outstretched hand with too many digits. The air was hot and hung with the weight of humidity. Probably no rain in the forecast even though sweat gathered under Belle's arms and at the back of her neck.

At the site, two large pole barns, apparently used as equipment and work sheds, were background to a low prefab building that housed the office. Bulldozers, backhoes, a crane and a trencher sat out in the yard along with two flatbed trucks for transporting them. Not a lot of storage, she thought. Some of the dozers must have to sit in the yard exposed to the elements. Belle stopped herself. What elements? She had to remember she wasn't in Cleveland anymore.

She drove her Honda into a space by the office, stuck the rest of her sandwich into the Baggie, and got out. In the yard a couple of workers, bandanas on their heads, sleeveless T-shirts, jeans so faded and dusted they looked white, and wearing beards – they loved their beards out here – were busy on one of the machines. They turned her way and stared. Not many women came around here, she guessed. She shouldered her purse and entered the low building.

The main office was very basic. A few girly pictures decorated one wall. A big calendar, a time clock for checking in and out, some notices, a couple of ratty looking chairs. Except for handprints and smears on walls and doors, that was the extent of the décor.

An old air conditioner chugged in a far window. At one end a long counter separated the office workers from the rest of the room and a door behind with a window indicated an inner office. The door was shut but Belle could see two men through the glass, one sitting at a desk, the other standing, engaged in a heated conversation. Even from where she was she could hear them swearing at each other. The glass door didn't keep much private.

A young man, no beard, clean shirt and jeans, stood behind the counter watching Belle's approach and ignoring the exchange in the office. "Need something, ma'am?"

"I want to talk to the person in charge," she told him, coming up to the counter. "Who would that be?"

He nodded toward the closed door. "Fred Preacher. He's busy. Whadaya need?"

"The person in charge."

He shrugged. "Have to wait." He went to the far side behind the long counter, pulled out some folders and began to sort. The conversation in the office continued.

Belle watched the man sorting a moment, then walked over to where the chairs were, eyed them doubtfully and decided to stand.

In a few minutes the office meeting was climaxed by the door being slung open so hard the glass in it rattled. One of the men stalked out. The fellow at the counter gave it a beat then peeked in the office door.

"A lady here to see ya, Fred."

The man at the desk looked over and glared. Finally he nodded. "Send'er in."

The young man looked at Belle, motioned toward the inner office and went back to his sorting. As Belle entered the room, cigarette smoke assailed her. The office was big enough but it was obvious they didn't hire a cleaning staff. Waste baskets overflowed, walls showed streaks from a leaky roof, the desk was in need of paint, and the big ashtray at the side reeked with a mountain of butts. Some, she guessed by the smell, were a week old at least. She turned off her senses.

Fred Preacher looked to be in his fifties, skin sun-hardened to the consistency of leather, iron hair thin and pulled back in a ponytail. No beard, but he wore a work shirt and jeans.

"Mr. Preacher?" Belle began as she stepped toward the desk. There was no place to sit down. "I'm Belle Evans from the Granite School District." She didn't bother holding out a hand, doubting if he'd take it.

"Whadaya want? I'm pretty busy."

She picked her words. "One of our high school students is very upset over the death of Julio Morales and I –"

"Cops already been here. Told 'em I didn't know nothing."

"Of course. The sheriff's concerned about who committed the crime. I'm concerned about Julio's girlfriend."

His glance was suspicious, guarded. "The Poole girl."

"Lily, yes." She stepped closer to the desk. "I thought perhaps if I

knew a little more about Julio Morales I'd be able to comfort her better."
Almost the truth.

Preacher picked up a pencil, pulled an invoice toward him. Not
promising. "I don't know nothing about Morales."

"He worked for you."

"Yeah, so?"

He wasn't going to make this easy on her. "Lily said Julio liked
working for you very much. Was he a good worker?"

"Sure. He took to them machines like he invented 'em. Worked
damned hard. I could-a used him regular, but he wanted to go to school.
Hell, I never finished school and look where I am."

She wasn't sure where that was so she refrained from commenting.
"I understand his salary was sufficient."

"Hell yes." He pulled out a cigarette and lit it. "I pay good wages.
Ain't had no complaints. I started up in this business driving dozers." He
blew out smoke into an already saturated room and sat back. "Bought my
first dozer when I was thirty-five. Got me a backhoe after that and I was
in business. Built up from there. Now I own the biggest damn company
in these parts."

"No wonder Julio liked working for you," she conceded. "You
must have taken part in a lot of the projects around town, the way it's
grown up the last ten years."

"You bet. The one got me started big was the Tucker Highway
project. Started working that one eleven – twelve years ago. Took 'em
three years to complete. After that, I was in the big leagues."

"I'm impressed."

He blew out smoke and Belle stifled a cough.

"Mr. Preacher, Lily said that Julio thought he might come into a
fair amount of money soon. Would you know anything about that?"

Now the man stiffened. He sat forward. "Don't know what you're
talking about. How the hell should I know what Morales was up to? He
worked for me. That's all."

Belle watched him. He pulled in a drag from his cigarette like a
drowning man pulling in air.

"I just wondered," she said mildly. "Lily seems sure of two things,
that Julio thought he could get enough money to take her away, and that
her father killed him."

"Look, lady, what're you after?" he burst out. "I only know about
Morales 'cause he drove for me. Nothing else." He jammed out his
cigarette in the overflowing ashtray, sending butts spraying over his desk
top. "That's all I gotta say." Now he got to his feet and came around the

desk, eyes hard and body a threat. "So why don't you just get the hell outta here?"

Belle shrugged. "Well, thank you for your time." Heart racing with a combination of alarm and elation, she somehow made herself move with unconcern.

Out in the Honda she sat staring at the building before her. Damn, if she hadn't struck a chord.

That afternoon Belle visited Monroe Middle School again, checking on the situation from Tuesday. Then at the board building she had a conference with Superintendent Cummerford and several of the board members to discuss her job success so far, and what she planned to accomplish for the first semester of the year in the way of special programs for the students.

"Your plans sound ambitious, Ms. Evans," Cummerford told her, getting nods from the members present. "We hope you're able to carry them out with success."

Cummerford asked her about the Lily Poole situation and Belle cited Morgan Andrews' commendation on her involvement. The superintendent seemed impressed. She didn't mention her interview at Mile Hi Earth Movers.

After the conference she cleared away paper work in her office and was setting up Thursday's schedule when the phone rang. Ned Stambaugh's voice had that slight edge of panic in it that seemed to accompany any crisis.

"You talked to them before," he said. "I thought maybe they'd listen to you if not to me." Jeremy Gibbs and Tom Kelliker were apparently stewing for a fight.

Belle wished to God Ned could handle this, but that was asking for the unattainable. Heaving a sigh, she agreed to come. Schedule finished, she drove back to the high school, ready to do her best.

Verna Reilly, Ned's secretary, was a tall, spare woman of few words and fewer emotions. Except, of course, disdain, which seemed to pour from her like a fountain. A high counter separated her work area from the student 'Bull Pen' as the kids called the waiting area. She looked up as Belle entered and from her place behind the counter nodded Belle in without breaking stride on her keyboard.

The boys were in Ned's conference room. Mr. Burke, the gym teacher, had referred them to Ramey who had handed them over to guidance. Apparently they'd been bragging to some of the students about how they were going to punch out Poole's lights good and proper.

"Man, he killed Julio," Jeremy insisted when she got them settled in the back room. He squeezed his chunky form into the chair, belly protruding, hands on the arms, fingers drumming a rhythm.

Ned hovered at the door of the cramped room while Belle talked to them. She looked them both over, saw their anger, their grief, their need to do something solid and physical. Their friend's murder was finally hitting them hard.

"Jeremy, we don't know for sure that he killed Julio."

"He done it, all right. Didn't he, Tom?" He swung his blond head in his friend's direction.

Tom Kelliker sat next to Jeremy, tall, thin, sullen. "Done it. Killed Julio. Everybody knows that."

"And the police ain't doing nothing about it, man. Just letting him get away with it." Jeremy punched his hand with a fist. "It ain't fair. He's a lousy, drunken killer. Even hit Lil. Man, he killed his wife. Gonna kill Lil, somebody don't stop him. Know what I'm saying? He's a bastard, don't deserve to live."

Belle watched him as the red diffused his round face, as he pounded his fist on the arm of the chair, as his eyes moistened with emotion. Tom leaned back glowering and looking away, also on the verge of tears. Two softies who talked big.

She eased forward in her chair, her voice gentle. "Jeremy, Tom, we understand how you feel. All of us do. The frustration is sometimes unbearable." She looked them over. "But the law has to handle this. It's one of those times when we have to sit back and allow someone else to deal with it."

"Man, that's just ghetto. Them cops ain't gonna do nothing. Should-a had him in jail by now."

Tom glared off across the room, long dark hair in his eyes. The acne brighter with his effort not to cry. "Needs to have somebody mess *him* up for a change, the sonofabitch. Needs to see what it's like to be on the other end for once."

A jolt of alarm ran through Belle at the sound in the boy's voice and the look on his face. "Tom, you have to let the police take care of this."

"They ain't gonna do it," he insisted, bringing his gaze to her, eyes swimming. "Been done already if they was."

"Man, Julio's got friends," Jeremy said. "What'er friends for if they can't fight for ya? Know what I mean?"

Belle glanced at Ned for help, but he shrank away from the door, giving her an 'I told you so' look.

She turned back, picking her words carefully, trying to penetrate the thick heads of these teenagers. "Fellows, let me tell you something. If Ralph Poole was able to hurt Julio, he'd be able to do the same to you."

"There's two of us. One-a him," Jeremy told her.

"He has a nasty tempered Doberman," she said. "And, according to the police, an even nastier shotgun. And who knows what else? I'm telling you, Jeremy, Tom, the man is dangerous. We don't want what happened to Julio to happen to you. Bad enough we lost one person. Let's not make it three."

Mention of the shotgun appeared to give them both pause. Jeremy glanced down at his hands gripping the chair arms, his expression one of consideration. Belle waited.

"He's got it coming," he said, but with less conviction in his voice.

"No one's disputing that. But there are ways to do it, ways that don't get more people hurt. I'm working on it myself."

Tom sat up with a look of dawning respect in his face. "You, Miz Evans?"

She nodded. "But I'm not putting myself in danger." Well, maybe she was a little. The memory of her own confrontation with Poole sprang to mind. "And I'm not interfering in the work of the police." Of course, she'd gone to talk to Julio's boss which wasn't exactly in her job description. But these boys didn't need to know that. "So I want you to do the same. You can keep your eyes and ears open, be a friend to Lily once she gets back to school. Please, though, let's let the law handle Ralph Poole. What do you say?"

The two studied her question. Looking at each other, they appeared somewhat deflated. Youthful anger and indignation was like a narcotic, easy to whip up, hard to lick the habit of the high it gave you. Finally they glanced at her again.

Jeremy flopped back in the chair. "I guess you're right, Miz Evans. But, man, he deserves to get his lights punched out good. You know?"

"Tom?" she asked.

Tom nodded. "Leave 'em to the cops. But if they don't get him –" He left the implication dangling.

When they had gone back to class, Belle didn't feel the relief she'd hoped for. Neither did Ned.

"Well, at least you fared better than I was able to," he told her. "With me, they just kept talking about beating him up – like it was the manly thing to do and I ought to understand."

"Some things just need a woman's touch," she grinned. And some plain old common sense, she hoped.

God help those boys if they went out to Poole's place. That dog and that shotgun loomed ugly in her mind.

After talking to the two boys, Belle went to Building E to see what Ronald Burke, the gym teacher and football coach, had to say about Jeremy and Tom, find out why he'd felt it necessary to send them to the office.

Burke was short, burly, with thinning hair, looking more like a counselor than a coach. Belle had met him on several occasions, a quiet man who seemed too gentle to enjoy something as brutal as football. And yet the school was proud of him, since he won them a record number of victories.

He had his freshman class out on the basketball court in back, drilling them on lay-up shots when Belle came out. He waved at her, said something to one of the boys he gave his whistle to, and walked over to join her.

"Here about Gibbs and Kelliker?" he asked.

Belle did a sad half smile. "Are they always this much trouble?"

"Maybe because they're seniors. Kids get antsy their senior year. Want to get out of school and try their wings. Trouble is, most of 'em can't fly yet, so they fall to earth with a painful bang."

"These two seem to be hitting the sod a record number of times," she told him. "Can you tell me what this thing was about?"

Burke shook his head, scratching above the hair line. "If I was a guessing man, I'd say they're starting to feel Julio Morales's death. Itching to do something about it. Kids, they always think there's an answer. Go fight somebody and the pain'll go away, right?"

"That's the way they think." She watched the students doing lay-ups, one row boys, one row girls. The girls were giving the boys a run for their money. "You knew Julio fairly well, didn't you?"

He glanced away then back. "Good kid. He took a lotta heat when he first moved here. Could hardly speak English. Got into a few fights himself. But the others learned to respect him. He worked hard and played fair. Couldn't help but win them over in the end."

"Did he have many friends?" she asked.

"Friends? I don't know. He kept to himself pretty much. You could tell there were things he didn't talk about. Besides, I think he was too busy to make a lot of friends. No time and no money to go to games and parties. These last few years he worked his tail off earning cash to send back home to Mexico. Earning money was important to him, that and graduating. No real time for friends. But the kids, they thought he was pretty cool."

"He made friends with Jeremy and Tom, didn't he?"

Burke laughed. "Those two meatheads. A couple of jerk-offs. But no harm to them. Julio took them under his wing. Stood up for them, spent whatever time he had with them." Another laugh, deeper this time. "He even took the blame for some of their shenanigans. Those two got mad at the football team last year because the fellows were making fun of them. So Gibbs and Kelliker soaked all the jock straps in kerosene. Lord. When I went to nail them, Julio said he'd done it. Took the blame. Got suspended for it. I knew it was them that did it, but what the heck."

"They told me about that one." She studied her hands, then looked up. "I'm worried about those two boys. And Lily Poole."

He nodded. "Heard about that. Heard you confronted her ole man. Against Ramey's orders."

"Yeah, well –"

"Good for you. Time we had a counselor with guts. Just don't get yourself fired for it, you hear? I'd hate to see another casualty of this thing."

The kids at the basketball net were starting to tussle over the ball so Burke excused himself. Belle watched. How could a boy who engendered so much respect from so many people get himself killed? And what was the likelihood of his friends sharing the same fate?

11

Mac had two surprises when he got back to the station Wednesday afternoon. Semi surprises, actually. When he thought about it, he could have predicted both. One was a message that Belle Evans had called and wanted him to call her back. The other was waiting for him in his office.

"Morgan, how've you been?" he said hanging up his Stetson and holding out his hand to the man in the big chair. Paul Cochran, in the other seat, he only knew slightly.

Andrews got up to grip the hand and pulled Mac into a bear hug. "Mac, you old war horse, it's good to see you. I was in town checking on the rally we're having on the courthouse steps and had to stop by."

"And find out about the latest murder? I know you pretty well." Andrews had gone serious and Mac changed his tone. "How're Mary Jane and the girls?"

"Mary Jane's playing grandma and loving it," Andrews told him. "Aggie gave birth in January and Mary Jane thinks *she's* the rightful mother. Carrie's back at Harvard getting her law degree."

"Like her ole man?"

Morgan nodded. "Mac, you know my manager, Paul Cochran."

Mac took Cochran's hand. "Good to see you again, Paul. You keeping this fellow in line?"

"I don't need to."

Mac looked him over. A tall man, as tall as Mac but at least ten years younger. Thin and pale from too much time spent indoors. He wore a suit to Morgan's jeans and shirt. Interesting contrast.

Cochran had an intensity to him that radiated through the outward covering. He seemed devoted to Morgan like a dog to his master. Married to a woman dedicated to the church, Mac knew, and no children to bring a little humanizing chaos to the home. He and his wife each seemed to have their separate areas of commitment.

"We keep hearing good things about you, Mac," Cochran told him, taking his seat again and adjusting thick horn-rimmed glasses. "And since we've been back to Arizona, Morgan spends a lot of time reminiscing. So I get all the old stories of your years together."

Morgan laughed. "Paul's a Massachusetts man. Can't get used to our wild and wooly ways. Rough country out here. Tough people. Paul's from a gentler set and more refined. Wouldn't say 'shit' if he had a mouthful."

Cochran blushed slightly. "We have a couple of tall tales from Massachusetts, too," he insisted.

"What do you think of Arizona?" Mac asked him.

Cochran shrugged. "It's not the East, of course, but it's where Morgan is." He scratched the back of his hand. "My wife has found her niche here, working with some of the Indian schools through the church."

"And Paul likes the fishing and hunting well enough. Wouldn't take him for an outdoorsman, now would you? Most of the time he's got his nose in a book."

"History, primarily," Cochran explained. "I've learned a lot about the history of this state. It's pretty remarkable. Especially the tribal histories. My wife pushed me into that."

Sarah, Mac's civilian aide and tech assistant, knocked on the open door. He motioned her in, introduced her to the other two. Sarah nodded but her demeanor was one of cool poise. Tall, thin, wearing glasses and a man's haircut, she was called 'Ice Maiden' by the other employees. Mac knew better, but he never disillusioned anyone.

"I've checked on the Morales bank records," she said and handed him the report.

"Thanks." He glanced at it. A couple thousand. Nothing remarkable. Just what you might expect from a working person. No sign he banked any large amounts.

Sarah turned and exited, leaving a little frost in her wake.

"Interesting assistant," Andrews commented.

"Best I've ever had," Mac told him.

He took his chair behind the desk and he and Morgan talked of the old days in Tempe while Cochran remained the polite audience.

Mac and his two brothers had been born in Arizona and had grown up around Phoenix, their dad a cop. The Andrews family, Morgan an only child, had moved here from the East when Morgan was in high school. He and Mac had played high school football together and become fast friends, standing up for each other, double dating. They'd been referred to as the Hardy Boys by some of their teachers because they seemed to tackle problems together, both school and personal.

Morgan's parents had money and made some lucky investments in Arizona real estate. Mac's family had struggled for as long as he could remember, he and his brothers working part time all through high school.

After their senior year, Morgan's parents had sent him to Harvard Law School. Mac had gotten a scholarship to his local community college for two years then had done a stint in the Air Force – been a chopper pilot during the Nicaragua and Grenada confrontations. But with the genocide in Guatemala and the scandals over U.S. involvements, he didn't enlist again. When he was discharged, the government helped pay his way through his law enforcement degree – following in his dad's footsteps.

Morgan had stayed in Massachusetts – a lawyer who made a name for himself in state politics. Mac had gotten a further degree, worked his way up, finally he was hired by the US Department of Justice in Washington D.C.

Both had lost a son – for Morgan his only son, for Mac his only child. Both had come back home to Arizona – Mac eleven years ago, Morgan eight. Morgan was still married to Mary Jane and had two grown daughters. Mac was divorced and lived alone. Remarkably the two men had stayed in touch over the years, had gotten together whenever they could, usually during Morgan's campaigns.

Morgan had run for the U.S. Senate seat here in Arizona six years ago, but the incumbent, Hank Grisholm, was a good ole boy and easily won the day. Grisholm was retiring from public office, though, and the primary this fall was wide open. With very little opposition from an uninspired Democratic candidate, it was a sure thing that whoever won the Republican primary would win the seat. So Morgan was back campaigning again and, not so surprising, here to see his buddy Mac.

Mac didn't really mind. He stayed out of political affairs except to run for sheriff, but Morgan was a good guy, one of the few in politics today. He'd make a strong senator. Rattle some of the old independent cowboy ways, bring some modern thinking into a state that was in desperate need of change.

Lloyd Pruitt, Morgan's major opponent in the primaries, was a replica of Grisholm, Mac thought. A man who couldn't seem to break out of that old mold of separatism. As far as Mac could see, he was a fierce defender of rights without responsibility. No laws, no restrictions. Do whatever you damn well please and screw the poor bastard who gets in your way. And Mac and his kind had to deal with the results. Like he had down in Glendale. Like he had in D.C.

Morgan Andrews was made of different stuff. So what if he used Mac a little in his campaign? Like standing up for a poor Mexican kid who got himself shot.

"How can I help you, Morgan?" he asked. "Got some scheme up your sleeve?"

Morgan laughed. He had a good laugh, one that laid the joke on himself. "I hate that you can always see inside me."

Mac gave a half grin. "What? An open book like you?"

Morgan ran a hand through gray hair, thick as a boy's. "This rally a week from Saturday. Mac, I need your help with it."

Mac shook his head. "It's not my jurisdiction. Chief Scott would aim for the balls if I tried to take over something in his town. You know that."

"He's going to screw it up," Morgan insisted. "Not only is he a Pruitt man, he's the biggest damned fool in the state."

Mac rubbed a hand over his face. "Well, not the biggest."

Cochran came to attention, his intensity a physical pressure. "Mac, we need help with this. Scott's moving like a snail, botching up all our paper work, purposely getting directions mixed up. We need this rally, one last chance to get out Morgan's message to the people."

Mac studied them both for a moment, took in air, let it out. "I'll see what I can do. But Berry's hell to work with."

"Tell us something we don't know," Andrews barked. He sat back in his chair. "Now, about that Morales killing – a hate crime, do you think?"

Mac shook his head. "We haven't been able to prove it yet. But it looks like the girlfriend's father did it. We're working on it."

"Hate." Morgan's whole body quivered at the word. "It's a sadistic, debilitating cancer in our civilization, Mac. We've got to do something about that in Arizona. Our state can never move forward if we don't work to change the old hatreds and prejudices. We're just standing still until we do."

"No argument here," Mac said. He knew Morgan's anger rose from personal reasons as well as political.

Paul Cochran adjusted his glasses. "That's a big part of our platform, hate crimes and how to put an end to them. Right, Morgan? We're going to put an end to the Lloyd Pruitts of this state, too. No looking back. Move us on through the twenty-first century - get this country on its feet again."

Andrews glanced at his manager, a warm glow in his eyes. "By the way, we were at the high school this morning. Met with the principal there. Tell me, Mac, did I misread him or is he a horse's ass?"

Mac gave him a one-sided smile. "At least Ramey stays out of my hair."

"And I met the lady who's been helping the Poole girl. Quite a heroine, isn't she? I told her so, too."

Oh hell, Mac thought, falling back and rubbing his face wearily. Let's encourage her by making her Woman of the Hour.

Belle got McFarland's return call mid afternoon. He sounded rushed.

"I thought you might want to know," she told him, "that Morgan Andrews – who's running for the U.S. Senate – came to talk to me." She couldn't pass up the chance for the barb.

"So I've heard." Whatever he was feeling, he kept it out of his voice.

"I'm wondering, should I call you Mac or Eli?"

"'Sheriff' will be just fine."

Did she hear a tinge of irritation this time? Good.

Belle's gaze moved to the window of her office. Some mourning doves cooed in the branches of the willow. The small courtyard grew mellow with the slanting sun.

"I wanted to know what the status is on Ralph Poole. I'm going to stop by to see Lily on my way home and I thought I should find out for her."

A sigh on the other end? "Mrs. Evans, you're interfering where you don't belong. Go see Lily. Fine. Kindly leave the police work to my department. That's what we're being paid for."

"Your friend Mr. Andrews commended me for interfering." She cringed at her own dig.

"My friend Mr. Andrews is a politician. He's after votes. I'm after a killer. Back off, Mrs. Evans. I don't need any more dead bodies on my slate right now."

Belle brought her glance back to her desk. "I – um – I went to talk to the manager of Mile Hi Earth Movers."

Now there was exasperation in his voice. "See? That's what I mean. You're stirring up trouble. Damn it, if there's trouble to stir up, let me do the stirring." Another breath, a calmer voice. "Mrs. Evans, I'm a pretty fair officer, with a pretty good group of deputies. I've worked in law enforcement for more years than I care to count. I'm grateful for your help with Lily. I'm glad you're staying in touch with her. But for Christ's sake, leave the leg work to me and my people."

Her back went up. "I just thought –"

"Don't. Don't think. Not about this. You seem to be good at what you do. Stick to it. Deal with Lily. Leave the Morales killing to me."

"Yes, sir," she said with acid in her voice

"Thank you," he blurted and hung up.

Belle closed her tiny office, walked out to the parking lot with Janice Purcell, Superintendent Cummerford's secretary, then drove down Ocampa Street and over to the Pines Halfway House on Forest and North College. Mrs. Rivera was out front on her knees, checking her flower beds, but her generous bosom heaved when she saw who it was. She rose to her feet, wincing with the effort.

"Those javelina," the woman protested, heading toward Belle. "They come like a thief in the night and eat all my petunias."

"Maybe you should just grow cactus. They wouldn't eat them, would they?"

"That would not help. They love the fruit and trample the plants to get to it." She looked forlorn.

"How's Lily?" Belle asked.

"Lily, she is better today. Tomorrow, I think, she will be ready to go back to the school. She is a strong girl."

"She's had to be, hasn't she?" Belle remarked.

Lily brightened when she saw who'd come. The girl's strength was returning and Belle began to understand the qualities Julio and Rosa Perez had seen in her.

"Miz Perez was here today," Lily said, sitting beside Belle on the couch in the parlor. "She said everybody missed me at school. She's so awesome."

A couple of girls walked through, school books in their arms, talking about science class.

"I think she is," Belle agreed.

Lily's eyes met hers. They were still sad but had strength behind the sadness.

"She was afraid for me and Julio. When my dad threatened us, we could always talk to her."

Belle moved closer. "Your dad threatened you? What kind of threats? What did he say? This is important."

Lily appeared to concentrate, to pull out memories. "Well, at first he told me I had to stop seeing Julio. That I'd be sorry if I didn't."

"Anything specific?"

She thought some more. "Mostly threats to Julio. He'd say things like 'That Spic's gonna end up with a knife in his back,' or 'his brains blown out,' or 'his legs whacked off.' Always some delightful thing like that." She squeezed her hands. The effort to keep tears back was in her face.

Belle suddenly felt hopeful. "I think we need to tell the sheriff about that."

"You figure he'll arrest my dad just because of some threats?"

"I don't know, but it's worth a try."

Lily didn't appear to hold out much hope. "Julio's cousin Carlos came by this morning. I almost called you."

"I haven't met him. What did he want?"

Lily flipped hair behind her shoulder. "He was talking kind-a crazy about revenge and stuff. He scared me a little. Mrs. Rivera sent him packing before he could say much."

"I'm glad. Revenge is *not* the way to go."

"Oh yeah, and Jeremy and Tom dropped by last night after supper."

"I had a talk with them today at school." She didn't explain that they wanted to beat up her father.

Lily gave a short laugh. "They don't mean no harm – *any* harm. They're just a couple-a dips, but they're good friends. They really loved Juli –" Her voice broke in a quiet sob and she studied her hands. When she looked up again, she said, "You got any kids, Miz Evans?"

"Two," Belle told her. "Will is married and going to law school in Michigan. He wants to be a lawyer like his dad."

"Wow, you got a married son? I didn't think you were that old."

"I'm old, all right," Belle assured her.

"Your son's gonna be a lawyer? So that means he can send killers to jail and stuff?" There was an edge to her voice.

"Well, actually, he's studying corporate law. Very dull. That is, unless you get a case like Enron."

"Like what?"

Belle smiled. "My daughter Ellie's at college, too, back in Cleveland where I come from."

"My mom used to talk about me going to college."

"You've got good grades. Maybe it's something to think about."

"You mean, now that I'm not going to marry Julio?"

Belle glanced away.

"How come you're here and your kids're back there?" Lily asked. "Where's your husband?"

"That's a long story, Lily. The short version is, my husband and I needed a break from each other. So I came out here."

She had a look of such sympathy Belle's heart hurt. Lily said, "It must be tough being away from your family. I thought I'd die when I lost my mom."

Belle suddenly moved in and put her arm around the girl, whose pain became her own.

Lily took a deep breath. "You know, when the sheriff was here with you and asked me all those questions, I forgot something. I guess I was just too upset to remember it. I mean, it's such a dumb little thing and when my dad showed up that night with Julio it totally skipped my mind."

Belle could see the whole canyon scene in Lily's face. Then it cleared and stubbornness set in. Belle had to hand it to her, the girl had resilience.

Lily grabbed Belle's hand. "Julio gave me something when we met at Lame Horse Canyon."

"He gave you something?"

"Wait here. I'll get it." She took off for the hall and up the stairs, two at a time.

A girl, maybe twelve, sad face and stringy hair, came from the back room and crossed the parlor to the dining room. Her expression, when she looked at Belle, was part curiosity and part apology – and in her demeanor were all the signs of an abused child. Belle smiled at her, her throat catching. Damn it, how could people do the things they did to children? Times like this she decided the human race had only a bare veneer of civilization over their feral exterior. And with many, that veneer had worn off – or had never developed in the first place.

Lily appeared two minutes later, prancing down the stairs and into the parlor, hair flying with each movement.

"This isn't much," she said. "I found it last night when I was going through my jeans to wash 'em." She held out a business card to show Belle. "He gave it to me when we met that night. Told me to hold on to it. I don't know why. Doesn't mean nothing – *any*thing to me."

Belle took the business card. It was badly worn, one corner ripped off, and a staple on the top edge where it had been attached to something else. The word 'Titus' was fairly clear on the front and 'Land Development' and a phone number at the bottom with an area code she didn't recognize. She could make out a four after the area code and a thirty-five after that, but the rest was hard to distinguish. Belle puzzled over the memento Julio had left with Lily.

"What did he tell you when he gave you this?"

Lily shook her head. "Not much. He just said to hold on to it for him. So I did."

"Could I borrow it?" Belle asked.

"Sure. You can have it if you want. I really don't want it. It reminds me of –"

Belle stuck the card in her purse.

Mrs. Rivera came in to say supper was ready. "Would you like to eat the meal with us?" she asked Belle.

Belle thanked her but declined. "Things to do tonight," she said.

Lily grabbed her hand. "Miz Evans – could you – would you go with me to – to Julio's funeral tomorrow? I don't think I can do it by myself."

Belle pulled the girl into a hug. "You bet," she said in her ear.

They held on a moment longer, then Belle said good-bye and headed for her car. Fishing for her keys, she came up with the card again. Titus Land Development? What was that? She decided to tackle the land records at the courthouse. It would be closed by now so tomorrow – another lunch hour spent searching for answers.

12

Belle sat on her couch, feet on the coffee table, watching the ten o'clock news. She sat in her pajamas, nodding a little after so much stress during the last twelve hours and ready to call it a day – or three. But she jerked up suddenly when Morgan Andrews came on the screen with Harold Ramey standing beside him. The high school principal looked as though someone had stuck an iron rod up his butt, his body erect and his face full of pain.

Andrews said pretty much what he'd said at the meeting in Ramey's office. He gave credit to the school for responding to Lily Poole's needs and to the sheriff for working hard to solve what looked like another heinous crime of hate. Then his spiel about his campaign and a plug for the rally he was planning that would take place on the "Historical steps of the Crook County Courthouse in Granite a week from this coming Saturday."

Belle rubbed her tired eyes, sighed heavily, and wondered about politicians and principals playing with other people's catastrophes.

News over, she now sat wide awake. Why had she watched it? Why let it get to her? She started in on the book she'd been reading, trying to regain some of that exhaustion she'd felt BA – Before Andrews. But when you faced real life crises it was difficult to be enthusiastic over fictional ones. John Grisham just wasn't going to do it for her tonight.

The phone ringing startled her so that she actually jumped. Who the hell could that be? Ellie with yet another problem? Oh God, not Larry. Then she relaxed. Almost two o'clock back in Cleveland. Even Larry wouldn't call at that hour.

Another ring and she got up to answer it.

"Sorry to call so late, Ms. Evans." The man identified himself as a sheriff's deputy. "Sheriff McFarland asks if you could please come down to the station. These guys, they been asking for you. Said they wanted you instead of their parents. Mac said call and see if you'd come."

"Guys?"

"Two high school kids. Gibbs and Kelliker. They look pretty bad. Had to have a medic patch 'em up."

Oh my God, Belle thought. What had they done? "How bad are they?"

"Not too serious. Just got the stuffing beat out of 'em."

"Are they in trouble?"

"You might say."

Belle told the deputy she'd be there and hung up. In three minutes she'd thrown on jeans and shirt, stepped into some nearby loafers, and was out the door. Thank heaven the county jail wasn't far, she was shaking enough to run the car off the road.

As she reached High Street she found the town nearly empty. Most of Granite pulled up the sidewalks by six o'clock. Except for the bars, of course, and a few restaurants. And the more conservative ones along the town square weren't open much later during week nights.

The street lights glimmered pink against the fluttering leaves of alders and maples as Belle drove past the back of the courthouse on Ventura and three blocks further to the Crook County Sheriff's Office and jail. She pulled into a parking space along the street, got out and walked to the front door.

After identifying herself, she was let in by the night man. The deputy from the phone call came around the bullet proof glass cage and led her down a hall to the interrogation room, opening the door for her.

Belle's heart took a plunge when she saw the two boys sitting at the table in the bare room, a large, red-headed man in plain clothes and a deputy in uniform flanking them.

The big man rubbed his copper moustache self-consciously. "Detective Carter, ma'am," he introduced himself. "These guys here had a little trouble, you might say."

Jeremy, gripping an ice pack in his hand, had a bandage over part of his face and an eye nearly closed that already looked sickly yellow. Tom held ice to his head, one side of his face swollen red and purple beneath the scars of the acne. They both sagged in relief when they saw her. Jeremy looked sheepish and uncertain, Tom bullish. Belle stood and studied them.

"What happened?" she asked.

The two boys glanced at each other, then down.

Detective Carter stepped forward, his bulk and red hair dominating the room. "Bar fight, Ms. Evans."

"*What?*" She stared at them, uncomprehending. "What in the name of God were you doing in a bar?"

When they still didn't answer, Carter said, "Trying to pick a fight with Ralph Poole."

Belle closed her eyes, muscles tense. They hadn't heard a thing she'd said today.

Jeremy sat forward, grimacing at the movement. "We're sorry, Miz Evans. I know you said we shouldn't. But we figured when he come into the bar, he wouldn't have no dog or gun."

Belle slapped a hand over her mouth. Had she encouraged this? "Are you telling me you confronted the man in a bar? And he did this to you?"

"No," Tom told her. Apparently it hurt him to talk. "His buddies was there. Didn't figure on that."

Carter, with a telling twitch to his moustache, said, "Our guys here started themselves a real bar brawl with the leather crowd – bikers. Granite police had to break it up. Took the others involved off to their own station. Sent these two and Poole to us. Knew we had the case under investigation."

Between the boys and Carter, Belle got the story. What Jeremy and Tom didn't tell her, the deputy filled in. It sounded as if the two of them had worked themselves into a rage over Julio's murder. Finally, with nothing better to do, they'd decided to confront Poole.

"Lil said he always hung out at the Sidewinder Bar over on Jackson," Jeremy told her.

"So you went looking for him?" she asked.

He glanced away.

"Poole was there, all right," Carter explained, "and pretty well into a bottle of Jack, according to Phil the barkeep."

Jeremy turned back to her. "Man, we was just gonna talk to him. Warn the dickhead off-a Lil. You know what I'm saying?"

"Turned on us," Tom said. "Gonna hit us. That's harsh. So we hit him first."

When they said no more Belle turned to Carter.

Carter shook his head despairingly. "According to Phil, that's when all hell broke loose. You know what it is, I mean, taking a swing at somebody in the Sidewinder after ten at night, it's like turning on the switch to a giant power generator. Everybody joins in."

"Some big creep jumped me," Jeremy hissed. "Man, he was big as a bear. Hairy, too. And a couple of 'em started on Tom. Just kept beating the crap outta us."

"And each other," Carter added. "By the time the cops got there, the whole place was one big brawl."

"What about Ralph Poole?" she asked.

"Phil says he'd slunk off to a corner to watch. Never threw a punch. Never took a serious one himself. We've got him in the other room. But he's clean, except he's drunk as a skunk."

Apparently Jeremy and Tom, being the youngest and most inexperienced, had taken the brunt of the melee. Carter seemed to think the tale was funny. Belle was just plain scared for the boys.

"Why did you have the police call me?" Belle asked Jeremy. "Where are your parents?"

Again that hangdog look which appeared pathetic behind the swollen eye. "We figured you'd understand better. You know what I mean?"

Just then the side door opened. McFarland in jeans and plaid shirt – evidently having been called in like her – held it for a man and woman, obviously not a couple.

The woman took one look at the boys and burst out crying. Jeremy turned away, acutely embarrassed. The man advanced toward Tom who suddenly looked afraid. He slapped the boy on the side of his head so hard the sound echoed in the bare room. Tom cried out. McFarland reacted but Belle was faster.

"Hey!" she yelled, moving around the table.

The man glared at her. "Whadaya want, lady?"

Belle sucked in her anger. "Mr. Kelliker, I take it. I'm Belle Evans, school counselor. I came at the boys' request to help them out."

"Don't need no counselor." He slapped Tom again.

This time McFarland was quicker. He grabbed the man's swinging arm. "Mr. Kelliker, unless you'd like to spend the night here, I suggest you leave the boy alone."

Kelliker pulled his arm away. "Damn it, he's my son. Look at him. A goddamn bar fight. Cops had to bring him in. Shit."

It looked like he might hit Tom again, but one look at the sheriff and he restrained himself.

Meanwhile, the crying woman had skirted the table and had hold of Jeremy's battered face. She bawled openly while Jeremy squirmed to get away.

"Leave me alone, Ma," he said, knocking over the chair in his struggle to distance himself from her.

"Oh Jeremy, honey. How could you do this to me? I work so hard to make a good home for you. And you do everything you can to break my heart."

Belle glanced at McFarland who raised an eyebrow at her as if to say, 'See what we deal with?'

13

Lily went back to school Thursday morning. Belle dropped by to check on her. The girl looked older than her seventeen years now and fragile, her eyes deep with sorrow. Somehow the tragedy transformed her, making her even more lovely than normal, and the other students gathered round her in a kind of awe.

Rosa Perez met Belle in the hallway. "Don't worry," she said. "I'll keep an eye on Lily in case she finds the going too difficult."

Belle was grateful. She spent a few minutes talking to Ned. They discussed the meeting the day before with Morgan Andrews but it was obvious Ned wasn't easy with it.

"Did he stay long after I left?" she asked him.

"Not long. He asked Mr. Ramey to do the spot with him on television."

Belle gave a laugh. "I caught it last night. Ramey looked pretty uncomfortable, didn't he?"

Ned straightened some papers on his desk. "It wasn't one of his better moments."

"Really? And I thought it was." She pulled at her ear. "Andrews not only put the school on the spot, he stuck the sheriff right smack in the hot seat. Makes you wonder how friendly McFarland feels toward his ole buddy Andrews at this moment."

Once again, Belle munched a sandwich while on the road. This time it was to the Crook County Courthouse on the square. The courthouse fronted on High Street, only a few blocks down and over from the board building and her office on Ocampa. But she had a funeral to attend after this, so she drove.

The downtown area of Granite was considered historical. Soon after General Crook, for whom the county was named, established Fort Malone during the Civil War, the ranchers moved into the area. The cowboys, weary and dry from the desert range land, would ride into Granite on a Saturday night to get drunk and shoot up the place. Only a few establishments had survived since then, but they sported their ancient bullet wounds with pride.

Fire had destroyed the original courthouse. The new building was a relic of the early twentieth century. It sat in the middle of the town taking up two square blocks surrounded by lawn and alder trees and statues of military men from the fort. On fine days people met, or sat on benches, or walked their dogs out on the lawn. A gazebo sat at one corner for visiting bands or speakers. Shops, restaurants and bars surrounded the square. During the summer, tourists flocked up the mountains from Phoenix to frequent the establishments and enjoy the cooler temperatures at five thousand plus feet.

Several museums graced the town and a number of art galleries, one of them run by Belle's landlord, Adrian. And on most weekends during the summer there were festivals of one kind or another where an army of tents filled the lawn around the courthouse and people flooded the town like a monsoon downpour.

Granite was a congenial town, its nearly thirty thousand inhabitants stretching the seams of its boundaries with a mixture of types so varied Belle found herself always surprised. She'd discovered this gem of the Olmsted Mountains two years ago while visiting Louise and decided this was the place for her.

Now she grabbed a parking spot just being vacated along the edge of the square, stuffed the rest of her ham sandwich in its Baggie and got out. In spite of the intensity of the sun, a stiff breeze whipped the heavy branches overhead and destroyed what remained of her hairdo. She was fast learning the power of wind out here.

Holding down a skirt too full for this kind of weather, Belle mounted the steps of the courthouse, twenty-three of them leading to the top. Light posts sat on the concrete railings. Two sets of pillars framed the twelve foot double doors in front with a clock overlooking them like a portrait of Big Brother. The façade was repeated on the other three sides of the building but without the clock.

Inside she had to pass through a security check. Gone were the days of easy access to government buildings. These were the times requiring security jobs like her own. Too many weapons around, too many people willing to use them, threats of terrorists and extremists with causes.

The old wooden floors echoed her steps as she moved along the hallway toward the information desk. The place was busy. Lawyers talking to defendants as they headed for one courtroom or another, a couple of city policemen, people sitting on benches, maybe waiting for their court appearance to come up. Belle had spent many hours with her dad in courtrooms, seeing what it was like, getting to know what her father did in his line of work.

"I'm trying to find land records," she told the woman at the desk, a Hispanic, hair pulled back in a neat bun, good make-up job, dangling earrings that looked expensive.

"Basement floor," the woman said. Her voice was shrill and reverberated through the hall of the old building. "Down the stairs and to your left. That whole section is Land Development but the records are the first door on your right. You can't miss it. Peggy'll help you."

Belle thanked her and walked down the hall to the stairs. She met several people coming up, probably going to lunch, and her stomach grumbled in envy. Three bites of a sandwich didn't begin to satisfy.

In the basement her steps echoed less because of the concrete beneath the floor. She found the door that said 'Records' and went in.

Peggy turned out to be a little old lady, barely tall enough to be seen over the top of the counter. Gray hair was bobbed, glasses sat on the end of her nose, wrinkles nearly hid the features of her face. But the eyes were of a different age, something younger and shrewder and full of suspicion. Belle quelled the urge to explain herself to this woman.

Peggy had her fill out a form for access to public information, pointed her toward a table bearing several hefty looking binders and turned back to her work.

"No computers?" Belle asked her.

"Humph. Don't need those things. Do nothing but break down. Besides, this hasn't been much of a territory for long. All you need's in those books."

Several tables furnished the room along with one wall of shelves on the far side. It housed books and large cubbyholes with rolled up maps. An old man with a beard twice the size of his head browsed through some charts at one of the tables. Belle shrugged and went to the table with the binders of land records.

She spent almost an hour hunting through development records, ownership titles, looking for the name Titus on anything. She double checked and cross referenced. Nothing. No Titus anywhere. Well, here was a dead end.

She clutched the business card as though through osmosis it could tell her what she wanted to know. Why did Julio have it? Why give it to Lily to keep for him? Why was it important? And who or what the hell was Titus?

* * *

The funeral was a pitiful affair. The whole thing took place at a tiny graveyard up on a hill outside of town. A fenced in piece of land, bare of anything but a dozen or so small gravestones and plastic flowers faded from the sun since Memorial Day or perhaps last Christmas. Some cholla cacti rimmed the fence and the Olmsteds loomed distant and unconcerned. The heat was intense with nothing to shade them except a few errant cumulus clouds heading toward a larger gathering along the distance hills. Even the wind had stopped for a while.

A young priest led the ceremony beside a plain coffin with a few people collected on two rows of folding chairs before the grave site. Belle thought it seemed indecent for the sun to shine so brightly on such an occasion as this. Where was the sympathizing rain?

Lily sat in front of her, huddled inward, silent sobs rippling her slender body in a gentle rhythm. Belle was struck by the amount of poise the girl possessed.

Julio's aunt sat next to her – a short, heavy woman who looked young, maybe in her late thirties. Her black hair hung straight and long and her flowered dress had no shape of its own. Flats on her feet, legs crossed at the ankles, hands busy with a handkerchief, she teetered between wailing sobs and silence while drops of perspiration streaked the sides of her face.

The aunt's husband and three of their children – all in their teens – perched on her other side, stiff and uncomfortable, as though they had no idea what was expected of them. The oldest boy sat off to the side, a brooding anger in the way he held himself and in the very air surrounding him, heated further by the sun. Rosa Perez was beside Belle, watching the proceeding with a stone countenance.

A furtive look passed between Lily and the oldest. Carlos, Belle supposed, the one responsible for upsetting Lily, for flaring up around town about his cousin's killing. He was short like the rest of his family, had a small moustache, his dark eyes intense. Belle watched him, saw the grief and impotent rage overtake him.

The ceremony was brief as if the young priest were in a hurry, or didn't know how to conduct a funeral. When the coffin was lowered into the ground the women set up a wail of crying. Belle had seen such things on television and found them tasteless. But here, now, with these people, the display moved her more than she cared to admit.

Julio's family lingered at the grave site with Lily. The few others in attendance began to leave. Since Lily had come with Belle, she waited at her car, giving the girl some time with her grief. Rosa stopped to say a few words to Belle then headed back to town and her afternoon classes.

After a while Carlos grabbed Lily's arm and moved off with her. His conversation was animated, the electricity of his anger heating the air, sparking off the ground. Lily began to cry again, this time at what he said, Belle thought. Not good.

She approached the two of them.

"Where I come from, my people do not let some gringo *maleton* get away with killing one of our own," Carlos hissed at Lily. "We take revenge. An eye for an eye. We do not sit by while the *stupido* police pretend to care about a Mexican boy who was beaten and shot to death."

Lily looked on the verge of hysterics.

"Carlos Hernandez?" Belle asked, interrupting the tirade. "I'm Mrs. Evans, Lily's counselor. She's told me about you, how close you were to Julio, that you've been like brothers."

Carlos was temporarily silenced. He looked at the hand she held out to him, hesitated, finally took it in a feeble grip. The rage in his eyes diminished only slightly. Belle braved through it.

"Your anger's understandable. A lot of us are angry about this. Especially since it seems as though the police haven't been able to do anything." She glanced at the small gathering around the priest, then back at the two.

Carlos' face became distorted. "He deserves to *die* for killing Julio."

"I suppose you could see it that way," she said. "But if everybody got revenge for someone killed, one killing would lead to another and soon we'd be emerged in death." She held up her hands. "Which is why we have to let to the law handle it, no matter how slowly they work. I really believe Sheriff McFarland cares about this. But we have laws, we have procedures."

He sucked in air. "To protect the *guilty* ones."

"Carlos, how would you like it if you were found guilty without evidence? These laws are designed to protect everyone. At least that's the theory."

"That man did this thing," Carlos spit.

Lily had seemed to calm down. Now she wept harder. Belle put her arm around the girl and faced the young man.

"You're forgetting he's still Lily's father. Maybe a little consideration for her might be in order."

He jerked his head away, anger powerful but uncertainty in his manner. "I did not mean for to hurt Lily."

"Grief sometimes makes us forget," Belle nodded.

Mrs. Hernandez left the priest and joined them. Her husband trailed her. "Carlos, what you been saying to these people?" she asked. "You been upsetting Lily?"

Carlos didn't speak so Belle did.

"They're both upset," she said. "This is a terrible thing. I'm so sorry for your loss."

The woman wasn't far from weeping again herself. "Lily says you been good to her. Did you know our Julio?"

Belle shook her head. "I wish I had. From everything I've learned, he was a fine person – strong, caring, determined."

Mrs. Hernandez was unable to speak for her emotion. Her husband stepped forward.

"He was a good boy; he was like our own son. Carlos and Maria and José and Roberto, they make him their brother. Julio, he work hard, never no trouble. Always treat us good, always make us feel proud he is ours." The man had trouble finding the English words for what he wanted to say, which made it that much more poignant. Belle was near tears herself.

The other three Hernandez offspring joined the group. Belle gave her condolences again, they parted, she walked Lily to the Honda.

The next moment, the aunt hurried back. "Lily, I have this for you." She held out a battered Nike shoe box. "These are Julio's things. Perhaps you would want to keep them."

Lily hesitated, considering. Then she took the box and hugged the woman, her tall, thin body encompassing the short, squat one. Some quiet sobs as they held on. Finally Mrs. Hernandez, wiping her eyes, tossed a shy, grateful glance at Belle and returned to her family and the battered Ford coup, probably from the late 80s or early 90s, the finish faded to a non color.

Lily held the box in her arm. "I don't know if I can look at this."

Belle reached out and squeezed her hand. "Give it time, Lily. Time is the universal healer of all things."

But not, she thought, if they didn't get Ralph Poole locked up, and quick.

14

After dropping Lily off at The Pines Halfway House, Belle was restless. Instead of heading back to her office, she took Miner's Creek Road out beyond town to the north turnoff for the Juniper Mountain Range and Lame Horse Canyon. She'd never been there herself but knew it by reputation. Lily and Julio weren't the only ones to meet at the canyon in a clandestine fashion. The spot was renowned as a rendezvous for teens who wanted to get laid. She'd even heard it referred to as the Love Canyon. Not anymore, she suspected. Now it would probably acquire a new moniker.

Only a small green sign along Miner's Creek gave the direction to the place. The dirt track in was rutted and rocky so that her poor Honda had a rough time. Her tires threw up stones that whacked against the car which twisted on gravel and bumped over the washboard surface. She had to take it at a snail's pace.

The road ran through grassland dotted with chaparral: scrub oak, beargrass, cholla, prickly pear. An occasional juniper colored the stark landscape. Copper Mountain to the east heaved over the distant vista and up ahead the cliffs of Piñon Peak gave the canyon its background. A small herd of pronghorn, grazing nearby, looked up at the sound of her car.

The dirt track climbed for a while, veered to the right, then headed downhill toward the cliff that seemed to rise higher the closer she got. Finally the road took a plunge down into the canyon and made a sudden left behind huge boulders to a secluded opening, maybe five acres in area. Granite cliffs walled the space on three sides like a corral.

She'd been told by an old timer that in the past cowboys had tried to use the canyon to round up wild horses but had given it up. The pitted landscape, gullies gouged out by torrential rains, had caused more injuries than the haul was worth. Hence the name for the place.

Belle stopped the car and got out, coughing at the dust she'd raised that blew her way like transgressions catching up with her. The cliffs stood mainly to the west so that now, at 3:30 in the afternoon, the canyon was mostly in shadow. But the warmth of the sun had been captured by the rocks and she wiped sweat from her neck.

Slowly she made a 360 degree turn, taking in the place; the sheer cliff forming the canyon, Copper Mountain off to the east, and far to the north a glimpse of the San Francisco Peaks above Flagstaff. It was like a travelogue picture of the rugged Southwestern mountains. How many kids had lost their virginity here among the rocks? And where was the spot Julio had lain dead?

Tire tracks crisscrossed each other, old ones embedded in the dirt after a rain, some marked in the dust. And there were definite signs of trampled grass and bushes telling her where to look. A deadening wave of sadness swept her as she walked over and stared down at the place. Dust smeared the large areas of blood where the boy's body had been. So much blood. She hadn't realized anyone could bleed that much. Where had the fight occurred? Where had the man pulled out a gun and shot him?

The rattle of an engine made her look up. After a few moments a pickup rounded the bend to the canyon rocking gracelessly over the bumps and pits in the road, its body battered and rusted, it's engine clanking. It jerked to a stop just behind her Honda. Belle wondered if this was what happened the night Julio died, Ralph Poole coming up behind Lily's Jeep.

She stood waiting for the driver to emerge, the windshield too dusty to see who it was. Almost a minute passed before the door creaked open and someone got out.

The old felt cowboy hat appeared first. Probably light in color at one time, now dirt-smeared and sweat-stained and ragged along the brim. Then she saw the beard and the emaciated body and her heart stopped. God, what was he?

He started forward and she took an involuntary step back. He didn't seem to notice as he came on, his eyes squinting, his gait arthritic, elbows jutted out as though he couldn't straighten them anymore. When he got too close, she backed up again.

"You here for a rendezvous with a lover?" he cackled. "Or you interested in where that there boy was shot?"

She cocked her head. "I'm Belle Evans. I'm a counselor in the Granite School System. I've heard a lot about this place and wanted to see it for myself."

He searched her face in the manner of a man with poor sight. "Yup. Lots-a folks interested in this here place nowadays. Killin's always good for business." He eyed her again. "Ya ain't with the newspaper, are you?"

"Just the school system."

He scratched the side of his face where the beard began and Belle was sure she saw dust rise. A strong odor of his unwashed body, tobacco, and some urine wafted her way on the breeze then mercifully moved on past.

"Thought maybe you was news. Thought you might wanna interview me 'cause it was me found the body of that Mex out here. Name's Virgil Hibbits, case ya want to write that down. Get it spelled right, hear?" And he spelled it out.

"Thanks, but I'm with the school."

She started to head for her car but he stepped in front to bar her way. She backed up once more.

"It was Poole done it, all right. Put that in the headlines. And me, Virgil Hibbits what found the Mex. Get that in there, too."

Now Belle stepped toward him, fighting the odor that threatened to overwhelm. "You know this for a fact? You saw Ralph Poole shoot the boy?"

"Didn't have to. Knowed it. Sure as I seen it. Told the sheriff, but he don't listen to nobody."

"What makes you so sure it was him?"

His cackle sounded unbalanced. "Hell, I know Poole. Him 'n me, we're drinking buddies. He's a good ole boy. Got a dime to spare, he buys me a snort. Not many'll do that for ole Virgil."

"Were you out here the night the boy was shot?"

He shook his head irritably. "Damn it, I told ya. Didn't need to be. I got me that ESP stuff. Took it when I lived up in Flag. I can *see* things."

Belle eased away from the man. "Well, it was nice talking to you. I'd better get back to my office."

Suddenly Hibbits grabbed her arm, fingers like a vise, and stuck his face into hers. His pale eyes glinted. The sound of him, the look of him sent a streak of alarm up her back.

"Ain't you scared-a Poole? Got him a gun, he does. End up shootin' you, you get in his way, news lady."

Belle tensed, mentally readying herself for defense. But he let go and backed off, setting up a cackle that echoed through Lame Horse Canyon.

In that moment she took off for her car, started it up, did a bumpy U turn around the pickup, and headed back to town.

Ralph Poole sat on the doorstep of his single-wide, torn T-shirt filthy with sweat and dirt, the last of the bottle of Jack Daniels in his hand. In the distance early evening sun streaked low just above the hills and turned the bank of clouds a blood red like the fire that burned inside him. His dog was off chasing up rabbits or some other damned thing. And he was feeling no pain.

That cop car was finally gone – son-of-a-bitch went off to take a leak or something. It'd been sitting out at the head of his lane, didn't give a shit if it was seen or not. Ralph stared out into an unfair world. Even the damned sun glared in his eyes.

Life down in Casa Grande had been one big pile of guano for him. A drunken son-of-a-bitch for a father who beat the crap out of him and his brothers whenever he could. His mother who slunk away every time his old man got the belt out. Left her own kids to take it all.

Earlier he could remember some good times, before his old man took to the bottle so much. When his mother was softer, prettier, happier. He could remember going out fishing or swimming in the reservoir or running with one of their dogs to beat a train. The Brown kids down the way would bring a sack of green apples and Ralph and his brothers would hole up with them in a little mining cave they'd discovered, eating the apples and telling jokes.

Later, though, when the drinking got worse, when his father got more violent, it was hard to recall any good times. His two brothers had stayed and taken the beatings, but he'd gotten the hell out of there when he was fifteen and never looked back.

The jobs he'd had to survive on in Phoenix were chicken shit. Sometimes he'd slept in alleys or in ditches. He'd stolen whenever he had to. Finally when he was eighteen he'd joined the army with three squares a day. Boot camp was hard on him, but he'd learned a lot of things about fighting and for once he'd felt like he belonged some place, like he had a real family.

When he got out, he'd worked in construction. Those were good years, too, especially up here in the mountains. He'd felt like a real man, not like a mangy dog being kicked all the time. He'd gotten married, had a kid. Bernice, his wife, had been a pretty woman, soft like his mother in her early days. And Lily, she'd been a good kid back then. Not a pain in the ass like some.

But all that had come back when they'd busted his leg for him out on the Tucker Highway project. That dozer crushing him'd done him in. Might as well have crushed his chest, killed him outright. That's when he'd started drinking like his ole man. Bernice'd begun criticizing him, become more like his mother later on. And Lily had grown into a smart-mouth. No way around it, disability sucked.

At least he could black out some of the worst stuff with his good buddy Jack. Only friend he'd got. He lifted the bottle and took another swallow.

Damn Lily. She should be here getting his meals, taking care of him. He needed her, depended on her, couldn't get along without her. He was her dad. Instead she'd gone whoring with that Spic and planning to run off. He knew what she was up to.

Now that bitch of a lady from school took Lily away, had her hidden somewhere in town. Thought she was going to keep his own from him.

"Look out, bitch lady. Ole Ralph learned a thing'er two back in the army."

He set the bottle down on the step, pulled the Ruger pistol from his belt and cradled it in his hand. Smooth. Cold. They hadn't found it. He knew where to hide it. He had a good hiding place, one they'd never find.

A sound in the distance made Ralph look up. A car. He started to move, then waited. Not the cop car. Dark and low. A dust snake followed it up his lane. Fucking time they came with the rest of it. Better hurry before the cops get back.

The car stopped two thirds of the way. Ralph stared. The last of the sun shone in his eyes so he couldn't see well. A man got out and stood beside the car. What the hell? Ralph shaded his eyes but couldn't tell what the man was doing. And the Jack Daniels made his response time slow. Something glinted in the dying sun.

A loud crack filled the air and Ralph felt a hammer strike his chest, knocking him back. The pistol dropped from his hands. The bottle of whiskey teetered and fell to the ground, breaking on a stone. Ralph was stunned, bewildered.

Another report in the distance and the last thing he ever felt was a blow to his head.

Off on the horizon the sun sank behind the hills as the dust snake started back in the opposite direction down the lane, leaving a blazing sky and silence in its wake.

15

"Honest to God, Mac, George wasn't gone more'n five minutes. Maybe ten." Rolly Carter scratched his copper moustache. "Ten goddamn minutes. That's all."

Mac stood in front of the single-wide with Carter, George Hornby hunched behind them, a light breeze of cooling air. Hornby was a small man, bald, in his early sixties with the drooping eyes and dewlaps of a basset hound. Headlights from the two cop cars and Mac's Cherokee illuminated the scene in the dim twilight. They stared at the body of Ralph Poole sprawled beside the steps. Butch Taggert, Carter's younger partner, was hunkered down beside him. Taggert was short and thin, half Rolly's size and wore glasses. They made an interesting pair.

"At least we found his gun," Hornby told them, as if this might lighten his guilt at having left his post.

Mac looked at the gun lying beside the dead man's right hand, and the bottle of Jack Daniels broken on the ground.

The sound of more vehicles coming up the lane took their attention. Mac hadn't bothered to call an ambulance, only the medical examiner and the crime scene tech crew. Twilight was fading fast, dimming to a fiery blaze across the western horizon as more headlights brightened the scene. Albert Yazzie, the medical examiner, stepped out of his van and came forward. He stood looking at the dead man.

"Got some of his own, did he?"

Al Yazzie was in his late thirties, barrel chested, his Navajo blood stark in his features. Mac liked working with him. He was thorough, to the point, and smart – one of the best in Mac's experience with MEs.

Electronic flashes glared from the tech crew taking pictures of the body and the surrounding area. Taggert got up and moved to the side as Yazzie snapped some latex gloves on his hands and knelt down to look at what was left of Ralph Poole. Blood had gushed from the chest wound in puddles on the steps. The bullet to the forehead had opened up the back of the skull, spilling brain tissue and bits of cranium on the steps and ground. The eyes stared into the flashlights in unbelieving surprise.

The ME looked at the gun beside the body. "Not a suicide," he said.

Mac shook his head. "With two holes in him? Couldn't be."

"Wrong kind of holes, too," Yazzie told him. He picked up the gun and smelled the end of the barrel. "Hasn't been fired recently."

"So he didn't try to defend himself."

Carter moved in, his bulk blocking some of the light. "Think he was expecting this, Mac? Had his gun ready?"

Mac shrugged and tipped the Stetson back with his forefinger. "Al, how far away do you think the shooter was?"

Al Yazzie used a flashlight to get a closer look at the head wound. "Not sure, but probably a good hundred-fifty yards. Rifle with a scope, maybe. Good shot. Chest first. Kept him upright for the shot to the head."

Mac went to talk to his tech men, two of them, who got out flashlights and a camera and started down the lane.

George Hornby came over, guilt still pulling at his basset eyes. "Honest to God, Mac, I wasn't gone long. I been watching this place good. Earl would take over 'bout three in the morning. We kept a good eye on him."

"I know," Mac said.

Hornby was having prostate problems, but not severe enough to go on disability, which meant he couldn't afford to lose his job. Still, he needed to relieve himself often. So the department kept him on the easier assignments. Surveillance was one of them.

"Don't worry, George. Nobody could've seen this coming." He walked back to the steps. "Rolly, Butch, get a crew on this place first thing in the morning. No sense ruining your eyes now. And make sure it's not disturbed."

Carter walked with Mac to his Jeep Cherokee. "You think the same guy killed 'em both?"

"Morales was shot with a .38 close range. Looks like Poole's gun could be the weapon."

"Payback then, from the other side?"

Mac rubbed a hand over his face, weariness engulfing him. "Who knows?"

"Daughter probably got an alibi, you figure?"

"Probably. Besides, she'd have to be a damned good shot. And have access to a damned good rifle. Couldn't have been any pawn shop special," Mac told him. "Not from that far away."

"Maybe that pair we had the run in with from school? Or one of her friends?"

Mac glanced off at the streak of fire across the horizon. The clouds themselves had turned an iron gray, beyond the reach of the sun's reflection. Night was fast enveloping the desert. "That's going to be a hard one – interrogating a bunch of minors. Damn."

"Or the oldest Hernandez kid? He's been talking vengeance and all that."

The two tech men came up the lane toward Mac's Jeep. One had something in his gloved hand and held it out.

"Rifle shell. The other one's probably still in the gun. A .270. This wasn't any amateur from that far away," he said.

Mac nodded. "Seems like he was in a hurry, though. Didn't bother collecting evidence. Expert rifleman, amateur killer. Maybe."

The man holding the shell shrugged. "Yeah, but half the hunters in the county use a .270. So that leaves us with a blank."

As Mac got into the Cherokee, another car pulled up the lane. The Granite Daily Sentinel.

"Thank God," he told Carter with a smirk. "We sure wouldn't want this killing to go unpublicized, would we?"

Belle wasn't entirely surprised to hear the sheriff's voice on the phone at this hour. After nine at night.

"Mrs. Evans, I need your help again." His usually unreadable voice sounded exasperated this time. And tired.

"What can I do?"

"Well," he started out slowly, "Ralph Poole's been shot."

Belle was silent, taking it in.

"Did you hear me?" he asked.

"Yes." She pulled in a lungful of air. "Lily's father was shot? How is he?"

"Dead."

"Good Lord." More air. "What happened?"

"We don't know yet. Trouble is the news people are all over it. I figured the girl ought to find out first." Silence on his end. "You seem to have a connection with her. I thought it might come better from you."

Belle considered the request. "Do you suspect someone?"

"Not yet."

"Lily?"

She heard a sigh. "Not likely."

"Her friends?"

"We'll have to question them."

"I see. Could it have been the same person who shot Julio?"

"Doesn't look that way. Different guns. We found Poole's. Looks like his could be the one that killed the boy." He waited a beat. "So, will you do it? Tell the daughter?"

"Sure."

"I hate to send you out tonight, but it'll be all over the news first thing tomorrow morning."

"No problem," she told him. "Can I tell her anything about his death?"

Another beat. "You can tell her two bullet holes, one in the chest and one in the head. Like Morales."

Belle called Mrs. Rivera before she left to make sure it was all right to come. Once again she drove down nearly empty streets, taking Quail Run over to Sanford and then to North College. Low clouds reflected street lights. Stars peered through the cracks with no moon to dim them yet.

When she got to the halfway house the woman was waiting with Lily, dressed in a bathrobe, and Belle asked her to stay. Mrs. Rivera cleared out the parlor, sending the girls to their rooms or to the library in the back of the house, and the three of them sat down, Belle on the couch next to Lily.

She wasn't sure how to brace the girl for the news. Lily may have been angry at Ralph Poole but he was still her father. Correction – had been. In Belle's career as counselor she'd had several occasions to prepare someone for the announcement of a death. But each one was different and therefore new. No rules. No known method.

She took the girl's hand, pausing a moment, then glancing straight at her. "I was asked by the sheriff to tell you about your father, Lily."

Lily shot forward, face hopeful. "He's in jail?" the girl cried. "They've locked him up?"

Belle chose her words carefully. "Not exactly." She studied the girl's face, locking onto her eyes as if to support her. "You father has been shot."

"Shot?" This from Mrs. Rivera.

The girl looked confused.

"Someone shot him, Lily. He's dead."

Belle had expected a strong reaction. Surprise, anger, elation. Instead, Lily was quiet. Mrs. Rivera seemed more agitated, but she stifled it in front of the dead man's daughter. Regardless of how much Lily had disliked her father, dismissing him as dirty laundry seemed out of the question.

Silence reigned for several moments. Soft mutterings at the back of the house, a car passing in the street, a chorus of crickets from the front yard were all that broke the stillness.

Finally Lily spoke. "Who did it?" she asked. "One of Julio's friends? Carlos?"

But Belle couldn't tell her. She gave the only details the sheriff had given her.

Lily sat still for a long time, no exultation, no tears, just a stunned look in her face. "Am I supposed to feel bad about this?" she asked. "I used to care about him. He was a good enough dad when I was a little kid. Sometimes even later. I guess he loved me. I don't know what to say. What am I supposed to feel?"

Belle decided it would take her a while to digest the fact that her one relative as well as her threat was gone. She'd lived too long with both to write them off so easily.

Driving back home, Belle reached for understanding. Poole was gone. That should mean Lily's danger was gone, too. And yet something jabbed the back of her mind like a cattle prod.

Had a kid done this? Jeremy or Tom? Retribution? It seemed possible. Anybody could get hold of a gun these days. She thought about Carlos Hernandez at the funeral, his black rage, his demand for vengeance. She suspected Carlos could do this.

She also remembered Fred Preacher's reaction to her questions when she'd gone to talk to him at Mile Hi. He'd been over the top with her. Why? What had she said that had sent his blood pressure soaring?

And the business card for a development company that didn't exist. At least not in Crook County. What was that all about? She thought she should probably tell McFarland what she'd found. But she resented his accusation of interfering. And what was it anyway? Some company that had meant to go into business and never made it? How many times did that happen?

Julio had thought it was important, though. Did he plan to work for Titus? The card was old, worn. Maybe the company was planning to start up again. Did Julio think he could get a job with them? One that paid a bigger salary than Mile Hi?

So, was this a hate crime, or merely Ralph keeping the boy away from his daughter? Poole's killing certainly looked like payback. The gun shots were the same according to the sheriff.

In the sky a corner of moon escaped the cover of clouds. A blast of wind whipped up, scattering the debris in the street as Belle drove through the neighborhood. Occasional streetlights burned a dull yellow circle on the pavement. A few porches glimmered through the darkness, like desperate beacons showing the way home.

Belle blinked hard at the strain in her eyes. This whole thing was becoming a puzzle. Too difficult to understand. Except that two people were dead and a young girl was left on her own to survive. It was Lily's survival that most concerned Belle. Furthermore, those dead were the two who were closest to her. Could that possibly mean Lily might be next?

16

Belle had another sleepless night. She imagined Adrian and Bern on the first floor counting the number of times she got out of bed. The floor did creak, after all.

Ralph Poole was dead. Why couldn't she let it alone? Wasn't Lily safe now? Did it matter who killed the man as long as he no longer posed a threat? So why rehash the whole thing? Why not just be glad it was all over? Let the sheriff worry about who killed Poole. It wasn't her concern. And yet she couldn't let it go.

When she finally got up for work she was groggy and irritated at herself. Even the sun splashing against building and tree didn't lift her mood. Why didn't the weather out here ever mirror her feelings? In Cleveland it constantly supplied you with a sense of gloom and morbidity.

Belle did her daily exercises learned from the police academy with more vigor than usual, hoping they might clear her mind. Then she got ready for school. Poole's murder was on the news, bright and early, just as the sheriff had predicted. Janice Purcell, the superintendent's secretary, greeted her with it when she entered the board building.

"Think it was the Mexicans getting him back?" Janice wondered.

"Who knows," Belle said, weary from a night of wondering the same thing.

"Wouldn't blame them if they did. It's time civilized people felt safe around here. Everybody and his mother owns a gun these days."

"Hence, my job," Belle reminded her.

"That's right. Without all those guns, you could go back to being a regular counselor. Sure would be a better world. Especially for our kids."

Once in her office, Belle phoned Ned and found out Lily was absent from school again. No surprise. After Julio's funeral and her father's death, who would expect her to show up?

"So, he really was killed?" Ned asked.

"He really was."

"Good grief. It makes you wonder who did it. One of Julio's relatives? It's so hard to believe that kind of thing goes on in this day and age."

She let him talk a little longer without comment. When she hung up she looked at her schedule. Not much on. This was going to be a long day.

But a little before ten Jenny called from the high school. "Mr. Ramey would like you to come as soon as possible."

"What's up?" Belle asked her.

"I wish I could tell you but he never confides in me."

Small wonder, Belle thought as she got ready to leave.

"Oh yeah, and a couple of sheriff's deputies were here this morning. Wanted to talk to some kids."

"Jeremy Gibbs? Tom Kelliker?"

"Yeah. What's that about?"

"Hopefully nothing," Belle told her and hung up.

Lloyd Pruitt, one of the Republican senate candidates running against Morgan Andrews, was sitting in Ramey's office when Belle entered. She was prepared for it. Jenny had told her the minute she hit the door. Why he was here, she didn't know. But why not? His opponent, Andrews, had come to the school. Hell, they could have a regular candidates' night out in the courtyard.

Unimposing was her first impression of him, harmless her second. But that changed quickly. He sat stiff and sulky in the seat provided for him. Another man sat in a chair away from the table, almost like a bodyguard, watching over things. A 'suit' was the feeling Belle got. An invisible presence.

Pruitt seemed fairly mild for a politician, almost baby-faced. But there was some malicious little glimmer in his eyes that caught Belle off guard. Medium height and barrel-chested, he wore a dark gray jacket and string tie held by a clip with the emblem of Arizona on it. He kept his white Stetson on instead of taking it off like most men would. Maybe he didn't plan to stay long.

Ramey had that steel rod-up-his-butt look, face grim as he watched Pruitt. Ned wasn't present to soften things this time.

"Mrs. Evans?" Pruitt began, and introduced himself. He didn't offer his hand, or get up from his chair. No Morgan Andrews manners in this man. When she was seated, he nodded at Ramey to begin.

"Isabel," Ramey started, "Mr. Pruitt is here because he's concerned that rumors have gotten out of hand. He – uh – he thinks people have the wrong idea about Julio Morales's – uh – death."

Pruitt sat forward, taking over. "People are calling this whole thing a hate crime." He had a Southwestern twang to his voice, a little Texas, a little Arkansas. "But nobody knows what it is for sure. They haven't even figured out who killed the Mex– the boy. And now we hear news that the girl's father was killed."

Belle nodded.

"But they don't know who did that one either?"

She shrugged.

He glanced back at his man, a tinge of satisfaction on his baby face. "A lot of opinions have been bandied about over this thing – a lot said on television that suggests more than is known. The sheriff has flung out misinformation. And then I learn that you people at the school are doing amateur detective work."

At first Belle was too surprised to be defensive. But gradually the man's words began to sink in. "Mr. Pruitt, I don't think the sheriff has been flinging out *any* information – mis or otherwise."

"He has. Where else would his good friend Andrews have come up with these allegations?"

"On his own perhaps?"

Pruitt glared at her. "Andrews would need a source. Maybe his source was here. I understand he had a meeting with you."

Belle's ire rose. "Right. Mr. Andrews would be likely to go on public television with information he'd gotten from a high school counselor about a murder. Smart."

"Isabel." Ramey gave her a warning look.

Pruitt's glance was cold. "You teachers, you're all alike. Involving yourselves in people's personal lives when you're being paid to teach our kids. Why can't you stick to what we hired you for? Maybe if you'd do your jobs our kids would be better educated. Instead, you think you've got a license to snoop and pry and put restrictions on everybody. You lobby for more government control, want to take guns away from responsible citizens, want to add more taxes to pay you higher salaries so you can do everything but teach."

"Can we back up a minute, Mr. Pruitt?" she said. "I take it you're upset about the news broadcast two days ago."

"Isabel," Ramey cautioned her again.

"Damn right I am," he said. "Where do you people come off getting involved in the law's business?"

Pruitt's face took on color and he sat forward. The 'suit' behind him did, too, like a Fred Astaire dance duet.

"I heard you're the one who's digging around in police business,

Mrs. Evans. Sticking your nose where it doesn't belong. Is that what we pay you for?"

"Actually, yes," she told him. "I've been hired as security counselor to the school system. A kind of semi police officer, you might say. I've had police training and I carry a shield." She pulled it out of her purse to show him.

Ramey's face cleared a little. "That's right, Mr. Pruitt. It's something new we're trying. There's been such an increase of violence in the schools throughout the country, you know."

The mean glitter in Pruitt's eyes amplified. "That's 'cause schools don't have discipline anymore. Back when I went to school you didn't have that kind of thing."

"Guns weren't so prevalent then, either," Belle said.

"Not a matter of guns," he spit out. "That's all you people can think of is get rid of the guns. Guns don't kill people – "

As Belle listened, she lost her anger. The man was a recording, an over-sized doll with buttons you pushed that spouted out all the slogans he'd been taught. So why bother getting upset? Still, she did wonder about one thing.

"Mr. Pruitt, I'm curious. What do you know about a group from Gilbert calling themselves the Black Falcons?"

Pruitt's face closed up. "Just a group. They've got their prejudices, sure. But that's not new in this country. People've got a right to their beliefs."

"Weren't several of them convicted last year of torturing and killing two Hispanics in a pretty gruesome way?"

He dismissed it with a hand wave. "Violent crimes happen. Which is why people should be allowed to own guns. They need to be able to defend themselves. Who knows for sure this boy didn't try to shoot Mr. Poole first?"

"Ralph Poole being such a pure, upstanding citizen who loved all mankind?"

Ramey started to caution her again, but she held up a hand and backed down.

"Look," Pruitt said, "I came here to talk to you people. To straighten things out. And you throw it back in my face. I guess I should have expected this." He adjusted his white hat and glanced at the man in the chair behind them.

Ramey got to his feet. "Mr. Pruitt, I believe you've gotten the wrong impression here. We are *not* involved in this investigation. Mrs. Evans is merely helping Lily Poole through some troubling times." He threw a look at Belle as if to say 'See what you've gotten us into?'

Pruitt stood, too. So did his man. "Is that why you were on the TV news with Andrews the other night?"

"I was there as a representative of the school the boy attended. I had no political agenda and neither has the school system."

"The school system's always got a political agenda," Pruitt barked. "You want our money – as much as you can get."

Belle almost jerked to a stand herself, but Ramey's glance made her change her mind.

Pruitt started for the door, his 'suit' hurrying to open it for him. "One thing's for sure. When I get elected to the senate, you people who want money for the schools can go begging."

The next moment he shoved through the door followed by his man, and leaving behind him the stale odor of animosity.

Mac turned down Poplar, a narrow street with small houses built in amongst the scrub brush and stunted trees. Garbage cans stuffed to over-flowing decorated front yards, an old couch or armchair on the porch, a car on blocks at the side. Here and there a sad effort at a flower garden. The neighborhood smelled of oil, over-spiced food, old rags, poverty. Too many people living in too small a space.

The Hernandez family lived in one of the nicer homes on the street. No furniture on the porch, no garbage can in front, a few hollyhocks and geraniums at the side. But it was small. Maybe two bedrooms for six people, plus Julio.

Rather than send a deputy, Mac decided to go see the family himself that afternoon. He'd thought of taking Carter along again, but he didn't want to set up defenses with the people over too many cops.

"Watch out for the dogs," Carter'd reminded him.

Mac heard the furious barking of the animals the minute he stepped out of his Jeep. When he knocked, the noise increased, the animals heaving themselves at the door. This was not promising. After what seemed like a long time, the noise was muffled as if the dogs were being sent out. They started up again once in the backyard. This neighborhood was a big area for dogs. Guard dogs, barkers. Nervous people owned big, hyper dogs; people new to the area, people coming from tough neighborhoods.

The small bungalow had paint peeling on the outside, driveway cracked, roof tiles missing. Mrs. Hernandez peeked out the door leaving the latch hooked, her eyes round and scared. "What you want?"

"Sheriff McFarland, ma'am. I was here before about Julio."

"What you want now?"

"I'd like to talk to you or your husband, if I may."

She didn't unlatch the door. "My husband, he is not home. No one is home."

Four o'clock, and according to Sarah's sources her husband was through with his job as janitor at Red Rock Elementary at three.

"May I talk to you, Mrs. Hernandez?"

She considered him a long time. Finally she stepped back, unlatched the door and opened it wide. The dogs continued to bark from the backyard.

Mrs. Hernandez, short and squat, long black hair caught behind her ears, stood uncertain in the doorway. No wonder, after his first visit when he'd told them about Julio's death. Finally he invited himself in. She seemed uncertain about letting him pass the threshold, but stepped back and allowed him to enter.

Inside, the place was cluttered, smelling of dogs and day old food. Worn furniture and religious pictures hemmed in the living room. An ironing board stood in a corner with a half ironed man's shirt lying on it.

She didn't offer him a seat but kept stiff and distant with suspicion.

"Mrs. Hernandez," he said, pulling off his Stetson, "I wonder if I could ask you some questions."

She looked dubious. "Why you ask more questions?"

He thought about how to put it. "I'm sorry to burden you so soon after Julio's funeral, but I need to know where your husband and Carlos were yesterday evening around sundown. Between five and eight."

"Why you need to know?"

This was always the tricky part, how to elicit cooperation at the same time you accused them. "Can you tell me where they were?"

She lifted her chin, glaring at him. "That man Poole, he is dead. And you think my husband or my son kill him?"

The dogs set up a new onslaught of barking in the backyard.

"I need to check all possibilities."

"They no kill him. He is the one who kill. It is good he is dead. Now we can rest. Julio has been avenged."

Mac shifted his stance. "I still need to know where they were."

She considered him, pride and suspicion glaring in her black eyes. "My husband, he is here with me. All my family is here."

"Carlos was here all that time?"

Her gaze wavered. "Yes."

"Mrs. Hernandez, we can check Carlos out, but I'd rather hear it from you."

Now she glanced away, tears starting. "My boy was with his friends." She swept her glance back. "But he did not do this thing. He would not kill. He is a good boy."

A good boy with a nasty temper, Mac thought. He was face to face with an adobe wall.

Suddenly all hell broke loose. One of the kids stumbled in the back door, a young boy, and the dogs came bounding in with him. Two huge, mixed-breed canines, one black, one multi-colored, raced into the room and faced Mac. Teeth bared, emitting barks and ugly snarls, they moved in closer, snarling in his direction.

The woman and boy just stood where they were as though frozen. Mac's heart was in his throat. He didn't move except to ease one hand toward his revolver. The other he kept at his side, gaze on the woman and her son, not making eye contact with the dogs. He knew better than to challenge them. They continued to bark and snarl, but didn't come closer. Finally the woman spoke.

"Blacky, stop. Blacky, come here. Stop."

They paid no attention until another figure appeared on the scene from the kitchen, a teenage girl.

"*Dios!*" she cried. "Blacky, cut that out. Camilla, stop that!" She went for the dogs and they backed away from Mac, still barking, but with less venom in the sound. She grabbed the black dog's collar and pulled him toward the kitchen. "José, get Camilla. Get her!"

The boy jerked to attention, took the other dog by the collar and the two were led out, still barking intermittently, as though to give Mac a final warning not to screw around with this family.

At last he stood alone in the living room with just Mrs. Hernandez. His pulse wouldn't settle down, but he made his voice sound calm. "I'm going to have to check on the whereabouts of both your husband and your oldest son, Mrs. Hernandez. I'm hoping they'll cooperate."

"You must ask them yourself," she said and went to hold open the front door.

Mac knew they were through for this round. She'd won it. He put on his hat and left.

Belle had made her circulation of the schools for the afternoon. She'd had a brief meeting with Superintendent Cummerford, and purposely hadn't told him about the Lloyd Pruitt scene that morning. He'd learn about it soon enough. She was back in her office when she got the call from Ned.

"I'm really sorry to bother you," he told her, "but it's Jeremy Gibbs and Tom Kelliker again. They've been in a fight."

"Another one?" she sighed. "Can't you handle it, Ned?"

Silence, then, "They won't talk to me. I can't seem to get through to them."

Belle liked the drive from her office to the high school but it was getting a little tedious this week. Why in hell was Ned even there? Probably because he was one of the few people on the faculty who didn't argue with Ramey and pogo-sticked when the principal told him to.

Belle parked in the teachers' lot and walked across the courtyard, heading for Building A. She let Jenny know she was here then went on down the hall to the counseling office, irritation nibbling away at her mood.

A teenage boy holding an ice pack on his left eye slunk sullen and aloof in a chair in the Bull Pen. Sandy hair fell in his other eye and his long legs sprawled out across the floor nearly tripping Belle as she entered. He didn't bother moving them.

Verna Reilly sat behind the counter as usual, typing at the computer. She tossed the boy a disgusted look and motioned Belle back to the inner office with a nod.

Worry colored Ned's features. "Mr. Ramey was ready to suspend them for a week but he settled for a day. Now I'm supposed to find out what the fracas was about. Gym class again. They picked a fight with one of the boys – Nick James. Nick won't tell me anything either. He's suspended because he took the first swing."

Belle shook her head. "Maybe Mr. Burke needs to offer boxing in his classes. Give these boys a release for all that pent up testosterone."

She entered the small conference room to find 'Tom and Jerry,' as she was beginning to label them, seated and looking belligerent if somewhat apprehensive. She studied them. They still had pathetic scars from the beating they'd gotten Wednesday night at the Sidewinder Bar. But there was a new cut on Jeremy's lip and Tom held an ice bag to his jaw.

"You fellows get prettier every time I see you," she said.

Tom gave a half smile, then winced at the pain. Jeremy hung his head.

"I understand the police were here to talk to you this morning."

They both nodded. Tom said, "We didn't kill that bastard."

"And your talk with the cops apparently didn't leave much of an impression on you either." She considered them. "What did the police ask you about?"

Jeremy turned his head sideways to look at her. "Wanted to know where we was last night."

"And where was that?"

"Out riding in Tom's truck. He's been working on the engine so we wanted to see how it'd ride. That baby's sweet. Right, Tom?"

Tom nodded without saying anything.

"A '48 Chevy pickup. Man, what a classic. He found it last year out on one of them old dirt tracks up by Copper Mountain. Just left there. Had a messed up engine but good glass. Boy, I love that thing. You know what I'm saying?"

Belle sighed. "So you fellows don't have an alibi for last night?"

"Got an alibi," Tom said around the ice bag. "We got no gun. How could we shoot him if we got no gun?"

Belle let it go. She was sure these two couldn't have done Poole in. And apparently the police didn't think so, since the boys weren't in custody. She sat down in a chair.

"Mr. Stambaugh has been very patient with you. So have I."

Jeremy sat forward, his face contrite. "We're sorry about getting you down to the police station, Miz E. Just that, you know, my ma, she's always crying. Anything I do, she cries, man. She makes me crazy with her crying."

"We'll let that incident pass," Belle said. "But we'd like to know what set off this latest in a growing series of fights."

Silence.

"Come on, boys, tell us. Did Nick James pick the fight? Did you?"

Jeremy's eyes teared. "Man, we was just asking him some stuff. He didn't need to get nasty. He's such a prick. Nick the Prick, that's what everybody calls him. He starts saying we're f-ing jailbirds, starts laughing at my black eye, says we major in bar fights and get beat up by a bunch of ole drunks. That's harsh, man." His anger bulged and he fell silent again.

"So you decided to show him? Two against one?"

"He hit first," Tom told her.

"I see. And what did you say to bring this on?"

They looked at each other, not quite so indignant in their anger now. Jeremy hung his head again.

"What did you say?" she asked. "You might as well tell me. I'll find out from him."

Jeremy shuffled in his seat. His voice was almost too low to hear.

"We – we called his ole man a butt wiping crook."

She nodded. "And why was that?"

He raised his gaze to her, defiant once more. "He's a crook, all right. Man, everybody knows that. He cheats people all the time. You know what I mean?"

Ned, standing in the doorway, said, "Mr. James is a realtor. He owns his own company."

"He's a crook," Tom insisted. "Julio told us. Said he knew for sure. Said he had the goods on James and somebody ought-a rub the guy's nose in it."

Once again Belle went to talk to Ronald Burke. He was in the gym, instructing a girl's volleyball practice. She watched as he demonstrated the serve, holding the ball on fingertips, bringing his fist up under it and sending it sailing over the net. When it was returned he handed it to the girl next to him, watched as she made a successful serve, then came toward the door to where Belle stood waiting.

"Volleyball," she said, "one of my favorite sports in high school – a hundred years ago. My daughter played on a volleyball team."

"Was she any good?"

"Actually, yes. She played varsity her junior and senior years. I went to all her games."

Burke stood, hands on hips, not much taller than her with a benign look to him. "You want to play or are you here about the two meatheads again?"

She looked at the girls on the court hopping three feet in the air, arms and legs reaching, twisting, gyrating. "I don't think I could do that anymore. So I guess we'll have to talk about Jeremy and Tom."

Burke shook his head. "What a pair. I have to tell you, James egged them on. He's a trouble maker. He pushes kids because he knows Ramey won't do a thing to him. Ramey was going to suspend Gibbs and Kelliker for a week until I told him James threw the first punch."

"Why is that? What's Nick James to Mr. Ramey?"

Burke shrugged. "I heard Ramey was friends with the dad. Both of them Elks or something. I'm not sure. What I do know is that the James kid has gotten away with more than anybody's got a right to."

"I understand the father's in real estate. The boys said Julio had called the man a crook."

A ball bounced in their direction. The gym teacher scooped it up and tossed it back to the server. "Don't look to me to deny it," Burke told her. "If Nick's a chip off the old block, then Julio might very well have been right."

17

"Did you see him on the five o'clock news?" Belle demanded into the phone. She couldn't stand it any longer. Ten o'clock on a Friday night but she had to talk to her sister Louise. "What a horse's ass. And malevolent, too. You can see it in his nasty little eyes."

"Don't over react, Izzy. You know how you over react. You've got too much of Nate in you." Louise always referred to their father by his first name. She was the calm older sister, Belle's cushion. She was also the only person on earth who could get away with calling Belle 'Izzy.'

"Did you see it?"

"Yes. And he sounded like every other politician I've ever heard. The only difference with Morgan Andrews is that he's better looking, has more style, more Eastern polish. Neither one of them are Democrats, are they?" A sin in Louise's eyes.

Belle flopped back in the armchair. "Oh, come on, Lou. The difference is enormous. Andrews stands for something worthwhile. Pruitt is a snarly little Gila monster. You should have heard the things he said in Ramey's office." She recited them all, described Pruitt's bodyguard. "No wonder he needs one. I might've permanently impaired his ability to produce kids right there."

"Now, that I'd like to see," Louise laughed. "Still, I doubt if the other man was a bodyguard, Izzy." She took a drink of something, probably a double scotch. She was a late-night drinker, when the day was finally over. "So, is this young girl all right?"

Belle took a swallow of coffee herself, then laid the cup on the side table. "I dropped by after school to check on her. I think she's still in shock. Too much has happened to her."

"She ought to see a doctor. He could give her something to settle her down for a few days, a week or so," Louise the nurse told her. It was the nursing at an underfunded hospital in a bad neighborhood that drove her to double scotches at night.

"I doubt if she's got insurance. I know she hasn't any money. I gave her fifty today. She didn't want to take it but I could tell she was grateful."

"So, how was her old man killed? You say he was shot?"

Belle took in a deep breath and explained what little she'd learned from McFarland.

"Revenge, you think?" Louise said. "That means it should be all over. I wonder if they'll catch the killer in a situation like this. He could have skipped across the border by now."

"Good Lord, Lou, I never thought of that. It sounds like an old Western." Belle sat back on the couch, pulled her feet under her and thought about it. "Maybe not Mexico. His two best friends at school aren't Hispanic. Neither is Lily."

"What about the aunt he was living with? The husband? One of the kids? Maybe a relative who still lives down there."

Belle rubbed her neck. "Something else bothers me. It could be nothing. Still –"

"What? What've you stumbled onto now?"

Belle told her about the business card Julio had given Lily for safe keeping. "I looked up the name Titus under land development at the county courthouse, but no go. Nada. A company that went bust before it ever got started, maybe?"

"It wouldn't be the first," Louise said, taking another swallow. "We've got enough of those babies in Arizona alone to fill half the state. It's the ones that've made it that're giving us so damned much grief. They wanna make big money off the land, use all the water and give nothing back."

"That's everywhere, Lou." Belle changed positions on the couch. "I guess the thing that gets my ass out of kilter is this guy I went to see on Wednesday. Julio's boss, or ex boss. Fred Preacher. A real piece of work, that one."

"Not living up to the name, I take it."

"I find it hard to believe the kid actually liked working for him." She described the episode with Preacher. "Told me to get the hell out."

"Christ, Izz, what're you trying to do? Get your head blown off? Stay away from people like that. Everybody carries guns these days."

"I've had training, Lou."

"Sure you have. That makes it all fine and dandy. Damn it, you sound more like Nate every day. Just please don't run off to Florida with some bimbo like he did."

"You're my bimbo, kiddo. I ran off to Arizona to be near you."

Louise gave a laugh, took another swallow. "Speaking of which, how are Lare and the kids? Talked to any of them lately?"

"You mean that SOB who's spent his life wringing me out and

hanging me up to dry?" It'd been Louise who'd campaigned for the marriage break-up, long before it actually happened.

"What? Ole Sweet Dumplin'? You're not sorry you left, are you?"

"Only because the kids are so far away," Belle admitted.

"And were too damned busy to see much of you when you lived in Cleveland."

"They have their lives. Will's a married man now. And school is demanding for Ellie. Besides, Ellie calls every Sunday. And Will once a month, pretty regularly. It's more than they talk to their dad."

Will still didn't understand Belle's choice to break up the marriage. Ellie, on the other hand, had actually joined her Aunt Louise in promoting it. She'd seen early on what the problems were. Even sworn that no man, much as she loved her dad, was going to treat her the way he'd treated Belle over the years.

Not that Larry was a bad man. He'd never meant to hurt Belle. He felt what he'd done was for her own good, making sure she wasn't put upon by the parents of students or over-worked by demanding bosses. Belle, being too much like her mother in the early years, had put up with his criticism and nagging and interfering. And later on because she couldn't bring herself to break up the family and because, in some weird way, she cared about him. He just was so godawful hard to live with.

Over time, though, she'd done a lot of maturing, becoming stronger, more self confident, changing in some ways from her mother to her father. The grand flip-flop. But Larry hadn't grown. He'd remained the same. Maybe this separation would force him to change. Whatever, she needed to get away, to live her life as she thought fit. The new, emancipated Isabel.

"How are Pete and the kids?" Belle asked, turning the subject away from the painful. "How was work this week?"

Louise lived in Paradise Valley. She had two grown kids of her own, both out in the world working. Her husband Pete managed a string of warehouses on the north side of Phoenix and Louise was a full time intensive care nurse at St. Jude's Memorial in south Phoenix. The horror stories she told Belle over the years were enough to curdle the blood in her veins, and Belle, along with Louise's family, had tried unsuccessfully to get her to find a nice private practice, preferably in Scottsdale. But instead of making the change, she just drank at night.

Louise finally cut off Belle's recriminations over the hospital job. "You're not through with this Lily Poole thing, are you?"

"What do you mean?"

"Come on, Izzy, this is me, ole Lou. You and me, we're connected at the hip, remember? I can read you like yesterday's headlines."

"Yeah, I know," Belle said. She stretched out her legs and propped them on the coffee table. "You have to admit I'm an object of interest to political candidates. Do you suppose they figure I have some special influence? Something about the Midwestern technique that grabs votes for them?"

"Or maybe the way you bat your baby blues. You always were the pretty one." A swallow again. "Look, Izz, don't start digging. Let it alone. You remember what happened with that Reynolds kid back in Cleveland."

Belle remembered. It was plastered indelibly in the scar she carried. She'd gone to see his abusive father when Family Services wouldn't do their job and the father had actually shot her. Luckily she'd moved and the bullet had entered the flesh of her upper arm. Otherwise she'd be dead. Then, of course, Larry's explosive reaction – worse even than getting shot.

"Lou, this isn't the same."

"Isn't it? Didn't that bastard Poole threaten you with a gun?"

"He didn't have a gun at the time, and besides, he's dead now."

"Right. And now you've got this boy's ex boss after your ass."

"It's not like that."

"Damn it, Izz, you're my only sister and my best friend. Let the authorities handle this, will you? For me? For my peace of mind?"

The scotch was making Louise maudlin.

"Lou, don't pull a Larry on me."

Silence, then, "Sorry, Izzy." A big swallow this time. "Guess I was, wasn't I? The person I really blame is that old man of ours and those policeman genes he passed on to you."

Louise had always resented Nate Bronson anyway for his philandering ways while their mother was alive. Even more when she died three years ago. And shortly after, he went off to Florida with a new young wife. In fact, everything bad that happened in their lives she attributed to him.

"At least will you get yourself a gun? Just to be on the safe side. I know you know how to use one. So what's the point of knowing if you don't own one? Come on, Izz, think about it."

Belle thought about it. "Maybe you're right. I'd probably feel more comfortable if I did. Any more suggestions for my protection? Think I can manage to live up here all by my lonesome?"

"Look, it's just hard not to give advice to my little sister."

"Some bloody nerve when you don't take it yourself. Get the hell out of that city hospital and maybe I'll start listening to you more. All you need to do is stick someone's HIV positive needle in you by accident and it's all over. My job? It's a romp in Disneyland compared to yours."

Saturday morning early, Belle took her usual trip to the shooting range on the outskirts of town off Route 47. Her conversation with Louise had left its mark, the insecurity of not being able to defend herself, of being vulnerable.

She had never owned a gun herself. Hated the damned things. Nate Bronson had touted his weapons at home too often and she'd sworn never to have one in her own home. Larry had agreed, one of the few times.

But the situation was different now. No kids, no Larry. She'd learned how to shoot during her training and was actually pretty good. And right now with all her frustration she felt the urge to blast the heads off a few targets.

The morning was clear and cool. Pearly cirrus swept across the blue of the sky like lace on a lady's ball gown. Traffic was heavy on the hills and curves of 47; Saturday mornings were a busy time for Granite residents. The highway cut through stands of piñons and junipers, small businesses dotting its edges: window and carpet wholesalers, fast food restaurants, an insurance office, a moving company, a car wash.

The shooting range was especially busy on a weekend. Belle's weren't the only frustrations pacing the room. She'd gotten there by eight-thirty and had to wait. Now at nine o'clock the place was full: independent and biker types toting their own side arms – it was allowed in this state – business men in Izod shirts and designer jeans, and quite a few women.

She rented a small Glock nine millimeter, ear muffs, aviation glasses, and paid for ammunition clips and a couple of targets. When a stall was vacant she walked down to the lane and pressed the button to bring the target string forward. She attached the cardboard version of a man and sent it back down the lane. Taking aim, she let off three rounds from the semi automatic before she paused.

"Not bad shootin', little lady," the man at the next lane said as he glanced at the damage she'd done to her target. She'd blown the left eye out of the thing and hit the heart several times. "You done this before, I take it."

"Some," she said, removing the glasses to rub her eyes. "I guess it doesn't hurt to know how."

"S'what I always think."

She spent the rest of her clip and began to feel the tension lift. The precision of the skill, the concentration required, helped her blot out the world. She changed targets and fitted the second clip into the Glock.

Belle was taking aim when she felt a large presence loom behind her. Turning, she encountered a man, six feet tall, brawny like a bull. Tattooed arms stuck out of a sleeveless T-shirt, jeans hugged skinny hips, and graying hair was pulled back in a ponytail. The look on his face wasn't pleasant.

"You, huh?" he spit out.

Belle was at a loss. Who the hell was he? "Do I know you?"

His expression was mean. "You're that lady got Preacher all upset the other day, ain't ya? Bastard took it out on me. Thanks a lot, bitch."

Belle's jaw dropped. Words wouldn't come.

The man in the next stall edged over. "Got a problem with this lady?" he asked the big fellow with the ponytail.

The ponytail moved in his direction. "Ain't your business, mister."

"Actually, it is," Belle said, finding her voice. "He's my husband and he happens to be a very good shot. So am I."

Both men stared at her. After a moment the ponytail moved on down the aisle at a respectable pace and the man next to her gave her a half grin. "Like I said, not bad shooting."

Belle used up her second clip with more intensity than before. Afterwards she checked in her equipment and headed for the Y on the other side of town to finish her regular Saturday morning workout. Her encounter with one of Fred Preacher's employees had started up her agitation all over again and she needed to work it off more than ever.

It was almost noon when she finally got back to her place, spent but not lulled. She climbed out of her Honda, waved to Bern and Adrian out back fixing a loose gutter – Bern on the ladder, Adrian below giving directions – and climbed the stairs to the second floor. The first thing she did was call Nick James' father, the realtor. At the gym, the fight between Jeremy and Tom and the boy had begun to bother her, what they claimed Julio had said about the man. The coincidence of realtor and Titus Land Development piqued her interest. Harley James answered but it was a machine recording. She had no idea what message she could give, so she hung up.

A shower calmed her tired muscles, though nothing seemed to help the agitation in her mind. She sat on a stool at the counter in old jeans and T-shirt, and chomped on a sandwich. She didn't like shooting a gun at the range, didn't like the idea that it might be necessary to use a weapon. And yet a wayward sense of power always slipped in unbidden. This was what people felt universally, this sense of control, like speeding down a race track, leaving all the other cars behind, like making a killing on a business deal before the other guy even saw you coming. Power. More important than money. Was that what Poole felt killing Julio? Was it what someone else felt killing Poole?

The phone rang and Belle reached for it, hoping to God it wasn't Larry. She just couldn't handle him right now. But the voice was Lily Poole's. She sounded a little stronger today, a little more determined.

"Miz Evans, I need a really big favor. I can't ask Kimmy or Monica 'cause they'd freak out."

"Thanks for the vote of confidence," Belle said. "What's this favor you need that's too gruesome for your friends?"

"I need to go back to my house. Gotta get some things. With my dad – you know – killed there, I didn't figure the girls could handle it."

"Can you?"

A deep breath. "Yeah. I'm fine. Anyway I will be if you go with me."

Belle wondered if the sheriff's people would still be there and decided to chance it.

"Got keys? The place might be locked."

"Got 'em."

"Okay, Lily. I'll pick you up in fifteen minutes."

Belle gulped down the rest of her lunch. Her digestive system was taking a beating these days. She debated calling McFarland's office and decided not to. If she asked, he'd probably tell her they couldn't go, and this itching to find out what had happened wouldn't let her rest.

"Sorry, Lou," she told the air. "Izzy's not taking your advice."

18

Dust in the lane off Stagg Road trailed behind as Belle drove her Honda toward the Poole place. Lily sat tense in the passenger seat, her face taut with suppressed emotion.

Clouds were already accumulating, moving in a bank that looked dark along the horizon. A hopeful sign since rain had been sparse during this year's monsoon season. The land was parched, dead trees up in the ponderosa forests and brown growth in the valleys. The green that was said to characterize this time of year hadn't appeared. No raging downpours, no flash floods, just the relentless sun and heat and taunting clouds.

When they neared the trailer, they could see the yellow crime scene tape flapping in the wind that cordoned off the area. But no police cars were in sight. Evidently the sheriff's department was about finished with their investigation or else taking a break. She wondered if she'd be in trouble for disturbing the scene of a crime, but decided Lily's needs were worth a little discomfort. What could McFarland do? Throw her in jail?

The main parking area, if you could call it that, was blocked off with the tape. So she pulled into the space behind the large alligator juniper. Lily stepped out of the car, wind blowing hair across her face, and looked around in a dazed fashion. Belle got out and watched her. The wind soughed through the branches of the juniper and the pine nearby. Ricegrass and squirreltail rustled throughout the open space, the seeds scattering into the air to race across the rangeland. Finally the two of them walked to where the tape obstructed them. Belle stepped over it first.

Lily looked at it, then back at Belle. "You sure it's all right?" Belle nodded so the girl crossed it. "It seems so quiet," Lily said.

"Well, for one thing, your dog isn't barking to raise the dead." McFarland had told her they'd taken the animal away.

"Poor Taffy."

"Taffy? That creature's name is Taffy?"

Lily shrugged. "When he was little he was cute. But my dad trained him to be mean. After a while I could hardly go near him."

Blood seemed to be everywhere. It had pooled on the ground and splattered the steps leading to the door along with some other indefinable substance. Lily froze when she saw it, her eyes wide, her mouth open. Remembering where Poole's bullet wounds had been, Belle hurried her past it, up the steps and to the door. Lily pulled a set of keys from her purse with shaking hands and unlocked it.

Inside, the mobile home still reeked of liquor and stale sweat. And the place looked like an animal's nest. Belle doubted all this was the work of the sheriff's department.

"You can sure tell I was away from home, can't you?" Lily said. "It only took him a couple-a days to do this to the place." A shudder made her body shake.

The trailer was one of the old models, long and narrow. Belle doubted if these were even manufactured anymore. Kitchen at one end, living/dining room in the middle, two bedrooms beyond with a small bathroom off to the side, the second door to the outside across from it.

Not all mobile homes held up well. And this one showed every year of its age. Even the furnishings were old and stained, the curtains faded, the table propped up on one side by an improvised leg. The ever-present wind whistled through cracks in the structure, singing a mournful song like ghosts in an ancient castle.

But in spite of the mess Poole had left behind, there was a homey quality to the interior. A few pictures on the walls, the drapes neat, knickknacks on some of the tables and shelves, lamps, a few books.

"Let's do this fast," Lily said and went straight to her room, the smaller of the two. The door was shut on the other. This was the only neat spot in the house. Traces of the police search were everywhere, even in here. But they'd been surprisingly careful not to trash the place.

Lily sat down on her bed, a twin with a pink flowered bedspread on it. Belle stood in the doorway watching her, wondering if the girl's composure would break.

This room was not only neater, it came alive. Framed photographs filled half of one wall. Stuffed animals surrounding a large teddy bear overflowed a dresser with a mirror, her closet was neatly arranged including the boxes on floor and shelf.

Belle went to look at the pictures. Several were of a young woman and a girl at various ages. The woman was a pretty thing with soulful eyes like Lily's. Fairer than Lily and sweet. Evidently Lily had gotten most of her features from her father, a fact Belle didn't intend to comment on.

As she studied the pictures, she saw that the older the girl got, the more haggard the woman became and the less they both smiled.

"Your mother?" Belle said, still studying the pictures.

Lily got off the bed and joined her. "She was so pretty, wasn't she?" Her voice had love and heartbreak in it. "I was eight when we got this one taken. At Wal-Mart. I don't have any pictures of her after that." A catch in her throat. "She died a year and a half later."

"Who are some of these other people?"

"Aunt Joyce." She pointed to a chubby woman, young and jovial looking. "That's Mom's sister. She was killed in a car accident in Texas five years ago. And that's an old picture of Grampa and Grandma Setter."

"No pictures of your dad up here?"

An ugly laugh. "Yeah, right. I'd want to go to sleep at night with *his* face staring at me." Then she seemed to relent. "I've got a few of him when he was younger, one when he and my mom got married. They're in one of the boxes."

She went back to the bed and Belle joined her.

"You've had a rough life for someone so young," Belle said.

Lily shrugged. "It wasn't all that bad. Can't remember much before I was five. But we used to live in town in a big old house. Victorian, over on Willow Street. Somebody with money bought it a few years ago and fixed it up real nice."

"Things were pretty good when you lived in town?"

"I remember when my mom used to take me down to the square to this little restaurant and we'd get ice cream. Just sit in there and order ice cream. I'm pretty sure she couldn't afford to buy a whole meal, but she loved sitting at the table and ordering. Like she was a queen, or something, like she was as good as other people." Lily hung her head, gazing at her hands. "Crazy, huh?"

She glanced out the small window in her room. "My mom cleaned people's houses. It was like she was their servant, you know. The pits." She turned to Belle. "But she was very careful how she talked, to sound educated. She made sure I didn't talk like I was ignorant, like my dad. And she made sure I did good in school."

"What about your father? Back when you lived in town? Was he drinking then? Was he abusive?"

Lily thought about it. "He might've been drinking some. I never saw it much. Maybe a beer or something. I don't remember him getting drunk." She took in a breath that sounded painful. "It seemed to me he was working pretty steady doing construction, building houses and roads and things. And Mom worked so we had enough money to live in town. I didn't see them argue a lot. Maybe a few times.

"Come to think of it, I do remember once when he hit her pretty bad and she was bleeding. But she said he was sorry for it and cried and – and begged her to forgive him." Tears stood in her eyes.

Belle touched her hand. "It seems your dad had a softer side. Look who he picked to marry. And she must have loved him, don't you think?"

"Yeah, she did. He could really be sweet when he wanted. It was when he got his leg busted up. About ten years ago. He had to go on disability. That's when he started to change, started drinking a lot."

"Drinking changes people. It makes them lose sight of their better self." Belle looked around the room again. "When did you move out here?"

"About a year before Mom died. We couldn't afford the house in town anymore. Some old man sold my dad this piece of junk for practically nothing. He fixed it up pretty good, the best he could with his bad leg. 'Course, he never owned the property, but I don't think the old man was charging anything. I mean, would you charge anybody to live on this God-forsaken piece of land?"

The tears started again but Lily stifled them and hopped off the bed. At her closet she began pulling clothes out and tossing them where she'd been sitting, then rummaging on the top shelf for items. Belle got up and walked back through the house, leaving Lily to her privacy. From the kitchen the ripe odor of week old garbage stung her nostrils. She thought of opening windows to get rid of the stink but decided against it. Don't give McFarland any more to jail her for.

Except for Lily's bumping around back there and the moaning of the air through the trailer, silence prevailed. Used to the noises of suburban life, Belle was always surprised by the silence. Out here in this deserted place, it made the hairs on her arms prickle.

After a while the bumping in the bedroom stopped and Lily emerged. "This is gonna take more time than I thought. Do you mind?"

"Fine. Can I help?"

Lily sighed. "I need a break."

She went into the kitchen, opened the refrigerator, edged back at the first whiff, then plunged her arm in and retrieved two cans of Coke.

"Want one? They haven't been opened so they should be okay. I won't offer you a glass. God knows what's been in 'em this past week."

She came back into the living room area, handed a can to Belle, brushed crumbs and a dirty shirt off the couch and sat down. Belle took a chair, popped the top and took a swig of Coke, looking Lily over for signs of giving way to hysteria. But the girl seemed strong, if pale.

Lily drank some of her Coke. "I never saw any of this coming," she said. "Stupid, wasn't I?" Another swallow. "I really loved Julio. He was so sweet. I guess he kinda reminded me of my mom. And maybe what my dad was in the beginning. Is that strange?"

"Not at all." Belle said.

"I mean, he came from a really poor family. Poorer than me even. And he moved up here to Arizona to make something of himself, you know?"

"Quite an ambition."

"Yeah. But he had a hard time. Couldn't speak English at first, so they held him back in school. He was going to be twenty in a couple of months. Still, he stayed in school. Some of the guys made fun of him for being so old. He just told them to piss off, told them they were the losers."

Lily was finally talking, getting out her emotions. Belle took another drink of Coke and settled back to listen to the girl.

"My God, the things he had to go through in his life. But at least he had his aunt and uncle. I guess they were pretty good to him. They had their own kids but they took Julio in so he could get educated and help his family back home."

"And he was going to take you away," Belle said, that old question needling her.

"I guess. Every time my dad got mad and hit me, Julio would start planning where we could go. At first he wanted to take me back to Mexico but we'd be as poor as his family was. So then he tried to think of other places where he could work and we could live. Maybe Phoenix. Still, he knew if he didn't finish high school he'd never get a good job."

"But Sunday night he thought he had a way?"

Lily sank back on the couch. "I don't know. Maybe he just wanted it so much. Maybe I did, too."

"Could this scheme have had anything to do with work, do you think?"

Lily shrugged. "He didn't say."

"What about the business card he gave you? Would any of this have to do with the development company on that card?"

Another shrug. "I don't know, Miz Evans. It all happened so fast." She wiped her face with one hand as though obliterating some image in her mind. "He got paid good at work. Maybe they were gonna give him more hours. But he'd have to stay here to do it, and he told me we were going to get away. So that couldn't be it."

She bounded off the couch, a kind of sickness in her face, sloshing the Coke she held. She laid the can down on the coffee table and started for the bedroom.

"I'd better finish. I don't want to stay here any longer than I have to."

A sharp wind whipped up and whistled through the rafters of the mobile home, making a racket. Not so quiet out here after all, not in a house of tin.

A few minutes later Lily came back out of the bedroom carrying a couple of paper bags, one stuffed with underwear, the other with odd items, presumably from a dresser drawer.

"You think Mrs. Rivera will let me stay another week? I just don't know if I could come back to this place."

"We'll talk to her and see what we can do. Is there any other place you can go? Any relatives?"

Lily rested the bags on the arm of the couch. "Aunt Joyce's husband. He and his kids live in Texas. I told you about her dying in that accident. But I don't know if I could go there."

Belle set the Coke aside. "Anyone else?"

"Mom had a brother, went up to Wyoming. I don't know much about him."

"Any address for the uncle in Texas?"

"Maybe. Somewhere." Lily rubbed at her forehead with her hand. "Uncle Bill isn't much of a writer, but he did write me a few years back. Let me know he and the kids were doing okay. Man, he hated my dad. They knew how my mom died." She sucked in air along with a sob. "Want me to find the letter?"

"No hurry," Belle told her. "I'll go get some of your clothes and we'll pack up."

Lily grabbed the bags and started for the door. Belle headed for the bedroom.

Belle thought afterwards she heard something like a car door slam and wondered if it was one of the sheriff's men. She'd just grabbed up an armload of Lily's clothes on hangers when a shot rang out across the landscape, stunning and shrill.

Her mind groped for an explanation. Suddenly her eyes widened; she dropped the clothes. "Lily!" she cried and raced back through the trailer to the open door.

A dust cloud made a furious retreat down the lane, obscuring its creator, obliterating the desert silence.

"Lily!"

Then she looked down at the girl lying at the bottom of the steps, bags and contents strewn on the ground and caught up by the wind.

"Oh God, Lily!"

19

Movement from the girl nearly stopped Belle's heart. She stumbled down the steps. "Lily, oh God, Lily."

A moan emanated from Lily. Belle knelt down to her. Blood on the ground stunned her until she realized it was old and dried. Ralph's, not Lily's. Whoever fired that shot must have missed her.

"Oh man," Lily groaned. "Jesus, what was that?"

Belle gulped air and sat back on her heel, trying to control the shaking that had begun. Some of Poole's blood had wiped off on the knees of her own jeans.

Lily pushed herself to a sitting position and seemed to take stock. As she moved her legs, she cried out, "Oh damn," and grabbed her left ankle.

Belle came out of her stupor and took hold of Lily's arms. Had the shot hit her after all? "Where are you hurt? I don't see any blood on you. Let me check."

"My ankle. I think I twisted it when I fell."

Belle examined her all over. No sign of a bullet wound. When they'd both gotten the chance to settle down a little, she asked Lily what happened.

"I don't know. I was just coming out to put those bags – oh damn, look at the stuff!" Bras, bikini pants, a shirt, some notebook paper, odds and ends caught up on weeds, flapped in the wind.

"I was just coming out and I tripped. I heard this loud noise. I fell down the steps and the bags went flying. I was so surprised, I guess I just laid there."

"Thank God you tripped," Belle muttered. "Whoever's looking after you up there, She picked the right time to glance down from Her cloud."

McFarland came with one of his deputies, the huge, red-headed man, Rolly Carter. Belle recognized him from her encounter at the jail over Jeremy and Tom's bar fight. Carter went outside to take a look around.

McFarland sat down with Belle and Lily in the trailer's living room, Stetson in hand, looking grim and fairly pissed. Belle braced herself for his disapproval.

"If you'd called the office, I could've sent somebody with you," he said. "Or were you afraid I wouldn't let you come?"

She shrugged a 'guilty as charged.'

"Why?" she demanded, putting him on the defensive. "Why would somebody shoot at her? Is there some crazy guy running around these parts taking shots at people? What possible reason does anyone have to hurt Lily?"

He glanced over at the girl. Lily sat back on the couch, her left foot propped up on the coffee table with a bag of ice resting on the ankle. The twist hadn't been as bad as they'd thought. Now she stared at McFarland with a bewildered expression, as though comprehending none of this. He rubbed the rim of his hat.

"From the looks of the bullet hole in the siding, the aim wasn't good if it was meant for her," he told them. "Lily, you must have surprised whoever it was. Mrs. Evans' Honda wasn't in sight so maybe he figured the place was empty."

"He? You have an idea who?" Belle asked.

"Could be a she. Usually isn't when it's shooting. Not unless a husband or boyfriend gets a woman furious enough."

"So, someone was after something here, you think?"

"That's a possible answer. We did a thorough search, but who knows?" He rubbed the side of his face with a broad hand and looked at Lily. "Anything here we should be looking for? Did your father have something somebody'd want?"

Still that baffled look in her face. "My dad never had anything valuable that I ever knew of. If he did, he'd've sold it to buy liquor. Most of his disability check went for that. I practically had to steal from him to get money for food."

McFarland looked around the place, his eyes squinted as though some x-ray vision would help him find what was hidden.

"Like I said, my people checked this place pretty thoroughly. Didn't find anything out of the ordinary. But then, the first time round we didn't find the gun either."

"Now you have it, though," Belle said. "The one he used on the boy."

He ducked his head away from Lily. "Poole – her dad – had it when he was shot."

"Did he shoot back at his killer?"

The sheriff shook his head. "The gun was cold. He didn't get a shot off himself."

Lily slumped listlessly, as though all interest in life were gone.

Belle edged forward, alert. "Meaning he was either surprised, or expecting someone."

McFarland threw her a narrow look. "Mrs. Evans, you're forgetting this is a police matter." He glanced at Lily.

Lily got up. "I'm gonna lie down in my room." She took the ice pack with her and limped across to the hall. McFarland waited until they heard the door shut.

"I told you, I'll take care of this?" he said.

"I just think Lily should know how her father was killed. And now she's been shot at herself," Belle insisted. "You said Poole was shot in the chest and head. From the front, I take it. So he'd have seen his attacker."

The sheriff nodded. "Apparently he was sitting on the front stoop outside."

"You said the two killings weren't done by the same person. Different guns. Are you sure Ralph Poole shot Julio?"

"Bullet matches up to the gun he had. It was a close range shooting."

"And Ralph Poole?"

"Rifle. From about seventy-five yards away. The shooter stopped down the lane. He left one of the shells behind, so I doubt he was a pro."

"Or she?"

His grinned seemed reluctant. "Sorry, didn't mean to be sexist."

Belle glanced away for a moment. She knew she was becoming too intense about the whole thing. She turned back, not sure if she should mention this. What the hell, he'd find out anyway. "I suppose you know I went to talk to Julio's boss, Fred Preacher."

"No, I didn't know that." He wasn't grinning anymore. "We already talked to him, Mrs. Evans. We're pretty thorough, despite the reputation of police in this country."

"I'm not criticizing, Sheriff. I told you before my dad was a cop. And a good one." She backed down. "My sister thinks I've got too much of him in me."

"Sounds like it."

She recrossed her legs, covering the knee with Ralph Poole's blood on it. "I just wondered why Julio thought he could get enough money to take Lily away. So I asked his boss. But the man got savage with me. Kicked me out of his office. I was just wondering why."

McFarland's face was unreadable. He got up and walked to the front window. Just then the door opened and Carter invaded the small space like a bear in a pup tent.

"Mac, looks like the vehicle pulled up over to the side so it wouldn't be seen from the road back there. Hard to tell much, ground's so dry. Got a feeling he figured nobody was around with this lady's car behind that big ole juniper. He wouldn't have spotted it right off. Then he saw the girl and got surprised, maybe."

"Thanks, Rolly."

The huge redhead nodded, checked out Belle in the chair. "Gonna see if I can dig that bullet outta the siding. Probably pretty messed up. Looks like a pistol shot. Maybe a .22." He moved with surprising grace back to the door and out.

Silence reigned for a moment. McFarland went to the window again and stood watching.

Belle broke the quiet. "I – um – have one other thing you might want."

She got up and retrieved her purse hanging on a kitchen chair; the table had been too filthy to set it there. Pulling out the business card Lily had given her, she took it over to McFarland. "I don't know if this is anything. Lily remembered it the day after we talked to her. She said Julio gave it to her when he met her in the canyon. Told her to hold on to it for him."

McFarland's gaze hardened as he took the card and looked it over.

"I checked the records in the courthouse," she said, caution in her voice. "Nothing on a Titus Land Development."

He looked down, scrutinizing her. "Like your dad, huh? Any more evidence you're withholding?"

"That's it," she said, hackles rising. "I'm just trying to give Lily some peace over this. Get some solution for her. I thought she could begin to heal with her father gone. But then this shot at her. Now I'm really scared for her safety."

"If you're scared, then keep her away from this place. You stay away, too, Mrs. Evans. Leave this whole thing alone."

Belle stepped away from his scrutiny. "Damn if you don't sound like my husband."

"Where is your husband?"

"I left him back in Cleveland."

"Divorced?"

"Separated."

"Too bad. He must be a level-headed fellow."

She laughed harshly. "Is it some male thing that you have to keep the 'little woman' out of trouble? Keep her wrapped up in a blanket and safe from the world? Let you men handle anything important?"

McFarland sucked on a tooth. "I sense a bit of resentment here."

"Hence the separation."

He nodded sagely. "Well, you and Lily gather up what she needs and take off. Don't come back here until I give the go ahead, Mrs. Evans. We're not to the bottom of this yet." He held up a defensive hand. "And, no, we don't need your help. We've muddled through before. We can do it now."

Belle agreed grudgingly, so the sheriff put on his Stetson and left.

She waited while Lily kept to her bedroom. The girl needed some time to herself. She still hadn't absorbed the enormity of her father being killed, and then to be shot at.

Not for the first time Belle wondered at the amount of pain and confusion some kids had to put up with in their lives. Being a guidance counselor was like any other social vocation. You had to help people work through the hurt and frustration of their lives. Only it was worse handling kids. They were so young, so ill-equipped to deal with these problems. Maybe her job wasn't such a romp in the park after all.

Feeling restless, she got up and looked out the window. The Crook County cruiser had disappeared down Stagg Road. She checked on Lily one more time then went outside.

She took the front steps quickly, avoiding the old blood stains, and walked around the empty dog pen to the back. The sun, playing hide and seek with a huge gathering of clouds, was still high but slanting to the west, casting shadows from the mobile home. Elements like wind and sun and shadow all fluctuated the temperatures during the day, here in the desert where little moisture was present to keep them constant.

A couple of ravens soared overhead, their sleek bodies dancing in the air. Some finches and sparrows chattered in the juniper around the front. And from the roof of the trailer a phoebe called it's sad little tune, then flew to a bush of scrub oak looking for insects or an old nesting site or, who knows, a friend and mate. Belle glanced around her at the solitude. In a place like this a man, sick at heart, could be alone and drink himself into oblivion. But it wasn't the place for a young girl to grow up. Or a wife to thrive.

She checked her watch. After three. Time to get Lily packed up and moved out. She pulled the Honda up close to the crime scene tape and went to help. When she stepped into the trailer Lily was already busy. She came out of the bedroom with an armload of clothes on hangers, limping but apparently not in terrible pain.

"How does your ankle feel?"

"Not too bad. I'll probably walk it off."

Belle didn't argue. "The car doors are open," she said and went for a load herself.

Lily didn't have much, though she'd kept a number of mementos squirreled away in her dresser and in boxes on the closet shelf. They found some grocery bags under the sink in the kitchen and filled those.

"You'll be coming back here before long," Belle reminded her. "You don't have to take everything."

Lily shook her head. "No telling what low-life would ransack an empty place like this. I just don't wanna lose anything important."

Belle noticed the pictures on the wall were gone.

They filled the back seat and trunk of the car and went into the house one more time to look around.

"What about important papers?" Belle asked. "Where would your dad keep such things?"

"Like what?" Lily apparently couldn't imagine Ralph Poole owning anything of importance.

"Papers on the trailer, insurance – "

"What insurance? I don't think my dad ever had a penny's worth of insurance."

Belle conceded the point as being likely. "Did he own this place?"

"Yeah, I think so. I mean, he got it for practically nothing. It was in lousy shape when we moved here."

"So he'd have a deed. You'll need that to prove ownership."

Lily threw her an incredulous look. "Why would I want ownership of this dump?"

"Because you have no other assets. Like it or not, kiddo, this baby's probably yours."

Lily made a sour face.

"He also might have some money stashed away," Belle told her. "So, where would he keep it?"

Lily concentrated. She turned toward the kitchen, scrutinizing each of the cupboards as though she could see into them, did a slow swivel around the living-dining room, then headed for the back to her father's bedroom. Belle followed her.

"I've been through every cupboard and cubby hole in the house," Lily said. "Can't think where he'd stash things like that."

"A desk?"

"Oh yeah, right. My dad spend money on a desk?"

When they opened the door to Ralph Poole's bedroom they were battered by a stench so strong it was like being hit by a high wind. Alcohol, old sweat, flavored with a soupçon of vomit. Belle hurried to open a window, then stood taking in the outside air like a drowning victim.

Lily held her nose. "God, he really had a binge while I was gone."

Belle shrugged. "I expect he was afraid he'd lost you for good." And killing the boy, she thought. That probably got to him.

The bed was a shambles of filthy sheets and blankets, a few clothes strewn on the dresser and the one chair in the corner, bottles scattered about. Belle didn't even want to think what might be under the bed. Something noxious that grew in dark places away from the sun.

The few clothes in the closet had been shoved to one side. So had the boxes on the shelves above. Lily pulled them down and they looked through each one.

Suddenly she stood up straight. "Hey, wait."

That got Belle's attention. "What is it?"

"Wait, I think –"

She turned and rushed out of the bedroom to the bathroom. Belle followed.

Another reeking wind met them as Lily opened the door. Ralph apparently didn't flush toilets when he was in his cups. Or else the mechanism was jammed and he hadn't bothered to fix it.

Stunned anew by the smell, they pulled back into the hall.

"Goes to show what happens when I'm not here for a few days," Lily said. She plunged back to the toilet as though facing the onslaught of a storm.

She pulled off the tank lid and set it on the sink, then jiggled a hidden panel on the wall behind it. Evidently, McFarland's boys hadn't found this place. The panel was loose but wouldn't come off.

Belle braved the foul air and went to help her. One screw was gone. Another was loose. She hunted through a drawer at the sink, found an old nail file and used it.

The panel was made of the flimsy wallboard that lined the entire inside of the trailer. Lily gave it a good yank and it cracked, revealing the plumbing fixtures and a rectangular, metal box wedged in between the pipes. The box was a foot by perhaps eight inches and maybe four inches high. A dull lead gray in color with a greenish tinge.

"I knew it," Lily exclaimed in exaltation. "He told me a long time ago he had a secret hidey hole. I just forgot where it was."

Belle pulled out the box and they headed back to the living room, breathing deeply in order to get the smell from their lungs. She set it on the coffee table and the two of them stared at it.

Perching on the couch, Lily took the box in her hands, handling it as though it might be housing for a rattler. "Can't be much in here. He never owned anything."

The box was old, made of some cheap metal, and had no lock. Lily pried it open and sat back with an odd smile. Inside was an envelope with a small stack of hundred dollar bills spilling out.

"Wow. Who'd-a thought?"

She pulled them out to examine. Five in all, new and crisp. Several envelopes lay beneath and a box of ammunition. There was room enough to hold a gun. Lily dropped the box of bullets on the coffee table as though it burned, staring at it with a stricken look on her face.

Finally she rifled through the envelopes until she found an official one and handed it to Belle.

Belle opened it and pulled out the folded document. "It's a deed, all right," she told Lily. "So your dad owned this trailer all nice and legal."

Lily's laugh was cold. "Wow, this place is all mine. I'm rich."

Belle looked through the other papers, a couple of letters, some old documents, then stopped. She held up the envelope that had been on top, the one with the money in it. Nothing written on it. She took it and flipped it over. "Oh my God!" she gasped. She hadn't noticed before, but on the back flap of the envelope was the company name, printed in small type yet perfectly clear. Mile Hi Earth Movers.

The money in Lily's hands was payoff.

20

Mac dropped off Rolly Carter at the station, told him he'd be back in an hour and headed the cruiser out of town to Mile Hi Earth Movers. The sky, as he drove, was heavy with fat, sullen clouds, teasing the dry earth with moisture it refused to release, or tempting it with strands of virga that never reached the ground. Sweat streaked down the sides of his face and filled the hollows of his armpits.

He hated to admit to it but the Evans woman was on the right track. Maybe because of her dad's police background, or because she had an analytical mind. Not that he wasn't irritated at her involvement. He didn't want to have to cart off another body to the morgue. But she had good instincts about this case.

He was beginning to doubt his own, though. Where the hell was this going? A hate crime? A father keeping his daughter from running off? For whatever reason, Poole had shot Julio Morales. Now Poole's killing. Jesus, that was cold blooded. Like a hit man. But where the hell would you find a hit man in these parts? And a sloppy one at that.

Why had Poole been killed? Payback, like Rolly said? Playback for a poor young Hispanic by someone with an expensive rifle and one hell of a good shot. That didn't set right.

And what was this business card? He pulled it out of his shirt pocket to look at. 'Titus Land Development' along with a partial phone number. He'd have to put Sarah on that. She could come up with a name if anyone could. He'd pit her computer skills at data finding against any expert in the state. Belle Evans said she hadn't found anything in county records. But she didn't have the resources of the sheriff's department. Or a Sarah at her disposal.

Now the shooting today. Who had been able to drive up without being noticed? Why had someone come? Lily Poole was there to get something. Maybe this other person was, too. What was in that place that Mac's people hadn't found?

Damn it all to hell. They'd scoured the trailer, looked through everything. But they hadn't found the gun, not in the first search. After Poole's death they'd gone through the place again, something he'd never hear the last of from Carter.

"Place was a stinking toilet!" Carter'd said. "Only three days later and it's a shit hole. Must-a been drunk the whole three days."

The second time they already had the gun, so they'd been searching blind, no idea what they were looking for.

What would Poole have that somebody wanted? Not money. They'd found a connection between Poole and Preacher. The Sidewinder Bar for one. But then, half the deadbeats in the county frequented the establishment. And the Tucker Highway project, they'd checked Poole's medical records and found it was one of Preacher's machines that had done the damage to Poole's leg. But what kind of connection that gave the two, Mac couldn't guess.

Now this thing about Titus. Had Poole known anything about Titus? Did Preacher? Did Titus have anything to do with why Morales was killed? Was Poole paid off as the hit man? No money was found. Or was his death the real payoff after having been promised money?

Mile Hi was closed up tight when Mac pulled into the parking lot. The hours said Saturday 8 till noon. Nothing Sunday. He could have called first and saved the trip. But then he'd needed this drive by himself out on the road to do some thinking, unfettered by business at the station.

He looked at his watch. Time to get back and check in with Carter. And he had to finalize plans for the political rally next Saturday. Morgan would be calling to find out about it.

There was historical precedence behind the rally being held on the steps of the Crook County Courthouse. In the last ten years a presidential candidate, a gubernatorial hopeful, and two men running for state senate had used this place to elicit support. Granite wasn't big if you compared it with some of the Eastern towns. But out here its forty some thousand plus the surrounding incorporations gave it significance.

So Morgan Andrews had decided to follow a tradition of sorts and take a stance on those very steps. Looked like it was going to be quite an event, too. Several other politicians would be there to cheer him on. And a crowd of over a thousand was expected.

Lucky for Mac, the Granite Police Department was in charge of this shindig. But Berry Scott, the Chief of Police, had a piss-poor record of keeping control during such events. And Berry could be a real cocksucker when it meant getting his department to cooperate with the sheriff's. Morgan had pleaded with Mac, though. And Mac had a hard time turning down a friend of such long standing.

So he'd called in all his extras for next Saturday and was in the process of mapping out their assignments. But right now he felt the burden of that rally like a huge pain across his chest. He had two people killed and the girl shot at. Why the hell weren't things ever easy?

Belle pulled into the driveway at The Pines around dinner time. Iron gray clouds hovered above them, covering the earth in shadow. Lily had been silent and thoughtful all the way back. Finally she turned to Belle.

"Do you think it was payoff money for something?"

Belle sighed. "Looks that way, though $500 isn't a lot. Maybe a first installment?"

Lily grabbed her lower lip in her teeth, eyes suddenly red and wet. "Was he –" Her voice caught. "Was he paid to kill Julio?"

Belle pulled in air, held it, let it out.

"But why?" Lily cried. "Why would anybody want to kill Julio? I mean except my dad. You think it was Julio's boss? You think he wanted Julio –"

Belle glanced at her, trying to think of something to say that would ease the pain and coming up with nothing.

Lily swiveled to look at the metal box they'd found, sitting stark and ominous on top of the pile of clothes in the back seat. Like watching a rattler to see which way it would decide to strike. Belle grabbed it and stuck it under the seat. "I'll take it to the sheriff if you want."

"Please. Just keep it out of my sight."

Mrs. Rivera came to meet them at the car, looking worried. "Is everything all right?" she asked.

Belle gave her a half smile and they got out. How much should she tell the woman?

"We were wondering if it's all right for Lily to stay here a while longer. I know you're crowded."

"Lily may stay as long as she has the need. The others will make room for her."

Some of the girls came out to help Lily transfer her belongings to the house. They were curious about her limp and asked her what had happened. Belle decided it was up to her how much of today's events she wanted to divulge.

Again Mrs. Rivera invited Belle to eat with them. Again Belle declined.

When the unpacking was done, Lily came out and got in the car, sitting silent as though reluctant to have Belle go.

Belle was reluctant to leave her. The girl had worked her way into Belle's heart deeper than she usually allowed with students. As a guidance counselor, it was always too tempting to grab up kids and take them home, give them the love and security they'd never had, feed them right, buy them decent clothes, comb their hair, teach them to laugh. Some of them never laughed.

But you couldn't give way to that urge. You had to maintain that objective partition. Trouble was, Lily had slipped under the partition. Or else Belle had dropped it somewhere along the way without noticing.

Lily turned to her. "I couldn't-a done this without you, you know. I couldn't-a gone back to that place. Not even with Kimmy."

"I'm not so sure," Belle told her. "You're one strong young lady. You've been through more than I could ever imagine doing myself, and look at you. You're managing. You're going on with your life. Don't underestimate yourself, Lily. Given time you'll do fine."

Tears welled in Lily's eyes and suddenly the dam burst. Belle grabbed her and held on while the girl sobbed into her shoulder. All her misery came to the surface, misery at losing Julio, at losing her mother before that, at being shot at, and finding herself without a family. Belle felt the weight of so much pain in that embrace.

Finally Lily got hold of herself and pulled back. "I'm sorry. I got you all wet."

Belle gave a laugh. "Don't worry. In this arid atmosphere, it'll dry in no time."

"I wish you didn't have to go just yet."

Belle hated the thought herself. But someone had to be resolute and she was the adult, after all. She said, "Honey, Mrs. Rivera's waiting supper."

"I know." Lily gazed out at the old house, its peeling paint harsh in the lowering daylight, the windows reflecting light and shadow patterns like eyes blinking. "You've been so good to me. Are you like this with all the kids?"

"Well, I try. Of course, you're kind of special."

Lily nodded. "All I can think to say is thanks."

"That's plenty."

Lily gave Belle one last long hug and climbed out of the car. Belle watched her limp up the porch steps then turn to give a soulful glance her way before going into the house. As Belle turned the key in the Honda, she noticed a dark pickup just down the street start up, make a U-turn and drive off down North College.

* * *

Belle stopped by the Crook County Department of Justice on her way home. She fully intended to leave the box they'd found containing the money and the Mile Hi envelope with McFarland. But when she asked for him he wasn't there.

She left her name with a woman at the desk, but not the box. She didn't want it getting lost in the shuffle. That was the trouble with having a cop for a father. You learned about all the screw-ups that could happen within a justice department.

Adrian was out front winding up the hose when Belle pulled in the drive. He glanced up at the sun along the horizon, a strip of gold just below the cloud cover. "When the hell is it going to rain?" he muttered. Then he took one look at her and said, "You need a drink, love. Get your fanny in here and let Adrian take care of you."

There was never any point arguing with him so she followed him in the front door of the house like an errant puppy. Bern slouched on a sofa in the living room watching a baseball game, a bottle of Michelob in his hand, legs sprawled out and stockinged feet resting on an elegant coffee table. His over-sized, gnarled body looked out of place in the Victorian setting of delicate furniture and knickknacks.

"Hey, Belle," he waved. "Adrian mothering you again?"

She laughed. "He's better than my own was." She paused before following Adrian. "Bern, you work in construction. Ever have any dealings with a man named Preacher? Fred Preacher?"

Bern glanced up from the game. "Preacher, the Mile Hi guy? Sure." He cocked his head, his boxer face quizzical. "You got something to do with Fred Preacher?"

"The student who was killed at Lame Horse Canyon worked for him. Julio drove those big earth-movers." She perched on a velvet covered chair. "What do you know about him?"

Bern straightened from his slouch and laid the bottle on the coffee table. "He's not the kinda guy I see *you* dancing with. Pretty tough character. Came up from the streets, so I hear. Still acts like it in my opinion."

"Are you connected with him on your present job?"

He shook his head, thick black hair falling into his eyes. He pushed it away. "Last time I worked on the same job as him was maybe a year ago. A new development up near Copper Mountain. His boys dug the blade roads in, then worked on the floodplain. They were a rough bunch. The rest of us kept our distance."

"Do you remember a young Hispanic boy driving for them?"

He shrugged. "Like I said, we kept our distance."

Belle considered him. "Bern, what do you think the possibilities are that Preacher could be involved in something illegal?"

Bern Wozak gave a harsh belt of a laugh. "Pretty damned good." Then he looked her in the eye. "You know something he might've done?"

"Maybe. I don't know for sure, but I think it's possible he had some hand in Julio Morales' death."

"No kidding?" Bern sat forward. "I'll tell you the truth, I wouldn't put it past him. Not if there was something in it for old Fred."

"That's what I'm thinking. Something in it for him."

She got to her feet, left Bern to get back to his ball game and headed out to the kitchen where Adrian was making one of his martinis.

"You've been a busy girl today," he said, giving the dried blood on her jeans a scrutiny. "Something heavy duty?"

He beckoned her to sit at the table and continued his work on the drinks, carefully adding the ingredients to the martini pitcher.

"I took Lily out to her house this afternoon to get her things."

"The sheriff didn't stop you?"

Belle winced. "I didn't exactly ask him."

"Ah." He paused in his operations to gaze at her, eyebrow raised, giving his face a sardonic appearance. "Those testy police officials, they almost never like you to enter crime scenes behind their backs. I hope he didn't find out."

Belle glanced away, the impact of the day hitting her like a fist to the stomach. Thank God she had Adrian to talk to.

Some people who weren't acquainted with Adrian Good would have said he was a gossip monger. But Belle had gotten to know him pretty well in the eight months she'd lived here. He and Bern had moved to Arizona from San Francisco six years ago, tired of the ultra 'gay' scene and seeking to lead a life of some kind of normalcy. They'd found Granite, a town of mixed extremes. Artists rubbed shoulders with ranchers, literary types shopped beside sun worshipers, liberals fraternized with conservatives, lots of retirees spent money on new home construction and art work. This was the perfect place for them.

Adrian's defenses had grown sharp over the years and his tongue could zap a foe below the belt with the skill of a scorpion. Anyone as obviously gay as he was had needed to learn such defenses. But his soft side was sincere, his sympathy genuine. And Belle was grateful she'd found him in a new and foreign land.

He turned to her, full face. "Okay, love, let's start from the beginning. Tell Adrian about the whole ugly mess. No, wait. Better get some gin in you first." He poured them each a glass, two olives, then sat down at the kitchen table, his attention entirely on her.

When Mac got back to his office, he had a message to call Morgan Andrews. That could wait. First he wanted to grab Sarah before she went home for the weekend.

"Get on this first thing Monday for me, Sarah. The phone number, the company name."

Sarah took off her glasses to look at the business card.

"Area code's an odd one," she remarked, eyes intense. "And the rest is partly obliterated."

"See what you can do."

Mac checked with Carter and the others working this case. Al Yazzie was gone for the weekend but he'd called in his final autopsy report on Poole. No surprises. Two .270 caliber bullets, one in the chest, one in the head.

He finally closed up his office and went home.

The sun lay on the backs of the mountains, painting the fat clouds in fire – yellow, orange and red that seemed to flicker like flames as Mac pulled into his drive. He lived northwest of town beyond the city limits. The two-story house was old but comfortable with a barn behind and surrounded by ten acres that belonged to him.

Situated in a small valley, it was bottled in to the west by mountains. Pine and scrub oak filled much of the area. A pasture of grama grass fed the three horses he stabled for a friend who lived in town. Ben and the kids came out several times a week to care for them and ride the mountain trails. Sometimes Mac went with them.

There was a dog that hung around the place, too. He belonged to the neighbors up the way. Bubba, they called him, part Lab and part German Shepherd, light brown and large, not given to staying home. Sometimes Bubba ran with the coyotes at night, a vagabond at heart. And he seemed particularly fond of Mac. Which made Mac wonder if they had something in common.

Mac didn't own any animals himself. Not since Jamie's death and the breakup of his marriage. In most things he supposed he had a fair amount of strength. His stint in the Air Force as a pilot had won him praise even though he'd believed what they were doing was philosophically wrong. His work for the District Attorney's office in

D.C. had brought him distinction. But the loss he'd suffered over his son's death and his wife's desertion had revealed his weakness. He'd closed up after that, allowed nothing and no one to latch on to him.

Friends he had aplenty. But his philosophy maintained that if one friend left or disappointed you, there were always others to fill the gap. You just couldn't allow them to settle into your affections too deeply. You had to maintain a distance, keep that guard up, just in case.

He stopped on the side stoop to rub Bubba's head and back. The dog leaned into Mac's legs, gathering warmth and camaraderie. He looked up with soulful eyes as if to say 'I understand you, Eli. We're two of a kind.' Finally, so as not to become too attached, Mac thought, the dog decided he'd had enough and loped off across the yard to the meadow and the freedom of the range land beyond.

Mac went on inside, hung up his Stetson on a rack, put his gun in a drawer, and headed for the kitchen. Dinner was a frozen meal heated in the microwave. He was too tired for more. The living room he'd decorated for basic comfort. Nothing fussy, no drapes, just a few pictures of landscapes on the walls he particularly liked. He ate his meal on the over-stuffed sofa, his feet up on an old trunk turned coffee table, and watched the news.

Andrews and Pruitt were both interviewed, were both on tirades giving their differing takes on some issue or another. The primary was a week away so the two of them were hammering it out to the very end.

As usual, Morgan made sense while Lloyd Pruitt sounded as though he came from an era long gone, when the good ole boys sat around a table in a room filled with cigar smoke and the smell of whiskey and hammered out deals. But since Mac hated politics all together, even Morgan seemed like a ranter right now.

In the middle of the sports report the phone rang. "Shit," Mac barked, wondering if he could let voice mail get this one. But on the third ring he pulled himself off the couch and answered it.

"Mac, I need to talk about the rally coming up," Morgan was saying. "Chief Scott's going to screw this whole thing up if he's left on his own."

Mac thought about it a moment. Finally he nodded. "I've got business in Phoenix tomorrow. I'll come by and we can talk."

Morgan thanked him, told him he'd pay him back once he got into office, and hung up.

Mac stared at the phone. Paybacks, sure. What he wanted, Morgan couldn't give him. Nobody could. Not unless they could hand him the answer to this double murder on a platter.

21

Sunday morning Belle lay in her bed, having tossed for the last hour and a half. Seven o'clock now and the sun shone in the east window of her room with a brilliance that made her wince. It was the beginning of September, for heaven's sake. What the heck was the sun so happy about? Back in Cleveland this would be indecent.

But back in Cleveland *everything* had been different. There had been Larry, for one thing. She could remember being so like her mother in the early days, giving way to her husband's superior judgment. Not that Larry was like Nate Bronson in most things. Larry the ultra cautious lawyer and Nate the quick-to-react cop were worlds apart. Except that both men ruled the family with a tight-fisted supremacy. Nate was the tough guy whose wife was there to serve him and understand his foibles. He was a man, after all, given to male weaknesses. Larry was simply always right and maintained his domination with the whip of guilt.

But gradually Belle had changed and the truth had begun to sink in. Larry was as much a bully as her father. Was it approaching forty that had changed her? She remembered a ferocious alteration in attitude about then. Forty years old and there she was still whimpering when Larry chastised her. Forty years old and she still hadn't told him to stick it up his ass.

That and his constant interference with her jobs finally made her shed the burden of her marriage. Get the kids raised and settled, finish the major duties of a mother, then good-bye, Larry.

Belle stretched and greeted the sunshine with renewed vigor. One good thing, tomorrow was Labor Day. No school. She tried not to spoil that brain wave by thinking about the events of the day before. But they kept intruding, the horror of the gun shot and seeing Lily lying on the ground, her confrontation with the sheriff, the discovery of that box with the money in it. And she still had the damned thing.

That brought her out of bed in a hurry. Where had she put it? The living room. She hurried out and there it sat on the library table near the door. With everything else going on the day before, the box hadn't seemed so menacing. Now it lay there, a dull metallic gray like a curse that waited silently to perform its evil. Giving the box a wide berth, she went past it into the kitchen to start coffee, then began her routine of exercise.

Afterwards she checked the clock. Ellie would make her Sunday morning call in an hour. Belle had laid down the law about when to call. "Remember, kiddo, I'm three hours earlier than you in the summer and two in the winter." This, after having her daughter ring her once at five-thirty in the morning. "God did not intend us to be awake at that hour on a Sunday," she'd told her.

An hour later, Belle had showered, dressed, and pumped some coffee into her system. Right on time Ellie called.

"I can't stand it, Mom. Dad won't leave me alone on this. He keeps calling and bugging me. He even showed up on campus last week. He tracked me and Mike down at the student center and started this majorly dramatic scene. I thought I'd die. He told Mike he was seducing a minor. A *minor*, for Christ's sake. He was freaking out. What's wrong with him? Is he Looney Toons?"

At nineteen Ellie was no longer a minor. But she wasn't exactly a major, either. Belle winced.

"Ellie, you know what your dad's like. He sticks onto an issue like gum on a shoe. Especially when he thinks you're going to get hurt."

"Yeah, right. He's doing it for my own good," Ellie muttered. "He thinks he's God. That he knows what's best for everybody. That's so bogus."

"So, what else is new, Honey?"

A disgusted sound. "Mom, you gotta talk to him. Make him lay off. I swear I'm gonna get a restraining order on him if he doesn't."

"Good luck," Belle said.

"Mom, *please*. Please talk to him."

"I could try, Ellie. But if I knew how to make him change his ways I wouldn't be living on the other side of the country from him now, would I?" She took a swallow of coffee. "There's still the possibility of a transfer. Your original plan was to start your second year at U of M. You've been accepted already. And heaven knows you've got the grades for it."

"Mike's *here*. And he couldn't swing the tuition even if he could get accepted."

"Well, there you are."

"Please, Mom. Please talk to Dad."

All Belle could say was "I'll try." But she dreaded like death to call Larry. "Tell me what else is happening."

They talked about Ellie's classes, about a lecture tour coming to campus, her friends, her professors. Belle didn't mention Lily Poole or the turmoil she was in. They caught up on news about Will and Lora and Aunt Louise and her family. Nothing new on Ellie's Grandaddy Nate down in Florida. He wasn't big on correspondence and his young wife didn't feel it her place to intervene. Louise maintained the woman couldn't read or write anyway.

Finally even Ellie's endless exuberance played out. Belle, on the other hand, felt invigorated.

"Promise me you'll talk to him, Mom," was Ellie's parting shot. "He's gotta chill."

When Belle had hung up, she sat staring at the phone. Ellie was the one and only reason she was sorry to have left Ohio. What she'd like is for her kids to be out here near her. But Will and Lora were ensconced in Michigan. And Case Western Reserve was a top notch school for Ellie. The University of Michigan even better. Larry's deal had been for their daughter to go to Case for one year so he could "help her out when she needed it," then she'd transfer the second and be near Will.

With Mike in the picture since last spring, though, Ellie had changed her mind about the transfer. At first Larry had gone along with her relationship when it meant keeping her close for another year. But now he was sitting on his daughter's back doorstep and monitoring every move she took.

Damn Larry. And yet Belle had to admit she wasn't easy in her mind over this Mike thing herself. But Larry's pounding wasn't the way to get Ellie's cooperation. Belle had intervened for too many years not to know that, having to make sure her daughter, in desperation, didn't go plunging off the deep end because of her father's interference. That was one of the main reasons Belle had stayed locked into that godawful marriage for so long.

"Stupid idiot!" she said. "He'll never learn."

Mac made it to Morgan Andrew's house near Scottsdale, coming for lunch at Mary Jane's insistence. Every time he drove down the mountain to Phoenix between May and October he got a stark reminder of why he'd moved out of the Valley. One of the reasons, anyway. Triple digit temps and oppressive pollution. Somehow he'd never noticed this while growing up in Tempe. Or maybe it hadn't been so bad back then.

The Andrews house was a large adobe that wrapped around a portion of Camelback Mountain. It was flanked by several full-grown saguaros reaching their arms for the blinding blue of the desert sky. Giant agave and bougainvillea graced the entrance of the house, perched as it was, overlooking the town. An eagle's eerie. Morgan was fond of saying he could 'watch over his flock' up here. He had a keen sense of responsibility for the people he served, or planned to serve.

Mary Jane was the most gracious woman Mac knew. Not beautiful but with a charm which made you forget that. Slender with graying hair swept back in a natural, clipped style, she epitomized the image of a senator's wife. She'd make a good one, he thought.

He'd liked her from the time they'd first met on one of his returns from Nicaragua. He'd just managed to make their wedding and been Morgan's best man. Though she hadn't known him, Mary Jane welcomed him as though he were family.

When Mac married Kathy, Kathy hadn't cared for the Andrews couple. She'd felt uncomfortable around such 'high in the instep' people. Their social position had put her off. But Mary Jane hadn't let that change her affection for Mac.

He'd been there at the loss of their four year old son Brian, shot by a stray bullet. In return, Morgan and Mary Jane had come to comfort him two years later when Jamie died of meningitis. And again when Kathy left him. The three of them had built a bond that had only strengthened over the years.

Mary Jane, cool in a beige pants set, handed Mac a Miller and sat down next to him on the over-stuffed sofa. The Southwestern motif played throughout the house; Indian rugs and Mexican pottery, cowhide chairs, pine floors, paintings of the desert. "How was your meeting this morning?" she asked.

Mac had met with several other sheriffs and the Attorney General at the Maricopa County Courthouse. Some law enforcement problems had come up that needed discussing.

"Nothing new," he told her, taking a swallow. The cold eased the dryness of his throat. "How's the campaign going?"

Andrews entered the living room wearing jeans, holding a bottle of Miller in his hand, and flopped in a chair.

"According to the latest poll, the third candidate doesn't even register on the scale. But Pruitt and I are neck and neck," he said. "So I'm counting on this rally in Granite to put me over the top."

Mac nodded. "Funny how people in this state grip the past that Pruitt peddles. You'd think they'd be ready to move on."

"People want the comfort of what they've known, Mac. Change is always scary. City people are more used to it, but a lot of city folk in this state are snow birds, not registered voters. Half the people who stick it out here, through heat and high winds and desert conditions, are the old timers, rural people. They're hard-nosed, suspicious of change, narrow and opinionated sometimes. They have to be bulldozed to move 'em. But they're also the kind of tough stock that settled the West for us city slickers. And they maintain the heartbeat of this country, keep us from moving too fast. Pruitt caters to that heartbeat. It's where his financing comes from."

"He's speechifying again," Mary Jane said. "Can you tell we've been on the campaign trail too long?" She got to her feet. "I need to help Tina get lunch on."

Andrews watched her go, then took a swallow from his bottle. "Amazing, isn't she? She sticks with me though everything."

The doorbell rang and he got up to answer it. In a moment he led Paul Cochran into the living room. Mac stood and shook hands. Paul was in kakis and a plaid shirt and looked relaxed for once, the intensity level turned down a few notches.

Cochran's wife Alice hadn't made it. She had some function at the Catholic Church they attended, administration of aid to one of the local Indian tribes. A devout member of the church, she apparently spent most of her time on committees or teaching Bible classes or visiting the sick and downtrodden.

"Unfortunately the church doesn't allow women into the priesthood," Cochran said. "Alice missed her calling."

Mac thought he detected a bitter tone in the man's voice. The Cochrans had no children. Maybe Paul blamed Alice for that. Whatever the relationship between husband and wife, though, Cochran was as devout a follower of Morgan Andrews as his wife was of the church. Which had come first? Chicken or egg?

Cochran was interested in how the murder case of the Hispanic boy was progressing. "Have you determined yet if that girl's father did the killing?"

Mac nodded, not really wanting to discuss the matter.

But Andrews picked up on it. "Damn it, Mac, we need to pass that legislation on hate crimes. We need to gut this monster. Did you hear about the latest in Gilbert? Another killing by one of the white supremacist groups. Some poor Hispanic fellow just leaving a bar, not giving anybody trouble, and four Nazi types jumped him for sport. Beat him to death right in front of witnesses and everything. Christ." He shook his head, face drawn, a stagnant silence hanging on the air of the room.

Mac knew Andrews was thinking of his son Brian, of the reason for the boy's death. Caught in the crossfire of a gang of skinheads taking out a couple of blacks who'd wandered into the wrong neighborhood. Morgan had his son in the car when he'd driven through that neighborhood to check on a client. They'd been in the wrong place at the wrong time. And his son had died for it.

When Andrews spoke again his voice was low with intent. "We've got to rip that kind of thing out by the roots, Mac. I swear to God I mean to change things. No more tolerance for brutality against the minorities. No more looking the other way because the killers happened to get pissed off, had a moment of insanity. If I stand for anything, I stand for that."

Mac looked down at the beer in his hand. "Morgan, don't plan on using my case as an example. Don't make it high profile. I don't know where it's going."

"What are you talking about? It's a perfect example. Crimes like that will get priority attention when I'm in office."

Cochran sat forward. "If this man killed the boy, then what's the hang-up?"

"Don't forget, the man was killed, too," Mac said.

"Retribution," Andrews nodded. "Just what you'd expect. It's another reason why this kind of crime is so heinous. It never stops."

"We don't know for sure what happened to Poole," Mac told him. "It's still up in the air. A lot of questions unanswered."

Mary Jane called them to lunch and put an end to the conversation. "You can't have a civilized meal and discuss business at the same time," she said. "Food never digests well that way. And Tina's cooking should *not* be wasted."

Afterwards the three men sat down at the round table in Andrews' office, got out location maps, and discussed the upcoming rally at the Granite town square.

Paul Cochran began, that intensity of his turned on again and ricocheting around the room. He insisted they keep the whole rally simple. "Townspeople don't like having someone come in and give orders. We have to act like guests in Granite."

Mac nodded.

"The town is known for its hospitality," Cochran continued. "At least here in Phoenix it is. We need to cater to that."

"Looks like you've got it figured out. So, what's the problem?" Mac asked.

Andrews sat forward. "It's Chief Scott again." He rubbed at his face wearily and glanced at his manager. "Paul, you can explain it better than I can."

Cochran gave Mac a pained expression. "Well, at first we couldn't get Scott's cooperation for security. Now he's going the other way with it, getting too heavy-handed. He's got security lined up like the Gestapo. Got the whole police force and city council in an uproar over this thing. My God, he's treating the rally like a parade of prisoners through the town. It's going to turn people off and end up losing us the votes we're trying to gain. Because he's a Pruitt man, we think he's trying to undermine the rally on purpose."

Cochran took his glasses off and pulled the map of downtown Granite toward him. "Here's what we'd like to do."

That afternoon Belle decided to try the James Realty Agency over on O. Henry off College. The man ought to be in today unless he was out with a customer, of course. Sunday was the biggest real estate day of the week.

She wasn't sure what she'd say to him. 'Why do people call you a crook?' and 'What business did you have with Julio Morales?' weren't likely to elicit the response she wanted. Funny, though, how something about a realtor and the Titus Land Development Company made an instant connection in the mind. And Julio had talked about James. How else would a kid know about the man?

James Realty was one of the little houses turned into shops and small restaurants and general places of business on O. Henry. Back in the fifties this had been a prominent middleclass neighborhood, the houses mostly bungalows, the streets lined with trees, some fences and gardens.

She found James Realty, a bungalow converted into a business like the others on the street. A Tea House stood beside it on the left, a bicycle shop on the right. A new Miata was parked in the drive, extra sporty in cherry red. She pulled in behind it.

The place had been painted a garish yellow and blue with the sign hung above the door which fronted on O. Henry. Belle entered, dressed in slacks and a blouse like a legitimate customer.

The front room of the house had been converted into an outer office. A large desk sat in the middle with a table at the side and a smaller desk in one corner. Listings of houses littered a bulletin board wall. A couple of framed K-Mart style pictures and some plastic plants softened the austerity. One door opened onto an inner office. What appeared to be a kitchen was at the back. And an air-conditioner hummed quietly in the window.

The front office was empty but Belle heard noises like dishes clattering in the back room.

"Hello," she said.

Immediately a head appeared around the doorframe, curly, reddish-blond hair combed over the balding spot on top, freckles on a face that sported glasses over pale eyes. A burley body came next, dressed in rust slacks that clashed with his hair color and a plaid suit coat. The man was a little taller than Belle.

"Hi there," he said, holding a cup in his hand. "Didn't know anyone was here. Should put a bell on that front door. Harley James." He came forward with his hand extended. "My co-workers are out showing a house today."

Belle took the hand and smiled. Used car salesman was her first reaction. He had that look about him that shouted 'deal.' She wondered if what the boys had said about him was true, that he was a crook. Or did he just give that impression because of his lousy taste in clothes?

"How can I help you today, Miss – uh –?" He laid his cup on the big desk.

Belle wasn't ready to give her name. "I'm renting at present, but I've been thinking more and more about buying."

Was that a hungry light in his eyes? He took her arm and led her to the wall with the listings.

"What type of home are we looking for? I've got all kinds. New, almost new, older homes, fixer-uppers. Some of my older homes are in mint condition and just waiting to be snapped up. A small home? Or do we have a growing family?"

We? "Just me. For now."

He nodded with what he probably thought was a sage expression on his freckled face. Sun caught his glasses and turned them opaque. "Probably not a fixer-upper, right?" He chuckled. "Take a look at some of my newer listings here on the board. I'll get my books out and we can check the computer listings."

Belle looked for a moment, feigning interest, then came over to the big desk where Harley James had gotten out several binders. He had them lined up, open to some smaller houses.

"How long have you been in business, Mr. James?" she asked, glancing through one of the binders.

He looked up at the question. "Been a realtor almost ten years. Bought this business close to seven years ago. Good business to be in out here. Place is growing faster'n a jackrabbit's brood. Real nice area to live in. Can't beat the sunshine, the climate. Lots of shops and museums and old west flavor. Did you get a look at the new mall going up on highway 47? Gonna be a doozy."

"I do like it here," she nodded.

"This is a great time to buy," he told her. "Interest rates are rock bottom and houses are going for pennies. A real buyer's market. Five years ago the real estate bust nearly did me in. But now - well, I got great deals right and left." He perched on the edge of the desk and took a drink from his cup. "We've got just about any kind of home you'd want. Take a look at some of these." He thumbed through the binder. "If you want a higher priced home, these up on the ridge are a real find. Fantastic views, privacy. Then we got homes in town, close to the shops, convenient." He turned some more pages. "And I can get you the best deal around."

He set his cup down, sloshing coffee on the desk, and went to his computer, going through files. "What do you do for a living? What kind of income are we talking about?"

Belle turned to face him, his freckled face practically in hers. Dandruff from his strawberry blond hair flecked his shoulders. "Actually, I'm a counselor with the Granite School System."

"Oh yeah?" He looked less enthusiastic. Because a teacher's salary meant a smaller home? "I know some of the teachers here abouts."

"Do you know Harold Ramey? He's the principal at the high school."

"Hal? You bet. Him and me, we belong to the Elks in town. We go hunting together every fall. Taught him how to use a rifle myself."

"So you've known him awhile?"

"Yup, I've known him a long time. We help each other out now and then, know what I mean?"

Belle did. "I've also met your son Nick."

His expression changed and he stood up, adjusting his glasses. Caution shone in his pale eyes. Most parents prepared themselves for a blow when a school official mentioned their child.

"What's Nicky been up to?" His chuckle rang false and he seemed to know it.

"Nothing that isn't normal for kids his age," she assured him.

He still didn't relax. He studied her, looking her over as though he'd just seen her. "Don't think I caught your name."

"Belle Evans. This is my first full year with the system. I started last January." She shrugged in a matter-of-fact way and leaned one hip against the desk, trying to ease the moment. "I'm from Ohio. I came out here on my sister's insistence and fell in love with the place. I didn't want to go back, so here I am."

The caution didn't leave his eyes, but his body slumped back into relaxation mode. He waved a hand toward the real estate books on his desk. "So, anything here appeal to you?"

She flipped a few pages in one of the books. "I like the school system. They're good people to work with. And, of course, kids are my greatest love."

He grinned, easing a little more, and sat down in the swivel chair behind the desk. "If you like 'em, you got a gift. Trying to raise my three is no picnic. That Nicky's a handful. Good kid at heart, though," he mentioned just in case. "But he likes to mouth off a lot."

She nodded. "Then they grow up and wonder why the younger ones are doing the same to them."

He chuckled, swiveling to find another file on the computer. "Isn't that the truth. They get what they give, huh? Guess we did that to our folks, too." He swiveled the screen to show her what he'd found.

"We just don't remember that part," she said, watching as he brought up house after house. "It's called selective memory. Very convenient."

Harley James nodded, his expression more relaxed, receptive again. He pointed to an entry with a question in his face, the pale hair catching light from the window and highlighting the bald spot he'd tried to cover.

Belle watched him carefully as she said, "There are always a few, though, that come to a bad end."

James dropped his grin, attempted the look of a sage. "Too bad about them. Breaks your heart, doesn't it?"

"It certainly does. Take that boy Julio Morales who was shot in Lame Horse Canyon."

As she watched, his whole body underwent a change. He stiffened, pushed back the chair, face suddenly guarded, eyes narrowed. But the next moment he recovered himself.

"Terrible case," he said, his voice changed in tenor. "Heard it was a racial thing. Girlfriend's old man shot him. Somebody got the ole man back." He got to his feet.

Belle shook her head. "That's the kind of problem I have trouble dealing with at school. The reactions of the other students are particularly difficult." She glanced up casually. "Did you know the Morales boy?"

"Me? Hell no. I stay away from those people." Realization dawned in his eyes. "I mean, I'm just in the business of selling real estate. They aren't looking for the kinds of places I sell, you know?"

She acted as though she understood. "I was just wondering.

According to his friends, Julio had mentioned you."

"Me?" Now the change was more pronounced. He pulled his heft up straight, eyes narrowed.

"Your son started a fight over the whole thing. So I was just wondering –"

"By God, you're the one," he snapped. "You're the one stirring everybody up over this, aren't you? You're that busy-body counselor that's giving everybody a hard time."

His face was dark, small eyes piercing. He didn't look congenial anymore. No more the used car salesman or the frumpy realtor. Something hard and ugly took him over. A bad feeling trickled through Belle's veins.

He stepped closer to her. "Lady, I'd mind my own business if I was you. Whatever that Mexican kid said about me's a damned lie. That girlfriend of his set you on me, didn't she?" His shoulders hunched like a bull ready to charge. "You aren't looking for a house."

"I'm looking for answers, Mr. James. Answers to the tragic death of a young man."

"Get out," he told her in a voice quiet and cold, and took another step in her direction. "Get outta my place. And tell that Poole girl she better stop spreading lies."

Heart racing like a steam engine, Belle turned and walked out. Back in her Honda she had to wait for her hands to quit shaking. James was watching her from the window. Finally she stuck the key in the ignition, started her car and backed out from behind the cherry-red Miata.

Her shaking was more from elation than distress. She wasn't sure what she'd just learned, but she knew for an almost blinding certainty that Harley James was somehow involved in Julio's murder.

22

If Belle thought she would get Labor Day off, she was mistaken. Harold Ramey called her at eight o'clock, telling her he wanted her in his office right away. "School or no school," he insisted.

Belle set down her coffee mug and rubbed at her face. What was so damned important that she had to give up her free day to face the principal? She halfway thought of ignoring the request, then shook her head. Her job was teetering enough as it was. No sense in pushing the envelope any more than she'd done already. She headed for the shower.

Ramey was stiff when Belle, dressed casually in slacks and a shirt, entered his office at nine. Ned Stambaugh followed her in, looking bewildered and nervous as a puppy that had to pee.

The principal got them seated at the conference table and sat down himself. He was dressed for lounging at home and his face showed extreme irritation, probably because he, too, had to give up his free day, Belle thought.

"Joe Franks called me last night," Ramey told them. "I don't like being chewed out by the president of the board of education on a Sunday night."

Ned stiffened.

Belle asked, "What's the problem?"

Ramey's heavy jowls shuddered. His small eyes shot daggers at them across the conference table. "It's the Morales case. And the Poole girl. The whole thing. Franks says we've got to stay away from it. In fact, he *demands* we let it alone."

Ned looked as though he were swaying on the edge of a pit of scorpions. Belle didn't feel far away from it. She'd put forth a lot of energy at Friday's meeting, assuring the superintendent and board members that their involvement with Lily Poole was good.

"I don't understand," she said. "What is it he thinks we're doing that he could possibly object to? We're looking after one of our students, that's all."

"School, Isabel. That's our jurisdiction. Just school. And Lily Poole hasn't been in school since the boy was – well, since he died."

"Since he was shot to death," she corrected him.

He grimaced. "The point is, none of that was school business. Nor was it your business to go to the county jail because of a bar fight."

Ned jerked back in his chair, eyes wide and anxious. An edge of anger began to suffuse Belle at this authoritarian male performance.

"Mr. Ramey," no one at school ever called him Harold, "I went to the police station at the boys' request. A good thing, too, the way Tom Kelliker's father treated him. The sheriff had to intervene."

"Mrs. Evans," Ramey said, leaning forward, his eyes even smaller, his face set, "what happens outside this school is not our business. Nor does it reflect well on the system when one of our faculty members interferes in what doesn't concern us. We aren't here to be all things to all people. Teaching the students, that's what our job is. Teaching the students. That's all."

Belle felt her cheeks heat up, but more from indignation than anything else. The narrowness of the man's scope made her wonder how in hell he ever decided to enter the teaching profession. But she already knew the answer.

Some people became teachers because they were dedicated to helping kids, to making the future better than the past. Some entered because they'd failed at what they really wanted to do. Then there were those who, probably having felt impotent in their youth, wanted to wield authority over others now that they were adults. Education was the perfect arena for them. They could manipulate kids who couldn't do a damned thing about it, and on a higher level, the faculty whose careers they could threaten.

Then there was the board of education, frequently made up of citizens who were ignorant of what went on inside a school and yet had the power to turn the whole system top over bottom on a whim.

"Has someone complained to Mr. Franks?" Belle asked. She thought of Fred Preacher and Harley James. Were they friends with the BOE president? Had one of them screamed bloody murder at her visit?

"Isabel, it's not our job to question the board. It's our job to follow their dictates."

In what other world? she wondered.

Ned hadn't spoken since they'd entered the office. He sat like a porcelain figurine, ready to be shattered at another harsh word.

Belle took in a deep breath. "Mr. Ramey, I understand the position of the school system. However, a girl's life is in danger here. She was shot at."

She told him about the incident on Saturday at the Poole place.

Ramey paled and drew back. But his determination only strengthened.

"I think the lesson here is that none of this would have happened if you hadn't taken the girl to the house in the first place."

"If I hadn't taken her, she'd have gone some other way. And could be dead by now. Maybe along with a friend."

His gaze hardened again. "Isabel, we're not here to save the world."

That brought her to her feet. She wasn't angry, just weary of his isolationist bullshit. "Do what you need to do, Mr. Ramey. But I won't let that girl get hurt if I can in any way prevent it."

He got to his feet, too, and gave her one more withering glare. "I understand you went to see Nick James' father yesterday. All on your own. With no authority to do so from me or anyone else."

Belle wavered in her indignation. She'd been out of line there and knew it. "I was simply trying to follow up on the fight Nick had with Jeremy Gibbs and Tom Kelliker."

Ramey's eyes narrowed, his jowls quivered, his voice was low and hard. "I will decide whose parents to talk to in this school. Until you're made the new principal, you will *not* make those decisions. Is that clear?"

Belle just shook her head. Without answering, she tossed an 'I'm sorry' glance at Ned, grabbed up her purse and left the office.

Mac had just hung up his hat in his office Monday morning when Sarah knocked on the doorframe and came on in. She was a no-nonsense woman. Her short, graying hair hadn't a strand out of place, her glasses were speckless, her slacks and blouse wrinkle-free. She had a sense of humor but it was subtle and she kept a tight reign on it. Except for once when she'd cracked a bitch of a case for Mac and he'd insisted on celebrating with a bottle.

After a few drinks Sarah became another person, funny, outrageous, horny as hell. She'd pulled off her glasses, unbuttoned her blouse several notches and done an erotic dance on his desk that rivaled the pole dancers at the Blue Devil bar in Janos. He'd gotten a view of the Hyde part of her personality he suspected few people ever did. It was their loss.

Sober, she could match any hacker on a computer and worm her way into files in minutes that Rolly and the other detectives took a week to ferret out. Now she held some printouts in her hand.

"Sir, I've got the info on your Mile Hi guy," she told him. "Fred

Preacher, forty-six, divorced, two children, wife and kids living in Pine Bluff, Arkansas. Grew up in Arkansas himself, moved to Arizona after he got married. Drove dozers in Phoenix, then came up here and started his own business. Nip and tuck until four years ago when he came into some money. No record as to how."

"Inheritance?" Mac asked.

Sarah shook her head. "Not likely. Family were share-croppers and itinerants. No lottery winnings. Maybe Vegas."

Mac didn't think so. Preacher hadn't struck him as a winner. "This money – how much? And was it a lump sum?"

"Looks like installments. The big deposits come to seventy-five thou."

"Not a hell of a lot, is it?"

Sarah shrugged. "Maybe to a man who's never had anything."

Mac perched on the edge of his desk. "What else do you have?"

Sarah checked through her printouts. "He did a few years down at the Maricopa County Prison in the mid nineties. Accomplice in armed robbery. Apparently they were caught immediately. Preacher got his sentence reduced for narking on his buddy who masterminded the job. Then parole for good behavior. After that, a few misdemeanors – traffic tickets, a drunk and disorderly. Drugs once. And he was arrested for beating up a woman, but the charges were dropped."

"I suppose you could tell me his brand of toothpaste, too." Mac took the papers, looked them over. "Anything on that business card?"

"I'm working on it, sir. It's a dead phone number. Cell phone. Those things are a bitch to uncover, but I've got my ways."

Mac's mouth twitched. "You certainly do, Sarah."

One of her eyebrows lifted slightly to acknowledge the joke. "I'll get on it right away," she said and left, a small but telling whiff of sandalwood tailing after her.

Mac glanced at the papers in his hand. Fred Preacher was no innocent. Time to talk to him seriously.

After the conference with Ramey, Belle tried again to drop off the metal box Lily'd found behind the toilet tank. Again McFarland wasn't there and wasn't expected back till the afternoon. So again she refused to leave it at the station.

Instead she did the very thing she'd been warned not to do. She went to pay another visit to Fred Preacher. She needed to see his reaction to the gun shot at Lily's place. Had he been there on Saturday? Was he after the envelope from Mile Hi in the metal box?

Someone else who worked there could have used the envelope. Or it could have been planted to implicate Preacher. *Or* Preacher could simply have been stupid enough to use one of his own envelopes. Belle had to find out for herself, had to see if he'd react in any way.

Preacher's office was closed for Labor Day but a couple of men lounged on the shady side of the building. They watched her as she parked her car.

"He's out in the garage," the younger man said. He apparently recognized her from the last time she'd come. "Fred's busy. Gotta get a job underway."

She nodded. "I'll go check."

"I told you, lady, he's busy."

"Thanks."

The temperature had climbed to almost ninety. She was nervous being here anyway, and her acute revulsion for Preacher extended to his men. What Bern Wozak had told her about them was vivid in her mind.

The huge garage stood dark and cavernous. Voices echoed over the sound of a loud motor and metal banging on metal. The odors of oil and smoke laced the air. After the bright sunlight, she was blinded by the dark. She pulled off her sunglasses and allowed her vision to adjust.

Belle walked over to a man working on a backhoe he had up on a hydraulic lift. It teetered slightly.

"Look out, Joe!" the man yelled at the one controlling the machinery. "She ain't steady!"

It wobbled a second time and Belle backed off in a hurry. She eyed the bulldozer, trying to judge its stability before moving forward again.

"I'm looking for Fred Preacher," she yelled over the sound of the lift.

He sized her up then turned his head. "Hey, Fred. Got a lady here to see you." He tossed her a one-sided grin and went back to work, swore as the lift jammed, and finally got it working.

Belle stood clear of the lift as she waited. In a few minutes she saw a figure emerge out of the dark interior. When he got close enough to recognize her, he halted, his face hard, his eyes venal slits. Then he came on more deliberately.

"What the hell you want, lady?" he snarled.

"I need to talk to you."

Hands on hips, he looked her over. "Got nothing to say. Just talked to the goddamned sheriff less than a hour ago. You sick 'em on me? Huh?"

Belle stood her ground, though she felt like a Jew at a Nazi stronghold.

"Mr. Preacher, I don't think the sheriff asked you about one of your envelopes found in Ralph Poole's safety box."

The man working on the backhoe at the lift turned toward them. Preacher grabbed Belle's arm painfully and rushed her outside, away from an audience.

"Goddamnit, you got some big-assed nerve coming here like you're accusing me-a something."

Belle pulled away from the claw-like grip. Her own face set. "You knew it was there, didn't you?"

Preacher's eyes got mean, his teeth bared like some rabid animal. "You ain't got no fucking proof. Sheriff didn't say nothing about no envelope of mine."

"Were you at the Poole place Saturday? Someone shot at Lily."

Preacher jerked his hand up, ready to strike. She was prepared for him, muscles tense. But at the last moment, he hesitated, then dropped his arm.

"Whadaya after, lady? A fucking payoff? You want money?"

Still on alert, she considered him. "I want Lily Poole safe. Just a warning, *Mister* Preacher. Any more attempts to hurt that girl and you're 'fucking' dead meat. You have my word on that."

She held his fierce gaze a moment longer to drive home her point, then turned on her heel to go. So she didn't see the hatred he shot in her direction.

Nor did she witness the sudden grip of fear that replaced it.

Belle shook as she drove back to her apartment. She may have been physically ready for a punch from Preacher, but mental readiness was never the same. And never easy. No doubt about it, the man could be violent. That's what she'd gone there to find out, and what she now knew, as well as his guilt in this whole affair.

But why? Was it something to do with Titus? Why else would Julio have given the business card to Lily? She should have asked Preacher if he knew Harley James. And about Titus. No chance, though. Her bombshell about the envelope had sent him flying off the handle. She hadn't meant to tell him about it. Damn her stupid mouth.

She needed to give all this information to McFarland. But right now she was too shaken for a confrontation with him as well, so she drove directly back to her apartment.

Lunchtime and Belle had taken a few bites of her sandwich, finding it dry and tasteless and hard to swallow, when her phone rang.

"I found out something," Ned Stambaugh said on the line, his voice different from the usual Ned. Conspiratorial was her first impression.

"I knew you'd be interested in this," he told her. "It's about Mr. Franks, the president of the school board."

"Ned, you rascal, what have you been up to?" She sat forward in the kitchen chair.

"I – um – I decided to find out what prompted the meeting in Mr. Ramey's office this morning. So I did some calling around."

"On the sly? Behind Ramey's back." She was stunned.

"Well, sort of, I suppose." A pause. "I had a feeling someone had been talking to Mr. Franks. Someone had gotten him to come down hard on this thing, so to speak."

Belle flopped back in the chair. "Someone who didn't want us poking our noses into Julio's murder."

She could hear him swallow on the other end. "Right."

"And you found out who?" she said, her voice grim.

"I did."

"Let me guess. Was it Fred Preacher of Mile Hi Earth Movers?"

Ned hesitated. "No. He was never mentioned."

"Harley James, the realtor. Was it him?"

"You mean Nick James' father? No, Belle. I haven't heard anything about him either."

Puzzlement replaced the grimness. "Who was it, Ned? Who's putting the muzzle on us?"

A pause, then, "Mr. Franks is a friend of Lloyd Pruitt. He's the one who's trying to get us to stop."

23

Mac thought afterwards that he should learn to keep the door to his office closed. He didn't even get a peremptory knock as a warning before Lloyd Pruitt stormed in, a snarl on his baby face and a tall man in his wake. Somehow Pruitt's big white Stetson made him seem shorter than he probably was - or else it was the tall bodyguard.

"I wanna know what the hell's going on," the man barked, his Western twang pronounced. He stopped in front of the desk, looking down on Mac in his chair, his eyes cold. "I'm sick of Andrews talking hate crime. He's stirring up trouble just to get elected. And you're helping him."

The tall man stayed in the background near the door like a mafia bodyguard. Mac would have laughed if he weren't so pissed.

He studied Pruitt. The man wasn't much to look at. Small in stature, his face chubby and weak. Not that Pruitt was a feeble politician. He knew how his supporters thought, what made them salivate or turn around and kick you in the ass.

Mac knew all about him. Pruitt's own family had been dirt farmers from Arkansas and Oklahoma, but he'd gravitated to Arizona as a young man. The baby face was deceptive. Lloyd Pruitt wasn't stupid. He had animal cunning and plenty of it.

Somehow he'd caught the eye of Lavinia Jackson whose father had made money in the early days down in Tucson selling black-market products from Mexico. By the time Lavinia was grown, Jackson had moved his family to Phoenix, cleaned up his money, and made himself look respectable. On the outside, at least.

Lloyd was an asset to the Jackson family business and before long had shown signs of becoming a strong politician for the far right boys. He not only had family money behind him, Daddy Jackson made sure there was corporate support as well. The big guys wanted their candidate, one they could count on.

Meanwhile, Morgan, the moderate, was struggling to keep out of debt.

Pruitt leaned over the desk, his belligerence a weapon pointed at

Mac. "Do you know what happens to a sheriff who skews the facts in a crime to fit his politics?"

Mac's eyes narrowed. "Are you going to tell me?"

"Damned right," Pruitt snapped. "Even better, I'm gonna show you. Just as soon as I win the election. Don't think your good buddy Andrews has a chance. I've got friends in this state. Important friends. That stinking rally he's planning for this weekend isn't gonna do him diddly. And you'd better be looking for a new job yourself. Night janitor's what I'm thinking. In another state."

Mac stood up slowly, his gaze locked onto Pruitt's whose wavered just slightly. The bodyguard was alert.

"I guess you'd know about skewing evidence, wouldn't you, Pruitt? The way you pulled Gibson Development out of the clutches of the law three years ago. Some skewing there, am I right?"

"I don't know what the hell you're talking about," he said.

Mac moved with an easy gait around the edge of the desk. The man at the door took a step forward. "Gibson was about to be put away for land fraud, if memory serves me. The state had the evidence, all tight and secure. Then suddenly you entered the picture and somehow the case never came to trial. Somebody got bought off, is what I heard."

Pruitt's face hardened, his eyes narrowed, he seemed to chafe in his cowboy boots. "That's a damned lie. No such thing happened. By God, whatever son-of-a-bitch says a thing like that –"

Mac came to face him. The bodyguard started forward but Mac cautioned him back with a look. He glanced down under the brim of Pruitt's hat. "And now I hear Gibson is one of the big contributors to your campaign."

Pruitt stepped back, his soft cheeks turning red. "Look here, you son-of-a-bitch, don't you try to –"

"Oh, and let's not forget the whitewash your people did on the suicide of your mistress. Was that four years ago or five? I can't remember. No matter. My girl Sarah can hack her way into the best of cover-ups."

"By God, you –"

"We also found out you have connections with that white supremacist group down in Gilbert. The Black Falcons, right? Were they the ones responsible for this latest hate crime?"

Pruitt sputtered something unintelligible as he eased away, nearly colliding with his man. "You watch your back, McFarland. You just watch it. Goddamnit, you haven't heard the last from me. I'll have your worthless head on a platter before I'm through."

He turned, ramming into Belle Evans who was standing in the doorway. When he saw who it was, his chest expanded dangerously. "*You!*" he bellowed. Then marched out, his man hurrying to catch up.

Belle needed to get Ralph Poole's safety box to McFarland. She had to leave it no matter what, sloppy government filing systems or no. She'd held onto evidence too long. Her father would have read the riot act. Probably McFarland would and she was prepared. This afternoon she found he was in and felt relieved. Until she got to the office door only to be rammed in the chest by an irate Lloyd Pruitt.

After the man had gone, McFarland looked over at her. "You all right?"

She wriggled her body. "It feels intact. Maybe a bruise. You've got an audience out there." She pointed to the receptionist and several deputies outside the office looking on with interest. "Was he threatening you?"

"Hot air." McFarland glared at the deputies crowded around outside his door until they left. He shot her a hard glance. "That bastard's got more dirt on him than the Olmsted Mountains. He's a nasty little prick whose testicles were neutered years ago by his Valkyrie wife and her father." He flicked a hand. "Sorry. Just venting."

Belle couldn't help a grin. "The real Eli McFarland at last. I thought nothing could move you."

His slow glance took her in. "What can I do for you?"

She came over to the desk and propped her satchel on it. "I've got something for you. Every time I started to leave it, you weren't here. I guess I've become leery of how easily things get lost in a big system."

She tried to look contrite, hoping he wouldn't take offense at the suggestion that his station wasn't well run. He didn't seem to react to either. The old, closed up Sheriff McFarland was back in place.

"What've you got?"

Belle opened the satchel and took out the metal box, handing it to him. McFarland turned it over, studying it.

"Lily found it at her place Saturday after you'd left," she told him. "We were looking for a deed to the trailer or any other important papers her father might have stowed away when she remembered a place behind the toilet tank where he'd kept things. There's a loose board where the pipes are. The board fits into the wall so you can't tell it's there. We wouldn't have found the place ourselves if she hadn't remembered her father talking about it."

He considered her, his mind working on something as she talked, his eyes narrowed. Glancing back at the box, he worked the latch and opened it. The envelope lay on top and a few of the new hundred dollar bills spilled out of it. He gazed at them, a frown deepening over his brows. He lifted them out carefully, held them by the edges to count, laid them on the desk and picked up the envelope at the corner, turning it over.

Belle waited him out.

Finally he touched the intercom. "Send Carter in," he said.

Belle cleared her throat. "Well, if you don't need me –"

"Sit down," he said. The steel was in his voice now.

She stiffened as she took a chair near the desk and watched him go through the other papers in the box. He glanced up, studying her, seemed about to speak when Rolly Carter, the big redhead, entered.

"What's up, Mac?" he said, rubbing at his moustache.

McFarland set the box down. "You and Butch go pick up Preacher at Mile Hi. We need him for questioning."

Carter's face lit up. "Something happen?"

"You might say so."

Carter nodded, winked at Belle, and took off. McFarland stood silent for a while before he took a seat behind his desk.

"All right, Mrs. Evans. It's obvious I'm not succeeding in keeping you out of this case, so tell me about the box."

"There's nothing more to tell," she said.

"You contaminated the evidence. You kept it to yourself for two days. What the hell were you thinking?"

Her back grew rigid and she sat up straight. "Lily was looking for her father's papers. We had no idea we'd find money and an envelope. So we couldn't help contaminating it."

"And you didn't leave it at the station. You kept it in your possession."

"Since the evidence was contaminated you couldn't use it in court," she pointed out.

"We could have picked up Preacher sooner," he said with a hard edge. Then he stared down at the box on his desk. "Any other tidbits I should know?"

She thought about telling him she'd gone to see Fred Preacher today, but that would come out as soon as his deputies picked the man up. McFarland would be even more pissed at her interference. Why make him go through that right now? After living with Larry she was gun shy to the point of hostility.

"Did you know Lloyd Pruitt came to the high school Friday? He wanted us to lay off, to leave Lily to the wolves, I suppose. He got in Ramey's face, told me off, practically threatened to cut school funding. The man's a real piece of dog doo, isn't he?"

"He's got the money interests on his side," the sheriff said.

"But what does he care about a killing that took place here in Granite? What possible interest could he have in this case?"

"Politics," McFarland said. "Morgan Andrews stuck his nose in it, trying to drum up an issue over prejudice. Wants to use it for campaign purposes." He sat back, eyes lowered, face drawn. "This has been a big concern of Morgan's. His son was accidentally killed in a crossfire shooting. Some white gang after a couple of black boys they didn't like."

"Oh, my God." Belle wilted in her chair, seeing Andrews in a whole new light, the pain she hadn't understood, the resolution that she now realized was genuine.

The sheriff looked up. "So now Pruitt's taking the defensive position."

"Insisting it wasn't a racist killing?" she said. "What do you think? Did Ralph Poole kill Julio out of his hatred for Chicanos?"

McFarland glanced at the money on his desk. "Beginning to look like he didn't."

Belle glanced at the money, too, then away. "Isn't Morgan Andrews going to have a political rally here on Saturday? I've been hearing about it on the news. No wonder Pruitt's upset if Andrews is trying to use Julio's killing in his speech, right here where it happened. Still – threatening everybody?"

His eyes narrowed. "Mrs. Evans, don't even think of interfering in the rally." The steel was back in his voice.

"Of course not, Sheriff." The good little citizen. She got to her feet. "But I have a nasty feeling about Lily Poole. If this whole thing wasn't about killing a Hispanic and revenge for it, then Lily may very well be in danger. Someone already took a shot at her. What if it wasn't a mistake? What if she really is a target?"

McFarland eyed her suspiciously. "I've already put a man on her until we figure this case out. Leave it to me this time, okay?" He got up, too, and his gaze softened a little. "You *can* do something for me, though." He glanced at his desk, pulled at his ear, as if trying to find a way of telling her. "The medical examiner is releasing Poole's body. We need to know what Lily wants us to do with it."

Belle studied her hands. "I'm not sure she has any idea what to do. And there's no money for a funeral that I know of, supposing she'd want to give him a funeral, the way she feels right now."

"The county can cremate him. We can even dispose of the ashes. Would you talk to her and see what she wants?"

Belle nodded. "I was planning to check on her this evening. I'll ask her."

"I'd appreciate it. And tell her we'll have a man on her, not to get spooked by him."

Belle thanked him, picked up her briefcase and left. Walking down the corridor toward the entrance to the county building she couldn't help the sickness in her stomach over Lily's safety. After all, they'd had a man watching Ralph Poole, too.

Mac sat staring at the metal box on his desk. Goddamnit to hell. Where was this whole thing going? A payoff to Poole by Preacher? Not a big surprise. The envelope gave them something to hold over his head when they questioned him. But even uncontaminated, it didn't prove murder, only involvement.

The man was a two-bit felon, but it looked more like a cover-up for something bigger than what Preacher could be capable of. The job ahead was to wring the truth out of him. Get to the bottom of things. Find out who he was connected with.

The box had been behind the toilet tank, for Christ's sake. Why hadn't Rolly and his boys found it? Probably where the gun had been stashed, too. If they'd found the gun earlier, Poole would still be alive, and talking to save his filthy neck. Shit.

Mac got up and walked to the window. The street was filled with afternoon traffic, people on their way to or from one place or another. A couple of county cruisers drove by towards the back parking lot, some kids on bikes took over the sidewalk, cars pulled out of the Wendy's down the street.

So what did they know about this case? Poole killed the Morales kid. Had to be him. No other prints on Poole's gun. Poole was then shot with a rifle. Then the girl had been shot at. A different slug than the other two. Three separate shooters?

The boy had given Lily Poole a business card for safe keeping. Titus Land Development. Who and what was that? Preacher, or someone working for him, had paid Poole off. For the killing? They probably knew Poole hated the boy so that his motive for the murder would be blurred. Had whoever it was planned all along to kill Poole? So what was Preacher's involvement? Earth moving - land development. An easy connection. But who or what was Titus?

His head ached by the time Carter called in.

"Wasn't at Mile Hi, Mac. They haven't seen Preacher since the woman came to talk to him."

"Woman? What woman?"

A pause. "Sounds like the Evans lady."

"Son-of-a-bitch." His head buzzed.

Carter cleared his throat. "Checked out his home, too. No sign of him. Think he split?"

"Looks that way," Mac told him. "Come on back."

He hung up the phone, closed his eyes, clenched his teeth. So help him, he'd lock up Belle Evans and throw away the key if he could. But it wouldn't solve these murders.

24

Belle dropped by to see Lily that afternoon. She was out in the backyard trying to feed an Albert's squirrel that sat barking at her from the branch of an old, gnarled cottonwood in the center of the yard. His tufted ears flicked as he talked. When Belle came on through the screen door, he barked one more time and skittered up to the higher branches, scolding them from a distance.

"He's not very friendly," Lily told her. "I've been trying for days to coax him down."

"Squirrels and people can be similar in that way."

Belle sat on the porch steps and Lily came to join her. The shade of the cottonwood cooled the air. A mild wind ruffled the leaves in a percussive dance. Out here on the edge of town the world seemed peaceful, apart from the congested race and scramble of daily routines.

Belle leaned her arms on her knees. "Mrs. Rivera says Carlos was by to see you yesterday."

Lily nodded, looking soulful.

"Are you two becoming friends?"

"Hardly," Lily snorted. "He keeps rubbing it in that my dad killed Julio. Maybe he thinks I'm partly to blame."

"Seems odd," Belle said. "I mean, now that your father is dead, you'd think he'd let it go."

Lily turned to her. "Miz E, you don't think Carlos – what if he –"

"Shot your father?"

She glanced away. "I don't think he'd, you know, kill anybody. He wouldn't, would he?"

Belle tilted her face to the wind. It lifted her short hair in its fingers. "I don't know anything about Carlos. He seems to have a temper." She softened at the anxiety in Lily's eyes. "I don't think he'd take a shot at you, though. That's something I can't imagine."

Lily's face cleared. "Well, I wish he'd leave me alone. If he comes again, I'm going to tell Miz Rivera I don't want to talk to him."

"That would give me some peace of mind, kiddo. By the way, if you spot someone in a car watching you, it's most likely the sheriff's man. He wants to keep an eye on you."

"Why? Does he think I killed Julio? Or my dad?"

"Hardly. He's worried because you were shot at."

"That was a mistake, wasn't it?" Lily looked worried now.

"Most likely a mistake, yes," Belle said, more to calm her than because she believed it. "But McFarland's determined not to let anyone else get hurt. I just wanted you to know so you wouldn't be bothered by it."

She didn't say anything about the dark pickup she'd seen parked down the street from The Pines on Saturday, the one that drove away just before she did. Scaring the girl further wasn't an option. Besides, now there'd be a deputy keeping an eye on her. Right.

Lily looked forlorn and Belle hated to hit her with the next item. But it had to be resolved. She took the girl's hand. "One other thing, you need to decide what to do about your father, about his - remains."

Lily looked startled, then slumped, running hair behind her ear. "I guess I knew that was coming." She glanced off across the yard as though seeking the answer there. "Are you gonna think I'm awful if I don't want him buried near my mom? I know he killed her even if they didn't convict him."

"I'd probably feel the same way," Belle confessed. "However, something's got to be decided about him. Sheriff McFarland said the county could cremate him and dispose of his ashes."

Lily studied on this for a while. The cottonwood leaves rustled, the squirrel chittered up on a branch, some birds visited the feeder Mrs. Rivera had put out back. Belle waited her out.

"No funeral ceremony?" the girl asked.

"That's up to you."

"Seems like something ought to be done. Even if he was a lousy bastard for killing Julio. And my mom. I guess it's not really his fault he was an alcoholic. It's a disease, right?"

Belle considered her. "You could have a memorial service for him later on when you're ready. When this whole thing is over. That would give you time to think about what you want."

Lily chewed on her lip, stared at her hands. Finally she nodded. "That seems like a good enough plan." She looked up at Belle and said, "I gotta go back to school tomorrow. I don't like being alone."

"I agree," Belle told her. "I don't like having you be alone. No matter how deep the tragedy, life has to go on."

Belle left Lily and came on home, her mind still in a turmoil. Fred Preacher, Harley James, Carlos Hernandez. And don't forget Lloyd Pruitt who was buddies with the BOE president. *And* somehow associated with the Black Falcons. What a guy.

McFarland had explained Pruitt's interest in this case. Political reasons. Still, he was a nasty piece of work, one who, if she'd heard right while eavesdropping at the sheriff's door along with the deputies, had covered up the suicide of a mistress. Had the mistress killed herself over him? Hard to believe, Pruitt such a rattlesnake. But stranger things could happen.

She sure would like to meet the man's wife.

After supper Belle and Adrian Good sat on the back porch in rockers, drinking his gourmet coffee, watching the fire of the sunset over the trees, and talking about old times back in Cleveland. The sound of Miner's Creek trickling below the hill drifted up to mingle with birdsong.

"So, love, how many years have you actually been a counselor, then?" Adrian asked, rocking back to gaze at the fans of orange and red reaching out across the sky.

"Well, two years before I married Larry. Then nine more years after the kids were in school – before I moved here. Three, three and three. Sweetie pie Larry managed to kill the last three jobs for me. By then I had to leave or seriously maim him."

Adrian lifted an eyebrow at her.

They talked in the quiet of the evening, a couple of finches chattering at the feeders, some robins chirping on the lawn, a phoebe calling mournfully from the roof of the garage. The wind died and the sky turned a deep, fantasy blue with carmine stripes shot through it. Belle looked at her watch and sighed. She'd better do it if she was going to. After all, she'd promised Ellie. My God, this was like sticking her arm in a grinder. On purpose.

"What the hell," she told Adrian, getting to her feet. "I need to get this call over and done with." She saluted him like a soldier going off to war and headed upstairs to the phone.

"Larry, I didn't call you so you could cross examine me," she explained after a full five minutes of his diatribe. "This call is not about me. It's about you."

"What *about* me, Isabel? I'm not the one who broke up our marriage. I'm not the one who went trotting off to the other side of the world, abandoning the children, the family, the friends. *And* a husband who's always been constant."

Belle squeezed her eyes shut, trying to keep her stomach from rebelling over the sound of his nagging voice. She let him go on another minute then cut him off.

"Larry, you've got to leave Ellie alone."

"She needs *somebody* to keep an eye on her. Now that her mother isn't here. *Somebody's* got to do the job, Belle."

"Look, if you push her, she'll do the same thing I did. Go off the deep end. She wants to get a restraining order on you as it is."

"*What?*"

"Larry, you cannot treat her this way. You'll lose her entirely. The way you lost me."

"You're just going through menopause," he insisted. "You'll see reason when it's past."

"Is that what you're telling yourself now?" She almost laughed. "Guess what, Lare. No hot flashes. My periods are still regular. You are wrong as usual."

"The signs just haven't appeared, that's all."

I tried, Ellie, Belle thought. "One more time and I'm hanging up. Leave Ellie alone. She's got a good head on her shoulders. She can work this through herself. But if you interfere, she'll do something drastic – marry Mike and quit school. I'm warning you, Larry, leave her alone."

After she'd hung up, she headed for the kitchen and the bottle of Cabernet in the pantry. Or maybe the Scotch would be better. Scotch it was.

She spent the next two hours trying to drown out Larry's voice, alternating between TV and the book she couldn't seem to concentrate on. Finally at nine o'clock she took a shower, letting the water beat against her bare skin to pump out the frustration, the anger and, she had to admit, not a little fear of her situation that seeped through the crevices of the wall she'd erected to keep it at bay.

Why did she continue to let Larry trounce her self esteem? Dance a Cha-Cha on her confidence, the belief in herself she'd fought so hard to attain? She'd moved out here to get past that portion of her life. The kids were fine. They could take care of themselves. Unless he goaded them into doing something stupid. Ellie could react that way sometimes.

Steam rose around her, filling her nostrils with that precious commodity, moisture. Heat melted the tenseness in her muscles and slowly drained the anxiety from her nerves. This whole thing with Lily Poole was wearing on her, taking its toll, and she needed to put it in perspective.

Finally, limp with exhaustion, she climbed from the shower and grabbed a towel. The bathroom was still steamy, the mirror clouded. She toweled herself dry, rubbing her skin until it tingled, then moved into the bedroom.

In the distance she heard it, someone climbing the outside stairs to her apartment. Adrian? Bern? It was late for a visit. Who else? Damn, had she locked her front door? Throwing on her robe, she eased out to the dimly lit living room, listening.

The door handle moved. No knock? Ohmygod!

The next moment it opened and Fred Preacher stepped into her living room, heavy boots drumming against the wood floor. In the spare light from the corner lamp Belle saw an ugly snarl on his face coupled with surprise. Fear sidled up her back and radiated around her ribs. She felt especially vulnerable in nothing but a robe.

"Guess you don't lock your door or nothing, huh?" he barked.

She tightened the belt of her the robe. "Guess you don't bother knocking, huh?"

In a bullish stance, fists balled, he glared at her. "You just can't leave it the hell alone, can you, lady?"

Belle sucked in breath, pushing back fear, readying herself for an attack. Adrenalin shot through her, making her muscles wobble then tighten.

Preacher strutted forward, cold anger in his movements. His voice was cigarette harsh. "I'm warning you to lay off. And you keep that Poole girl's mouth shut, you hear me?"

"Or what, Mr. Preacher? What'll you do? What you did to Ralph Poole?"

He was close now, his body blocking the corner light. His ponytail swayed with his movement. "You'll get hurt, lady, that's what. Don't you fuck with me no more."

"Don't try anything, mister. You'd be smart to turn around and walk out that door." She held her arms ready at her sides, kept her knees just slightly bent. "Sheriff McFarland knows about you. He knows about the payoff to Ralph Poole."

"By God, you're just asking for it, bitch!" Body puffed with anger, he moved in, one meaty arm lifted to strike.

Belle was ready for this. She let out a wild yell. In one swift motion she grabbed the man's arm, twisted underneath and came up behind him, shoving the arm toward his shoulder blade, her chest against his back.

Preacher cried out, a high pitched scream for such a big man, and fell to his knees. Belle pushed up harder, making him yelp again.

"I told you, the sheriff knows about you, Preacher. In fact he's probably out looking for you right now. You've got to be the stupidest fool in the world to come here of all places." She gave his arm one more jerk and he cried, falling into a whimper.

The next moment she heard clomping on the stairs, then her front door was filled with the large form of Bern, Adrian peeking around from behind.

Adrian shoved past his big partner to deal with the scene. "What in God's name is going on here?"

Belle held onto Preacher's arm. "Had a nighttime caller," she told them, her voice tight from the strain.

Bern moved further into the room. "Damn it, it's Preacher. He try to hurt you, Belle?"

"Get her off me," Preacher yelled. "Get this bitch off me!"

Adrian rolled his eyes. "I don't know, Belle. You play pretty rough with your boyfriends."

She let out a snort and released Preacher. He remained on his knees, rubbing his arm and swearing to himself. Finally he scrambled to his feet, glaring at the three of them. Bern took a threatening step in his direction and Preacher backed off.

"Want me to call the police, love?" Adrian said, moving toward the phone.

Preacher recoiled. "I ain't done nothing to her. She done it to me."

Adrian smirked. "Oh, I don't know. A small matter of breaking and entering? I suspect the police would like to know about that little tidbit."

All at once Preacher heaved himself between the two men, shoved through the door and down the steps. Bern started to follow but Adrian pulled him back.

"Don't bother," Belle said. "I don't think he'll try it again."

Adrian still wanted to call the police, but all Belle could think about was McFarland's insistence that she leave this case alone. Somehow, she couldn't face his displeasure, not after confronting Larry tonight.

Adrian and Bern stayed a little longer, 'just in case,' they said. But when they were gone, Belle fell onto the couch and began to shake now that the episode was over. Or was it really over after all?

25

On Tuesday, Lily went back to school and Belle was glad. She didn't like the idea of the girl spending so much time alone at the halfway house. Lily was better off with people surrounding her and friends to commiserate with her. And a deputy to keep watch over her.

The encounter with Preacher in her very own living room made Belle feel completely vulnerable. The man was a real and present danger, something she couldn't brush off. She might have over-powered him with that cute little arm twist of hers, but he wouldn't be caught off guard by her a second time. She decided to let McFarland know what had happened after all, know about the threat. The thought of his displeasure made her hesitate, but this was getting to be a mountain-sized phobia she needed to start hacking away at. Tell him, damn it, and screw his displeasure.

And Lily, how much of a threat was he to her? That dark truck she'd seen lurking near The Pines on Saturday – did Preacher have one like it?

She made her rounds of the schools she was scheduled to visit that morning, gave a talk to the fourth graders at Pines Elementary about anger and the right ways to deal with it as opposed to the wrong ways. One of the girls asked her about the Morales killing.

"My parents say it's 'cause he was a Mex. Is that what happened?"

Precocious little wench, Belle thought, and steered the class away from the topic. No need to get yet another administrator ready to feed her to the coyotes.

Finally she headed for the high school to check on things. Parking in the teachers' lot, she spotted a sheriff's cruiser off to the side. The deputy sitting behind the wheel looked over as she got out. He seemed young and stiff and overly prepared like a new recruit. This was McFarland's watchdog? The worry returned.

She walked across the courtyard to Building A and stopped at the main office to let Jenny know she was on the grounds. A couple of boys, floral underpants showing above bagging cutoffs, were waiting for the secretary to write them a pass. By the look of feigned contrition in their faces, she decided they'd just been chastised by the principal for some violation or another.

With Jenny's attention taken, Belle was able to avoid the usual probing questions. She gave the high sign to the secretary, shook her head at one of the boys who threw her a sheepish grin, and went down the hall to guidance and Ned's office. Verna Reilly nodded her in.

"I haven't heard a peep out of anyone so far today," Ned told Belle. "I've been checking."

She had to adjust her view of Ned. He'd ventured where angels didn't dare, braved reprimand in discovering the board president's connection was Pruitt. Perhaps his backbone had grown a size.

They talked about Lily and Belle filled him in on what had happened since yesterday's meeting with Ramey. She didn't mention her encounter with Preacher. For all his new-found courage, she didn't think Ned could handle that story just yet.

"I noticed one of the sheriff's men sitting out in the parking lot," she said.

Ned already knew. "He came in and introduced himself. Deputy Hollis. Mr. Ramey was upset but couldn't actually tell the man to leave. As for me, I'm glad he's here."

She agreed, though she wasn't sure what a cop out in the parking lot could do. She supposed he was there as a deterrent. But of what?

The bell rang for pass period and she plowed through the rush of students in search of Lily. As she left the building she spotted the commotion. Ronald Burke, the gym teacher, was breaking through the throng of students and two other teachers were headed in that direction from the opposite side of the courtyard. Belle pushed her way into the crowd.

Lily was at the center of the disturbance. Jeremy and Tom were part of it as well. The three of them confronted an angry Carlos Hernandez. Belle halted, muscles clenched, then came on. She and Burke had to bodily move students out of the way.

"I got to know what Julio said," Carlos cried, his fist inches away from Jeremy's face. "Did he talk about his boss? That Preacher fellow? Did that crook set Julio up? I want to know."

"Look, man, he didn't say a thing about his boss," Jeremy yelled back. His face still carried the battered marks from his two fights last week. "So just leave us alone. Stay away from Lil, ya hear me?"

Lily shoved at Carlos with both hands. "You leave him alone, damn it. He didn't do anything to you. And he doesn't know anything about Julio's boss. So just get out of here!"

Belle had angled her way toward the center of the group. Burke joined her. She started to speak when Carlos whipped a gun from his pocket. A huge gasp of surprise emerged from the crowd in unison and they stepped back in a wave. Carlos stuck the small revolver in Jeremy's face and Jeremy's cheeks went ashen. Belle froze a moment. Jesus, she thought, but her training kept her steady.

"You tell me," Carlos cried. "What did Julio say? I will shoot that son-of-a-bitch boss. I will shoot you as well. Julio was like my brother." When neither of the boys spoke, he reached out and grabbed Lily, one arm around her chest, the other holding the gun to her right temple.

At that moment Belle's heart stopped. Breath wouldn't come.

"Tell me or she dies!" he hissed.

The wave of sound this time had a physical impact on the air. Belle shoved down the worm that threatened to immobilize her. She swallowed to start her breathing, forced her hands not to shake.

"Carlos," she said quietly, "we can help you. What is it you want?"

He swung on her, waving the revolver in her direction. "What do I want? You have done nothing for to avenge my brother Julio. You say leave it to the police. *Murrda!*"

"Carlos, the man who killed Julio is dead. It's finished. You don't need to do this."

He swung the revolver back at Lily's head. Lily was pale and visibly shaking. But her eyes showed courage, a refusal to let this destroy her will. Belle's heart swelled for her.

"Let Lily go. She's not to blame for any of this. Let us help you. What do you want us to do? Tell me."

She watched the gun, watched the young man. Heart beating a deadly staccato, she held his attention while the other teachers eased students out of the way and into buildings. From the corner of her eye she saw the deputy appear at the far entrance to the school yard, his hand at his holster. He kept his distance and stayed in the shadow of the buildings.

"It is not finished if another is to blame as well. Julio must be avenged."

"I understand how you feel. It's all right to feel anger and frustration. But this isn't Lily's fault. It's not the fault of Julio's friends." She kept her voice calm, kept the fear out of her eyes. "Put the gun away, Carlos. We don't want to see innocent people get hurt. You wouldn't want to hurt these kids. I know you wouldn't."

"Someone is to blame!" he yelled, almost in tears.

"I know how hard this is for you. We all do. But the gun won't help. It only causes more problems."

The deputy had eased his way along the courtyard so that he was behind Carlos and moving closer.

"Please, Carlos, put away the gun," Belle said. "We don't want anyone hurt here."

Suddenly Carlos swung around, gazing at the diminishing crowd of students and teachers in frantic despair. Then he checked as his gaze landed on the deputy. With a cry of pain and frustration he swung back at Belle.

"Liar! You are all liars. You have all helped to kill my brother Julio." His voice was ragged, tortured.

He flung Lily away from him so that she almost fell. Jeremy caught her. Then Carlos plunged through the crowd in the opposite direction from the deputy and disappeared down a corridor between buildings. Belle nearly toppled in her relief.

Mac got the call from Deputy Hollis at the school.

"That Hernandez guy was brandishing a gun," Hollis said, breathing fast and heavy. "When he spotted me, he took off between the buildings. I lost him, sir. I'm sorry. What should I do now?"

"Stay there. Keep an eye on the Poole girl. I'll send some squad cars to look for him. We'll keep someone staked out at his home."

After he hung up the phone he sat back in his chair and rubbed his eyes with the heels of his hands. Dammit to hell. How many complications could you have to a case? They couldn't find Preacher. The man hadn't shown up at work today. Looked like he might have skipped town. And now the Hernandez son running around, pulling out a gun and threatening people. Dammit to hell.

Sarah interrupted his recriminations. Neat, unwrinkled, she stood before his desk.

"Sir, I'm having a time cracking this phone number you gave me" she told him.

Mac wasn't surprised. Nothing about this case was going well. He waited.

"It's dead, of course," Sarah said. "I knew that yesterday. And I'm pretty sure it's in-state. But the cover-up's extensive. Nobody'd go to that much trouble for something legal."

"So you're saying the Titus Land Development isn't?"

She shrugged. "Looks that way. I'll try a wider circle."

Mac sat forward. "What're we looking for?"

Sarah was in her element. "Dirt. Something under the table, maybe. Of course, plenty of developers are known for that. They have ways of obtaining parcels of land they didn't learn from Boy Scouts."

"Realtors?"

She flipped a hand. "Property has to be sold by somebody. Realtors know how to do it. All you'd need is one person to keep his mouth shut. One person who wasn't squeaky clean himself."

"Or herself."

Sarah's eyebrow lifted a notch. "Right."

"Maybe the land wasn't sold."

"Then why cover your tracks?"

"Maybe it was going to be sold but the deal never came off," he said.

Sarah thought about it. "Could be. In which case, this will be harder still." She glanced down at him. "Don't worry, sir, I'll find it. Somewhere out there in cyberspace is a clue."

Ramey's office felt crowded with so many people in it. After the incident Belle had gone to the teachers' lounge and sat alone in the darkened room to get a grip on herself. Two big threats in less than twenty-four hours.

Now, fifteen minutes later and a little more composed, she looked around at the assembly. The sheriff's deputy, Hollis, was there and Ronald Burke with two other teachers. Ramey glared at everyone without exception, but the coldest glare was reserved for her.

"How could this happen at my school?" he demanded, jowls shuddering. "How did this Hernandez person get in?"

Belle thought of the openness of the buildings ranged around the courtyard and wondered how the school could have kept him out.

Deputy Hollis stood at attention, hat in hand, hair in an army burr, utility belt heavy and clinging to his thin hips, his uniform tightly pressed but still wet with perspiration after the chase. He looked young and duty-bound. Even his voice was young when he spoke. "Hernandez didn't come through the main gate. I was there the whole time. He must have climbed over the fence in the back."

Ramey threw a glare at him. "What I'd like to know is why a police officer has to be parked in our lot."

"I explained that earlier, sir," Hollis said. "I was told to keep an eye on the Poole girl. It looks like the sheriff's worries were justified."

"And what good was your being here? It didn't prevent what

happened."

Hollis eased back toward the door, unable to answer that.

Ramey studied them all, his face livid. Finally he zeroed in on Belle. "This is exactly the kind of thing I've been trying to prevent, Isabel. I suspect your involvement with the Poole girl may have caused this."

"I don't see how."

Ramey started to answer her, then looked at the audience. "You three," he said to the teachers, "you go on back to class. As for you, Deputy, please report to the sheriff that I resent having you parked on school property, especially when I was never consulted."

Hollis the rookie looked caught between his duty and public disapproval. But he did as he was told and four people filed out of the office. Belle started to get up but Ramey pinned her.

"Isabel, you stay."

Burke threw her a crooked smile as he left.

When the door was shut Ramey placed himself opposite her, standing over her like an interrogator.

"Look, Mr. Ramey," she started before he could, "my concern over Lily has no effect on the actions of Carlos Hernandez. What happened might have happened anyway. Except that if I hadn't taken Lily home that first day, her father might have hurt her and she'd be in the hospital right now – instead of here at school."

Ramey stepped back. "Now, don't over dramatize this situation."

"Who knows what could have happened if we hadn't gotten Lily to the halfway house?" she went on. "Ralph Poole wasn't locked up, and in his drunken state he might even have killed her."

"Isabel –"

"And now we find out that a big politician is putting pressure on the school board to keep us out of this whole thing."

His eyes narrowed. "What are you talking about?"

"Lloyd Pruitt. He's buddies with Mr. Franks, our board president." She was on a roll. "That's probably why Franks chewed you out on Sunday. Pruitt was behind it."

"Wait, we don't know that," Ramey insisted.

Belle got to her feet, on the offensive now. "Did you know Pruitt also went to Sheriff McFarland's office to come down on him for the same thing?"

Ramey edged back to his desk. "That's not our concern." He cocked his head so that one jowl was lower than the other. "How did you come to know this?"

"I was there," she told him.

"Why were you there?"

"Because," and then she realized the tables were turned again, "because Lily found something at her house concerning Julio's death that he needed to know about."

"I see. And how did you find out Lloyd Pruitt was a friend of Joe Franks?"

Crap. She couldn't betray Ned. Not when he'd finally shown some spine. "I asked around. I couldn't help wonder why Mr. Franks was so adamant. I thought you'd want to know the source."

"Me? Why would I?"

"My mistake," she shrugged. "But the sheriff wasn't worried about Pruitt's threats. Evidently there's some dirt in the man's corner."

"And a great deal of influence," Ramey told her, glancing out the window. His expression had undergone a change, from condemnation to speculation. He glanced back at her. "Pruitt still has the power to do us harm, Isabel."

"Maybe," she admitted. "But don't forget, Morgan Andrews thought we were doing the right thing helping Lily out. Maybe he'll be the one to wield the power in the end."

"We can't count on that. I haven't heard that Andrews has much influence. Pruitt, on the other hand, has connections in high places. Lots of muscle."

Belle studied him. In that moment she could sympathize with Harold Ramey. Running a school was a political chess game and he had to play it, like it or not. It took a certain amount of rigidity to finesse the moves. Maybe that's what he'd been hired for.

She let out a sigh. "I should go talk to the kids. Find out what happened. And you're going to need some counseling intervention with students. The event was traumatic for them."

He held her with his gaze for a long moment. At last he said, "Isabel, stop making waves over this affair. We can't afford it. We have to think of the school system."

And the students? she thought. Let's not forget that minor item.

Belle found Tom and Jerry slouched on chairs in Ned's outer office, the Bull Pen – Verna Reilly typing away, unconcerned.

"Where's Lily?" she asked them.

Tom nodded toward the inner office.

Jeremy said, "Mr. Stambaugh, he's talking to her."

"All right," she said, pulling up a chair. "Tell me what happened."

"Jeez, man, that guy's a crazy," Jeremy began. "He pulled a friggin' gun. He was gonna shoot Lil. He's crazy."

"Start from the beginning."

The two boys looked at each other. Tom began. "Bell rang, see. Me and Jere, we was talking to some guys after class. Maybe get up a game after school. We went out and saw that creep yelling at Lily."

"She was ready to cry, man. Know what I'm saying?" Jeremy said.

"Did you recognize him?" she asked.

"Sure – Julio's cousin. They was pretty close," Jeremy told her. "But Carlos, man, he had a bad temper. Julio used to tell us about it."

Belle nodded. "What was he yelling at Lily for?"

"Who knows," Jeremy said. "Something about Julio's boss and about her dad."

Tom sat forward, pulling his long legs up. "Told him to leave her alone. Wasn't Lily's fault. Then he got in her face. Wanted to know what Julio said about that guy, Preacher."

"Man, we didn't know," Jeremy barked. "Julio just told us he liked his job."

Belle thought about it. "When Julio said he was going to get money to take Lily away, how did he plan to do it?"

Tom shrugged, picking at a scab on his cheek. Jeremy shook his head.

"What about Nick James' father, the realtor?" she asked. "You had that fight with him. What exactly had Julio told you about the father?"

Jeremy said, "Just that people're right. That he really was a crook. Said he knew it, man."

And if Julio knew it, Belle thought, maybe he extorted money from Harley James – blackmail.

And maybe, just maybe that was what got him killed.

26

Mac got the call at home. The sun wasn't over the horizon yet, the coffee wasn't done percolating, and he was only half shaved. When the phone rang, his razor slipped and he swore, dabbing at a spot of blood.

"Sir," Deputy Garrison said, "we found Preacher. I think you better come down here."

Morning twilight filtered across the sky, a pale blue melting into pink and then pearl above the western horizon then diminishing as the sun approached the top of the mountains to the east. By the time Mac reached Mile Hi, the sky was bright with the new day, the world awash with the virgin sun.

He parked his Jeep in the lot by the office. Two of his cruisers were there along with a couple of pickups and a Camry. As he got out, Garrison appeared at the door of the garage.

"Did you get hold of Rolly?" Mac called, walking over to meet him.

"He'n Butch're coming," Garrison said. He shook his head. "Couple of the men found Preacher when they came to work. Not pretty."

The morning light outside made the garage feel like a cave. Garrison led the way to where several deputies formed a semicircle. Three of the workmen stood off to the side. They surrounded a backhoe, a giant yellow insect shape that had fallen off the hydraulic lift and lay at a peculiar angle on the floor of the garage. Underneath it, his legs and one arm reaching out like the Wicked Witch of the East under Dorothy's house, lay the body of Fred Preacher. The workmen had IDed him.

Someone came into the garage behind Mac. Another employee. "Christ, what the hell happened?"

Blood pooled around the body. It smelled as though the man's bowels had let loose on impact. Part of the face had been crushed while the tidy ponytail at the back of his head looked incongruous. The workman stared in disbelief, then went to join his cronies. A low conversation started among them.

Mac turned to Garrison. "Who discovered this?"

"Gomez!" Garrison called to the circle of workmen and gestured.

The man came forward, a short fellow, barrel chested with a goatee and dark Hispanic features. He had a little strut to his walk. After all, he'd been the first to see this, which elevated his importance in the eyes of his fellow workers.

Mac took Gomez outside to talk. "Tell me what happened."

The man glanced back at the garage entrance, then at Mac. "See, I get here first every day. My job is to open things up, you know?"

"What time was that?" Mac asked.

"Five o'clock, every day like clockwork, that's me."

Mac nodded.

"So I get here, open up. Don't see nothing at first. Too dark in that hell hole, you know? Just go turn on lights, set up the coffee pot – that's my job, too. I'm checking the work schedule on the board up by the counter, what we got lined up for the day, that kinda thing."

From the corner of his eye Mac saw Carter's cruiser pull into the parking lot. He waited as Gomez told the story his way.

"So I'm checking out the board. Then I look over and see the backhoe on the ground. Christ, I'm thinking. The damned lift give out again. We been having more trouble with that thing. Now the backhoe is really broke, the arm knocked off center, you know?"

Carter and Taggert joined them, giving a nod to Mac.

Gomez went on. "So I go over to look at the wreckage. And, man, I see a arm sticking out. And then two legs. I think I'm going crazy, you know? Can't be. I get closer and sure enough." He shook his head as though the whole thing were too incredible to believe.

"Me, I wanted to get the hell outta there. But I gotta know who it is, you know? So I get closer and there's all that blood under the arm-a the hoe and a body all crushed – God, what a mess. But I know, sure as I gotta piss, it's Fred, all right. Old Fred – "

"Did you notice anyone driving away when you came to work?"

Gomez shook his head. "Place was deserted like always. Well, except –" He shot a quick glance at the building entrance.

Mac walked Carter and Taggert back to the garage as several more workmen showed up for the day, gathering inside the building and creating an echoing din.

"Where the hell was that asshole all day yesterday?" they heard, and, "Musta been fooling with the goddamn lift. Couldn't wait for Jonesy to get that backhoe working. Had to do it hisself," and, "Lousy hoe ain't gonna be doing no more work, or him neither." No sympathetic note for Fred Preacher.

Carter and his partner questioned the men. Al Yazzie showed up along with the techs. The job was to get that backhoe off the body without ripping it apart. Someone suggested they bring the crane from the yard to lift it, and the process began.

Mac stood back watching them work and wondering. Where the hell *had* Preacher been all day yesterday? What the hell was he doing working on a piece of equipment after hours, and with no help? Or maybe he'd had help.

The techs got busy dusting for prints at the controls. Not an easy job under the circumstances. The whole thing looked like an accident.

But this was no accident. Mac could feel it in his gut.

Belle didn't hear about Fred Preacher's death until lunch time when she got back to her office. Janice Purcell, the superintendent's secretary, told her.

"Heard it on the radio. Can you imagine? This big bulldozer just fell on him and crushed him. Lordy, what a mess that musta been. Blood all over, I'd guess."

Belle couldn't speak. She hurried to her office and shut the door, breathing hard, staring across the small room. Did her going to see Preacher have anything to do with him dying? Or his attack on her at her apartment Monday night? Had he been scared then? An accident, Janice said, but it didn't feel right, didn't fit.

She plopped down in her chair, her gaze moving through the window at the grackles squawking in the willow tree. First Poole got killed. Now Preacher. Retribution? Carlos was yelling about Julio's boss yesterday in the school yard. He had a gun. She wondered if Preacher had been shot first before being crushed.

Coming to a decision, she picked up the phone and dialed the sheriff's office. The sergeant who answered said he was busy at the moment and would call back. She'd barely hung up the phone when he did.

"What is it this time, Mrs. Evans?"

Belle hesitated. "I just heard about Fred Preacher. I - um - I can't help wonder if I'm somehow responsible."

Now he hesitated. "I don't think so."

"Did you know I went to see him Monday?"

"Yes." His tone was stiff, tight.

So. She grimaced. "I didn't tell you because I didn't want to hear another lecture."

"I see."

Belle chose her words carefully. "Preacher was very upset when I talked to him."

"I know. Detective Carter questioned his men."

"I also didn't tell you he threatened me Monday night. He broke into my apartment."

"Christ." Silence a moment. "What happened?"

"He said that I should fuck off – his words. That I'd be sorry if I didn't. And so would Lily Poole if she didn't keep her mouth shut."

"Then what?"

"He started to hit me but I subdued him."

A crack of disbelief. "You subdued him?"

She stiffened. "I know a few maneuvers. Then we were about to call your office when he suddenly bolted out the door. We didn't try to stop him."

"Who's we?"

"My landlords. They came up when they heard the commotion." When he didn't say anything, she added. "It's an old house. The floors aren't sound proof."

Finally he spoke. "That's it? He told you to lay off, you subdued him, and he left?"

Belle took in a deep breath. "Was Preacher shot?"

"Can't tell if he was shot. We'll have to wait for the medical report."

"I wondered," she said. "Did your deputy tell you about Carlos Hernandez making a scene at school yesterday?"

"Yup."

"Did he tell you what Carlos was asking Lily and Jeremy Gibbs about?"

"I understand he was waving a gun around. That he threatened to shoot Lily Poole. And he took off when he spotted my man. We haven't found him yet. The deputy said you confronted Hernandez. Pretty gutsy, Mrs. Evans. But then I guess you know some maneuvers."

"Sheriff, I'm a trained counselor and I've had police training, too. Give me some credit."

Silence.

She went on, glancing at the poster on the opposite wall about kids and gun safety. "The reason I called is because Carlos was demanding information about Julio's boss."

"What specifically?"

"He wanted to know what Julio had told them about Preacher. You'd think, since he and Julio were so close, they'd have talked about it between them. Instead, Carlos came to Lily and the boys. He seemed wild, like he wasn't sure what he wanted."

"He threatened them with the gun."

Belle sat forward, leaning her elbows on the desk. A raven flapped its wings toward the willow and the grackles took off. "He didn't show the gun at first. He was just yelling at them, a crowd of kids all around. Then, when some of the teachers and I advanced on the group, he got scared or nervous or something and pulled the gun out of his pocket, a revolver, and started threatening everyone with it. Finally he grabbed Lily."

"That's when you talked him out of using it," he said.

She eased back in her chair. "He didn't back down because of me. He ran off because of your deputy."

McFarland was quiet on the other end. Finally he spoke. "Anything else I need to know?"

Belle wasn't sure how to say this. "I've been meddling again."

"I'm aware of that. What else?" He didn't sound surprised.

"Well, the boys, Jeremy and Tom, got in a fight with a student at school the other day over a comment Julio had apparently made. They fought with the son of a realtor in town. Nick James was the student. His father is Harley James of James Realty."

"What was the fight about?" He seemed more interested now.

"Some remark of Julio's about the man being a crook. I got the impression Julio knew something about James." She hated confessing, but she had to under the circumstances. "So I went to talk to the man. I felt there might be some connection between real estate and Titus Developers, the name on the business card."

McFarland listened while she described her visit to the realty office. She was grateful he didn't reproach her, though she could sense tension in his voice when he talked. After she was done, he remained silent for a long moment.

"This is everything?" he asked at last. "No more tidbits you're keeping to yourself? You know that withholding evidence is a crime."

Belle didn't answer that. "Do you think Harley James could be connected with Fred Preacher? Earth mover – real estate agent?"

"Let me worry about that, Mrs. Evans. Look out for the Poole girl if you have to. Twist some arms in that direction. Leave the rest alone. Or is that a useless request?"

When she'd hung up the phone, she sat gazing out the window, past the willow rustling in the wind, past the building beyond, all the way to the mountains in the distance.

Where was Carlos holed up? How was Harley James involved in Preacher's death? How had Fred Preacher gotten himself killed?

Maybe she needed to go find out.

Mac contacted dispatch and put his people on the alert for Carlos Hernandez. This time it wasn't just for pulling a gun at school.

Carter called. He and Taggert had gone to search Preacher's place. "Found the .22," he told Mac. "Looks like it could be the one used to shoot at the Poole girl. We bagged it. Found a rifle, too, but it's an old bush gun, 30-30, no scope."

"Anything else?"

"We're going through his papers and stuff now."

"Look for something about Titus Development. I want to know if there's a connection."

"Will do, Mac," he said and hung up.

Mac decided he'd make the trip out to the Hernandez house himself, get the feel of the situation from the mother and whoever else was there. And talk to them at the door. No more confronting those goddamned dogs. He rose to his feet, about to set off, when Sarah came into his office.

"Got it," she told him, a tiny glimmer of pride in her uncrackable countenance.

Mac perched on the desk top. "Is this the phone number on the business card?"

"It is," she nodded, adjusting her glasses just a little more flawlessly and looking at the information on the printout. "It's a cover-up but not the smartest one I've ever seen. We're not talking pros here. Which is probably why I missed it the first time."

He thought of Preacher, of Poole, even the Morales kid. Pros? Not by a long shot. He wasn't surprised that a cover-up wouldn't be, either. "So what did you find?"

Sarah came closer, showing him the printout she held. "I connected with the phone company down in Phoenix."

Mac knew she'd been hacking into private files but didn't question it.

"Turns out this is the number of a title company. Has to be a fake one. 'Mountain Title.' I've looked everywhere. No such a thing, sir.

Never was." She glanced up at him. "Thought it was a dead end. But –
turns out the phone company wanted ID."

"Is that usual?"

"Most of the time your credit card's sufficient. But this yahoo
wanted to pay cash. So they asked for ID." She shook her head. "What
they say about crooks being dumb –"

Mac took the printout sheet from Sarah. He glanced through a lot
of garbled computer readout looking for the information. Finally he came
to 'Mountain Title Company.'

Sarah spoke. "The idiot man used his own driver's license as ID.
Can you believe that?"

Mac's eye followed down the page. And there it was. The name of
the man who'd set up the account. He gave a snort. If Belle Evans didn't
cause him such a pain in the butt, he'd offer her a job.

The ID on the account said 'Harley James.'

Belle stiffened as she held the phone, listening to Ned on the other end.
"Not at school?" she said. "They didn't show up today? Neither one of
them?"

Ned cleared his throat. "Well, the boys aren't exactly honor
students, Belle. They're probably sick or they skipped out for the day.
You know how that is. I'm sure Jeremy and Tom have done it before."

"I just don't like their timing," she told him. "That scene in the
school yard with Carlos yesterday. And now Fred Preacher turning up
dead."

"Preacher? Wasn't that Julio's –"

"Boss. Right." A cold shiver ran the length of her back and she
shoved it down. "Did you check their homes?"

"Of course," Ned told her. "But the attendance secretary didn't get
an answer. It happens all the time."

"And she didn't try again later?"

"We haven't got the manpower to keep calling back on students."
He was on the defensive now. "We leave a message if there's a machine.
What else can we do?"

Belle rubbed at her face with one hand. Tom and Jerry missing.
Not a good sign. "I'm sorry, Ned, but I'm worried. Three people have
been killed in this case. I don't want it to be four. Or five. Is Lily in
school today?"

"Just a minute." Silence on the other end while he checked. Then,
"She's here according to the attendance sheet."

"Would you go check? Until they solve this case, I want to know where she is every minute."

When she'd hung up, she checked the directory on her computer for the phone numbers of Jeremy and Tom. She'd call herself and find out where they were. She didn't like not knowing. Carlos was out there toting a gun and an ugly temper.

And someone, she was convinced, had done in Preacher.

Mac's back grew rigid as he listened to Carter on the Jeep's phone. He'd just finished talking to Mrs. Hernandez himself, dogs in the backyard yowling to wake the dead. Something was very wrong there. He'd seen panic in her face, and her husband was there, on a weekday, standing in the background glowering.

The wife was the communicator of the two, able to speak English more fluently and generally more accustomed to dealing with people than the man. But Mr. Hernandez's resentment and anxiety spoke loud and clear in the way he held himself. Still, nothing. Carlos wasn't there and they had no idea where he was. Not at work at his job with Thorne Landscapers the last few days either.

Now, back in the Jeep heading for the station, Mac got the call from Rolly.

"James Realty's closed up tight as a tomb, Mac," Carter told him. "And no sign saying he'd be back. So we checked out his home. Wife was there but no hubby. Claims he's on a business trip. Left this morning. Somewhere in California, but didn't know for sure. Maybe San Fran.

"Son-of-a-bitch," Mac barked. This was not what he wanted to hear. Carlos Hernandez on the loose, Preacher dead. And James nowhere to be found.

Were they going to discover James now, with one of his For Sale signs pinned through his heart?

27

Belle grabbed her purse and was out the door, holding a slip of paper with Jeremy's address. Lily was in school doing fine. Just not the boys. She'd tried calling both their homes. No one answered at the Kelliker place after eight rings. At Jeremy's house she got Mrs. Gibbs and a negative answer to her question. He wasn't there. He was at school. For heaven sakes, hadn't the woman gotten the school's message? She decided to talk to Jeremy's mother in person.

As she drove she became aware of an oppressiveness overhead, an accumulation of heavy clouds, low along the line of mountains, variations of gray and black, yet tight, as though unwilling to share their moisture with the parched earth.

Jeremy lived in one of the older sections of town, a little, low house on a block of similar homes. Spindly pines and cottonwoods, with some of the older branches dead, shaded the area. Spent hollyhocks and daylilies grew out of control in the yards. Several had a little grass – brown from the drought. A variety of fences and stone walls lined the street. She got the feeling of old shabby but with a streak of pride running through. She parked in front of the house.

Jeremy's mother came to the door in polyester slacks that bagged at the knees from long wear and a faded, flowered over-blouse. She was a short, chunky woman, face pallid, who appeared as though her main diet consisted of pasta and deserts. She looked surprised at seeing Belle, then added a touch of resentment when she recognized the woman she'd met at the sheriff's office the night of the bar fight.

"What is it you want?" she said, her words civil, her tone hostile.

Belle introduced herself and tried to ease the moment. "Mrs. Gibbs, I'm a little concerned about Jeremy."

"He's at school right now."

"Actually, he's not. The school must have called you." Belle said it as gently as she could. "I'm concerned that he's not there."

She watched Mrs. Gibbs shrivel before her eyes. Hostility gave way to fear. Her whole body went limp. "Nobody was home earlier. I didn't know somebody'd called."

"Answering machine?"

"We don't have none."

"I'm sure he's fine," Belle said. A lie. Why else was she here? "Could I come in and talk to you about him?"

Uncertainty reigned for a moment, then Mrs. Gibbs stood back to let Belle enter. The odor of fried bacon and eggs lingered from breakfast, faint but undeniable.

They sat on a couch, musty with age. A recliner in the corner looked worn on the arms, grease stains where the head rested. The table tops and hanging shelves were littered with knickknacks – mostly cute and small – and pictures – Jeremy and an older girl when they were young.

"Does Jeremy have brothers or sisters?" Belle asked to soften the tension.

"A sister. Jennifer. She's secretary at Horace Printing Company."

In Jeremy's records there was no father listed.

"Mrs. Evans, what's this all about? Jeremy, he went off to school this morning. Jennifer drove him. She picks up Tom on the way if Tom don't drive himself. He's got a pickup he's been fixing up. A rickety ole thing. Sometimes it works, sometimes it don't."

"Evidently the boys didn't show up for homeroom. They're on the absence list."

"Tom, too?" Her face crumpled. "Oh, Jeremy, how could you do this to me?"

"So far as I know," Belle said, "they haven't done anything to be overly concerned about. Being truant is more common than you'd think."

"But after that bar fight and the police and all –" She shook her head and took out a handkerchief from her pocket.

"That's my concern, too." Belle glanced around her, trying to think how to word this without having the woman get hysterical. "Mrs. Gibbs, has Jeremy talked about Carlos Hernandez recently? Since Julio's death?"

"You mean that hot-tempered cousin of his? I don't want Jeremy to have nothing to do with him. Matter-of-fact, I wasn't happy about his friendship with Julio Morales. Not that I got anything against Mexicans. But look what happened to him. There's something wrong with a person who gets hisself killed that way." The handkerchief came up to the mouth. The eyes puddled.

Belle watched her as she sniffed. "Did Jeremy mention a Mr. Harley James. Or his son Nick?"

Mrs. Gibbs paused, a suspicious glint in her wet eyes. "That fight, it was all the other boy's fault. Jeremy said so." More tears. She dabbed them with her handkerchief.

Belle tried a while longer but the woman was either very good at withholding the truth, which didn't seem likely, or knew very little about her son's escapades.

"Well, I suspect the boys are just out enjoying some freedom," Belle said and took her leave.

But she didn't believe that. And her talk with the mother only caused her worry over Jeremy and Tom to increase.

Distant thunder rumbled and lightning illuminated the clouds over the mountains to the east as Belle pulled into the driveway of the Victorian House on Quail Run. To the west the clouds were separating and patches of sunlight streaked through like pictures she'd seen in Sunday School classrooms depicting God in the heavens. There'd be no rain in Granite today.

It was four o'clock. Instead of taking the stairs to her apartment, she headed for the side door of the first floor.

"Adrian, I need to talk to someone," she told him when he answered her knock.

"Darling girl, you look absolutely hideous. What on earth has happened?"

He pulled her into the kitchen and sat her down, finding her something to drink.

Adrian had already read the news about Preacher's death. "According to the article, some kind of bulldozer fell on the man. Honey, I told you not to play so rough with your boyfriends."

Belle wasn't in the mood for humor. She explained about Carlos Hernandez and the incident with the gun at school, threatening to shoot Lily and yelling at the boys.

"And now Jeremy and Tom are missing. Missing, dammit! They didn't show up at school today and Jeremy's mom doesn't know where they are."

"Hold on a minute, love. Don't get your tail feathers in an uproar over this one. They're probably just playing hooky," Adrian said. "God knows I did it often enough."

"But after what they did last week, getting into a bar fight with Poole, then with Nick James, then this Carlos thing –"

"They do seem volatile," he admitted. "Two young peckerheads with half a brain between them."

"And I couldn't find them," she cried. "Dammit all, where are those twerps? What are they up to now?"

Adrian let her vent for a while. It was good to share her burden, but it didn't make her feel less anxious. This whole thing was looking uglier by the day.

It was almost five. Mac had just gotten back to his office and hung up his Stetson on the rack when Paul Cochran knocked on the door jamb.

"Are you busy?" Cochran said, a tired smile on his face.

"I didn't know you were in town, Paul." Mac pointed to a chair. "How long have you been here?"

Cochran settled himself in the chair like a man who'd journeyed long and hard. "I drove up yesterday to check things out for Saturday and brought a load of banners and handouts. I'm on my way back home. I thought I'd stop in."

"No flunkies to do that kind of work?"

Mac sat down in his own chair behind the desk. He studied Cochran's face, harried over the campaign. It had been the same six years ago when Morgan had run for office. This kind of career took its toll on a man – hectic days, sleepless nights. Even running for sheriff had been tough, but not as crazy as campaigning for the U.S. Senate.

"I can't leave the arrangements to a fledgling. That part has to be done right." Cochran folded his hands, elbows resting on the arms of the chair. "Chief Scott says you talked to him about security on Saturday. We appreciate it. The man's hard to move."

Mac scratched his jaw. "I'm not sure how much I helped. Told him he'd scare the tourists off if his security detail came on the heavy. So he's going to put some of his men in street clothes."

Cochran's expression was grim as he thought about it. "I suppose that'll have to do. We're lucky to get any cooperation at all from a Pruitt man."

"You've been at this night and day, haven't you?" Mac said. "I can see it's beginning to wear on you."

Cochran shrugged. "I'm not complaining. I'll do whatever Morgan needs me to do." He sat back. "Morgan's going to be our next senator if I can help it. And who knows, maybe more."

Mac cocked his head. "He's a good man."

"Better than good. Great. He's got what it takes to change things, to bring about a solution to the problems we face in this state. And in this country. He's got to win, Mac. It would be a tragedy if he didn't."

"Maybe. But we've weathered worst things than a Pruitt in office."

Cochran seemed to consider this. "How's the case of the Hispanic boy coming?"

Mac rubbed at his jaw. "Another death. Could be connected."

"Really? All I heard about was an accident with a bulldozer. You don't mean that one?"

Mac's eyes narrowed. "The media always grabs up something bloody like that in a hurry."

"They're bound to. You know how it is. If it's sensational, people love it," Cochran said. "So you think there was foul play?"

"Could be. He was boss to the Morales kid. Looked like he might have been involved in the killing. Now we'll never know for sure."

Cochran sat in thought for a long moment. "It's hard to believe something so complicated could happen in a town this size. The boy, the father of the girlfriend, the boss all tied up together. I thought you came up here to get away from that kind of sordid violence."

"I thought so, too." Mac sat forward. "Ever hear of Titus Land Development?"

Cochran's glance sharpened. "Titus?" He shook his head slowly. "But that doesn't mean anything. There's no end to land developers."

"No record on this one."

"Then how do you know about it?" Cochran asked.

"Something the Morales kid gave his girlfriend."

Paul Cochran was silent. Finally he spoke. "And you think this is connected to the boy's killing?"

Mac glanced out the window, his focus on the church building across the street. "We're still digging. Nothing's concrete yet."

"I'll ask around. Maybe someone in the Phoenix area has heard of Titus." Cochran's smile was sympathetic. "I don't envy you this problem, Mac. It's a big one. But then, Morgan and I have a pretty large one ourselves. That rally is going to be the deciding factor in our campaign. If it goes well, I think we're in."

He stood and so did Mac who came around the desk. "Good luck, Paul. I'll do what I can on my end."

Cochran nodded. "Morgan's lucky to have you as a friend."

They shook hands and Mac watched him leave. All candidates should have a Paul Cochran at their back.

His thoughts were interrupted by Sarah who entered his office. "Found something interesting, sir. Thought you might like to have a look." She had a letter in her hand. "I practically had to wrest it from that twitty clerk at City Hall. She wasn't going to let me see it. Finally I pulled out my ID and threatened her with jail time."

Mac's mouth twitched as he took the envelope. "What is it?"

"From the Tallmadge Company in Boston. It's a company that makes glassware. Seems they invested in some land around here a couple of years ago. But when they inquired about it back in June, there was no answer from the developer." She parked her hand on her hip, looking at him with head slightly cocked. "Would you like to guess what the name of the developer was?"

Mac's gaze widened and Sarah nodded.

"You got it," she said. "Titus."

28

Thursday dawned dark and dreary and airless. The storm system from the Baja Gulf had wound its way between mountain ranges, moving thick clouds to cover Arizona like a blanket, smothering the dry earth and teasing it with the moisture they held.

Belle felt the depression in the atmosphere as she got out of bed. It weighed on her almost as heavily as her worry. Did Jeremy and Tom get home last night? Was a deputy still keeping an eye on Lily? Had they found Carlos yet?

Belle had just gotten settled in her office on East Ocampa when the phone rang. It was McFarland.

"I understand the two kids from the bar fight are missing," he said. "Their parents called when they didn't come home last night."

"Oh my God," Belle breathed. "Still? They weren't at school yesterday. I talked to Jeremy's mother." She laid her head back, squeezed her eyes shut. Fear for the boys jarred her so badly she shivered. "My God, what's happened to them? All these people ending up dead –"

"Don't count them out yet, Mrs. Evans." His voice said he'd had practice calming frantic people. "We'll do some tracking. Could be they're pulling another stunt like the one at the Sidewinder Bar."

"But all night?"

"Kids never think who's worrying about them."

"Don't I know." Some of Will's exploits at this age had left her dry-mouthed with anxiety. She took a deep breath, eased the air out again.

"Any ideas where they might have gone?" he asked.

"I wish to God I did. I've been wracking my brain trying to think of some explanation. There was the confrontation with Carlos at the school. You haven't found him yet, have you?"

"Not yet," he said. "Did you get the impression Hernandez might hurt the boys?"

She shook her head, frustrated. "He didn't seem like he'd hurt any of them really, except by accident. But he was too volatile, so who knows what he's capable of?"

Silence on the other end.

She sat forward. "Will you call me if you find out anything?"

"Sure," he said.

As soon as Belle had cleaned up the work at her desk, she headed for the high school. She wanted to see for herself that Lily was all right. She caught her in between classes and used Ned's office to talk, shooing Ned out the door to Verna's domain.

Lily looked tired, her face drawn and pale, eyes full of sorrow.

"I just can't sleep, Miz E," she said. "The whole thing is like a nightmare. Except I wake up and it's real, you know?"

Belle looked her over. "I think we need to find you a good therapist to talk to. You're dealing with more than anyone should have to."

Lily ran auburn hair behind both ears. "I keep wondering how much of this mess is really my fault."

"Oh now, Lily girl, let's not start that. The answer is none. None of it lies at your door."

"But if I hadn't met Julio on the sly like that – Carlos said –"

Belle glanced away. "I'm pretty sure Julio would have been killed just the same." She brought her gaze back. "I strongly suspect he got himself involved in something ugly."

"I never thought Julio could do anything wrong," she said with passion in her voice. "Honest, Miz E, he was good. Ask anybody."

"Maybe something he didn't realize was bad. But it turned out to be. Or he was desperate to get you away from your father. And whatever it was got him killed."

Lily's gaze narrowed. "The payoff to my dad. Julio's boss paid him off because of – of what?"

"Something Julio knew about Preacher is my guess."

"Do you think that's why Carlos was looking for the guy?" Lily thought a moment. "The business card Julio gave me, did that tell you anything?"

Belle flipped a hand. "I don't know. Not for me, but I gave it to the sheriff. Maybe his department has found something." A tiny wince of irritation. "I'm not exactly in his confidence."

Lily sat back, looking as though she were carrying a huge burden. "What about Jere and Tom? Does anybody know where they are?"

"We're working on that."

The girl's expression showed her concern. "You think they got – hurt?"

"I don't know," Belle told her honestly. "But that isn't your fault either."

A knock at the door and Ned entered apologetically. "Just need some schedules." He went to a file cabinet, ruffled through a drawer and pulled out a couple of folders. "Sorry," he said and slipped back out. No hesitation as though he might want to stay.

Lily's eyes followed him without actually registering his presence.

"Has the sheriff's deputy been pretty visible?" Belle asked. "Have you seen him around The Pines?"

"Oh yeah," Lily nodded emphatically. "I'm glad, too. Last night Tammy, this girl I room with, and me, went for a walk out along Forest Road toward the elementary school and we nearly got run down by some stupid ass who was speeding. Hollis, he pulled up right after and walked us back to the house."

Belle's stomach lurched and she sat forward. "Somebody tried to run you down?"

"No, honest, Miz E. It was just some fathead with a new sports car, probably showing off for a buddy. It was almost dark so he didn't see us."

"How many people in the car?"

Lilly shook her head. "I couldn't tell. Too busy trying to get out of the way."

"What color was the car?"

Again Lily couldn't help her. "Too dark. And I didn't really look. Just a little sports car is all. It was no big deal, honest. But it shook Tammy and me up." She looked up under her brows. "Hollis was all right. He's one of the good guys."

Belle tried to quiet her anxiety but the incident didn't sit right. She remembered the sporty red Miata sitting in the driveway of the James Realty Company. No good making Lily worry more than necessary, though. It sounded as if Deputy Hollis was on the job. Please, God, let him be good.

Belle straightened. "I'm still worried about the boys missing. Do you have any idea where they could have gone?"

"I've been trying to think," she said. "Hollis asked me the same thing this morning when I got off the bus. So I've been thinking about what those two Bozos would do."

"And?"

Lily looked away. "I just don't know." Her voice caught and she took a moment to get a handle on herself. "Tom's got this beat up old pickup he keeps working on. It's a pile of junk but he loves the stupid thing. Painted it bright green." Another pause to get control. "Last year they took off with Julio and drove all the way over to Tuba City on the Navajo Reservation. Gone for three days. When they got back, Tom's dad did a number on him and Jeremy's mom cried for a week."

"What about Julio's aunt and uncle?"

"Funny. They were upset, I guess, but they didn't do nothing – *anything* – to him." Her face crumpled in horror. "Tom's dad's an animal. Not as bad as mine, maybe, and he's not a drunk. But he's always hitting Tom."

"That pickup of Tom's, Mrs. Gibbs said he sometimes picks Jeremy up for school in it."

"Yeah, when it's working."

Belle relaxed as a ray of hope shimmered. "Anyway, none of this is your fault, Lily. You didn't cause any of it, unless being alive and loving a boy who deserved to be loved could cause a problem. My being here this moment has ramifications of one kind or another. We move in this world; therefore, things happen."

Lily's eyes teared but her face relaxed. "I guess you're right, Miz E. I never really thought of it that way." A tentative smile. "I'm pretty lucky you've been here to help me. I just want you to know that."

"My job."

Lily shook her head. "I know you've been getting flack on my account. Mr. Stambaugh told me."

Belle grinned ruefully. "It makes life interesting."

Lily's smile grew. It was the first Belle had seen from the girl in all this time and it dazzled her. It also pulled fiercely at her heart.

"Oh, by the way," Lily said, "I got a job."

"Job?"

"Not a paying job. But somebody from the Andrews rally committee called and asked if I'd like to help out at the courthouse on Saturday."

"Help out how?" Belle couldn't say why she felt uneasy about it. "Who called you?"

"Some man called. He said Morgan Andrews figured I was kind of a heroine after all this. Said he wanted to meet me and asked if I'd help out." She saw Belle's expression. "It's okay, isn't it?"

Belle considered her. "I don't think Andrews should be using this case for his platform. But I guess he has some pretty strong convictions about such crimes. With reason, I understand." She cleared her face so as not to worry Lily. "Should be fine. What are they asking you to do?"

"Just hand out stuff, I guess. The man said Mr. Andrews wants to show me off in public, or something like that."

Belle still didn't feel comfortable about it. But under Andrews' protection and with all the police around, it was probably a safe place to be. Still, Carlos was running around loose with a gun and anyone could slip into a crowd unnoticed. She decided the best thing was to go there herself and watch out for Lily. And it wouldn't hurt to inform McFarland either. Just in case.

Mac stopped pacing his office. A useless activity that never accomplished anything. He had reports to fill out, had a meeting with Chief Scott in an hour to check out final plans for the rally. Why the hell did it have to come up this weekend? It was Morgan's last chance to gain votes, that's why. But the timing was lousy.

They'd notified the police from here to the coast to be on the lookout for Harley James in a red sports car. Hernandez, on the other hand, was probably still somewhere in the area. Gut feeling. Those two kids, though – what the hell had happened to them? Who else was involved in this mess?

Hernandez was on foot as far as they could tell, since they still had his truck in custody. Unless, of course, he'd stolen a car. Several had been reported missing in the last couple of days, but that wasn't unusual. Some were clunkers, easy to start and take for a joy ride. Others, top picks, were most likely headed across the border by now to be sold for parts.

Kelliker had an old '48 Chevy pickup, souped up with big tires and borrowed parts. Mac's people were on the lookout for it. The fact that they hadn't spotted it might be encouraging, unless Hernandez got hold of them and took the vehicle himself. Heading for Mexico? Mac had put the DPS on alert, but this was late, already a day after the boys had disappeared.

Dammit to hell. Why couldn't they find these people?

His phone rang and Mac reached across the desk to get it. "Yeah?"

"Yazzie the medical examiner's on the line," his lieutenant said and switched him over.

"Al, what've you got?" Mac perched on the edge of his desk.

"The guy's a mess, Mac," Yazzie said. "The backhoe did a number on him. And more when they pulled that sucker off him. What a job."

Mac rubbed the back of his neck. "What about bullet wounds?

Anything that shows he was killed before the backhoe landed on him?"

"He wasn't dead beforehand. Too much blood."

"Wounded?"

"No bullet wounds. He wasn't shot."

"So it was an accident? No evidence to the contrary?" Mac asked.

Yazzie hesitated. "Well, there is a wound on the back of his head. Hard to tell, but it's not consistent with the others. Different type."

Mac's jaw came up. "How so?"

Al Yazzie hesitated on the other end, always cautious. "I need to check out the site again, but it looks like a blow from a blunt instrument. And I found a couple slivers of wood imbedded in the wound."

"Wood?"

"Pine, like in building lumber. Don't think he could've gotten it from the fall," Yazzie told him. "I didn't see any wood at the scene."

"So you think he could have been wounded somewhere else?"

"I'm just telling you what I found, Mac. Whatever hit him didn't kill him. That backhoe did the work. Hell, how could it not?"

When Mac had hung up the phone he sat down in his chair, thinking. So, it looked like Preacher had been attacked – maybe. If so, what happened then? Had he somehow wandered back to the Mile Hi, fumbled with the machinery and gotten crushed? Or had someone brought him back and used the backhoe to make it look like an accident? That wound on his head, inconsistent with the others with slivers of wood, was the key.

Belle dragged herself home weary and disconsolate. Still no word from Jeremy and Tom. She'd checked at the sheriff's office before she left work. No sign of them, the lieutenant had said. Wind had whipped up and the weather was uncertain. "Where the hell are you boys?"

She felt like another one of Adrian's martinis but decided against it. No use becoming a lush over this. If she hadn't done it in all the years she'd lived with Larry then there was no point starting now.

At five o'clock she turned on the TV and went to the kitchen to start supper. She could see it from there when she turned the stand around. It was time for the local news. Local, of course, was Phoenix, unless she watched the Flagstaff station.

But not much went on in Flag. Maybe a protest by university students, or an accident on the mountain trails, or hunters shooting each other while stalking whatever was in season at the time. Flagstaff was a unique mountain town overrun by college kids, backwoods loners with their rifles and dogs, and sixty year old flower children still raising the banner of hippydom. Phoenix, on the other hand, was like every other big city in America – only hotter.

The big news was the primaries coming up at the polls next Tuesday. They had a story on Andrews at home, talking about the rally on the steps of the Crook County Courthouse in Granite on Saturday. Andrews, his appearance of calm assurance, told the reporter about the future, about progress, about a new awareness of people and of understanding for all cultures.

Pruitt was next. He highlighted Arizona's pride in the past, the dangers of encroachment and change, of losing the values of freedom and family. Between the two candidates, they covered both ends of the Republican spectrum.

Belle had the urge to call Louise and get her take on the campaign now. She had the urge to drive down to Phoenix, lie in the fetal position on Lou's couch, have her sister pat her like a baby and say soothing things to her. Life could be such a bitch.

She was turning down the heat under the broccoli when the item about the multiple murders in Granite came on.

"Still no suspect in the killing of Ralph Poole, though the sheriff's department is considering Poole as the one who shot Julio Morales, age nineteen. Poole's daughter was the girlfriend of the Morales boy. Some are looking at Poole's murder as revenge from a person close to Morales. Police are looking for the young man's cousin, Carlos Hernandez. Hernandez appeared at Granite High School Tuesday afternoon threatening students with a gun. When the sheriff's deputy appeared, he ran."

They showed a picture of Carlos and asked viewers for information about him.

The next story was from Granite, too. No picture this time, just a description of the accident at Mile Hi Earth Movers.

Belle's stomach turned over again. She switched off the heat under her meal.

By eight o'clock she'd finally calmed down enough to get into the book she was reading. So the telephone ringing jarred her. It seemed she'd been getting an inordinate number of late night calls recently. None of them good. Her immediate reaction was bile in her throat. What now?

Lily was on the other end and Belle's heart rate soared. "Are you all right?" she demanded.

"Sure," Lily said. "But I thought I'd better call you right away, Miz E." A pause, then, "Do you remember that shoebox full of stuff Julio's aunt gave me? The stuff that belonged to him?"

"At the funeral, you mean?"

"Yeah. I just haven't been able to look at it. I was afraid I'd start bawling."

"I don't blame you."

A deep breath. "Well, I finally got up the nerve to do it, take a look inside. I thought I might find something important in there." Another pause, this time longer. "I found something you might wanna see. It's a brochure and it tells all about that Titus thing."

29

Belle had to apologize to Mrs. Rivera for coming at this hour. Not quite eight-thirty but not a time for visits, either.

"I do not care to have my girls disturbed late at night," she said, but softened. "You have been a friend to Lily, though. I welcome you, Mrs. Evans. She has become stronger with guidance you have given her."

Belle talked to her while she waited for Lily. When Lily came trotting down the stairs holding the shoebox, Mrs. Rivera looked as though she might stick around. But Lily's fidgeting on the couch without disclosing anything seemed to give the woman a clue she wasn't wanted, and she left. Lily relaxed.

Belle waited, not pushing, though her pulse raced to know what the girl had found.

"Maybe it's not so important after all, Miz E," Lily told her. "I didn't mean to get you out here for nothing."

"You're not that far away," Belle said. "If it's nothing, then we haven't lost ground."

Lily nodded. "I guess."

She glanced around to see if anyone lurked nearby, watching. But the parlor they were in was empty except for themselves. And though they could hear female voices chattering in other parts of the house, no one came through to disturb them.

Lily opened the lid of the size eleven shoebox. Inside a pile of loose objects sat jumbled together. Belle spotted the handle of a wrench, a stack of pictures – one that looked like family on top – a pair of leather driving gloves badly worn, several envelopes, a small, plastic school trophy. Tucked into the side of the box was a brochure. Lily pulled it out.

The brochure on cream colored paper was smudged and wrinkled and had been folded in the middle at one time. Belle handled it gingerly but didn't kid herself that any prints could be pulled from it at this point.

Titus Land Development written across the top had a picture beneath it. A canyon with a cliff behind it – lush, full of color.

"Lame Horse Canyon?" Belle asked, though she didn't think so.

Lily shook her head. "I know Lame Horse like my own home. This isn't it. Never saw this place before."

It looked unspoiled, virgin. Beneath the picture was the usual blurb about the beauty and seclusion of the place and the home sites planned for it – single-family homes on two plus acre lots, built to suit the owner.

Unfolded, it had several other pictures of the location from different angles and one in the middle of a quaint cabin with the name on top, "Canyon Ranch Homes."

Several paragraphs told about the area and about the town of Granite, the usual things developers said about home sites. And the phone number at the bottom. Plain to read this time. Everything you'd expect on a brochure about a new development. But nothing unexpected. Titus could have been a hopeful that went belly up before it could get started.

And yet Julio had thought it important enough to save.

Belle looked at the front of the brochure again. It had been handled a lot and a small rip at the top told her where the stapled business card had come from. She turned it over to the back.

"Oh, my God," she said, sitting forward. "Will you look at this."

Where the page was nearly blank, someone had used a pen and drawn a map.

Too dark outside. Too late to see where the map might lead. Belle would have to wait until tomorrow to follow it up. And she needed to let the sheriff know about it. No more information held back.

She spent another night with dreams of frustration and waking to cold sweats. Did Adrian hear her downstairs? Morning twilight seeped into her window at five-thirty and kept her awake so that she finally got up, feeling groggy and useless. Luckily her Friday schedule was light.

Belle stared at the brochure lying on top of her briefcase on the library table. It looked so innocent, so normal. How many times had she picked up brochures like this? Gone through them blithely, wondering if she'd build here someday? Innocent. Yet lethal if this information had gotten Julio killed. And Poole. And Preacher. But why kill anyone over a land development that had gone belly-up? Mineral rights? A deal gone bad – a scam?

More important, how much of a danger was it to Lily?

The early morning had started out fine, but by eight o'clock the clouds threatened. The weather report had indicated rain now for most of the week, yet the clouds remained barren, never coming forth with their promise.

Before she went to work, Belle called the sheriff. He wasn't at his desk and she didn't leave a message.

The first thing she did when she reached her small office in the board building on High Street was to call Ned Stambaugh.

"Are the boys at school today? Jeremy and Tom?"

Ned's voice was tight. "I checked first thing. They haven't shown. A police officer was here yesterday afternoon making enquiries. And the deputy's still out there keeping an eye on Lily. Mr. Ramey's more upset than ever. He thinks this whole thing is giving a bad name to the school."

Belle's insides clutched. Were the boys lying dead somewhere on the desert floor like Julio? Was this turning into a massacre?

The morning ended up being busier than she'd planned on. One of the elementaries called her in for a consultation about legalities. Drugs were suspected in the lockers of a group of fifth graders and the principal needed to know the ramifications of a search.

She was just turning back into the board office parking lot when she got a call on her cell from Monroe Middle School. She answered and found another stir up between the Hispanic and white gangs. Thunder rumbled in the distance as she turned the Honda around and headed in the direction of the school. The meeting lasted the rest of the morning, the boys still belligerent and almost ready to take each other on right there in the office.

Belle pointed out the consequences to them, refraining from threatening the removal of certain body parts as she would like to have, and settled them down again. But she wasn't naïve enough to suppose it was over. How did you dispel hatreds that had been fed them by their parents since the bottle? Except maybe removing those particular body parts. It seemed to work with other animals.

She got back to her office by lunch time but couldn't eat. When she called McFarland she'd just missed him. This time she left a message.

The Titus brochure sat in her briefcase, out of sight but just as noticeable as if it had an active speaker system. She itched to find this place indicated on the hand-drawn map. Still, if the brochure was as old as it looked, the whole project might be dismantled and overgrown. She had to see what it was Julio Morales and the others may have died for. What it was that seemed to threaten Lily Poole, and caused the boys to disappear. Maybe all the events were unconnected. But they *felt* connected, felt like one long string of casualties brought about by a central cause.

Friday afternoon was busier than the morning had been. Three of the schools called her in for consultation. She had a meeting with several teachers and the principal at Pines Elementary, in conjunction with the drugs they'd found in the school she'd been at that morning. It kept her busy and her thoughts away from Tom and Jeremy and Lily. But at odd moments the realization would come slamming back into place with such a force she teetered on her feet. At her office she found out McFarland had returned her call. But when she called back, he was out again on another case. She wasn't privy to his cell phone number. But then, he wasn't privy to hers either.

Four o'clock, quitting time, was upon her when she got a buzz from Janice in the Super's office.

"Mr. Cummerford would like you at the meeting, Belle. He didn't say, but I'm pretty sure it's about the police hanging around the high school."

Belle passionately did not want to do this. She'd heard too much bitching from the administration already, and it always seemed as though they blamed her for causing this problem. They'd done everything but accuse her of shooting Julio. Maybe they thought she'd killed Poole. Who could fathom what they were thinking? Or maybe they weren't thinking at all, just giving knee-jerk reactions to something they didn't want to deal with. Hiding her feeling of foreboding and a good deal of tension, she walked down the hall to the superintendent's office and went in.

Ramey was at the meeting, of course, looking tight, small eyes squinted, jowls quivering. And a thoroughly uncomfortable Ned. Two board members were present. Joe Franks the president was one. And the administration director, a woman, second in command in the system.

Franks was short and thin, slightly balding, whose dress of choice seemed to be jeans and a sports shirt. A snarly little man, always ready to pick a fight. Lloyd Pruitt's friend, Belle reminded herself. Cummerford, on the other hand, was tall and broad, emanating strength of character and deep understanding, a façade, she knew, as much a deception as Ned's coach-like appearance.

"We seem to be in a bind here," Cummerford began after acknowledging everyone. "We've had several very disturbing events at the high school. Harold here has kept me informed of it all."

Ramey nodded, looking grim.

Cummerford glanced around the room, seeming to focus on Belle. Or was it her imagination?

"One of our students was killed, another one threatened by a violent parent, several others by a young man with a gun, now two of those are missing. And we've had the police there questioning our students and teachers and patrolling the vicinity. Very disturbing."

For the next hour and a half they hashed and rehashed the situation while the wind whipped up outside and whistled through the old bricks of the building.

Franks openly sniped at Belle for getting the school involved. Ramey was more general in his condemnation of events, but his eye kept meeting hers in a way that shot blame in her direction. Ned stayed as far out of the discussion as he could, actually scooting his chair back so he'd be less noticeable. Poor Ned, so beyond his depth, Belle thought.

She squirmed in her own chair, wondering when she could get out of here and do something constructive. Nothing constructive was happening here. Meanwhile, Tom and Jeremy were missing. Lily was alone. And somebody out there was a killer.

Mac got back to the station, weary from a long, hard day. Fridays were always a bitch, and this one stood at the top as a major pain in the ass. Nor had the weather helped. Something about a falling barometer seemed to wreak havoc among people and their lack of control. He'd spent too much time pussy-footing with Scott over this business of the political rally tomorrow. It was the jurisdiction of the GPD, not his. But both Morgan and Barry Scott had involved him up to his eyeballs.

To make it worse, they'd had three major accidents to deal with. A jack-knifed truck south of town on Route 95 that killed the driver of a Dodge minivan and injured three other people inside, one a two year old girl. That one twisted his gut. Another had happened out on Indian Creek Road. Some idiot in a big pickup trying to pass a line of cars had forced two oncoming vehicles off the road. One had rolled over, pinning the driver. The third accident had been a collision at a back road where an old man had run into the side of another vehicle driven by a couple of teens. Some injuries there but nothing fatal, thank God. Turned out the teens had stolen the car.

On top of that the department had to deal with two domestic quarrels, one near Janos and another at Blake Junction. A dog attack, a theft at the Wayside Gas station, a bar fight among some bikers out on Route 60. Jesus, the world was crazy. He and his people had been hopping all day.

He pulled off his hat, flopped down in his chair and ran weary hands over his face. The next minute Carter stuck his red head in the door.

"What's up?" Mac asked.

Rolly Carter moved into the office, his large frame filling much of the space. "Still nothing on those two kids we've been looking for. Suppose they bought it?" He ran a finger across his neck.

"God, I hope not. But they've been gone a long time. It sure doesn't look good."

"What I figured," Carter nodded. "We got word on that Miata of James the realtor. The DPS spotted it halfway between here and Flag, but lost it again. Still, we know now it's in the state, not California. Guess that's something."

Mac sat up at the news. "So maybe James didn't go too far after all."

"Looks like."

Carter, smoothing his mustache, gave a report on the bar fight. They discussed strategy on the other matters and he left. Mac sat staring out the window. Where to now? What was the next step?

He glanced through his messages. Belle Evans had called back. He tried her again. "Out of her office," the secretary told him. Damn. What was she up to now? Mac shuddered to think.

It was five-thirty before Cummerford broke up the meeting at the board office. And as far as Belle could see, absolutely nothing had been accomplished except to make her scream inside to be released. Franks had bitched some more, Ramey had become silent and sullen, Ned had retreated into himself. They'd gone over every aspect a dozen times, or so it seemed, and the final outcome had amounted to nothing. How like the administration, she thought.

When she got back to her office, she discovered that McFarland had called yet again. She tried him and found him gone. Dammit, why didn't he stay put? Then she grunted. He was probably saying the same thing about her. No matter, she was outta here. The inactivity had driven her nearly to the edge of sanity and she had to do something. She knew what that something was.

First she'd need sustenance. Clouds, heavy with a burden they refused to release, wind whipping the trees and people alike, she headed for the nearest Wendy's. After that she was on a quest. She would follow the Titus map and find out where all this violence had found its origin. Maybe then she could figure out how to help Lily.

30

Belle maneuvered down Ponderosa Avenue munching on a chicken sandwich and checking the hand-drawn map on the brochure. Not quite six on a Friday evening and the traffic was heavy.

Clouds obliterated any trace of the dying sun. Lightning flicked in the distance and she could hear a faint rumble of thunder. Would they finally get the storm that the weather reports had been promising? She had tried McFarland one more time before leaving her office. Not in but this time she left her cell phone number. Then she'd taken off on her treasure hunt. If she found anything interesting she could present him with that along with the Titus brochure.

Belle drove, looking from map to highway, afraid of missing the turnoff for Cave Road. A bad moment to go slow on these curves with no passing lane when everybody was in a hurry to get home or out of town for the weekend. An over-sized pickup on a jacked up axel hugged her rear, barely two feet behind her. She could see the driver, red-faced and swearing at her, in her rearview mirror and wanted to yell a few things back. But this wasn't the time to get into a confrontation with the owner of a vehicle twice the size of hers.

Calvin's Market and gas station stood at the junction for Cave Road and a sign pointed to Swanson's Lake. When she took the turnoff, the truck squealed past her with a blast on his horn and his middle finger raised high. She let out her breath. The road was almost deserted so she was able to relax a little. According to her atlas, it led to the lake surrounded by wilderness area, state owned land seldom used by anyone but ranchers for grazing cattle.

A chill wind whipped the trees and roadside growth. Without moisture to hold the heat, the high desert could become cold in a blink. In the last seven months she'd learned how unpredictable this climate was. Sandwich finished, she crumpled the paper and concentrated on her mission.

After a short time the road began to climb. Wind whisked through bear grass and shrubs, bending stalks of sunflowers and camphor weed along the sides. One blast whipped across the road, swirling dirt and debris in its cape and nearly cutting off her vision. She was looking for the Cactus Lane turnoff and almost missed it. Screeching to a halt, she backed up to where the lane began. Dirt road, but it looked fairly smooth. She hoped her Honda could make it. Belle pulled out her cell phone and checked it. Barely any signal. Damn, she'd forgotten to plug it in today. Small wonder, with all that was on her mind.

Cactus Lane, still climbing, moved through a forest of pines and gambel oak. The road twisted one way, then another, washboard in places enough to jar her teeth. The motor of the Honda scared a jackrabbit out of the brush to scurry across the road. Ravens circled overhead in a threatening sky. Wind tossed dirt in front of her and worried the dust trail she left behind.

Belle looked at the map again. From Cactus she was looking for a road that cut to the left. No name on it so she could only take a guess. About five or six miles up she found a left-hand turn off. This road didn't look so promising. Checking her phone again, she heard nothing - dead. Should she risk it?

"Oh, what the heck," she breathed and turned onto the road. She and her Honda had been through worse.

Potholes and imbedded rocks challenged her small car. She took it slowly, easing around the larger impediments. At one point a coyote emerged from the left. It stopped in the middle of the dirt track fifty yards ahead and stared at her, then trotted into brush and trees on the other side. Belle was too busy trying to keep her Honda in one piece to react.

Checking the map again, she figured the final turnoff was about four or five miles from the entrance of this lane. Would that road be even worse? Her poor baby would never forgive her. It would fall apart or rust just out of spite.

It seemed as though she'd been driving forever before the turn to the right finally appeared. This track wasn't any worse than the last and the climb was apparently over.

The area was maybe six thousand feet plus in elevation. Not as high as Flagstaff but higher than downtown Granite. The landscape wasn't spectacular, just the usual – live oaks and juniper. So why would Titus come out here? Why would anyone want to build in this deserted place?

Then bouncing over a rise she saw it, like opening Dorothy's front door onto the Land of Oz. She came to a halt out of sheer surprise. The road dropped down into a spectacular canyon. Rock walls a stark copper red, even in the dimming light, surrounded a meadow with a small stream thick with willows and cottonwoods lining it. She could hear water in the stream in this drought. The reality was better than the picture in the ad.

Lonely, secluded, with a blade road cut into it for access. And at the end, partially hidden by willows, was a short single-wide decorated to look like a cozy cottage, the picture in the Titus brochure.

Mac paced his office, face grim, jaw set, eyes dark with frustration. After six. Time to leave. But he couldn't. Where the hell was that woman? And what new surprise did she have for him this time? He'd called her office, her home, the cell phone number she'd left, no answer. Maybe she'd gone out to dinner, or shopping, or whatever else normal people did on a Friday after work. She'd tried getting him four times today. Not usual.

He'd spent the last two hours himself in a meeting at the Granite Hotel with Morgan Andrews and Paul Cochran and their people. Barry Scott and his men had been there, so Mac saw little reason to attend. In fact, Scott had been pissed about his presence, but Andrews had insisted.

So they'd sat in the conference room going over all the details of tomorrow's rally, Mac chomping at the bit because he needed to be here. He'd finally declined dinner with his old friend.

Now he was back in his office, but why? His people were looking for any sign of Harley James. The family had been questioned again. Nothing. But the DPS had reported the red Miata in the area.

Hernandez was still missing. No clues to his whereabouts. And no sign of the boys, Gibbs and Kelliker. No reports on the truck Kelliker would have been driving. Was that a good thing? And now that damned Evans woman had disappeared, for the love of God. Was the whole town of Granite getting swallowed up, one at a time, by some giant hole nearby?

He stalked to the window and stared out at the street. Traffic streamed by the old church, horns honked, the sky looked angry enough to pelt the earth with lightning. "Dammit to hell," he spit, "where is everybody?"

Belle thought of turning back, but the place was deserted, abandoned, no one here, so she eased her car down the dirt track that had been cleared through the canyon by a bulldozer. Fred Preacher's? Weeds had grown up along it. How long had it been unused? She glanced at the hand-drawn map that Julio had gotten hold of. How? Stolen from his boss's office? Was that why he'd been killed?

When she reached the bottom of the canyon the dirt track evened out, cutting across a meadow of grama grass and blooming camphor weed to the cottonwoods, willows and bushes obscuring part of the creek, and ending at the door of the single wide mobile home. Above, ponderosas stood atop the cliffs like sentinels in an eternal watch.

Belle stopped a hundred yards or so from the building, searching the area in the fading light for any sign of life. From here the trailer looked ancient and desolate, not nearly so quaint, left to rot like so much garbage in this virgin and pristine place. It seemed to her a sacrilege on the land, especially when she considered the havoc it might have wreaked.

Finally she drove closer, judging she'd still have enough light left to make her way out of here. Twilight didn't fade these days until nearly eight and it wasn't quite six-thirty. Time enough to take a quick look and get back on the road.

As though on tip-toe, she pulled up to the trailer, turned off the motor and got out. Wind whipped the trees, partially covering the sound of water over rocks, the onk of a raven above and the chittering of birds in the branches readying for the night. The raven's call echoed in the canyon as it floated on air drafts toward the pines that stared down from the cliff edge.

Solitude prevailed here. What a place to have a cabin. But a whole housing development? There wasn't nearly enough room for such a project.

The trailer itself had a façade that made it appear like a real cabin, the front covered with faux logs, a full covered porch and steps. The windows had been highlighted with green frames and there were flowerboxes along the porch railings, one hanging askew, all of them empty now or gone to weeds.

Up close she could see that the construction job had been slipshod. The porch roof tilted at an angle where one of the posts had fallen in. Some two-by-fours lay on the ground along with a pile of other construction debris. The porch railing had captured tumble weeds and leaves. Animal feces littered one corner. A coyote?

Belle walked over to the pile of debris on the ground and turned over what remained of a large sign. "nyon Ran" and below it "itus Buil" was all that remained. So, this was it. Who? Why? How?

She headed back to the steps of the porch. They looked none too steady. Carefully she tested the first one, then the second. They squeaked as she climbed. When she reached the porch, she crossed it in the same tentative way and looked through the window, shading her eyes from the little light that remained. The inside looked as bad as the outside.

A microburst of wind whipped through the trees and whistled up the canyon as she moved to the door. It startled her to find the door unlocked and responsive to her push.

"Hello," she said on the threshold. "Anyone there?"

No answer. The place was deserted.

She stepped into what appeared to be a living room/office/garbage dump. In the kitchen area a few dirty pans and dishes littered the counter and sink. Silence except for the wind soughing through the canyon.

Out of habit she turned on a light switch, then jumped when the overhead light went on.

"Ohmygod! What – "

She heard the boards creak before she felt the blow on the back of her head. Pain, then bright points of light dancing in her field of vision. Her legs gave way and she fell on hands and knees. A second blow came, but she moved and it grazed her shoulder.

"Interfering bitch," seethed the voice. "Just can't leave things alone, can you?"

By the time the third blow came, Belle's mind had cleared enough for her to roll away. As the cloud in her vision lifted, she looked back at the figure of Harley James, reddish blond hair, glasses over pale eyes, a garish shirt and slacks, and an ugly snarl on his freckled face. He held one of the two-by-fours she'd seen outside in both hands like a baseball bat.

Pain hammered in her head as she struggled to her feet. "No big surprise seeing you here, Mr. James."

She backed up until her hip met the refrigerator in the kitchen. James moved closer, wary, wielding the piece of wood. She looked for a weapon. A pan? Were there any knives?

"Lady, you're too damned much trouble to live. You and that Poole girl." He did a little dance around her as though picking a choice spot to strike.

Belle edged away, but he stayed on her

"The sheriff knows I'm here."

"Like hell he does," James sneered. "If he knew, he'd have been here first."

"I left a message for him." Did that sound like the truth?

Apparently James wasn't buying it. "Nobody knows where this place is. Lady, you're lying to the wrong man. I'm an expert in that field."

Belle stood her ground, allowing her fear to show, while he inched closer, the two-by-four waving in the air. Suddenly with a loud yell she kicked, aiming for his privates.

James moved and the kick landed slightly off center. But he yelped, dropping to his knees and clutching his testicles. In that moment, Belle dived for the door of the trailer.

The kick hadn't been effective enough, though, and he was too fast. He grabbed her leg, yanking her off her feet. Her head, still thrumming from the first blow, bashed against the floor. Stars once again threatened her.

Before she could shake off the daze, James fell on top of her. His fist connected with the side of her face, shooting pain all through her, and she lost the fight for consciousness.

Almost seven-thirty and Mac sat at his desk eating Chicken Lo Mein from a carton. Rolly Carter sat across from him stuffing Kung Pao Pork into his mouth. Several empty cartons had been tossed into the wastebasket. Mac had told Carter to go on home but the big Scotsman refused.

"You stay, I stay," he'd said.

So Mac had sent him out for Chinese at Lee Wong's down the street.

An hour before, Carter had come with the galling news that Lloyd Pruitt was in town, staying at the Ponderosa Inn, on the south side of town.

"Figure he's here to start trouble at the rally tomorrow?" Carter'd asked.

"Shit," was Mac's reply.

Whatever Pruitt's aim, it wasn't to ensure a smooth event. But that damned political rally wasn't at the top of Mac's list of worries. Still no word from Belle Evans, though he'd left enough messages for her to call. They'd checked for her at the halfway house and his people were on the lookout for her car – along with a string of others. Nothing. Not a single thing.

So now he and Carter sat in the office eating Chinese and discussing possibilities.

"Maybe she skipped town for the weekend," Carter suggested around a mouthful of pork. He wiped his moustache with his forearm. "Took off for Phoenix or Vegas or something."

"Who knows?" Mac rubbed the back of his neck. Who knew how

the woman thought? For that matter, her or any woman?

"Maybe she's out looking for those boys, the two dickheads got themselves arrested in the bar fight."

Mac snarled. "Those two dickheads could be dead. So could she. She sure as hell has done enough to piss somebody off big time."

Carter looked up from his carton, concern in his eyes. "Mac, you can only do what you can do. Don't go kicking your own ass."

"You're forgetting yourself, Carter," Mac barked.

"Yeah, I know. That's part of my charm. That and my red hair."

Mac took another bite of Lo Mein. No taste to it tonight. It might as well have been wet yarn. "Now we've got this damned performance going on tomorrow. And that lousy Pruitt appears on the scene. What's he up to?"

Carter polished off the carton of Kung Pao and tossed it into the wastebasket. "He's here for trouble. Gonna rattle somebody's cage, you can bet. Suppose Andrews knows he's here?"

"I'd be surprised if he didn't."

"Election's so close," Rolly nodded. "A lot riding on this. Gonna be a fun day tomorrow."

Mac banged the carton of food on the desk, sending the chop sticks flying. That on top of everything else. Where the hell was that Evans woman?

Stars pierced the blackness. Stars that danced and laughed and taunted. Pain like hot ice shot through Belle's head, then her arms and neck. Consciousness was elusive. Awareness frolicked just beyond her reach.

Noises moved in and out of her perception. A locomotive sound – or was it wind? A party – or was it just one voice? Some kind of engine running?

She fought for understanding, fought the pain that made her want to creep back into oblivion. Her head hurt the most. She struggled to move. Couldn't. Grimacing, she labored to make her mind work.

Arms – confined behind her. Something at her wrists. Then blinding reality hit her. She was tied up! Arms, feet. And she was hunched over in some small compartment. What on earth had happened to her?

Okay, she told herself. Calm down, think it through.

She blinked, trying to remember. The map. She'd been following the map. Good. And she'd come into a canyon. All right. Then what? The dirt track. The trailer partially hidden by trees. Her exploration of the place. And pain. The struggle with James. And his fist. That was the last.

Belle sat very still and listened. The wind. She heard the wind. And just barely the water over rocks. So she was at the site. And an engine. A generator of some kind? Then she heard steps. Oh God, someone was in the trailer.

She almost laughed. Of course someone was here. James. He'd knocked her unconscious, tied her up and stuffed her in some closet. That was it, a closet.

Mustiness and the odors of days old food met her nostrils. Old grease. So James must be using this place. Pain throbbed harder. She had to stop herself from whimpering.

More steps sounded. They came closer, then went farther away. Closer, away. Pacing. He was pacing. The footsteps stopped and she held her breath.

"Where you been?" The voice slightly muffled. "Damn it, I been calling for the last three hours."

Was that how long she'd been out?

"That Evans woman came here. She got hold of that brochure the kid stole. I found it in her car."

The next part was muffled again. She caught "snooping" and "hit her," then "I can't leave the body here, dammit! The sheriff might know she came."

Belle's heart took a sickening plunge. Body? Hers? Was that her future? To die here in this place? The reality wouldn't come. Violent death was something that happened to other people, not to her. Suddenly the pain in her head didn't seem so bad, not with this new threat.

She put all her effort into listening. What would James do?

"I got her tied up, but it has to look like an accident, same as Preacher."

An accident? Time? Did she have any? Time was the great white hope of the condemned.

"I'll do this one, but you gotta deal with that Poole girl yourself, *Senator*."

Belle's breath caught.

"Maybe not now, but you will be. You'd better be, after all this."

Then there was silence – while the wind rocked the single wide as though it were a cradle.

31

The hours stretched out as Belle sat cramped in confinement. Pain increased, seizing every part of her. And her head still throbbed, centering on the place she'd been hit. Was there blood? She had no way of knowing. The malicious beast of fear gripped her and she had to fight to keep it at bay.

She listened to the man pace and bang and talk to himself. He was angry and swore a lot, but didn't say anything to give her a clue about her situation. Finally he was quiet, probably asleep.

All the time she made herself think, tried to unscramble the puzzle before her. Had Titus Development been a huge scam? Three people killed already over this place. Preacher's death was no accident. How much money would have been involved? A lot if the number of deaths was any indication.

Had Julio Morales died because he knew about this place? He'd suggested to Lily that he could get hold of enough money to take her away. Blackmail? Had he held this over them? Over his boss? Was that where he'd gotten the brochure? Had Preacher drawn the map she'd followed?

So Preacher had paid Ralph Poole to kill the boy. Ralph, the hit man. Why would they have picked such an unstable entity as Poole to do the job? Because Preacher set it up and Preacher was a fool. He and Poole had both proven themselves a liability.

Was it Preacher who had used his equipment to cut the road into this canyon? So where did Harley James come into it? Land development. As a realtor, he could have set up the deal and gotten brochures printed. The company was now defunct. But Julio had uncovered the scam. So he had to die.

Her head hurt like hell. She tried to move her cramped body and couldn't. The closet was too small. She worked at the restraint around her wrists but it wouldn't budge. Not a rope. Tape? That's what it felt like.

Senator. That was the word that chilled her. "You will be," James had said. Morgan Andrews? Lloyd Pruitt? She didn't know who else was in the running. Was Morgan Andrews somehow involved in these killings? Hard to imagine, but stranger things were possible. After all, who really knew the inner workings of a man?

Pruitt was the one who stuck in her mind. Was more likely. Pruitt, who had threatened the school and her. Pruitt, who had come down on McFarland with more threats. Pruitt, the nasty piece who had been crooked in the past, if the sheriff was correct. She'd thought when she met Harley that he was a Pruitt man. Pruitt the killer, though?

Belle fiddled with this, picturing Pruitt's bodyguard pulling out a gun and blowing her brains out. She tried to make light of it but ugly fear crept through the cracks.

And Lily. According to James, she was a danger to them. She'd have to be killed.

Now the fear swept up Belle's throat and nearly choked her. Blind rage and panic took control. She shivered violently. Her head swam.

Easy, girl, she told herself. The sheriff has a deputy watching over Lily. But they'd had one watching over Ralph Poole, too, and he was dead. Shot from a distance by someone with a good rifle.

Besides, Lily would be going out in public tomorrow, exposing herself by helping at the rally. All those people, so easy for a sniper to pick her off. Panic seized Belle again, making her frantic with despair. Pruitt and his bodyguard were probably both marksmen, living out here in Arizona, the hunters' paradise.

James was a hunter, too. And Harold Ramey. Hadn't the realtor said the two of them went hunting together frequently? Ramey? No. She couldn't see that one. And yet, look at his anger over her involvement with this case. Gun shy from past criticism? Maybe.

After a while fatigue took over and she dozed. Each time she woke, it was with a jerk of pain and recollection. She told herself that Lily would be safe, that the sheriff would see to it. He might even be looking for *her*, since she didn't call him back.

But how the hell would he find her? He didn't know the map to this place existed – Because *she hadn't told him!*

"Way to go, Belle," she hissed in the dark.

Mac didn't go home. He slept on the cot they kept in a back room of the county jail. He paid the price for it. The cot was hard and his fifty some year old back hurt like hell. The body never gets better with age, he told posterity.

He'd passed the night in vivid dreams of frustration, jerking awake, trying to adjust himself on the cot to ease the throbbing in his back, running over the facts in his head then trying to dismiss them. Conclusions from a tired brain were never accurate. He'd been in the business too long to think otherwise.

Morning twilight broke through the small window in the back room. Five-thirty. He gave up on sleep and pulled his protesting body off the cot, wiping his face and listening to the silence in the station. Staying here had been useless. The sergeant in charge had orders to wake him if anything developed. Nothing had. He stood up, stretched, groaned at his aches and headed for the door. His office was dark except for the pale light from his window. He stood staring at it, then grabbed his Stetson and left.

"I'm going home for a shower and shave," he told the female desk sergeant. "Call me if you get any word on the missing people."

"Will do, sir," the young woman said.

So young and eager to do the job, Mac thought, wondering if there was ever a time he'd been like that.

Belle woke slowly, noticing a thin line of light penetrate the darkness. She'd actually slept, deep and dreamless. Gradually, as the pain took over, she remembered where she was. It wasn't the pain as much as the numbness in her feet and hands that bothered her now.

The bar of light grew slowly brighter. Dawn? She could just make out the contours of her cell – a closet. At her back she felt some kind of implement but couldn't tell what. The door to the closet hung slightly askew. That engine noise she'd heard last night was back. A generator? That would solve the problem of electricity out here.

If she dared, she might bash the closet door open with her feet. But what then? Harley James may not be up to killing her here, but he probably wouldn't balk at hitting her again and she'd be back where she started. Maybe worse with a crushed skull.

Where would he do the killing? Was "the Senator" still in Phoenix or would he come up the mountain to see the job done? Or maybe Pruitt would simply send his bodyguard. To kill her? To kill Lily?

Too many dark questions with no answers.

If Pruitt had done it, how did he set this whole thing up, this Titus Development? Money paid out for a false land investment. God knows it'd been done plenty of times. You make up a brochure, set up a false claim on some land, make it look attractive to people with money. Then dissolve it with no trace.

And no one had records for it. How easy to defraud the public. But who did he swindle? It would be hard to take people who lived in the area. They'd want to see the development site themselves. And this canyon, lovely as it was, was no fit place for development.

So who? Out of state people? People back East? Big companies who wouldn't bother to come out here? And if it fell through, they could use it as a tax write-off. Nobody gets hurt.

No, that sounded too considerate for Lloyd Pruitt.

Even more surprising that Pruitt would go to all that trouble for money. What could he make? A few million? Good God, he had all the big corporations in Arizona begging him to take their contributions. Why would he need to pull a thing like this?

And that's when it struck her – the senator-to-be who *did* need the money. Who knew people back East.

Oh my God, was it possible?

Mac had showered, shaved, grabbed a bite of breakfast and gotten back to the office just after 7:30. The young sergeant was still at her desk and looked up in surprise to see him.

"Early, aren't you?" she said.

Mac gave her a half smile that wasn't happy and went on back to his office. Through the Venetian blind he could see Saturday traffic picking up outside on Apache Drive. When Sarah showed up fifteen minutes later, he raised his eyebrows.

"I know, sir," she said. "I was going to take the weekend off. But I've got this thing cooking with Josh at the phone company."

"I thought we did that?"

She came on into the room. "We checked the calls from James's regular phone. But he's got a cell phone we didn't find a number for until yesterday."

"Sarah, everybody's got a cell phone these days," he barked.

"Not me."

This threw Mac. A techy like Sarah and no cell phone.

She shrugged. "I hate the damned things. People talking in cars, walking down the street, going through the mall with those things glued to their ears. Pain in the ass, sir." She shrugged again.

"So?"

"So I'm checking on the man's cell phone records. Should have 'em soon. We can see who he's been calling and when."

Mac thought of something. "Check on Belle Evans' cell phone

calls in the last twenty-four hours." He gave her the number Belle had left him.

Sarah nodded, "Gotcha," and left the office.

He eased back in his chair, his jaw set. Where the goddamn hell was that woman? Where were they all? Having a picnic somewhere in the wild?

The strip of light around the closet door grew brighter still. Belle figured several hours had passed before Harley James stirred. She heard the door open, heard him clomp down the porch steps, boards creaking, then silence except for the wind and trickle of the stream nearby.

She tried again to loosen her hands and feet. Needles stung them. At least there was still feeling, though not a lot. Her head didn't hurt as severely, but the dull pain made her feel listless. A concussion?

After a while James came back up the steps and into the trailer. He stomped about, slamming cupboards and what sounded like the refrigerator door. Pans clanked to the tune of his mutterings.

"Goddamn, son-of-a-bitch."

A sudden unbidden picture of Larry came to her, and that irritating way he had of saying "I told you so." She almost laughed out loud. But at the same time, tears came. It seemed as though that lousy SOB was right after all. What a satisfaction he'd feel when they told him she'd gotten herself killed.

"Damn you, Larry," she whispered at the closet door. "Always get the last word in, don't you?"

James moved around awhile longer. A radio sounded with the morning news. She realized it was nine o'clock already. Finally the door slammed open again, steps on the porch. Nothing for perhaps fifteen seconds. Then the sound of a vehicle revving up, motor running, moving away in the distance until it was gone. Her car? Or did he have one hidden in the brush? It occurred to her how acute hearing could become when sight was taken away.

Did she dare chance it? Where had James gone? Had someone else arrived? She hadn't heard anyone but him. When she thought about it, she had few choices anyway.

Bringing her feet back as far as she could in the small space, she rammed them against the door. Sharp pain shot through her legs. Bright light nearly blinded her. The door gave almost too easily. Flimsy place, this. No wonder it was falling apart.

Worm like, she inched her way out of the closet. Only to be

obstructed by the opposite wall. Somehow she got her body through the doorway and out, turned around so that she had some room to maneuver. The thought of Lily's danger almost paralyzed her, but she fought it down.

Duct tape was wrapped several times around her legs. The idea of slipping her bound hands under her to bring them in front came to her. How many times had she seen it in the movies? But when she tried, it wasn't possible. Pain jagged through her body and she cried out. Her arms were simply too short to do the trick. Maybe if she'd been tall and slender. And double jointed. Tears stung her eyes, more from frustration and defeat than anything.

She gave up the struggle and tried to think.

Easing the closet door shut with her feet, Belle inched down the hallway to the main part of the trailer. She sucked in air when a particularly sharp jolt knifed through her. Hands and feet stung as blood trickled into them. She could see now how white her feet were above the flats she'd worn to school. Somehow she contrived to get herself into a sitting position, then remained panting for breath.

What now? Sit here and wait for Harley to come back?

The next sound sent a shock through her. Soft steps on the porch. Jesus, she hadn't heard the car come back. Maybe in all her scrambling she'd missed it. Panic nearly choked her.

The next moment she saw a head appear around the doorframe. A round face, black-eyed and scared. Jeremy Gibbs. And then Tom.

Belle almost blubbered in her joy and relief.

Mac busied himself with affairs at the station until time to leave for the courthouse. Scott had called him and fussed over some damned thing. No word had come on the missing people. At the Ponderosa Inn Pruitt was being watched by Mac's deputies. No activity as yet. What was he up to?

Nine-fifteen. The political spectacle would begin at ten. The one thing Mac didn't need today was a fracas between candidates on the courthouse steps.

Finally he'd put it off long enough, strapped on his Smith and Wesson double action revolver, and grabbed his Stetson. Out in the hall Sarah waylaid him.

"Got something for you, sir. I think you're going to want to see this."

The tone in Sarah's voice told him he didn't. He paused for several heartbeats, dread crawling like a worm along his intestines. "Come in the office," he told her and led the way.

He propped himself on the edge of his desk, needing support, and nodded to her.

Sarah watched him cautiously as she handed him the first of the pages she held. "Cell phone records of the calls James made in the last week."

Three of them stood out. One on Sunday, the day Belle Evans had paid James a visit. One on Wednesday, the day James had gone missing. And one more, made last evening to the Granite Hotel, the place where Morgan Andrews had spent the night.

32

"Dear God," Belle gasped. "We'd all given you boys up for dead. Where in *hell* have you been?"

"Whoa, Miz E, look at your face," Jeremy cried. "Who hit you? And there's blood on your head."

"I'm okay," she said. "Just get me loose. Where were you?"

Jeremy worked at the duct tape around Belle's wrists. Tom, her ankles. She sucked in air as hundreds of needles stabbed her at the flow of blood returning.

"Sorry, Miz E," Tom said, the acne on his face red from embarrassment.

"Man, we didn't mean to worry you guys," Jeremy insisted. "Figured Tom's ole man'd smack him around anyway when we skipped school that first day. Probably pissed as all getout."

"More like scared to death that something had happened to you."

After they'd released her, Belle sat on the floor a minute longer, getting her bearings and trying to force her head to work. It pounded like a jackhammer, each beat a thrust of pain. The two boys squatted and watched her as though afraid she'd faint or maybe even drop dead.

"Help me stand," she said and they obeyed, each of them taking an arm and pulling her to her feet. She wobbled a little as she walked back and forth in the trailer, getting her legs back. Glancing around the place, she had the boys check the bedroom area.

"He's been sleeping back there," Jeremy said cocking his head in that direction. "Room's a pig pen, like a bomb hit it. Man, my ma'd shoot me dead if I left that kinda mess."

Tom came back. "Checked the bathroom. Don't think the water's hooked up." He looked in the small refrigerator. "Couple-a beers. Guess he's got electricity. Maybe a generator out back."

They listened and heard it go on, the same hum Belle had heard off and on during her confinement.

Jeremy looked out the front window. "Better get outta here 'fore he comes back. He could bring somebody with him."

Ice skittered down Belle's back. 'The Senator' needed her dead.

And if the boys were with her, they were in danger, too. And Lily – Lily was at the political rally this morning. Working for Morgan Andrews.

"Okay, fellows, here's the plan. Tom, you have your truck?"

He nodded.

"Then you two get back to town and find the sheriff. I'll drive my own car and stop at that corner store to phone."

She explained Lily's danger and almost regretted it when she saw the boys stiffen, Tom's expression fierce, Jeremy's becoming belligerent. Two unlikely heroes ready to save the damsel in distress. She would have laughed but for the fear that threatened to immobilize her.

Jeremy shook his head. "Can't take your car, Miz E. Tires're slashed."

Belle ran out the door and down the porch steps. A stiff wind and a low ceiling of mean-looking clouds met them. Her Honda was pitiful. Not one but two tires flat, making it lean dangerously to the left.

"Damn." She muttered. She swung the door open and found the contents ransacked.

She straightened, fought panic. "Okay, boys, plan B. We all go in Tom's truck. And hope to God we're on time."

Tom's pickup, his '48 Chevy with the old divided windshield, was painted a bright apple green and sported over-sized wheels. The miniature cab wasn't made for three people. Jeremy got squeezed in the middle; the open windows gave Tom and Belle some elbow room. Wind whistled through the cottonwoods and bent the willows along the creek. Tom backed up, then turned onto the blade road and started up the hill.

"Where have you been all this time?" Belle demanded.

Jeremy tried to shrug. "Man, we was up at the cabin. We found it last year up by Swanson's Lake. Deserted, you know, and broken down."

"Me and Jere stayed in it a couple-a times this spring," Tom said. "Kind-a like a hideout, away from my old man and his ma."

"Everyone's been looking for you," she told them. "We've been frantic."

"Yeah?" Jeremy asked, a lilt of pride in his voice. He lost the lilt when he saw she wasn't happy with him. "We was just trying to get away from Carlos and his gun. Scared the hell outta us, man."

Tom changed gears, jabbing Jeremy in the stomach with his elbow. A blast of wind rocked the truck as they reached the top. They had just made it to the old track when Jeremy let out another squawk.

"Look out!" he cried. "Here comes James!"

After Sarah left, Mac stood in the middle of his office staring not at anything concrete, but at memories. And regrets. Morgan, who had been a buddy in high school, Morgan who had stayed connected with him, been there when life turned rotten, not once but over and over.

Morgan, who'd spent so much money on the last political campaign and lost. Had he needed more to wage this push for the senate? Now that he had a real chance of getting elected since his nemesis Hank Grisholm was out of the running? Had Titus Land Development been his way of making money so he could save Arizona? Bringing it into the twenty-first century? "My God, Morgan."

Pruitt had most of the big corporations in the state tied up for campaign donations. Pruitt, the bastard who deserved to be thrown in jail and kept there for the next seventy-five years for all the crooked deals he'd made.

Mac couldn't get the truth to sink in. He was swallowed up by disbelief and pain.

In a little while Sarah came back into the office, her face showing caution, her eyes veiled. "Sir, I – uh – I ran bank records on Mr. Andrews."

Mac's gaze met hers. "On a Saturday?"

She shrugged. "Banks are electronic these days, remember?" When he didn't speak, she showed him the printouts. "This one was before the Titus thing started. And this is last year's – one year later."

Mac had to force himself to focus on the figures. Morgan had depleted his reserves by the end of the last senatorial election. In three years he'd managed to increase his bank account by six and a half million. No small sum since it was at the expense of three lives they knew about. Poole might have ended up dead in a few years anyway. Who knew about Preacher? But the boy, though probably dead through an act of stupidity on his part, didn't deserve this.

And what about Gibbs and Kelliker? Any connection? Suddenly Mac straightened. Lily Poole apparently knew too much. And Belle Evans. Disappeared.

"Christ," Mac hissed. Now he was in motion. He grabbed the phone and called dispatch. "Get me Deputy Hollis." He waited. "Where are you?" he asked when he was connected. He could hear the sound of people in the background and of a heavy wind.

"Down at the square, sir."

"What are you doing there? I told you to stay on the Poole girl."

"I am, sir. Somebody picked her up at The Pines and brought her here. But they took her on inside the courthouse."

Mac had to catch the breath that suddenly left him. "Who picked her up?"

"Didn't hear that, sir. It's crazy down here. Mobs of people."

"I asked you who picked up Lily Poole."

"Tall guy, suit and tie. I think it's that friend of Mr. Andrews."

Sickness. Cold sickness. Okay, calm down, he told himself. "Hollis, I want you to go into the courthouse, find her, and bring her out. Two of our units are already at the square. We'll alert them."

Mac swept a glance at Sarah still standing there. He set his hat on his head, adjusted the revolver in its holster, and strode out the door.

Belle and the boys stared at the bright cherry sports car blocking their way up the track. Total surprise registered in Harley James' freckled face and pale eyes. Then fear, then anger. Belle watched the changes in a disconnected way as though they were performed by an actor on stage.

Suddenly Tom jerked the wheel hard to the right. "Hold on," he hissed, wrenching the gear shift. Jeremy yelped at the elbow in his side and Belle grabbed the door for support as the truck swerved off the track and through the brush. It hopped and joggled over rocks and small bushes. She hung on for dear life while her head throbbed with each jolt. Jeremy's bulk shoved her against the side. When she looked back she saw the Ford sports car struggling to back up along the rutted track she'd taken the day before and remembered the condition of the road.

Tom looked into the rearview mirror and grinned. "Gottem," he barked.

The little Miata hit a snag. Useless to try backing down a road like that. James would have to find a place to turn around. Jeremy whooped and Tom jerked the truck back onto the track. Belle figured they could get a head start on James. And while Tom's truck was no match for the cherry red car on the highway, the situation would be different out here in the wild with the bigger tires and higher clearance.

Then she remembered Harley James had a phone. He could get help. She had to force down panic. Take it one moment at a time. Lily needed her.

"How in the world did you boys find me?"

The truck bounded over a rock, leaving them without gravity until they plummeted back to earth.

"We was out getting food at Calvin's Gas Station when we spotted Mr. James," Jeremy explained. "He was doing the same thing, getting food and stuff. He didn't know us but we seen him before, right, Tom?"

Tom nodded and kept his concentration on the track.

"Swanson's Lake's not far from here. So we followed him, you know. Found this place."

Another jolt sent them flying. Belle clenched her teeth against the pain in her head. She thought of Lily, of the girl's danger. She had to be strong.

"Last night we come to check him out," Jeremy continued. "Man, when we seen your car here – well, we was afraid he'd done you, Miz E."

"He did me, all right. I never spotted his car."

"Over in the trees by the creek," Jeremy said. "Guess he figured he was clever."

She gave a bark of laughter. "Too clever for me."

"Nah," Jeremy said. "You just wasn't expecting him. Me and Tom's been watching him."

They reached Cactus Lane and the ride was easier. And faster. The clouds hovered closer, black and heavy and sparking dry lightning. The wind increased, making the trees sway around them, the force bombarding the truck as they drove. Tom gave the small pickup everything he had. Before long they reached Cave Road and pavement. Belle had to quell her anxiety. The closer they got to town, the more it assailed her.

They hadn't gone far down Cave when Tom, looking in his rearview mirror, yelled, "Shit!"

Belle looked behind. The Miata followed not five hundred yards away.

Mac only got as far as the front desk when his cell phone went off. It was Carter.

"Okay, Mac," Carter said, "I think we got trouble. Pruitt's on the march."

"Tell me."

"He'n some of his boys just left the Ponderosa Inn. A crowd – a couple-a dozen people were waiting for him. We watched 'em gathering. Suddenly they got big signs. 'LEAVE ARIZONA ALONE,' 'TOO MUCH GOVERNMENT,' 'ANDREWS, GO HOME,' that kinda thing. It doesn't look friendly."

Mac wiped a hand over his face. That was all he needed. A riot on the lawn of the courthouse. "Okay, Rolly. I'll contact Scott. Right now I'm worried about the Poole girl. Hollis lost her. Cochran disappeared with her inside the building."

"What's she doing there anyway?"

"Working for Andrews, I gather."

Carter sounded relieved. "Then she's safe."

"No," Mac said, his voice flat with the sickness in him. "Get there, Rolly. Find her. I'm on my way."

He was grateful Carter didn't argue or ask for explanations. He got hold of Barry Scott, told him about Pruitt and his hecklers, told the chief if he didn't want a first class riot on his hands he'd better get his ass in gear. Scott didn't sound friendly and Mac didn't give a damn. He was just stepping into his Jeep when the car radio buzzed him. Deputy Hollis.

"Sir, Mr. Cochran and Lily just came outta the building. They're carrying a bunch of brochures or something. What do you want me to do?"

"Get her, Hollis. Just tell her she's wanted at the station. Don't make a fuss. Keep it low key. But get her. Carter's on the way."

Mac was out of the parking lot and turning onto the street when he got the next call. This one from George Hornby, on duty at the square.

"Mac, you're not gonna like this."

"I don't like anything I've heard so far, George. What now?"

"Well, you know that Hispanic kid, Hernandez? Name's Carlos? We just spotted him. He's here at the courthouse."

"Is the whole damned world coming apart?" Mac shoved down the knot that was filling his stomach. "Pick him up, George."

"We'll try, but he's disappeared in the crowd. You wouldn't believe the people here. They got this F-ing craft show going – tents all over the place. People like I never saw 'em – for the show, for the political scene. God Almighty, you'd think they were giving away a million bucks."

"Find him, George. For Christ's sake, find him."

Mac stuck the mike back in place and gunned the motor for the square.

Belle knew despair as the James' car closed on them. "We're not going to make it," she breathed. "He's going to stop us."

She thought of Lily, unsuspectingly agreeing to work for Andrews at the rally today. Blithely helping out, never imagining her danger. Who would? Morgan Andrews seemed the epitome of all that was fine and decent. Caring politician, family man, help to those in need, wanting what was right for the state and the country – and long time friend to

Sheriff McFarland.

A man like that a killer? How? Money, most likely – to run a campaign. Any means to a justifiable end. She almost laughed, but sickness choked her instead. Now Lily would die. And herself? And the boys? Wouldn't they all have to die for the greater good?

"He's gaining," Tom hissed.

Belle looked back. The Ford was almost upon them. She could see the ugly set of Harley James' freckled face, the anger and determination in his eyes.

He started to pull abreast of the small truck when Tom yelled, "*No way!*"

The next moment the Chevy pickup swerved off the road, plowing through a wire fence, and into a pasture – while the cherry red Miata sailed on by.

33

Belle thought her teeth would jar loose from the ride, but she wanted to kiss Tom for his initiative. Not too soon, though. This field could turn out to be a dead end.

Clouds rumbled overhead, lightning shot horizontally across the sky, and a blast of wind whipped to a frenzy, rocking the little Chevy pickup. Tom drove like a wild man. Jeremy yelped every time they hit a rut or a rock or a bush. Belle just clenched her jaw and prayed the boy knew what he was doing. Harley James' couldn't follow.

They'd gone less than three miles when they neared a line of houses. Tom didn't stop. He burst through the wire fence at the other end of the pasture and rammed through a backyard, plowing into a flower garden at the side.

Belle gasped as the truck mutilated the symmetry of the garden, ran over the burnished mound of mums and snapdragons, and threw up marigolds behind. Then he knocked over a fountain with a statue of a frog on top. When they hit the pavement, she wanted to hug Tom again.

"I love this man," Jeremy laughed. "Ain't he something, Miz E?"

In the side mirror Belle watched a woman explode from the house, yelling and waving her arms. Tom drove on, gathering speed.

"Maybe we should have stopped there to call the police."

Tom shook his head. "Faster this way. Almost to town."

He took a right turn, a left, then another right, ignoring traffic lights and stop signs. Belle thanked God few people were on the streets on this Saturday morning. Now she recognized where they were and her anxiety grew. Lily. Could they get to Lily in time? She kept urging the truck faster. Please let Lily be all right. Please.

They were doing fine, making time until they turned onto Ponderosa Avenue. And there was the traffic jam – a barricade across the road to the square.

"Damn it," Tom cried. "Now what?"

Mac, his Jeep's siren splitting the air, pulled past the east roadblock into the melee. A few people had sneaked onto the cordoned off streets to park around the square. The place was awash with humanity. White tents circled the square like a mushroom ring – the craft show in bloom.

Above, though, the clouds bore down on the earth as if to smother it. Lightning flicked and a heavy wind worried the tent flaps on the green.

A huge crowd filled the walkway leading to the courthouse steps. Some waved flags, a few carried signs of "TUCSON SAYS ANDREWS FOR SENATOR," and "A VOTE FOR MORGAN IS A VOTE FOR FLAGSTAFF." Looked like people from all over the state were here.

On top of the courthouse steps and to the side stood Cochran with Lily next to him in a bright red blouse. Mac breathed his relief. He couldn't spot Hollis but knew the deputy would be close. At the mike in the center was Senator Greyburn giving the introduction. The man looked tall and confident and all-American. At this distance and in this crowd Mac only caught snatches of the senator's words. All the usual things politicians said about their colleagues, he supposed.

He thought of Morgan and a new wave of sickness washed him like polluted water. Damn you, Morgan, how could you do this thing? Betray everyone who's ever believed in you.

Mac left his Jeep in the middle of the street and strode toward the square. He spotted Carter's red head at the other end and then the Pruitt mob, signs raised above the crowd, larger and more prevalent than the Andrews banners. Thunder growled a warning note at the crowd as he made out Pruitt, off a little from his people and flanked by a couple of his bodyguards, it looked like.

The introduction on the steps came to an end. The audience applauded while a small band assembled in the gazebo played "Hail to the Chief" as Morgan emerged from the doors of the courthouse. The applause increased, swelling even over the sound of wind, and he stepped up to the microphone.

"Thank you, thank you," he told the people. "My, what a warm welcome. You touch my heart."

More applause.

"We're here today to talk about changes in Arizona. We're here to talk about the terrible destruction caused by hate crimes and their revenge. We want to make this a safer place, a better place for future generations."

Then two things happened. Paul Cochran, phone to ear, scowled, took Lily Poole's arm, and slipped back into the building.

At the same time Pruitt and his crowd, banners raised, voices piercing the din of the speakers, started pushing and jostling to get through to the steps of the courthouse.

"Hold on," Tom said, an echo of before.

"Tom, they'll stop us for sure if you try it," Belle insisted.

But he didn't listen. He swerved to avoid the center of the sawhorses cordoning off the street, caught the edge of one and knocked it over as he shoved past with his pickup. Then he started down the street, beeping at anyone who barred his way.

"Jeeze, Tom, you got balls, man," Jeremy laughed, the sound a touch maniacal.

Belle's grip on the window frame made her knuckles white. They had to slow down to avoid hitting those who ignored Tom's horn, losing precious moments. She wanted to yell 'Murder! Life and Death! Get out of the way!' So many bodies. So much confusion. A short distance from here a young girl would be killed.

Just two blocks from the square it happened. A couple of squad cars descended on Tom's truck. He screeched to a halt as the officers got out and came forward. Granite police. Belle's stomach tightened.

"Hey, kid, whadaya think you're doing here?" the older one demanded. "You got a permit to be driving down this street?"

"Carl says he rammed right through the blockade," the younger one told them. He had his hand on the shoulder mike.

"We need to see your license, buddy," the older one told Tom. "Step outta the vehicle."

Belle didn't hesitate. She jumped out of the truck and confronted the two cops. "I'm Isabel Evans. I'm with the Granite School System. This is a matter of life or death!" she snapped. "A young girl is going to be killed if we don't hurry."

"Lady, just calm down," the older one said. "Outta the truck. All of you."

"We need help," Belle insisted. "Now. Can you get hold of Sheriff McFarland? We need him."

The younger officer looked scornful. "Not his jurisdiction, lady. We're in charge." He looked her over, her wrinkled clothes, hair tangled and bloody, the bruise on the side of her face. "You been in a fight or something? Drinking?" And moved toward her.

"Your license, kid," the first one insisted.

Belle glared at the obtuse young man. "You asshole. Lily Poole is going to be killed if we don't get to her."

"Lady – "

"Screw you," she hissed. With stomach churning, she took off for the square and the crowd around it.

She heard him yell after her, then heard Jeremy's voice raised in abuse, probably to take the patrolman's attention away from her. Jaw set and tears stinging her eyes, she ran.

Thunder rattled the sky, the sound ricocheting among the buildings. She shoved through groups of tourists blocking her way, praying Tom and Jeremy would keep the two cops occupied.

"Excuse me, excuse me," she said. Some of the people were irritated and muttered snide comments. A few swore at her. Someone's dog barked as she passed it. No matter, Lily needed her.

Out of breath and panting, she made the square. Was a cop following her? Where was McFarland? Her head swam. Some kind of fracas was going on, people with signs shouting, angry.

Then she spotted Andrews on the top step of the courthouse. And Cochran. And Lily in a bright red blouse. Her breath came at last.

But Cochran was talking on a cell phone. He looked out at the crowd as though searching, then he took Lily's arm and led her into the building.

"No," Belle hissed. "*No!*"

A deafening crack of thunder shook the ground. The lightning flash that followed lit the sky like flood lights.

Belle's race took on a nightmare quality, trying to make it through a sea of molasses, desperate to go forward but hindered by the cloying stickiness of the substance. People swarmed the square, obstructing her way. "Let me through. Please. I have to get by."

Somehow she wound her way to the west corner of the building. Andrews' voice came over the speakers, the senatorial quality laced with compassion, understanding and determination. But the crowd grew rowdy. She heard descent in its midst, shouts of protest. Some yelled, "Pruitt!"

Then she saw him, the baby-faced little man, the edges of his white Stetson flicking in the wind as he stood three steps up, pointing at Andrews. Blue uniforms tried to subdue him and his people without success. A fight broke out on the fringes. Then another.

Suddenly Belle's gaze was caught by the two emerging from the side entrance. Cochran, and he had Lily in tow, her red blouse easy to spot. Down the steps they went, Cochran almost dragging the girl, until they were swallowed up in an ooze of people and craft tents.

Belle took off in that direction, swimming her way through the crowd, cursing, sobbing, praying, diving between and around. She thought she saw his head above the ocean of humanity. And a flash of red. But it disappeared.

"Oh, God!" she cried in despair.

That last crack of thunder staggered the crowd. They looked anxious now, as though they might pull back. If there were anywhere to pull back to. Mac wasn't sure which way to go himself. Scott's blues were scarce. What happened to that huge force he'd been threatening? Hell, let that be his problem. He was in charge of this fiasco. Screw it. Screw Pruitt. Mac's job was to protect Lily Poole.

He got a call on his cell phone and yanked it out of his pocket. "Deputy Hollis, sir. I've lost the girl again. She went inside."

"Yeah. I saw it," Mac said. "Get in there. Find her."

"Sir, I don't want to disturb Andrews' speech."

"Disturb the speech, Hollis. Get into the courthouse. Find that girl."

The next call was Rolly Carter. "Mac, there's no way in hell to stop Pruitt's people. Already got some fights breaking out. This thing's crazy."

"I told you to forget Pruitt. Carlos Hernandez was spotted in the crowd. Find him, Rolly. We've gotta put a cap on this thing."

"And Pruitt?"

"Barry can get his fat ass off his chair and deal with it. It's his problem now. Ours is Hernandez and the Poole girl."

Mac, with his sheriff's badge, was able to break through the crowds on High Street to the west side of the square along Ponderosa. Carter's patrol car was parked at an angle but he and Taggert weren't in it. Mac pushed his way through the onlookers. Morgan's speech came across the speakers but was garbled by the yelling from the crowd – Pruitt supporters yelling at the Andrews people. Another clap of thunder and flicker of lightning.

Morgan looked nervous on top of the courthouse steps. Mac could tell he was trying to maintain his composure and suspected it was a struggle. Hurt and disillusionment jabbed him and he clamped his teeth against it. Why, Morgan? Why you?

Shoving his way through the crowd, he reached the gazebo off to the side of the lawn and climbed the stairs. Between the band and onlookers the stand was full to bursting, but he used his badge to move people aside and stood searching the courthouse steps. He was just in time to see Cochran disappear into the crowd at the west side. He pulled out his cell to call, then paused.

A curly brown head moved in that direction. Belle? Belle Evans? A hard knot he hadn't realized was in his throat dislodged.

But it formed again the next moment as he spotted Carlos Hernandez, not far behind and heading in her direction.

Belle felt as though she were caught in a bog, moving in and between people. A blast of wind whipped the flaps of tents and made them sway dangerously. One woman cried out as she grabbed a display easel before it fell. Several others were too late. Pottery shattered somewhere.

Belle saw Cochran and Lily cross the street at the far end of the square. Her view was blocked for a moment by a large man with a dog, then she saw them disappear down Ventura Avenue. She shoved past more people and hurried after them.

By the time she reached the corner, there was no sign of them. She took off in the direction she'd seen them go. Please let her find them. Please, oh please.

Starting down Ventura, she knew panic. Where were they? Where had they gone? She kept moving because she didn't know what else to do. Crossing the next intersection she looked both ways. Now where? Three blocks, four blocks. If she guessed wrong, Lily was dead. Or maybe she was anyway.

Then she spotted Cochran's head and a splash of red down an alley. She took off after them. Breath came heavy as she ran. Purpose gave her the energy of a younger woman. What if that were Ellie? What if someone were trying to hurt her daughter? Lily had no one to protect her, no mother to race like a crazy person to her rescue.

The sky split with a giant crack and flash of light. And the first heavy drops of rain hit the ground.

As Belle ran, she heard the clatter of some kind of generator, growing louder the closer she came. She shot around the corner to the alley and came to an old factory for Langley Vitamins, still in sporadic use, the ancient generator deafening. The building covered half the block. It's windows grey with dirt, brick walls stained with age and industry. But the back alley was deserted. No sign of them. And no one around to help.

Slowing slightly, she searched right and left for some indication they were here. No movement, no life. Large drops, heavy with their burden, danced on her shoulders and wet her hair. Where could Lily be?

Then she spotted an old warehouse down at the end of the alley. It was behind the factory, windows boarded up, weeds taking over what bare ground there was, the place no longer in use. A cottonwood grew between the two buildings, huge and bent, one large branch of it dead.

Belle stopped, gasping for breath. She crept to the door of the warehouse. Wind rattled the leaves on the cottonwood and swept dust and rain across the street. The factory generator clanked and vibrated. She couldn't make out any sounds in the building. Then a cry. Lily's.

"No, damn it," she barked and shoved open the door.

Her eyes took a moment to focus in the dim light from cracks at the windows. The room seemed empty. Over the din outside she could barely hear voices. Careful where she stepped, she moved toward more light where the inside door stood partially ajar. Her steps had a muffled ring in the hollow room.

She reached the door and eased it open. Then peered around the edge into the muzzle of a Remington rifle with Paul Cochran on the other end.

34

"Don't hurt Lily," Belle begged. "Please, Mr. Cochran. She's not to blame for any of this."

Wind, carrying a few large splatters of rain, whipped at the old roof of the warehouse. Thunder cracked and lightning lit the windows, illuminating the features of the occupants and of the Remington hunting rifle the man held.

Paul Cochran's face showed a burden almost too great to carry. "I'm sorry, Mrs. Evans. You can't possibly know how sorry I am."

Lily stood several yards away hugging herself, lit by an electrical flash of light from a partially boarded up window. The factory generator next door whined in the storm.

"Is he gonna kill me, Miz E?" Lily asked in a small voice that shook. "Like Julio?"

"Mr. Cochran, you don't have to do this," Belle insisted. She remained before him, his rifle pointed at her chest. Despair swept her but she fought it off.

Cochran motioned for Belle to move next to Lily. "Sacrifices have to be made. It's for the good of the country."

Belle wrapped her arms around Lily then stared at him incredulously. Anger shoved at the fear, anger at this impossible situation. "We're dying for the good of our country? Oh please. I suppose you'll give us a ceremonial burial in Arlington National Cemetery." She gave a harsh laugh. "What do you know about the good of our country? You ran a scam to cheat and steal."

"You don't understand. Morgan needed that money. He couldn't have waged the campaign without it. This state needs him. This country needs him."

Lily shivered against Belle and Belle held her tighter.

"Needs a man who cheats and steals and murders? Mr. Cochran, what planet are you from?"

"No," he cried, moving closer, his face filled with pain. "We didn't hurt anyone. Not with Titus. And those companies got a nice tax write-off when it didn't pan out. This way they were doing something valuable for a change. Good God, they'd been milking that money from the public all these years. Time they gave some of it back for an important cause."

"The old Robin Hood story, right?" she said. A huge clap of thunder rattled the warehouse followed by a blinding streak of light.

"Morgan is a great man. He needs the chance to do something with that greatness." The intensity in his words was almost convincing. "Lloyd Pruitt is a sewer rat. You know that, Mrs. Evans. You've met him. His ways of getting money are far worse than what we did. He doesn't deserve to be garbage collector, let alone senator."

Belle had to shake herself at the man's reasoning. "You committed murder, for the love of God. You killed people."

"Julio," Lily sobbed, shoving forward, that strong will of hers surfacing. "You bastard, you killed Julio!"

Cochran straightened to attention, rifle aimed, but she didn't ease back.

"That was terrible," he said. "We never meant for that to happen. The boy – he stumbled onto the Titus deal. He was going to report it." Profound sorrow etched his features in the flash of light.

"You paid Lily's father to kill him," Belle said.

Cochran filled his lungs and glanced from Belle to Lily. "Julio was blackmailing us. He shouldn't have done that."

Lily's features wore outrage. "Julio was trying to get money to take me away. He was working hard to help out his family who lived in *poverty* in Mexico. Damn you, *you* should be the one dead. Not *him*!"

When Belle saw Cochran stiffen again, she took Lily's arm and pulled her back. As rational as the man sounded, she knew he wasn't. He stood on the edge of a precipice, trying to justify in some weird logic the people he'd had killed, or killed himself.

"Ralph Poole?" she asked, nodding at the rifle. "You did that?"

"He was no loss. You were better off without him, Lily. If only you'd left it alone."

The cold logic sent ice moving through Belle. Panic fought for dominance. But her need to save Lily and her own self-preservation held sway.

"Fred Preacher?" she asked. "Your doing? What was his part? Did he cut the road into the canyon for you?"

Cochran winced. He shifted his weight, tightened his grip on the weapon. "Sometimes you have to deal with scum to get things done."

"And Harley James was part of it, too."

His gaze narrowed. "How did you find that place? What led you there? Why couldn't you just leave it alone? This is your own fault. You did this to yourself."

Now he brought the gun up and his eye to the sight. There was no mistaking his intent. The man was a fanatic who believed completely in his cause.

"No!" Belle screamed and gave Lily a terrific shove, knocking herself off center in the process.

An earsplitting report filled the warehouse. She felt something slice through her upper left arm. The impact brought her to her knees. This had happened to her in the past, back in Ohio. Before she could react, another shot deafened her, but with a different reverberation.

"You murderer!" came the cry. "I heard you. You killed my cousin. Now I kill you!" Carlos stood in the doorway, his face fiery, his revolver in his hand.

A third shot sang out and Paul Cochran slumped to the floor while the warehouse shook with the storm.

As he ran, Mac used his cell phone to get hold of Rolly Carter. "Hernandez. I spotted him. And Belle Evans. Cochran, too, with Lily. They headed west down Ventura. Get a squad car to follow me."

He ran, shoving his way through the crowd of people. Morgan's voice over the speakers faltered as the chaos in the crowd increased. Wind whipped the tents. Large splashes of rain pelted him. A crack of thunder shook the earth beneath. When he got to Ventura he moved faster, making it to the corner, then down. Christ, he thought, the whole world was coming apart. The storm raged around him as though adding truth to his thoughts.

Where would they go? He tried to picture that area of town. The Langley Vitamin Factory was down a few blocks. And the abandoned warehouse. He ran faster, his Stetson staying on in spite of the wind. When he reached the alley to the vacant warehouse he slowed, checking left and right. His man in the squad car phoned and he told them where he was. Then, over the din of wind and the factory generator, he heard the shot. He took off. A moment later and there were two more.

"Oh Christ!" Too late?

He moved fast, his heart pounding in his head, trying not to think, still wanting to hope. Three shots. He'd heard three shots. The rain started in earnest, washing the dry landscape, plastering his shirt to his chest. Two blocks later he reached the warehouse, turned the corner and pulled out his revolver.

At first he heard no human sounds. But when he pushed the door open the girl's voice echoed softly through the building. Then came the siren from the squad car. Slowly, easily Mac stepped into the building, scanning left and right. The darkness blinded him. He listened. Lily's voice was more distinct. He caught snatches of words over the wind and the generator next door. Then Belle Evans' voice and the muscles in his chest loosened. No sound of Cochran or Hernandez.

As his sight adjusted he made for the inner door and more light. Flashes from outside aided him. He kept his gun poised. When he reached the doorway he saw two legs sprawled on the floor, Paul Cochran. He stepped around the man and entered the room. The other two were squatting on the floor, Lily doing something to Belle Evans' arm. Mac let the air out in a rush.

"Damn it, Belle, where the hell have you been?"

She looked up at him with a wavering smile. "Sorry, Eli. Didn't mean to worry you."

"She's hurt," Lily told him, her panic barely contained. "Mr. Cochran shot her."

"I'm all right." Belle glanced at the man on the floor. "Cochran's been shot and I don't know if he's alive. Carlos did that. "

Mac holstered his gun and knelt beside the man, feeling for a pulse in his neck. Cochran was alive but bleeding badly. Mac grabbed his mike. "Secure in the warehouse but Hernandez is on the loose and armed. He just shot a man. Get an ambulance over here."

The next minute two of his deputies entered through the door. "Ambulance on the way," one said.

Mac nodded then went to Belle. "How bad is it?" He squatted on one knee to take a look. Her left sleeve was covered with blood. He paused at the bruise darkening the side of her face.

"I think he just winged me, as they say in the westerns," she said. "Don't worry, this has happened to me before." She slunk back against Lily, losing strength. "I believe I've got some bad news for you about your friend."

"Yeah, I know." He looked away, betraying nothing in his demeanor.

He concentrated on her arm, pushing the other thing aside to be dealt with later. He couldn't tell for sure in the intermittent light but Lily seemed to have gotten the bleeding stopped, or at least slowed.

Then his cell phone rang. It was Carter. "Mac, we spotted him. The Hernandez kid."

"Grab him, Rolly. But be careful. He's got a gun and he's willing to use it. Just don't let him get away."

"Gotcha." Suddenly three gun shots sounded over the phone. "Oh shit!" A pause. "Oh Jesus."

"What? What, for Christ's sake?"

Silence on the other end. Then, "You better get up here, Mac. It's pretty bad."

Mac's stomach knotted. "What happened?"

Another hesitation. "It's that Hernandez kid. He just shot Andrews."

Rain whipped the town square, battering tents or sweeping them off their foundations. Most of the people had run for cover already; a few others stood transfixed by the drama being enacted in spite of the torrent. Thunder and lightning bombarded the town.

Mac, unconscious of the drenching, knelt on the top step of the courthouse beside his long time friend. He held Andrews by the shoulders, close to him, trying to shield the dying man from the rain. Morgan had been shot three times in the stomach and chest and was grabbing onto the last moments of his life.

Deep and aching sorrow washed through Mac until he swayed with the impact. Carter and the others kept back, giving him room.

"Why, Morgan? I never knew a better man than you. Why would you do this?"

"Mac." Blood gurgled in his throat. "Mac, – so sorry. Just wanted to – to help our state – help people – needed money for – campaign. Meant – right. Got out of hand. Paul?"

"On his way to the hospital."

"Did he – shoot –?"

Mac shook his head.

Andrews' face seemed to clear. "Told him not to – told him not the girl –"

Mac gazed down on his friend, the ache in his throat so huge he couldn't swallow. Andrews looked up at him, his eyes warm and caring, then concerned. "Mary Jane?"

"I'll take care of it."

The man relaxed, his body went limp, his head fell back and his heart stopped. Mac held him, not sure he could let go as the wind and rain slashed across the courthouse steps.

After a while, though, he stood and looked around. Down below, Barry Scott finally had his force out, holding back the few who braved the weather. Where the hell had he been when Morgan was shot?

Cameramen struggled to get by but were kept at bay. They always seemed to smell out disaster the way a vulture found carrion.

His people had picked up Hernandez, evidently in no hurry now that his cousin had been avenged. One of Mac's units had spotted the cherry red Miata heading for Flagstaff and nabbed James. Cochran was being helicoptered down to a Phoenix hospital, his wounds severe but not critical. And Belle and Lily were alive. Carter had even grabbed Gibbs and Kelliker away from the GPD who wanted to throw them in jail for running their barricade.

He glanced down again at Morgan, that familiar face in repose, washed clean in the deluge. How could he break the news to Mary Jane? He'd have to hurry if he didn't want the newscasters to get there first.

But what could he tell her? What could he say? How could he explain what this man, a man they'd both known for so many years, both loved and trusted, had done?

Mac looked out into the storm and let the rain wash down his cheeks.

35

"I'm coming up there," Louise threatened over the phone.

"I'm all right, Lou," Belle insisted. "Come on up. I'd give anything to have you here. But my arm isn't that bad. And my head will recover."

It was Sunday afternoon. Belle had gone to the local hospital Saturday morning for medication and a tetanus shot. They'd checked her head where James had hit her, put her arm in a sling and sent her home. All she had to show for her ordeal was an interesting bandage on her arm and the bruise on her face for the kids at school to exclaim over.

Saturday evening Eli McFarland had come to talk. Apparently they were now on a first name basis. She'd explained her actions on Friday and Saturday and had expected him to chew her out. Instead she was struck by the mantle of sorrow surrounding him. She found out he'd had to break the news to Andrews' wife.

"We checked out the canyon," he'd told her. "Found the two-by-four with Preacher's blood on it. Not quite washed off by the storm we had. It's public land up there, but hidden away. Nobody would find it. Well, without a map." A little edge to his voice that time. "This wasn't a hate killing, but I guess in the end it was revenge, a kind of harsh justice."

The storm that took place had been cited as one of the memorable ones. A 'gully-washer,' lasting over two hours. It drenched the parched earth, filling up the streams and arroyos, causing flash floods across back roads and washes and taking off roofs with the wind. Afterwards it had drifted on into New Mexico, leaving the land soaked and the air clearer, less constricted with suffocating apprehension.

"The main thing is, Lily's all right. And so are the boys," Belle told her sister. "The three of them came over this morning to see me. Adrian ushered them up and insisted on staying to hear the whole story. Poor Adrian. He said he had a migraine worrying about me."

"Yeah, poor Adrian."

"The boys brought me flowers," Belle laughed. "What a pair they are."

"A pair of assholes," Louise muttered. "But heroes, too. Damn, I love those guys and I haven't even met them. They saved your life, Izz."

"They did indeed. And inadvertently Lily's. If I hadn't gotten to her in time –" She glanced out the window, then back. "I was afraid of what their parents would do to them after they ran away like that. But they told me Mac had a long talk with Jeremy's mom and Tom's dad. Emphasized their sons' part in saving lives. Explained to them that the boys deserved a medal. And, I gather, he told the Granite police to take the warrants for running the police blockade and destroying property and 'stick 'em where the sun don't shine.' Jeremy's words, of course."

"So, what happens to Lily?" Louise asked.

"She has an uncle in Texas. We're contacting him. I hate to see her move away, but it's best. She doesn't need this place as a reminder." Belle pulled her legs under her on the sofa. No point getting sentimental over this.

"So Andrews, the great white hope, was a swindler and a killer, huh?" Louise said. "If my belief in politicians wasn't already low, that'd do it for me."

Belle slumped. "The terrible thing is, I don't really believe he meant to hurt anyone. Cochran and the others did the actual killing. Saturday morning Cochran had stowed his rifle in the warehouse, ready to use on Lily." She wriggled the arm in the sling. "Apparently Andrews just wanted to pull in enough money for his campaign from businesses who could afford the loss. I understand they were some he knew about from his years as a lawyer back in Massachusetts."

She looked out the window again, the sunlight bright as though the storm had never happened.

"Julio Morales' interference was the glitch in Andrews' scheme," Belle said. "After they killed him it went from bad to worse. Andrews tried to make Julio's death look like a crime against Hispanics. He used it to go along with his own campaign. But Ralph Poole was unstable, so they set up Poole's death to appear to be revenge. Trouble is I began pestering Fred Preacher, who then became a problem as well. After that I started poking around and got Lily involved. Lou, I was the one who put Lily in danger. It was my fault. If I'd just left it to the sheriff to handle –"

"Ease up, Izzy. Don't go acting like you're God," Louise told her. "So how did your sheriff friend come up with the truth?"

"Phone records, bank deposits. I think Harley James' connection was what did it."

"And who found out about the James connection?"

"Me."

"Right."

"It had to be hard for Mac to envision a friend like Morgan Andrews being the kind of person who would kill people. Or condone their killing. No wonder he didn't come up with it sooner."

"The papers ran the story but it sounds hushed to me," Louise said. "Evidently Cochran takes most of the blame – a confession. Whoa, is that ever a whitewash."

"Paul Cochran's doing, not Mac's."

"And Lloyd Pruitt's having a field day with this. My God, Izz, can you believe that man's going to be our next senator?"

Belle remembered the uncontrolled fracas at the courthouse square and how much of it was Pruitt's doing. She didn't speak for a moment.

Finally she said, "They've got Carlos Hernandez locked up. Mac says the parents are pleading for mercy one minute and insisting on his innocence the next."

"What's Carlos saying?"

"That he's proud to have avenged Julio's killing."

"Yeah, well –" Louise sighed on the other end. "What about your Honda?"

"My baby? It's back. New tires. Had to pay for that myself."

"It's your own fault for following that damned map," Louise barked.

"But if I hadn't, I wouldn't have known the danger Lily was in."

"For God's sake, Izz, you could have been killed. Nearly were. Twice."

Belle didn't know what to say about that so she didn't say anything.

"Got a message from Larry," she said instead. "Friday night and again Saturday morning to call him. I didn't. But Ellie phoned this morning and told me all about the crisis."

"Which was?"

"Well, it seems she broke the news to her father that she and Mike were running away. Then hung up on him when he got hysterical and hid out when he came to the campus looking for her."

"God, that girl's got spunk. Takes after her Aunt Lou."

Belle laughed. "Thank God Mike doesn't. She must have scared the hell out of him because he dropped her like hot coals."

"You're kidding."

"Nope. The worm decided he couldn't handle such a strong woman, so he called it quits."

"I'll be damned. Does Larry know?"

"He didn't when she called. But I insisted she tell him or he'd have a stroke and it would be on her head. So she said she would. Tomorrow. Or the next day."

A bark of laughter came over the phone. "Girl after my own heart."

On Monday Belle was nervous when Superintendent Cummerford called her into his office. There goes my job, she thought.

Instead, he congratulated her. Apparently Sheriff McFarland had phoned him first thing that morning to commend her actions and praise the school administration for their foresight in forming her position. She wasn't sure how much of that Mac honestly meant, but she didn't ask either.

The primary election occurred on Tuesday. On Wednesday the report was that record numbers came to the polls that day. Morgan Andrews' name was stricken from the ballot. Lloyd Pruitt's was the only prominent one there.

But the two main camps had forgotten about a little known business man also running. He was William Rodriguez who owned a small hardware chain in Chandler. Apparently the great majority of Republicans in Arizona decided that Pruitt's strong-arm tactics went beyond the bounds of senatorial behavior, so they voted for the only other possible candidate.

It was later said of Rodriguez, though never confirmed, that his sole purpose in winning the candidacy and eventually the senate was to give Arizona back to the Mexicans to whom it belonged.

Other books by the author,
also available on Amazon.

In the vein of Nora Roberts, *Harper's Bluff* portrays a quiet Ohio River town turned deadly over greed and a long-buried secret.

A Romantic Suspense with a touch of Sci Fi, *The Danesboro Line* portrays a southern Ohio farm community that harbors a bizarre secret.

With a supernatural slant, *The Day of the Beast* portrays an Ohio town in a frenzy over a preacher who appears able to cure people.

A historical suspense novel, *Imperfect Union* takes place at the end of the Civil War Reconstruction era when the South again threatens secession from the union.

3473112R00135

Made in the USA
San Bernardino, CA
05 August 2013